# MARTIN CAIDIN

# KILLER STATION

P9-DEJ-064

BAEN FICTION BOOKS

KILLER STATION

This is a work of fiction. All the characters and events portrayed in this book are fictional, and any resemblance to real people or incidents is purely coincidental.

Copyright © 1984 by Martin Caidin

All rights reserved, including the right to reproduce this book or portions thereof in any form.

A Baen Book

Baen Enterprises
260 Fifth Avenue
New York, N.Y. 10001

First printing, December 1985

ISBN: 0-671-55996-6

Cover art by David Mattingly

Printed in the United States of America

Distributed by
SIMON & SCHUSTER
MASS MERCHANDISE SALES COMPANY
1230 Avenue of the Americas
New York, N.Y. 10020

# RUSH FEARED HE WOULD BE TOO LATE.

*Pleiades* shuddered with a renewed sickening motion. There could be no mistaking that dangerous wobble, no escaping the deep groaning sounds emitted by the enormous strains on the structure. A shrill alarm stabbed his ears and the emergency speakers sounded through the station.

*"Red alert! Red alert! All hands! All hands! Pressure seal break in the station! Pressure seal break! All emergency crews on the double in suits to Tube Three, repeat, all emergency crews on the double in suits to Tube Three."*

There came a momentary pause as if the speaker was trying to get his wits together—no, it was a woman's voice, Rush realized, Dianne Vecchio's. "We are on full alert," she went on, calmer now. "All personnel into pressure suits immediately. All personnel into pressure suits immediately."

Rush saw Steve Longbow just outside Control. "Steve! Get your crews into their suits and then get some fireaxes and cut those goddamned cables from the computer! We can't wait for the lasers!"

He saw Longbow gesture to acknowledge the command and then Rush was jerked roughly by the shoulder. He flailed with his arms to regain his balance, then saw Christy just behind him. "Get into your suit!" she screamed at him.

Beyond Christy's face lights flashed wildly and he saw plumes of the nontoxic red smoke released automatically whenever the pressure dropped. The smoke would follow any air leak and indicate just where they would find the breach in the pressure seal. And the triple-damned smoke *was moving*, snaking its way through the air, showing long tendrils in a spiraling motion . . .

## novels by MARTIN CAIDIN

Killer Station
Marooned*
No Man's World*
The Cape
Four Came Back
Starbright
ManFac*
Jericho 52
Aquarius Mission*
Cyborg*
Operation Nuke
High Crystal
Cyborg IV
Devil Take All*
The Last Dogfight*

The God Machine
Anytime, Anywhere
Whip
The Last Fathom
The Mendelov
   Conspiracy*
Almost Midnight*
Maryjane Tonight
   at Angels 12*
Wingborn
The Final Countdown*
Three Corners to
   Nowhere
Deathmate

*Sold as a major motion picture or TV series

for **POPPA JOHN**

he was there

# Chapter 1

"I never thought it would be possible. Never."

Christy Gordon shook her head, surprised at her own feelings. She turned suddenly from the invisible glass sheet that gave her a vertiginous view of infinity. A blonde ponytail swirled about her head and weightlessness kept her hair in a languid stroke of visual poetry. She was too beautiful to be a scientist, Rush Cantrell judged in thoughts he kept strictly to himself, and a figure sensual and athletic, even in her jumpsuit, seemed out of place hundreds of miles above the world. The men with Cantrell in the Astrophysics Laboratory of the great space station *Pleiades* seemed puzzled by her abrupt and uncompleted remark.

Ed Raphael smiled tolerantly. Christy Gordon was a brilliant research scientist in her own right, but brilliant women, even if they were beautiful, were prone to emotional outbursts. "Christy, what's so impossible it's never?"

She gestured, pointing with a finger at what was inescapable—a sun roiling with fury within its savage heart, ripped with monstrous currents, pulled and tugged and twisted by tides of gravity and time beyond the comprehension of mere man. These people, nevertheless, tried.

"The sun," Christy said abruptly. "Maybe I never realized what I've been looking at all my life—bright and shining and warm. To a little girl that means flowers and soft grass and beautiful clouds and glorious sunsets, and you don't really lose any of that when you understand it's a star and it hasn't changed hardly at all since the first man looked at it millions of years ago. Oh, Christ, forgive me. I don't know how I ever got on this soapbox in the first place. But suddenly the sun *frightens* me."

She has good reason to be frightened, mused Cantrell. He held an oblique regard of things and events that were or could be dangerous. It provided an interesting perspective and gave always renewing birth to objectivity. Rush Cantrell nodded to Raphael. "Ed, give me third-level filter, please." Raphael was a tall, slender man with a brooding, hawklike face, but embedded in that fierce countenance, between a sharp, hard nose and a shock of curly dark hair above, there were eyes of intelligence and warmth. Had he lived centuries past, this man who was a brilliant astronomer and astrophysicist, and the First Executive Officer of *Pleiades*, would certainly have worn the trappings and hood of a monk dedicated to searching out God's wonders in man's world. But his monastery was an enormous tangle and assembly held in a delicate but superb orbital balance three hundred and forty-six miles above the earth. No monk's trappings here, but a comfortable jumpsuit, sneakers with velcro fasteners, computers, and exquisitely sensitive instruments. He would be equally comfortable in either setting, judged Cantrell. He pondered the thought for a moment. Well, he had, but did not need, justification for such thinking. Interpreting and judging the men and women of *Pleiades* was second nature to the man who was commander of the great scientific and engineering arsenal hurtling about the planet.

Ed Raphael's fingers slid across the control panel of the laboratory and a filter snapped into place across the full surface of the thick armorglass sheet. With that single movement, the sun attained a visual signature barely resembling the bright star they had been studying. The blinding, stabbing light faded and presented an optically painless, silvery-copper rim of the star ninety-three million miles distant. Through the filter, they saw splotches on the stellar surface—angry red and black welts, whirling suddenly, and hurling thin streamers far into space from the rounded edges of the disc. Thin streamers from their tiny bird's-eye view, but in reality howling storms within which a thousand earths would be instantly crushed and exploded and vaporized as an atomic explosion might incinerate a snowflake.

"See?" Christy thrust at them. "It's . . . well, malevolent. *Ugly*. It has worms crawling on it."

Joe Svec burst into laughter. The burly engineer of *Pleiades'* power and engineering systems with the perpetual five o'clock shadow on his squared

chin lacked poetry, it seemed. He saw things and
events in strictly mechanical and engineering terms
which, of course, was just as well for all the lives
on the station so dependent on quite specifically
that kind of quality engineering. To Joe Svec's
world, nothing worked or mattered if it couldn't
be measured in pounds per square inch or metered
flow or radiative current or ohms and watts and
joules and amperes; ugly didn't exist. It was like a
flower, as expressed in Joe Svec's particular view
of life. There it stood, pristine in color, texture
soft and gentle, glowing with life. When those elements waned and the texture crumbled and color
faded, Joe Svec saw not decay or death but a
natural progression of events. A maggot wasn't
ugly. It was the next step in a life pattern, just as
surely as steam rises from water treated with fire.

Joe stepped closer to the screen. Pragmatist he
might be, but Christy Gordon's emotional reaction
was starting to reach even his own monolithic
mental order. He'd been in this station for a year
and not during that year, or ever, had he seen a
sun like *this* one. By God, there was something to
it. Joe considered it from his longstanding views.
Something was screwed up, because stars didn't
show wheals and open lesions and—

He heard Rush Cantrell's voice addressed to Hank
Markham of Life Support Systems. "Hank, what's
the index on the alert scale?" The others turned to
watch Markham as he went swiftly through an
instrument-packed console. The radiation specialist shook his head slowly. "I've seen it this high
before," he said, glancing at Rush, "but I've never
seen it climbing so rapidly. We're starting to indicate a sharp upcurve."

"Think we're ready for an alert?" Rush Cantrell went on calmly.

"*I* want an alert status," Christy Gordon broke in.

Rush glanced at her again, and once more the feeling of distortion struck him. The station of superpowerful alloys, glass, plastic and ... this woman with the golden ponytail and the orange-beige flight suit and the swift, intelligent gaze, and behind that a brain as capable as any he'd known. He pushed the thoughts out of his mind.

"It's more than just what the instruments show," Christy added hurriedly. "We're picking up a strong electromagnetic pattern and it's beginning to have a physiological effect. *I can feel* it. And if it's got me edgy, that means we're going to go over the safe exposure limits—and a lot faster than we may anticipate."

Rush Cantrell looked at Raphael and Markham. Raphael nodded slowly; so did Markham. "I never argue with the lady," Raphael said. "Not for courtesy, you understand, but," he sighed, "as we all know, she's always picked up such things before anyone else. I say alert status immediately, so that if Miss Picture Perfect over there is right again," he grinned at Christy, the expression warm and teasing, "we won't be reminded at dinner of just how sluggish we are between the ears."

Christy offered a modest bow. For the moment, genuinely pleased with the hawk-faced scientist's remarks, she'd forgotten weightlessness. When she bowed, her body arched, but her feet didn't remain planted to the deck. Her eyes widened as she realized she was floating, bent over like a Raggedy Ann doll. The men laughed as Rush leaned forward and placed his hand gently atop her golden hair to push her down. "That's a good doggy. Remember the rules, okay? No floating when we bow." Christy flushed, but grinned with the moment of sharing. Brief enough; they all saw the new flare begin, like a bright spark on the solar rim, and start its great lofting jet explosion into space. They saw it only briefly, for *Pleiades* was plunging down the curving mountain of the earth. Sunset sped swiftly beneath them, and in a convulsive gasp and stretch of color swallowed all sight of the sun.

All save that lingering finger of stellar hell that seemed to mock them.

"Okay, people, all ears," Rush announced. Their conversation fell away as he switched to earthside transmit. His voice would flash upward, higher through space, to a geosynchronous communications satellite, and beam with the speed of light halfway around a planet into a familiar room at the Johnson Space Center in Houston, Texas. The same control room that had guided and nursed Gemini, Apollo, Skylab, and Apollo-Soyuz through incredible moments carving new niches and heights in man's history now played technical big brother and nursemaid to the fifty-two men and women aboard the fourteen-hundred tons of space platform the world knew as *Pleiades*. A touch of whimsy had retained the long-outdated call sign for Houston Control—*CapCom*. The name had originated in the primitive days of manned space flight in the early sixties when America's thrust into space was the diminutive, archaic, barely survivable capsule known as the Tin Can to its sole astronaut, and as Mercury to the world. Capsule Communicator—CapCom. It seemed to fit, like old socks, and they'd hung on to it. There was, after all, precious little heritage to this business of living and working away from *any* world. Instinct, perhaps some Darwinian tremor in the subconscious, led to a deep-rooted clutch at the familiar.

A spiderweb cap pressed into Cantrell's hair, molded to his skull and free of pressure, with a thin earpiece and lip mike, made up his entire communications ensemble. His mike was voice-actuated and he spoke as easily to the NASA control center as he did to anyone scant feet from him. "CapCom, *Pleiades*. You guys on the line?"

"Roger that, Rush. Jeremy here. You people calling about our rambunctious star?"

Rush grinned, picturing Bill Jeremy's measured movements and considering his southern drawl giving the sun its own "star" status. "That's affirm, Houston," Rush answered. "Christy Gordon says Old Sol is getting downright ugly. I've got Raphael, Markham, and Svec with us in the solar lab, and it appears Christy is well ahead of the instrumentation and the computers. She'll get with your solar rad people right after this conversation, but right now her intuition, and we're agreeing with her, says we're in the initial phase of a super magnetic storm."

That last remark brought hesitation from Cap-Com. "Uh, *Pleiades*, you did say *super* magnetic storm? Over."

"Affirmative, Houston."

CapCom didn't reply for a moment. Rush knew that Bill Jeremy had already pressed the alert buttons for the science duty crew, because anything that exceeded 100 on the storm scale meant immediate warnings throughout the entire earth to prepare for serious disruption of power, communications, travel, and industry. When you got into the "super" class you could expect, and certainly you were going to get, violent disruptions in power transmission facilities *everywhere* on the planet. The sun-generated magnetic storms triggered severe surges and breakdowns of currents in power lines. That meant, simply, that if you didn't get off your duff and start cutting the power loads, and drastically, you were facing complete disruption of power-line transmission, and that itself led to complete breakdown of the system. The magnetic storms severely overloaded the system, and what had been a problem many years past was now far worse because of changing conditions Earthside. With the vast increase in numbers of power lines, and those lines carrying more powerful loads than ever before, their vulnerability to magnetic disruption had simply escalated. The two situations were about to join. More demand for power and more power lines on earth meant greater vulnerability to widespread breakdown. At the same time, in the late 1970s, the sun had just eased past its peak of a particularly severe sunspot cycle registered in planetary events as Cycle 21.

*That* boded serious problems for the future, for the sun had a nasty habit of celebrating the close of a sunspot cycle with a vicious super magnetic storm. Ever since the early satellites had shown a clear path to monitoring such events, spaceborne satellites, and now the *Pleiades* station, always kept an electronic ear cocked for such violent events, and stood ready to flash warnings to earth of their arrival and predicted effects. In August of 1972 a "healthy" magnetic storm caused thousands of minor power outages around the world and brought on a distinct rise in crime rates because of physiological reactions to electromagnetic fields arising from the solar storms. The effects of an angry sun on human emotions, criminologists believed, were much more severe than a full moon.

"CapCom, you still there?"

"Ah, roger that. It's just that we've had no indications from any satellite monitors of a storm of such significance. Over."

Rush shook his head with this sign of instant official escape from reality. "So next time buy better goods," he said, with no playdown of his sarcasm. "You want to complain about your equipment or stick to the point?" Rush Cantrell was not always known for shining protocol, but he *was* known to cut the mustard, and quickly. And right now he was even more quickly seeing his own patience evaporate. The sun was building to violence, faster than they'd ever known before, and Bill Jeremy was hiding behind official platitudes.

"CapCom, move your butt. Notify Global Alert and do it *now*. I want voice confirmation and I want the full television pickup, using all wavelengths, on the line for both real-time monitoring and recording. Got it?"

Standard procedure in the space flight business is for the man closest to the problem to run the show, and Rush Cantrell was definitely on the run with his authority. "Yes, sir," Bill Jeremy said at once. "Stand by while we carry out notification and bring up all systems on the line."

Rush looked about him in the solar physics lab. The men were grinning. Christy Gordon blew him a kiss. "Bravo, bravo," she added. "You just carved another notch on your unpopularity pole."

"You know I'll be up all night worrying," he tossed back. "Okay, okay. Let's get to work. If Christy is right, and all instrumentation is backing her up, you know what we're looking at? The great-granddaddy of all super magnetic storms. The sun is about to go ape. The only way to convince the groundlovers is to give them the full treatment in different wavelengths. Global Alert knows what to do with the stuff. By the time Milt Berghoff is through orchestrating a worldwide news interruption, he'll turn this thing into a complete real-time horror show. Get busy. We have maybe another twenty-five minutes before we come out of darkness into direct view of the sun. I want everything on the line."

He didn't expect sudden resistance from Christy. "Hold it, Rush," she said, openly. "I haven't time for your televised theatrics, even if the sun is on center stage. I've got a job to do. I need to bring my staff on the line and—"

"They can do everything without you being there," Rush broke in. "I want you here. I want you—"

"That's ridiculous," she snapped. "My job here is research, not broadcasting. "If we have all these satellites and the equipment on this station, you don't need anyone hamming it up."

"You're wrong," Rush said quietly. "We look like we're on the edge of the biggest solar event since the South Pole melted away from what's now the Sahara. People down below are going to be frightened. They need reassurance, they need information, and they need it dramatically." He cocked his head and held her gaze. "Besides, if we're so neatly wrapped up with automatic sensors and equipment, what the hell are *you* doing on this station? If I follow your reasoning, Christy, you're excess baggage. Fortunately," he went on quickly before she could again interrupt, "you're a better scientist and dramatist than you are a logician. Hold it, *hold it*, lady. I'm serious about this. The world below us doesn't trust instruments, per se. People are frightened and resentful of being reduced to ciphers. The computerized world is a bitch. They don't *want* to be told by instruments. We've been up here eleven months and if it's taught us anything it's that the human touch carries the ball. Human interpretation, description, dramatics, recognizable fears and convictions. The whole gamut. You're a scientist *and* you're a woman. So you go on camera when we come around darkside, and you tell the people down there, just like you're a poet, that the sun's about to poke them in the eyes with a couple of sharp sticks."

She held a stubborn line to her face. Rush sighed. "Christy, don't you understand what I'm saying to you? They're going to be scared out of their minds and they need your help."

She chewed her lower lip, an instinctive reaction to contest within her own mind. Damn, she was here to study and research, not to play nursemaid to the billions of people down below. But she knew what she'd hear from Rush if she voiced that opinion. *Who the hell do you think paid to get you up here, lady?*

Since she knew the answer, she didn't parade the question. "All right," she said, nodding. "Let's get with it. I'd like to have Chuck Gambrell on the

TV monitors. He worked for NBC for a couple of years and he could teach the Disney crews some tricks."

They went to work, setting up a live dialogue with words and special TV-transmitted instrument scans of the sun that would show the world what the pitifully inadequate human eye couldn't encompass.

They fell around the darkside of the planet, looking at the glittering jewels of great metropolitan areas and the gleaming pearls of cities along coastlines. Great thunderstorms flickered like light bulbs across oceans, and for a long moment they all paused as meteors streaked the darkness like living diamonds scratching across dark velvet.

At seventeen thousand miles an hour you don't remain long in darkness. They plummeted upward around the great curve of the planet, watched the incredible first pink wisps of the swift dawn, the spreading orange and red and golden light following behind, and the sun heaving itself over the sharply curving horizon.

In that brief turn away from the star that was the source of all life on earth, it seemed to have swelled with new anger, raging in what was to them utter silence and impossibly far away. But it wasn't. Christy felt a cold shiver through her body. She could almost hear and feel that terrible solar thunder booming through space.

# Chapter 2

They needed to give vision to the earthsiders. That, mused Rush Cantrell, was the crux of the whole issue. Warning a blind man to be careful about a vision-stabbing glare was ridiculous, as was telling the deaf not to turn up their wind chimes excessively. Throughout history, it has been man's nature to ignore danger signals that his immediate environment is about to undergo serious dislocation or even violent rattling. Down through the time-compressed strata of history the signs have been unmistakable—millions of people buried beneath the raging waters of collapsed dams, millions more killed from earthquakes because their cities were almost guaranteed to come tumbling down about their ears. How many entire cities had been buried, burned, gutted, and incinerated by volcanoes their very victims watched, studied, heard, and slept beneath? Disasters of every nature visiting suffering humanity have almost always been preceded by advance warning. Man, being a curious sort of social beast, usually protected himself by killing whatever temple priests survived the immediate debacle, as a satisfactory solution to utter catastrophe and holocaust.

And today, as Rush Cantrell observed, those of us in *Pleiades* are the temple priests. He studied the sun through a small telescope filter from a control room in the lower core of the space station. It was kaleidoscopic in its virulence, and— He brought himself up short. If he tweaked his imagination just a bit, he could be observing a nuclear fusion explosion under a microscope, or so it seemed from the slow motions of viral and bacterial forms he watched through the filter. But some of those forms were, literally, lesions in the surface of the sun tens of thousands of miles long, and they raged and struggled to tear away from their own stellar furnace.

A dark-haired girl wearing a blue-and-gold jumpsuit eased down the vertical slide pole into the control room. Here, in the station core they called Saturn, Dianne Vecchio was both beautiful and weightless, a combination Rush found immensely appealing. *Not now, not now*, his scientist's eye growled at him.

"Commander, I understand we're on special call," Dianne said as openers. She was a very professional space officer, and unless she and those about her were off duty, Dianne was *always* all business. Rush could ask no more; he shifted mental gears to the moment.

"You updated yet?" he queried.

"Yes, sir. Ed Raphael gave me the word and

then," Dianne couldn't resist the tug of a smile at the corner of her mouth, "Commander Gordon gave me a brief lecture on the asininity of the world being spoon-fed their ABC's."

Rush met the last remark with a smile. "Christy Gordon is one of the best scientists I know," he told Dianne. "She also is well insulated from reality. She has a habit of forgetting that this station came from millions—no, make that billions—of coffers called pockets and purses. You know, that dirty old stuff called taxes. Spoon-feeding ABC's is just part of the repayment."

"Raphael said we're on the edge of what could be a super magnetic storm."

"And he in turn got that from Christy Gordon, who has the most incredible scientific intuition I've ever known. If the lady had graced the court of Camelot, then in her time she would have been a female Merlin, or whatever is the name for wizards of the other gender."

"I wonder, Commander, if she knows how you feel," Dianne smiled.

"Ah, not her business, Dianne, or yours, for that matter," he said easily to bring them back to the reason for her presence. "I could have done this on the videophone but I wanted to add a few touches between us. From this point on, until I consider us off this solar alert, you're standby Exec around the clock. If you're not actually holding the watch as Station Commander, be ready at any moment to assume that watch. You may not get much sleep, but then—"

"I know," she smiled, "it goes with the job."

"Okay. You get back to central. Right now you're strictly an observer and on watch standby. But I don't want you to miss any part of what's going on. If you take over as Exec I don't want any misunderstanding on your part. You haven't much time."

"Yes, sir." Dianne floated upward from her position close to Rush, extended a foot, and pushed gently into a slow drift toward the entry hatch. She caught herself short as two legs slid down the pole. Brooke Allen slid into view, grinning, as usual, with an infectious smile spread wide beneath wild curly hair and a great handlebar moustache. Dianne gestured her greetings and goodbyes and disappeared through the entryway.

Brooke Allen pushed downward toward Rush and did a beautifully controlled slow somersault to ease into a chair that snagged the velcro strips of his jeans. "Presto," he said. "At your service, Mr. Cantrell."

Rush nodded. No time to pay compliments to weightless acrobatics. "You confirm Svec on the monitoring?"

Brooke caught the tone, harsher than usual, from the station commander. "Yes, sir," he answered promptly. "He's off the station line. His instructions are to contact only you, or me, if we start getting any danger signals."

"You're both aware I want full security status on this?"

"Right. No civilian notification."

"Okay, Brooke. While we're here, our job is strictly monitoring. You contact Joe on the security line so we know for sure he's on safety comm between him and us. The rest of it is watching. I'm letting Christy Gordon, as Science Lead for this station, along with Raphael and the others, handle

this whole affair." Rush gestured to the display of
television monitors surrounding the larger central
screen. "Everything they do from the TV cast we
can see here. I want us to see just what earthside
gets. If any questions come up later we'll be one
jump ahead of them."

"Yes, sir."

Rush checked the digital time counter. "They're
about ready. Sit back and enjoy the show."

Chuck Gambrell was in his element operating a
complete television broadcast studio. He had twelve
camera positions from which to choose the picture
that would go out live on international "real time"
broadcast. Every camera would also be recorded
for later editing into repeat broadcasts, but there's
nothing so effective as a live news broadcast and
press conference that hundreds of millions will see
breaking into their favorite sitcoms or movies or
football games. You get their attention that way.
You also piss off a lot of people, but they have a
habit of watching what's angering them. There
had been a last-minute decision to include a hand-
ful of world-known newsmen in the scientists' group
at Houston who would carry on the charade of
querying Christy Gordon in the *Pleiades* station.
That way they'd avoid charges they knew were
going to be made that the whole affair was trumped
up to gain public support for the space program
by scaring the bejesus out of everyone on earth.

The live broadcast could also be picked up by
any receiving studio in the world. It wasn't like
the old space days. Then, you had to be line-of-
sight with the earth's surface, and that meant that
any spacecraft on the side of the earth away from

Houston would have its signals transmitted through complex systems of ships, aircraft, microwave towers, and land lines. Now, Gambrell sent his television signal by microwave from *Pleiades*, not to the earth's surface, but in the opposite direction— farther out into space—to be relayed by the communications satellites orbiting at 22,300 miles. The global comsat network permitted TV transmissions in both directions between *Pleiades* and earth in less than a second's time.

Rush Cantrell and Brooke Allen watched the on-station monitor, listened to Gambrell's instructions. "Christy, CapCom recommends you dispense with any hellos or hi theres for your broadcast. They feel you'll be more effective with the meat and they can handle the potatoes. You just get right into the swing of it when you start. In fact, you can watch the intros on your own monitor. When they wrap it up, they'll have a break in between that'll show *Pleiades*, a couple shots of earth, and then the sun. You'll hear them announce coming in to us for your pickup. Okay with you?"

Christy, well surrounded by computer banks, consoles, and instrument panels, looked the role of the brilliant mad scientist. Rush smiled at the visual impression—brilliant, yes, but also as unemotional when it came to her work as the computers with which she delved into astrophysical mysteries.

The center screen picked up the "WE INTERRUPT THIS PROGRAM FOR A GLOBAL ALERT" announcements. There was something visceral in a program break that might be telling you the world was about to go *blam*. The digital counter on the screens everywhere showed less than two minutes to go, and the screen filled with different

scenes of the sun, including several eclipse sequences with computer enhancement of fiery spears
climbing slowly but impressively away from the
star. They cut finally to a shot of NASA Administrator Dr. Luther Grenville, looking very official,
very imposing, and, Rush was certain, very much
of a pain in the ass to those people whose home
entertainment was being mangled in this fashion.
This was pure hype and a waste of time. It wouldn't
get people to keep their television sets on to see
what might follow. Rush sighed; the bureaucratic
piper must be paid.

Grenville finally faded from the screen and a
panel of three scientists appeared. Dr. John Schefter,
Dr. Albert Millikan, and Professor Yuri Romanenko.
And the three newsmen: Robert Stanton, representing the four major North American networks;
Toshio Toshimura for Asian News; and, a dark and
angry fellow from AfroWorld Live. His nameplate
read Ali Liam.

"Boss, where the hell did they get that name?"
Brooke Allen queried Cantrell. "AfroWorld Live, I
mean. Sounds like something out of Disneyland or
Busch Gardens."

"Same place he got that afro bush on top of his
head," Rush replied. "But don't let that wild and
woolly look kid you. I know Ali. He's got two
Ph.D's, he flew a lot of combat in the African bush
wars, and *then* he trained with the Russians and
made one of those joint flights in a Soyuz. He
stayed up three weeks in their old Salyut station."

"*He* was an astronaut?" Brooke was openly disbelieving. "He looks like he forgot to bring his
spear with him."

"That's the idea. Everyone, except those of us

who know him, underestimates him. In a straight one-on-one debate he'd eat you alive."

"He looks like he has the teeth for it," Brooke murmured.

Rush considered telling Brooke Allen to zip his lip, but they weren't saying anything worthwhile on the screen. It was still introduction time to impress the audience. If this didn't put them all to sleep down below, they still might have a few hardy or patient souls watching their sets when Christy came on. They went through their introductions, and then the stock footage, to bridge the gap between serious, pontifical faces and live from *Station Pleiades*. Rush came up straighter in his seat when he saw what Chuck Gambrell was doing. He'd made a decision somewhere along the line to select the transition footage personally. They ran through the usual dramatic shlock of earth from different angles, drifting in to see *Pleiades* with the earth below, and the run-of-the-mill scenes of the sun on different scopes and wavelengths. Then Gambrell pulled his sneak punch. The screen shifted to absolute black, then a thin hazy line stretching from the lower left to the upper right of the screen with a tiny black dot in the center. The camera closed in steadily, and it became evident this was no studio special-effects presentation, but a film made from a spaceship approaching at great speed to the earth, with the sun directly behind the earth. As the planet swelled in size, the viewer also saw that the thin white lines was actually the zodiacal light, gases and dust reflecting sunlight in a beautiful scene.

The view wavered, seemed to shimmer, and as it came back into focus, burning letters were superimposed on the still-expanding shot of the planet. Chuck Gambrell knew how to grab his audience. You didn't easily ignore a live show from space that began with the words "TARGET: EARTH." The scene dissolved into a stunning shot of *Pleiades*, the sun blazing through the great center tank, the radial arms, and the huge rim, reflecting brilliantly off the cables, tanks, assorted laboratories, and small spacetugs in the scene.

"Jesus, but he's good," Rush murmured. The camera fell toward *Pleiades*, then the scene blurred into another dissolve and came out sharp and clear on Christy Gordon in a deep copper-gold jumpsuit with blue trim and the *Pleiades* patch prominently over her left breast. Her name and title appeared beneath her dramatic opening shot. For the moment, she sat quiet and dignified before the camera; then they heard Bill Jeremy's voice come in as CapCom.

"Our first question will be from Mr. Ali Liam, representing AfroWorld Live. Mr. Liam?"

"Doctor Gordon, I appreciate this opportunity to speak directly with you and to allay the growing fears of the African people," Liam began. Rush watched his old friend intently. Ali Liam threw the best first punch of any debate. "Is it true, Doctor Gordon, that the sun is exploding?"

Laughter burst from Rush. "I told you the son of a bitch was beautiful!" he chortled to Brooke Allen. "He's already grabbed his audience by the short hairs."

Christy Gordon didn't miss the golden opportunity Ali Liam had offered. She paused just the right time for dramatic effect and then nodded somberly. "Yes, Mr. Liam. It is." Another pause

while untold millions sucked in their breath. "The
sun is exploding, but not quite so fast as many
people have feared. There are many kinds of explosions involving the star that provides all life and
energy on our world. Most of them have little
effect. Others have caused ice ages and then melted
the results of catastrophic eras on our planet. The
sun has caused the earth to shift its magnetic poles,
turned the Sahara Desert from a frozen wasteland
into both sand and oases, and transformed what
was once a lush jungle paradise of meadows and
mountains into what we know today as Antarctica."

*Bang*. Just like that, Christy had snatched the
cudgel and run with it. Beautiful; just beautiful.

". . . we are facing is known as a super magnetic
storm. We have every reason to believe it may be
the most violent such storm ever known in recorded history. Let me explain that we use a solar
index to signify the intensity and danger of such
events from our star. In August 1972, the Earth
went through the effects of a solar storm that on
our scale index had a rating of 220. Until recently,
we believed this storm level was particularly dangerous and close to the maximum we might expect
in terms of effects on the way earth's people live
and work. You may recall that during that violent
episode of solar flares and magnetic fields crashing into the earth, we suffered thousands of inter-
ruptions to the power grids of the planet. The
aurora, which we all know remains in the polar
areas, seemed to have gone crazy then." *Pause;
shift in mood. A gentle floating to enhance the zero-g
effect. She rippled fingers across a console before her
and the computer bank lights responded in angry*

*colors. She was masterminding every second. Rush gave her a silent whoop of congratulations.*

"The 1972 storm came on the heels of severe sunspots, when our star seems to suffer brutal and grievous open lesions. That's just what they are, enormous wounds ripped by uncontrollable forces within the sun. These heave trillions of tons of subatomic material into space. The vast majority never comes even near to our world. But a very small percentage arcs across space in an invisible flood. This solar typhoon, which is as good an explanation as any, mixes with the electrical portions of our atmosphere. The solar wind reacts with the higher reaches of earth. They clash, soundlessly and even beautifully. That's why, in 1972, the aurora that has so long been a beautiful mantle for our polar regions seemed to have gone crazy. It raced down from the poles with unbelievable swiftness, valkyries riding the magnetic winds of earth. It stabbed into temperate regions and, to the astonishment of hundreds of millions of people, in the United States it flared and shone over states as far south as Kentucky. Much the same happened in parts of the world that had never seen an aurora. It is beautiful, even breathtaking, and . . . it may contain a message of danger. If we prepare for its effects, we can ride out the storm with minimum discomfort. If we choose to ignore what is happening and what is yet to follow, first there will be disorganization and, afterward, an inevitable chaos to our way of life.

"This . . . is 1972." Christy's voice remained strong as a light orchestral strain became barely audible. She dissolved from the main camera as Chuck Gambrell worked the films he had waiting to roll, and a ghostly picture showed a darkened earth in space, coming alive through bands and streamers of green and blue colors flashing across the top of the planet. The dazzling light show went on for exactly sixty-five seconds, rippling through the spectrum, pale silvers and reds and orange hues, the aurora showing as a gossamer veil, then waving curtains, a fascinating interplay of light and movement.

Christy's voice came over the changing scenes. "That was 1972. The intensity of the great magnetic storm was seen in these lights. More realistic, however, was what happened on earth." Power lines stretching across a darkened countryside appeared on the screen and almost immediately began to flash and spark. Intense green light flashed from overloaded transformers. Gambrell had a full series of fast cuts, from exterior lines to control rooms flashing danger signals. In several minutes, with Christy narrating the high points, the television screen made clear just what a solar magnetic storm could do to earth power facilities. The camera dissolved out of furious arcing and spitting lights to Christy.

"On the measuring index we use to rate major solar magnetic storms, anything that reaches 100 is considered to be dangerous. The 1972 storm, the effects of which you have just seen, reached 220 on this index. At this moment, the growing solar magnetic storm is approaching the danger mark of 100. However, our instruments and laboratories aboard this station indicate clearly that it is growing swiftly in intensity, and will soon be of the class we consider violent. Over the past century, we have recorded more than seventeen such violent storms—the super magnetic solar storm—that registered on our index well over 350."

Gambrell went to a fast cut of a closeup of the sun taken from a solar probe. It was fast and it was terrifying, taken with a long lens from a distance of only 28 million miles, a raging flare leaping toward the camera like demented furies. As soon as the solar closeup showed, Gambrell cut back to Christy.

"We don't know how high on the index this new storm will reach, but we estimate at least 300 on the storm scale. The effects of such a storm, and it may well go even higher, are so severe that it is critical to prepare for what it will do to disrupt power systems on earth. What we on *Pleiades* stress to you is that a storm of this intensity is far more dangerous now than it ever could have been before. During the past twenty years, we have increased our dependence on power grids. They are longer than ever before, they have more interconnections, they are riddled with elements far more susceptible to magnetic storm damage than we have ever known. Those of you who are familiar with the family Christmas tree will understand immediately what we are saying. The lights on such trees have many interconnections. If any one section fails, then the entire tree is blacked out like—"

She paused, and Gambrell cut in tight to Christy snapping her fingers, boomed the snap, and cut away to Houston, where they were rolling film of the great blackouts that had plagued the more concentrated and industrial sections of the country. Again there were scenes of power lines and transformers arcing, one connection after another breaking down, and they rolled the film into montages of cities ablaze with lights and dying of electrical starvation before the cameras. New York, Washington, Philadelphia, Atlanta, Chicago, Detroit, San Francisco, Los Angeles, and others, all gasping their last breath of electrical life, dissolving into darkness broken only by the feeble fireflies of cars and trucks and what lights emerged from gasoline-driven generators or batteries.

"If this new storm reaches the intensity we believe it will, what you see now could be much worse. Unless," she paused again for effect as the picture dissolved out of the city scenes to a closing shot of the space station and another dissolve to Christy, "we take immediate steps to begin unloading the demand on electrical power sources."

Christy was a natural. She had three scientists and three of the top newsmen in the world sitting on their hands in Houston, and only Ali Liam had been given the opportunity to say a word. His question had been precisely the catalyst Christy needed to be off and running. Rush Cantrell turned to Brooke Allen. "Now she's going to drop the piano on them."

"You mean she's got more?" Brooke asked.

"The piano," Rush repeated.

"I don't get it."

"You will. Watch."

"The human eye, marvelous and serving us all our lives, can't see the solar storm," Christy continued. "Unlike the storms of clouds and wind and rain, or dust and sand, unlike hurricanes and tornados and storms of this nature, the super magnetic storm is invisible to us. There are only two ways of knowing such a storm is raging all about us. One way is to suffer the consequences of massive power failures, disruption of nuclear reactors, even wiped out memory banks of computers. The other way is to use the instruments of this space station. We're now going to show you the storm by using our instruments to make the invisible become visible to the human eye. Remember, we can't see radio waves, but we hear them. We can't see television waves, but we can see and hear them by having a proper receiving terminal—the very set you're watching at this moment. We can't see even lethal nuclear radiation, but we can measure its presence and its intensity through the use of special instruments. Many of these instruments are on *Pleiades*. Others are in orbit much closer to the sun than this station. We'll combine the many instruments and their sensors into this unprecedented look at what's happening on the sun, and to the earth, right now."

Rush grinned. "Here we go."

# Chapter 3

They handled it like pros. But then, Rush judged, they had the greatest stage the world had ever known. First the moon, cratered and lifeless except for hundreds of instruments located strategically across its dusty and rock-littered surface. The camera point-of-view began with an approach to the moon until it seemed whatever ship was carrying the camera must crash into that forbidding surface. At the last moment, a heady rush brought the camera lunging over high lunar mountains to a shocking view of the sun, with light painful to the eyes even from a television screen. The camera turned slowly until a small blue-and-white marble came into view, glowing softly, and with the sun now out of camera range, against black velvet. Christy was no longer interested in the sun as the primary subject, but in what was happening in space and to the earth because of the sun. As the camera slowly changed its viewing point, Christy's voice off-screen filled in with terse statements to explain what appeared to the viewers. Wisely, her comments were cryptic. Nothing could match the incredible display offered by reality.

The screen held with the earth on the lower right. Just the beautiful blue-white marble glowing in a crescent line, with the terminator between night and day pulsing its yellow-orange of sunrise about it. Gambrell held the shot long enough for its effect to sink in and, when he figured the viewers would begin fidgeting, he cut in the filters that gave man sight of what his own eyes could never show him.

The sight was stunning, a shock. It was almost unbelievable that this could be *real*. But this *was* the reality, as the swirling energies between star and world snapped into view, transformed by electronic magic to fit within the spectrum of the human eye. Vast radiation storms rushed across the screen, a fantastic vortex of energy within which the earth seemed pitifully tiny in size and hopelessly unable to survive the glowing silent thunder inundating the planet. The view began to shift, film movement greatly accelerated to meet the limitations of human viewers who would never understand the long periods of time during which a camera must be transported along gravitational spirals connecting worlds.

The distant sun swam slowly into view. Pouring outward from mankind's star was a howling maelstrom of energy particles, but the particles appeared as flashes of lights and waves, much as a hurricane made up of individual droplets of water presents a solid front of furious winds hurling rain with devastating force before its path. What the viewers saw as surging currents and eddies was the continuous blast of protons and electrons spewing forth in a relentless, ceaseless, raging stream. Christy's voice almost startled Rush, for even he found himself thoroughly enraptured by the maelstrom unfolding before his eyes. "What you see," he heard, "makes the tiniest whisper of every explosion that ever took place on the earth since our planet was born."

There was no need to say more; not for the moment. The screen, as best as might be presented on a flat or curving surface, was displaying energy on a scale the viewer could only look at and gasp or simply marvel and wonder. Again Christy's voice joined the picture. "Look well, for what happens to this energy as it thunders toward and against our earth teaches us a grim lesson, indeed—that our planet forms a magnificent shield against these solar blasts. Without this natural barrier of the earth against such intense energy, no creature would ever have struggled to life in the four billion years of history we can measure. Understand, also, that life thrives on earth for many reasons. One is that our world is the densest of all the planets surrounding the sun. It also rotates rapidly, spinning with a speed measured at the equator of a thousand miles an hour. Because of these two forces, density and rotational speed, we live on a truly extraordinary magnet. The forces that radiate away from earth are so powerful they create our own natural space barrier against the radiation flooding down to us."

*Click.* A new filter changed the view. Instantly the screen showed great sheets of blazing energy streaming toward but not able to sear the earth. Fifty thousand miles ahead of the shimmering marble, in the direction of the sun, appeared a great, glowing band of blue-white light, so intense it seemed to be the curving edge of an incredible mirror glowing along its surfaces and from within its own substance. This was the shock wave—literally—glowing brightly from a clash of energies: radiation from the sun crunching into the magnetic field barrier of the earth.

This was the line of battle for life, between the outreaching magnetic field of earth and the continuous tides of the stellar energy avalanche. It was here, along that curving band of blue-white light, that the clash was joined and the immense radiations of the sun hurled aside and away from man's home world.

Ten thousand miles closer to earth appeared another line of demarcation. "This is the magneto-pause," came Christy's voice, subdued as if she too were overawed by what was now visible. "We never see this with our own eyes, but it is truly the dazzling yellow-gold you are now seeing . . ." That it was, a celestial fire flaming along the shimmering surface of a darker burning royal purple within. "Forty thousand miles out from our planet is our bulwark. This is the closest the intense magnetic field of earth permits the radiations from our sun to reach us. Notice the glowing lines of demarcation. On the inward side of the magnetopause, toward earth, is the magnetosphere. It is literally a solid boundary of magnetic force enveloping earth like a shield of massive armor."

Christy's voice was no longer heard, but the screen was almost mesmerizing as colors rippled and shimmered with changing intensities of solar forces. The camera swung toward the sun and zoomed steadily inward to catch a storm erupting from the interior of the star, tearing apart the liquid flame of the surface, and spewing forth a frightening silent explosion. Camera views changed, pulling back to show both the sun and the earth, space between the two globes, one massive and the other tiny, and all of what could be seen raging with energy. Tidal waves and currents blazed toward earth, and the invisible line of the magnetopause *was* now a visible barrier, forming a huge bowl of coruscating, brilliant colors deep within which spun that small, dense marble.

"There are other energies surrounding us," came the off-screen voice again, a priest leading an awestruck group through these temples of the gods. "Many of the streaming particles from the sun do get through the magnetopause, but earth is yet kind to us, for these high-penetrating particles are trapped in other shifting bands of magnetic fields. They are whirled about earth so high above us they present no danger to our lives. Never forget, however, that this enormous conflict goes on day and night, ceaselessly, and it has been fought for eons—before man first walked on this world."

Something happened to the great rivers of energy flowing against and around the magnetic defenses of the planet. In all directions against the glowing marble, moving backward along the boundaries created by the magnetopause, there appeared a gossamer fire, like a thinly glowing teardrop extending for a hundred thousand miles above and below earth, then spinning and whirling back to form a magnetic tail that fanned out, becoming thinner with distance, for more than a million miles from the globe. It was a plume of utter beauty, a softly glowing veil through which stars could be seen.

"For a moment, back to our myopic sight," came Christy's voice. The special filter screens were turned off, and as of that instant, what had entranced all who watched vanished. "We are now seeing what is to us the visible light of the spectrum. It is obvious that we might just as effectively have been struck blind. Until the first satellites, and then Skylab and Soyuz, and now *Pleiades*, we were as blind to these energies as the Neanderthals were to what we now call radio waves." The blue-white marble hung suspended in the screen, terribly naked and alone. "I would like you all to consider that our sun is an energy engine of such violence and magnitude that *every second it destroys four million tons of its substance* and transforms that substance into raging energy. Again, to regain the sight we have enjoyed, here is our star as it exists, and which we could see if our eyes gave us sight in the ultraviolet band."

From two hundred thousand miles distant, with film taken from a moonbound Apollo, the screen showed earth through the modified ultraviolet filter. A visual miracle burst outward from television sets across the planet, showing the distant world embedded within a geocorona made up of glowing hydrogen gas that reached out more than fifty thousand miles in every direction from the turning marble. It was as if earth now had become a completely dark sphere rolling silently through a fog that glowed and shimmered through all its substance.

Christy remained the superb master of ceremonies. The screen dissolved to darkness and her face appeared ghostlike on its surface. "Now we'll see earth without that glow of hydrogen gas that produced the utter beauty you just witnessed, the geocorona. What you will see now as radiant energy is atomic oxygen and molecular nitrogen."

Christy's face dissolved, then the screen went dark and burst into life with the earth transformed into a magician's crystal ball. One half of the globe, that side facing the distant sun, was a blinding white-gold light. The other half remained in darkness. One word came from Christy. *"Wait."* Eyes adjusted to the unusual picture, adapted to the new light intensities, and then fingers of golden light gleamed forth from the lighted side to reach around to the darkened side of the planet. The fingers unraveled at their edges to form swirling tendrils of gold and orange and red that whispered across the dark side, swirling gently around the edge. The scene became an interplay of just this special part of the spectrum—colors of earth no eyes had ever seen from the surface of the world.

Chuck Gambrell dissolved the special screens and the familiar blue-white marble dominated the screen. The camera pulled back steadily until earth had become a small sphere with its magnetopause etched thinly but unmistakably well sunward from the globe. Gambrell was a fine-tuned maestro. The camera swung again toward the sun, covering tens of millions of miles in seconds, the film once again from the solar probe that had raced by the star only 28 million miles distant. Another series of convulsions ripped across the solar surface, jets of flame arced hundreds of thousands of miles above the solar atmosphere, and a subatomic hurricane rushed against earth. In fast camera motion, the earth was again in the distant, remote vacuum of space, and the furious outpouring of the sun smashed into the thinly defined magnetopause. Hurricane violence exploded across the screen. Savage blue-white light sprang into being, and whorls and eddies of shifting, sparkling, raging energy seemed to try to burst from the screen at the shaken viewers.

The in-space violence faded, and out of the dissolve came the control room in Houston. A light blinked on the table by the microphone before Robert Stanton, representing the four major television networks of North America. Bob Stanton was sharp and a veteran of the news game, but he was just a bit eager to stub his toe. Rush Cantrell nudged Brooke Allen. "If Christy has played it right, this guy's going to step right into her little trap."

Brooke was openly puzzled. "Trap? I don't understand what—"

"Listen, damn it," Rush snapped.

"Commander Gordon, I'm Robert Stanton and I'm speaking for all the major news networks of North America." *As if we didn't know*, Rush murmured to himself. "I assume, from these very impressive solar fireworks, that we have been watching the super magnetic storm that caused you to announce a Global Alert."

Chuck Gambrell saw his opportunity and he snatched it. A digital panel before Stanton, out of camera view, flashed "STAND BY." He paused, glowering, and Gambrell punched in the camera for a closing tight view of Christy. He played his lights perfectly, and the world saw a beautiful and competent scientist, who showed a tolerant smile on her face that might have been reserved for a small boy.

"Why, no, Mr. Stanton. You've missed the point entirely. What you have been watching *is a normal, quiet sun*. You see, this is what goes on all the time. Our magnetic fields function quite well against what is really serenity on the part of the sun. The super magnetic storm, which we expect will peak well past our index of three hundred, is just beginning. And against what we expect will hit us from the sun, the barriers will collapse."

Gambrell studied his monitors with his index finger poised, saw what he wanted, immediately punched in the Houston camera, and showed the world a great profile shot of Robert Stanton with his mouth open—and wordless.

# Chapter 4

"Okay, okay, hold it down. The damned show's over." Christy Gordon stood behind the control panel she had used for the television broadcast and news conference between Houston and *Pleiades*. She'd had those earthside idiots right up to her ears. "Everybody listen. From now on we're on a constant double shift for all personnel and that's around the clock. No more solos for duty watch. Those who stand watch, and all sections involved with power, communications, radiation, space environment, and station life systems, will send live reports every two hours to Houston." She ignored the chorus of groans. A distinct separation had been noticed by herself and Rush between station personnel and what they called the earthsiders. In moments of stress or high workloads required from the ground, they became even more insular in their attitude. The concept of *colony*, at least to these people, was steadily eroding the reality of *station*. No matter that they were tied to the earth's apron strings and existed solely at the sufferance of political demigods, their solidarity as a unit had become a dominant force in their lives. Christy, observed silently by Rush Cantrell, stepped quickly into what could become a "mood breech."

"Everyone understand me? I'm well aware that everything we have to say is registered on instruments aboard *Pleiades* and a whole school of satellites orbiting up here with us, as well as what we've placed on the moon. I know that; we all do. And my order for personal contact by each section with CapCom, every two hours, still stands. The station commander made that very same point to me not very long ago. If all they have to talk to up here is something that computes instead of talks, they don't need us, and you'd better remember that. *And*, just in case you think the instruments can do it better, you're not here for a sightseeing tour, and I'll also remind you that no matter what you heard me say on that staged broadcast, the human eye is one hell of a lot more versatile than even you people believe."

She took a deep breath and gestured easily to relax their sudden tension. "How many of you remember who Aleksi Leonov was? He was the cosmonaut who did the first EVA in the old Voskhod program, and he pioneered much of their work with Soyuz and Salyut. He took crayons with him into orbit, as did many of our Gemini and Apollo astronauts, because there isn't a camera made that can capture subtleties like the old Mark IV Eyeball. In a single glance we have an instrument that can scan a wide spectrum, including all objects within range, compute the colors, variations, the faintest whispers and brightest hues, figure out shapes, reflectivity, light source and angle, decide what's right or wrong with it, and a few dozen other things, and all in the blink of those eyes resting atop your noses."

She exhaled noisily. "Enough. Ed Raphael will handle all science board assignments, Ron Doyle leads the power engineering crews, Jamie Knight runs the show for industrial test systems, and I want Bill Ottley for global weather service. Other shifts will maintain their regular assignments, and station management will also be handled by Raphael with final word by Commander Cantrell. Normally I'd ask for questions, but I don't want to hear any from all you good souls. I am sick to death of questions, of baiting newsmen and screwing my poor fellow scientists earthside, who by now must be convinced I am a renegade and should be cast out of their highdome territory."

She saw the smiles and grins catching on about the conference room. "And now, I am going to accept the kind invitation of our station commander for a drink. I understand the bar is closed, so I'll settle for coffee." Abruptly she became Science Lead again. "Mr. Raphael, you have the command."

Raphael's eyes shone in that dark and brooding face, but his smile was warm. "Aye, me good Captain Ahab. Be off with ye."

She placed a thumb on her nose and waggled her fingers at him.

She lifted away from the control panel, floating gently toward the top of the conference room. Moments later they saw her feet disappearing through the hatch into the transfer area that would take her to an outward tube of *Pleiades*. In the transfer area, she studied the life support systems of Tube Three leading away from the Saturn core of the station. Pressures and temperatures were normal. She spun the wheel of the entryway to the tube, pushed up gently, turned to secure the pressure hatch. Ahead of her stretched a long cylinder, glowing softly, with a grip pole in its center much like the old firehouse poles, leading from the upper to the lower floors.

At station center she was weightless, and even a sudden exhalation of breath would cause her to drift ever so slowly in the direction opposite that gentlest of breezes. But the tubes rotated on a giant bearing around the Saturn core and, leading outward to the station rim, a huge wheel that made up the main outer edges of *Pleiades*. The farther she went toward that rim, the greater would become the effect of centrifugal force. Once she reached the rim, the ceiling would become the floor and the floor the ceiling. Outward acceleration would keep her head *down* toward station center, and that same acceleration, the centrifugal force of rotation, would impart a slight but very effective artificial gravity to everything in the rim.

Lifting upward from station center was literally a dream, an incredible sensation of floating. It was something other than zero gravity because the closer she came to the rim the greater the rotation and the more she felt this acceleration. The old law of physics hadn't changed. If you resist acceleration you gain resistance, and the human body interprets resistance to acceleration as weight. But here, just starting upward in the tube, she was light as a feather, and that's something more than weightlessness. It was every dream sensation of floating come to reality, the body relaxed and drifting outward. She grasped the center grip pole and pulled herself toward her outstretched hand. She floated, adrift in body and an all-too-brief daydream, felt herself beginning to accelerate, and gripped the pole. She felt friction enough barely to indicate the first warmth in the palm of one hand, and then the deeply padded contours of the upper hatchway of the tube touched skin.

You *never* opened a hatch in *Pleiades* without instinctive checking of pressures and seals. She studied the gauges and pressed the OPEN panel. The hatch flashed a green light and opened away from her into a riotous airlock. She lifted into the airlock, closed the hatch behind her to seal the tube. Almost hysterical warbling and chirping greeted her. In every airlock there was always a large cage with canaries and parakeets, lighter than any feathery hummingbird on earth, and the station crew had made it a habit when moving through the airlocks of shamelessly spoiling the birds. Christy smiled as the feathers spread and the little creatures hovered, studying her with sharp little eyes, waiting for the morsels she selected from the tray beneath the cage and presented to them. Pavlovian response or not, human and bird had come to accept the arrangement as part and parcel of life in space.

And you always wanted to hear these little darlings or see them move. If they didn't, you had good reason to suspect an air leak somewhere in the area. Space at 346 miles above earth was regarded in a manner different to the earthsiders. They didn't consider danger to lie in air escaping

from *Pleiades*. Far safer to consider any leak as
permitting vacuum to enter, and vacuum was dead-
lier than the most horrible poison gas ever created. It did nasty things to the body and ended the
ordeal with a bloated, frothing corpse. So if a bird
sang or flew, you didn't sweat it.

Who ever would have imagined, thought Christy,
that these same little creatures men once carried
deep into mine shafts to warn them of deadly
gases would also be carried far beyond the earth
to warn of vanished life-giving air? She scanned
quickly along the food and water troughs to be
sure everything was in proper working order,
brushed her hand lightly across the riotous covering of outsized pumpkin leaves along one entire
wall of the airlock, marveling again that so common a terrestrial plant should also be one of man's
dearest allies in space. Algae took in human waste
as nutrients and produced great quantities of oxygen as its reward, but algae demanded all sorts of
water and temperature and pressure controls and,
in the long run, was a bother that drove the station botanists near to distraction. The mutated
pumpkin vines were another matter. They flourished in low gravity, went wild with growth, and
produced enormous quantities of oxygen.

And added fresh food for the packaged meals
and real, live pumpkins to be carved into jack
o'lanterns—well, at least through one Halloween.

Christy went through the security motions of the
far hatch of the airlock and moved into the great
circular tube, the enormous pressurized wheel, like
some gigantic bicycle tire studded with metal and
reinforcing material, that made up the outer rim
of *Pleiades*. She closed the airlock hatch behind

her, and for a moment, closed her eyes as well. *Now* came that moment of adaptation, for the world turned topsy-turvy. Here was the true effect of their rotation around the Saturn core of the space station. Since she was being spun outward, she had to turn the position of her body. Now her feet were on the outside and her head was inside. It took a few moments to adjust, but with walls, ceiling, and floor, with signs, pictures, lights, furniture, and all the visual elements so vital to equilibrium, seconds later she had completed the turnover in mind as well as in body.

She flexed her knees to adjust to the suddenly strange sensation of body weight. Beneath her sneakers she felt the trembling life, the shuddering flows of *Pleiades*. The station was alive in every way one might imagine, inhaling and exhaling, carrying fluids and gases and pressure and bulk through man-made arteries and veins constituting an exquisitely complex network. Machinery thumped and pumps groaned and gurgled, voices carried along the rim. She heard music, the singing of birds, the hissing sighs of pressure locks at work, time gongs, hatches and doors opening and closing. It was the muted and sometimes the louder sounds of mechanical animal, and human life in a splendid harmony.

*Pleiades* truly was an exquisite creature, a living abode of fourteen hundred tons falling effortlessly, *always* falling, around the planet. And it was neatly balanced in its speed and curving angle of fall—as fast as it fell, in mathematical terms, toward the center of the earth, the surface of the earth 346 miles below fell away exactly along the same curving line. The final result was a circular orbit about the tremendous mass of the earth, the huge station and all its people, liquids, machinery, laboratories, birds, and dreams falling endlessly at 4.71 miles *every second* around the world.

Like pilots who never ceased to marvel at the miracle of moving air that gave lift to their wings and flight to man, she never thought of this ballistic motion without her own sense of deep and approving wonder. Fifteen times around the world every day. Each round trip of ninety-six minutes meant a sunrise and sunset in just over an hour and a half.

She thought of a young Christy Gordon, so very long ago as a teenager, looking into the heavens and watching a great satellite sailing soundlessly, unblinking, chrome-gleaming-starshine as it moved across a starfield. How could one imagine that right now, at this instant, people looked into their own starry skies and saw *Pleiades* in precisely that same fashion? But it was *true!* That was the miracle of it all—no sense of motion, of plunging around a globe with the dizzying speed of more than 282 miles every minute.

How did you compute a speed of seventeen thousand miles an hour in terms of *really* understanding that speed? The fastest rifle bullet ever fired was a slow-motion, near-death crawl compared to her speed at this very instant. She shook her head with the wonder that never left her. She stopped by a window hatch, undogged the protecting metal cover. The urge to look outside, to look *down*, at least to get that feeling of down, was almost overwhelming.

*Pleiades* was on the downswing of an orbit, plunging over the southern edge of Africa. The great station circled the planet at an angle to the equator of precisely 63.8 degrees, a sharp slice across the invisible equatorial girth of the world that brought all of mankind's home within view. Far below, giant thunderstorms cast long shadows across the continent. Somewhere below there was wind and lightning and lashing rain, people huddling in huts and other people, a stone's throw, away ensconced in great apartment buildings, but from her lofty advantage they were all invisible from the opaque wand of distance.

*Storm* . . . She thought for a moment of her own words on the TV-cast, of the reality that another invisible storm was raging all about them. *The hell with it*, she told herself, dogging the window hatch and walking in easy, flyweight strides along the rim. She was hungry, she discovered with some surprise. She stopped before the sliding, curving door with the gold seal embossed on its surface and tapped lightly. The door slid away before her. Rush Cantrell greeted her with a mocking bow.

"For our worldwide celebrities, madam, step inside, if you please. Be careful not to leave your autograph on the walls. We're short of cleanup sponges."

She offered Rush an extended middle finger in exchange, then stopped short. Christy looked about her, eyes wide. "What in the name of God do I detect in here?"

He grinned like a kid, enthusiastic, revealing a secret. "A pet project of mine with Ali Rajai, the supreme chef of *Pleiades*. Dinner tonight, m'lady, is filet mignon, done just the other side of medium rare."

She shook her head. "You're crazy." She sniffed gently at the air. "But it *smells* like steak."

"The advantage of command. Ali had it smuggled aboard on the last shuttle delivery. It *is* steak, and it's in the microwave charbroiler. You going to stand there forever or sit down to dinner?"

"All you need to destroy me, Rush, is wine."

"Our smuggling service knows no peers. Coming right up."

The wine glass was plastic, but the wine was heavenly.

# Chapter 5

She sat back, sipping coffee, every taste bud in her body thrilled and still disbelieving of the gastronomical wonder Rush Cantrell had sprung on her. He refused to have her so much as lift a finger. "It's like the condemned woman enjoying a hearty but last meal," he said lightly, pushing dishes and utensils into the ultrasonic dishwasher. He pushed the activate button, a low hum reached her, and in seconds everything was sparkling clean and being moved crisply into its storage racks. "I'm pleased you enjoyed it, Christy," he went on. "You may be on fast rations for the next several weeks until this storm business is behind us. So, while we still have the time, take advantage of it." She nodded as he sprawled in the deeply cushioned seat across the table. He turned on several exhaust fans on the bulkhead behind him, went through a brief ritual of preparation, stretched out his feet, and lit à long, slim cigar. He closed his eyes, savoring the taste of fine Jamaican tobacco, then smiled with pleasure.

"In the old days," he observed quietly, "this would not only have been sacrilege but downright dangerous. Breathing pure oxygen for months . . ." He let the thought hang, shaking his head. He didn't need to explain further to Christy. The smoke was pulled into the exhaust outlet—into charcoal scrubbers, cleansers, and a brief ultrasonic bath—was doused with a precise quantity of water vapor, and then was separated—clean, fresh air back into the commander's quarters, and the carbon dioxide and other waste products shunted through long lines to the algae tanks and pumpkin farms. Very neat, indeed.

He tapped a grey ash into the suction disposal on the table, looked up at her. "How do you feel that show of yours went?"

Christy showed him a sour expression. Then she forced herself to relax. She hadn't realized that deep beneath her obvious enjoyment of dinner and the unexpected personal attention of Rush, she was still rankled with the idiotic demands of the earthsiders. "How did you know?" she asked. "I mean, have I been irritable or something like that?"

He laughed easily. "No, not at all. You've been the absolutely charming dinner companion, even if we're missing candles. It's just that I've been with you for a long time, and you have beautiful skin, and I'm not accustomed to seeing lumps where there shouldn't be any."

"Lumps," she echoed.

"Not the ones that are in the right places," he told her. "They go with the curves."

"Commander Cantrell, I would never have guessed you noticed."

"That's my job."

She stuck out her tongue at him. "You must mean the bumps on my forehead. Would you believe I *did* get one during that press thing . . . or whatever it was we were performing? I became *so* frustrated with that pompous ass, Stanton, that I leaned forward to emphasize something and banged my head on the microphone." She rubbed the barely visible swelling. "Damned fool," she murmured.

"Well, you *did* nail his hide to the barn door," Rush said. "I watched the whole thing. First you nailed him up, scraped away the skin, and then gave him the rock salt treatment. What did you expect him to do? Bless you for stripping his poor little brain naked before half a world watching television?"

"No, no. I didn't care about his cupping his ego in his hands," Christy came back quickly. "What I *do* find objectionable is his using this whole situation, the magnetic storm, I mean, to make brownie points with his advertisers. Baiting the issue deliberately to court public opinion to regard him as a savior for the helpless peoples of earth is as close to throwing up in this game as I could imagine."

"Well, he was right. It worked. You're still hot under the collar. Didn't anyone ever teach scientists about the reverse use of semantics?"

She stared at him. "You lost me on that one."

"You're smarter than he is. You're faster on the uptake. You opened the door and showed him uncompromisingly on the john, so to speak. Took away his precious little old dignity. So he resorted to the tried-and-true methods of old. Like the old

saw about are you still beating your wife? No
matter what you answer you're a loser. He figured
you right and you fell for it, that's all."

Her forehead creased. "How do you figure that?"

Rush gestured with his cigar. "Look, you offered
up something that would choke an elephant. An
intolerable situation. You gave the world a rotten,
stinking super magnetic storm. You—"

"Wait a moment! Whoa there, mister. *I* gave the
world a magnetic storm? That's ridiculous." She
sat bolt upright. "I just told them the *truth*—"

"And the truth," he laughed easily, "does not
make you free. In the old days, Christy, a messenger of bad news to a king was usually put to death
for having the audacity to bring to the court the
truth. Do you really think things have changed as
far as mass human behavior is concerned? To the
great unwashed hoi polloi, good entertainment,
even if it means someone slipping on a banana
peel and breaking his back, is preferred to bad
news arising from good science. Stanton is more
an entertainer than a newsman. Ernie Pyle is a
memorial to discipline, Walter Cronkite retired in
an effusion of realizing he may have been the last
of his breed, and so-called newsmen like Stanton,
who might even be damned good if ever they had
the chance, are forced into a ratings runoff with
comedy and shlock."

Christy stirred uneasily. "I'm not sure I agree.
To me there's a difference between dramatizing
the news and deliberately inciting to unrest."

Rush let cigar smoke float gently from his nostrils, savoring the tobacco. "You're wrong," he said
after a pause. "Dramatizing the news is the same
as building a propaganda machine to get what you

want. Comes a war and the enemy of the moment, no matter if he was yesterday's friend, is vilified, condemned, cursed, and raked over the coals, all to make us hate the better and sacrifice more for the so-called common good. It's always been that way. The methods are different because we've gone through technological change, but that's all. You think we don't go through dramatics to sell our own space program? You think our people don't gloss and shine up everything they present to the temple priests who control the purse strings in Congress? If we didn't do it, you and I wouldn't be here, and I," he added the light touch, "wouldn't be floating about the earth with a fine cigar and a lovely lady."

"Thanks for the order of preference," she said drily.

"Hush. You're fighting historical reality," he chided her. "George Bernard Shaw said it. A woman is only woman, but a good cigar's a smoke. Don't knock me; I'm only trying to use a little education in such charming company."

"*And* you're changing the subject," she poked at him. "Let me make one point."

"I'm all ears."

She ignored his lopsided grin. "Look, do you remember what Stanton said? He made sure he was looking straight into the camera and—"

"I watched, listened, and understood."

"Then how can he get away with attacking us by demanding to know why, as he put it, 'they bloody well don't *do* something about this terrible problem?' Then he went on—"

"I heard it," Rush repeated quietly.

"—and on about our spending all those billions

of dollars and all they got for their tax money was a corny television show from space." She tightened her hands into fists and grimaced. "If I could get my hands on that, that—"

"You miss the whole point, lady."

She came up short with that remark. "*What* point?" she demanded.

"Down there," he said, gesturing with his cigar. "The Earthsiders. Don't you understand? No matter *how* Stanton acted or put on the dog, the people listened to what you had to say. They listened, they heard, your visualizations were right on target, and now they're all talking about it. Sure, they'll ignore it for a while, putting aside bad news until tomorrow. You know the power companies, all the telephone and television people, the computer outfits, airlines, and shipping, everybody who's going to be affected, *they're* already making preparations to get through the geomagnetic fields. That's what counts, not the great unwashed."

She looked at him carefully. "You've dropped that great unwashed routine on me several times. Do you really hold the common man in such low repute?"

"This is the liberated age, Christy. Make it the common man *and* woman." He shook his head. "No, not at all. But I understand their position. It's one massive confusion being shoved down their throats and they can't do anything about it. All you could hope to accomplish was to make them understand *why* their TV sets are blowing snow, why they can't hear Aunt Maude on the phone because of static, why all their computer-processed bills are all screwed up, and so on. So you did what you wanted to, but you don't realize it yet.

What would you have the average Joe or Jane *do*? There isn't anything they can do about it. That's why they listen to Stanton. He's the modern-day Archie Bunker against the world of science, and while you're a hell of a lot better built than he is, he's the better entertainer."

Christy sipped a second cup of coffee. "Is that your official evaluation, Commander Cantrell?" She peered with smiling eyes over her cup at him, watched Rush shake his head. He put down the cigar for more coffee of his own.

"Nope. Not mine to appraise, fair lady. This man runs a tight ship. *You're* the one who upholds public confidence in us." He was back with his cigar again, studying the ash before letting it fall gently into the suction tray. "I wouldn't have it any other way."

"You know, just a few days ago I would never have believed this about you."

"Believed what?"

"Rush, are you aware that this is the first time in almost a year on this station that I've been alone with you? I mean, alone on a personal basis. One-on-one. I've *never* seen you wearing the skin of a warm, companionable, very decent human being. Where have you been hiding for an entire year?"

"Right in front of your eyes."

"Did it have to take a Grade-A emergency with the sun to make you visible?" She detested the slight exasperation she knew he must detect in her voice, but she knew of no other way to seize this rare advantage of finding a man instead of the human machine with her.

"Could be," he acknowledged, and she knew he was puzzled by her emphasis on the suddenly warm, pleasant relationship they were sharing. "But maybe I've been here all the time and you were looking for somebody else."

She felt herself tighten, the instinctive move when she was handed personal criticism. Just a bit coolly, she offered her protest for his remarks. "I don't know how you mean that, Rush."

"Damn it, Christy, anybody watching you right now would see you clambering atop your high horse. For Christ's sake, *you're* a warm and sensitive human being, even if you *are* so gung-ho on this female equality bit. Since no one is trying to dilute your equality, why are you always so ready for a fight on the subject?"

She was amazed. "Are you serious?"

He nodded. "One moment we're enjoying a beautiful time together. The next you're trying to psychoanalyze me. Why?"

A dozen responses leaped to her lips and a dozen times she fought them down. She took a deep breath. "Maybe you're right. Maybe I was looking all this time, not *for* someone else, but *at* someone who was there."

He grinned. "Now you've got me confused. Spell that out."

"Rush Cantrell, you're the man most likely *never* to be taken for an astronaut I've ever worked with since I joined the NASA program seven years ago."

He blinked at her. "You're serious?"

"I am."

He laughed. "You're right. I know it. I didn't think you knew it."

"Are we playing the games people play?" she threw back at him.

"Takes two to tango," he offered.

"All right. I hate to rain on your parade, especially after you've been the perfect host, and all that," she said, "but the truth of the matter is—" She drew herself up short, her lips pressed tightly together. "Forgive me. I really had no right. I imagine I sound rather prissy right now."

"You don't, and if I didn't care to know your thoughts I wouldn't have led you on, and I have a skin that's impossible to puncture." The cigar described a lazy, gestured invitation. "Have at it, fair lady."

She studied him before going on. That old familiar picture of astronauts the public clutched so dearly was of the young and lean, sharp of eye, flat of tummy, adorned with both jet pilot helmet and academician flatboard, and interested primarily in flying into space and tumbling with someone else's girl or wife in bed. The more dedicated the hero impulse, the more likely was the pilot preference to win out, even if briefly, over the skin-on-skin routine. But *this* man wasn't any of these things.

She looked at him openly and frankly and he held her gaze, unabashed by what was now so clearly a penetrating inspection of his own self. That in itself told her much about this man who was thirty-eight years old. A man's age in this business was almost always a paradox. Anyone under forty couldn't possibly gain *all* the qualifications for so complicated and demanding and responsible a position as commanding a fourteen-hundred-ton space station. He *had* to be at least partially a genius, in excellent physical condition, a skilled engineer, scientist, meteorologist, at least a passable astrophysicist, steeped in fluid dynamics and aerodynamics, more than a paramedic, know astronomy and the higher math, be an absolute whiz at navigation, geology, and oceanology and, after all that, have a steely grip on his own emotions and be able to command not only the men of *Pleiades*, but also its women. That last thought startled her. She had never entertained just how difficult it would be for *her* to command this station. As Science Lead she had headaches enough, but not until this moment of studying Rush Cantrell had she taken a look into the mirror of her *own* psyche.

She studied him from this new vantage. "Lean and mean" didn't apply to Cantrell, and space cadet he definitely was *not*. He was stocky in build, powerful in musculature and, she had noticed several times, adorned with a thick matting of body hair. Astronauts, she sighed to herself, are satin-smooth of skin, and here I am with an extremely intelligent and talented grizzly. This is the only man I know who could float about nude in a weightless chamber and collect all the loose dust particles floating in midair.

"You have a reputation," she said abruptly, "of being meaner than a wolverine when you get ticked off."

" 'The Guide to Good Manners' is worthless when you're in a situation where an instant decision means life or death for many people," he said, his face expressionless. "Command is not and has never been a popularity contest."

She felt a chill wind. "Did I just get bitten?"

He laughed. "Good Lord, no. I suppose my verbal reaction was like pressing a switch. You don't think I haven't heard that about myself before, do you?"

"It doesn't bother you?"

He shrugged. "What for? Popularity never changed the facts of a situation. A popular commander who clouds his judgment with popularity yearnings cheats himself and his crew who depend on him."

"I have the feeling that every time you speak on this subject your answer comes as automatically as pressing a button," she noted.

"Then what you're looking for isn't so much a desired answer as a desired *manner* of response, isn't it? You know what that sounds like? Being in the water after jumping from a sinking ship and complaining that the life raft someone threw to you is the wrong color." She listened and nodded, at the same time noting that his voice didn't rise or fall. He *was* responding with courtesy to what he obviously considered to be a question built on sophomoric reasoning.

"Did you always want to be up here?" she asked in a sudden change of subject. "I mean, you know how some kids are. Stars in their eyes from the first time they ever saw a plane or watched a rocket. That sort of thing."

He laughed. "NASA asked me that same question when I joined the outfit. At least their sharp-eyed little public relations staff, always on the lookout for good press copy, did. For the space administration, good public relations is the keystone to getting appropriations for missions like ours. There are plenty of qualified pilots and mission specialists, but the real demand is for those with a great public relations image. I never saw

myself that way." He relit a cigar. "At the same
time, by then I began to have a sneaking suspicion
that I'd been groomed for years for this job without ever having been made aware of that fact. So I
went in that direction. Work at my job and ignore
the flash bulbs and press conferences. I told the
NASA public affairs people to kiss off and stop
bothering me."

Her eyes widened; she recalled the enormous
hype that had followed her and her science team
along for years before *Pleiades* ever left the Earth.
And he was right. She had known precious little
about the man who would command them all in
orbit, while everyone else was practically a neon-
lit open book. "Then," she said slowly, "what got
you up here? I don't mean to be pushy, but you
very neatly sidestepped my question."

"I didn't mean to," he told her quickly. "Look,
Christy, it's just not that romantic and made for
bright lights on a marquee. I went to high school
in Marietta, Georgia, and it's difficult not to be
drowned in aircraft when you live near the Lock-
heed plant, as well as all that air traffic in the
Atlanta area. Science, astronomy, and geology were
the big things for me as a kid, and I didn't even
have to work at it. It just came naturally. The idea
of flying appealed to me and, like a lot of other
kids, I learned to fly out of a grass strip about ten
miles from home. Did the whole routine, first solo
when I was sixteen. That's where I met Barbara.
She didn't fly, but here was this beautiful girl who
loved jumping out of airplanes—she was into skydiving. Whatever clicks between people clicked between us. We were kids but it got better as it went
along."

She had never heard of Barbara, and she felt a pang within her. Then she clamped her mouth shut. Time for questions on that subject later. *If any*, she warned herself.

"From Georgia, I decided to try a different area, so I went to the University of Florida in Gainesville. I majored in hydrography and nuclear engineering, and I also decided to get in a lot of free flying, so I joined the Air Force ROTC, which gave me the chance to become professional at what I was doing and fly some of the hotter military stuff. I had also gone bananas about the ocean, and there were plenty of opportunities for scuba diving and learning more advanced systems. I must have been crazy because I had little enough time as it was, but I added submarine studies and deep-ocean exploration to my schoolwork. On top of that, Barbara and I decided to get married. We'd been living together while I went to the university. So," he said, his voice a touch huskier, "we did. Get married, that is."

"Rush, I've never heard about your wife before. Do you have a picture of her?"

He shook his head. "No." An awkward silence followed, then he leaned forward, passing through a deep reflective moment. His head lifted and he held steady eye contact with Christy. "That's all in the past. We were scuba diving in a quarry. Barbara's air tank malfunctioned." His face was stone. And she understood, just a bit better in these few moments, why he was known as bullwhip tough when it came to any of his crew operating equipment in space that meant life or death. *Barbara died from equipment malfunction.* Christy resisted the suddenly powerful urge to touch his face.

"I guess," he went on slowly, "I took out a lot of my grief on the gridiron. I'd never been very much for competitive sports—before I lost Barbara, I mean. This terrible pressure was building inside me to *do* something about losing her. I wanted to strike out and yet I knew I couldn't blame anyone. But something was twisting around inside my head, and psychological need was overpowering any rational thought."

She smiled, gratified with the upswing of mood. "I think I know what happened. Football, wasn't it?"

"Uh huh. The Gators. I played for two years, and I transformed every man on that field from the opposition into a very real, hated enemy. Carrying the ball became my thing."

"Your real name is Rick?"

"Until I went crazy on the football field. They stuck me with the name of Rush."

"That's self-deprecation," she chided gently. "You set an all-time record for rushing for Florida."

"Not important now," he said with an easy wave of his hand. "Not important for a long time. The name just won't go away and I quit fighting what people liked. It didn't ask much of me."

*So he does bend!* "Do you mind if I ask what happened later? After finishing school, I mean?" Then she added hastily, "Forgive me. I sound like I'm interrogating you but I'm really not."

"What are you doing, then?"

She didn't hesitate an instant. "Learning more about someone whom I've respected for a long time and have come to admire very much during a much shorter time. Feminine and personal curiosity on a most intense level, Commander Cantrell."

"Fair enough." He glanced at the digital timer on his cabin bulkhead. "We have a little time before we go to work. Full station inspection. You and me."

"Please. Go on. After school?"

"Would you believe I earned my air force wings, fighter pilot, the whole package, and the day I was commissioned I was tapped on the shoulder for special duty by the navy?"

"I didn't know you flew from aircraft carriers."

"That's just it. I didn't. Here I was all ready to soar off into the wild blue yonder like the rest of the young tigers, and I ended up in special schools. Very hush-hush, no public fingers pointing us out. Nuclear engineering, ocean sciences, submersibles— that sort of thing. Seven days a week for eighteen months. And one day, when the cram courses and the fog cleared from my head, I stepped into the sunshine as a Lieutenant S.G. in the U.S. Navy, of all things. They didn't waste any time. Gave me a thirty-day leave, and the moment I reported back for duty, they buried me. Got to admit I loved it, though. Research submarines, patrol and attack subs, underwater demolition teams—the works. It was a crazy crosshatch. They kept me flying and put me through jump school, so I ended up with paratrooper wings as well. There were ten of us who remained together. You know one of the other men."

"I do?"

"Sure. Our fiery redheaded Irishman—Marvin O'Leary, our Boats Officer. We did the whole routine together for years."

"But how did all this lead to," she gestured in a sweeping move of her arm, "this?"

"For a long time I didn't know, either. I mean, I spent two years as engineering officer, nuclear power systems engineer, and then exec officer, and finally as the skipper of a nuclear-powered attack boat. Two years in subs. I swear, I hardly saw daylight the whole time. A killer sub with a nuclear drive is an incredible world unto itself. You live with the reactor *all* the time until it's second nature, as common as a coal-fired boiler. You operate with high speed, under tremendous physical as well as mental pressure, you've *got* to get along with your crew, and you're always playing death tag with the Russian killer boats. When we came home from patrol, I went on a long leave to clear my head. In the mountains, of course. Hiking and camping. Me and O'Leary. It was marvelous. When we reported back in they had our orders ready and waiting. Houston, of all places. Detached duty and assigned to NASA."

She showed her surprise. "Just like that?"

"That's what it seemed like, Christy. But they'd been planning this project all along. When we reached Houston, we were put into underwater construction in the big training tanks there. We figured it was for SeaLab or some other underwater ocean-living habitat. But we knew that wouldn't hold together. They didn't make things for underwater systems. Not the stuff we worked with. Then it struck us we were working under an environment intended to produce neutral buoyancy." He snapped his fingers. "Click; we got the message. This wasn't for down below. It was intended for upstairs. Here."

"But why didn't they just *tell* you?"

"Part of their program. Figure things out for

ourselves. The moment we did and confronted the big boys, they just smiled and added to our workload. O'Leary and I divided our time between working underwater and assembling parts of what would become *Pleiades*, and flying jets and spending days in the shuttle and station simulators. I didn't really believe I was scheduled to go, to end up here, because when you looked at the whole NASA program, what the hell, I was about the worst selection for an astronaut. These other guys are the tigers with the tailored flight suits, shining faces and pearly teeth, and all that garbage. Well, NASA figured that was great for going up and coming down but awfully fragile for the long run. To boss this big wheel, they wanted someone long accustomed and proven in working and living within severely enclosed spaces, under pressure-seal conditions, and working with people where some sticky tensions could build up. All this time my training had been for this job and I didn't even know it. One clue, for sure, came in the neutral buoyancy construction work." He laughed. "Before we started wearing the pressure suits, I mean. I almost spit out my mouthpiece one day when the construction engineer assigned to work with me swam up in a bikini. She was a knockout. Dianne Vecchio."

She joined his laughter. "And here we are. Eleven women out of your crew of fifty-two." She hesitated a moment. "Straight out, Rush. Do you mind women aboard your station?"

"Its not *my* station, Christy."

*Just like that, he's switched to his official stance again. Damn, I've got to watch how I ask him anything . . .*

"How would you compare working underwater to being up here?"

"You mean being here as compared to those tanks in Houston?"

"That'll do."

He shrugged. "Well, we all worked underwater in the station replica. You were part of that program. To me, this is a hell of a lot easier. Inside the station, under normal conditions, we don't need heavy pressure suits or clumsy gear, and we're either zero-g or light gravity at the rim—that sort of thing. Of course, there's nobody just outside this tank to haul in your ass if something goes wrong."

She smiled. "There are other compensations, I daresay."

"Sure," he responded. "You, for example."

She shook her head. "Not what I meant."

"What, then?"

"No sharks."

He boomed with laughter. "Was that a professional or a personal judgment?"

# Chapter 6

The cigar was long gone in the arc incinerator, reduced in a flash of dull blue light to ionized particles. And the warm, gentle Rush Cantrell with whom Christy had spent the last several hours seemed to have vanished with the same finality. He turned from their conversation to his communications board, contacted a selected group, and gave his orders with all the inflection of a bored computer. They were to conduct a complete security tour and inspection of *Pleiades*, just as a captain and his top officers might personally scrutinize a ship they knew was about to be engulfed in a violent storm at sea. If Christy hadn't seen and experienced the man who'd wined and dined her, she would never have believed that "other side" of Rush Cantrell even existed. But she *had* seen the other man, the face he kept averted from all those about him, and now, despite the seeming harshness that attended his orders and work, she knew what lay behind it. She hurried off to her own quarters where she outfitted herself with instruments and tools, and was surprised to discover how eager she was to return to Rush's cabin before the others met there as a group. She had a thousand things she wanted to talk about with this man, and here they were about to conduct a station tour with a small technical army. She felt like a starving girl with her nose pressed against a bakery window.

At Christmas time, yet.

She walked quickly along the rim corridor, tapped on his door, and announced her name. The door slid aside with a quiet hissing sound and she went inside. Rush was buckling on a heavy belt, much like that of a powerline engineer, with instruments, tools, and communications gear hooked and clipped to the belt. He nodded at her. "The others will be along in a few minutes. We'll start our inspection tour from here."

She walked up to him, almost face to face. His eyes narrowed at the sudden familiarity. "I'm glad they're not here yet. I didn't thank you for dinner."

"Oh, that's—"

*It's now or never, Christy, old girl.* Her inner voice compelled her movements and she leaned her lips against his, holding the kiss long and tenderly. Before he could say a word, she stepped back and eased slowly into an armchair.

"I don't really believe you did that," he said after a struggle to find his voice.

Her face froze. "I didn't mean to—"

"You don't understand. I've wanted to do that for longer than I care to remember."

They remained that way for several moments, more said with their eyes than words might have spoken for them. He started to her and they both heard the knock at the door. He didn't hesitate an instant, a move Christy observed and judged. *He doesn't waste even a split second in shifting mental and emotional gears. I'll have to remember that.* Rush pressed the door release, left it on *Open*. Gale Bowie stood before him, in a work jumpsuit with her own belt of radiation and other medical monitoring instruments. The girl with curly blonde hair smiled at Rush and nodded to her own commander. Christy gestured her greetings. "Anyone else from MOT?"

She shook her head. "Not unless Commander Cantrell called after I left," she said easily. She was lead MOT, the head of the Medical Observation Team. Gale, along with their Canadian astronaut technician, Bruce McCandless, were not the most popular people aboard *Pleiades*. They carried the burden of their title—medical observation. They were medical doctors but their primary field was psychology, and they were regarded by the others as snoops doing their best to pry into people's behavioral patterns and emotions. Their job was understood, but few people take well to the role of guinea pig, no matter how realistic or lofty the need. Christy understood Gale's position, understood also why Gale had not accepted her entrance as *not* interfering with what Christy and Rush had been doing. No matter that they had enough equipment hanging from their belts to clank loud enough to awake the dead. Sometimes, Christy mused, *I believe the observers are the ones on the edge of falling over an emotional cliff.*

"Gale, sit down," Christy said, leaving no room for argument. This was the best way to communicate with the MOT people. If you offered pleasantries, they looked for something the giver was trying to conceal. "Commander Cantrell and I were talking about Pleiades."

Trained or not, Gale Bowie's raised brow told all. She didn't believe they were talking about the station, and she wasn't that hard for Christy to read. "For God's sake, stop jumping to conclusions," Christy said, more snappish than she intended. "*Not* the station, girl. The original Pleiades."

An order was an order; Gale sat. "Oh, you mean the stars. The constellation."

"No, she doesn't," Rush tossed into the uneasy conversation. "We were talking about the original Pleiades. Do you know about them?"

Gale shifted uncomfortably. "No, sir; not really. They're of the Greek mythology, I believe."

"You *believe?* Don't you *know?* You intend me to believe that you're here to observe how we kneejerk and bend to and fro and you don't even know how this station got its name? You haven't been doing your homework, Bowie."

Christy watched and listened, aware that Rush was putting the girl in her place, but not really understanding why.

"Sir, NASA named the station and I didn't believe it was that important to know the why of it, just that it had a mythological source, and—"

"Bowie, *every* manned vehicle sent into space by your country has that historicity behind it. Or hadn't you recognized the pattern? Mercury, Gemini, Apollo, Skylab—"

Gale Bowie bit hard. "Sir, Skylab is hardly Greek mythology in its original form."

"True," Rush admitted. "But it was also *un*-manned when it was launched, if you'll dig into your memory cells."

Gale struggled to keep up. "But what about the shuttles, Commander? Columbia, Enterprise, Falcon, and the others. They're not from mythology."

"Shows how stupid NASA can be, young woman. They broke the chain. Bad luck and that sort of thing. That's why I named this station, called it *Pleiades*. It has mystery to it. Makes you think." He held his eyes on her. "Or it *should*."

"I—I don't understand, sir."

"Gale, the Pleiades were the daughters of Atlas, and there were seven girls in that godly family. If you knew your mythology, you'd know their names were Electra, Maia, Taygete, Alcyone, Merope, Celaeno, and Sterope. Apparently they were something very desirable because Orion exhausted himself chasing them. Maybe he was just horny, or whatever, but he refused to quit and he hounded them. Zeus watched the whole caper from the top throne, took pity on them, and to get Orion off their backs, committed them into the heavens as stars. And if you'll picture the constellations, you'll notice, as mythology records, that even then Orion kept after them. After all, they had a pretty good track record when they were earthsiders. Maia, for example, was the mother of Hermes, and no one knows if there was a marriage license involved. Electra birthed Dardanus, who went on to found the race of Trojans. Did you ever see the constellation, Gale?"

"Pleiades? Yes, sir."

"How many stars?"

"You said there were seven sisters—"

"How many *stars?*"

"Uh, seven—"

"Six. That's why I named this station *Pleiades*. Six stars are visible. The seventh is visible only to those with unusually keen sight. How is yours, Gale?"

"Why, I see perfectly, sir." She was thoroughly off balance by now.

"Well, perhaps the problem is your insight— maybe it's lacking something. Not to fret, girl. Ah, you're now in good company. We have our protector with us. Come in, Sam."

They turned as Sam Hammil crossed the doorway. Rush Cantrell had picked this man personally. He'd watched him in training. Sam was tall, almost cadaverous, yet strung tight with long and powerful muscles. He shaved his skull and looked all the world like a naked Abraham Lincoln, except for his perpetual five o'clock shadow. Sam Hammil ghosted his way through life. On earth he seemed to levitate instead of walk. He never got out of a chair; he unfolded. On *Pleiades* he seemed to walk in zero-g. And above all his other qualifications as a mechanical, plumbing, electrical, electronic, and other systems genius, he had something even more important—a strange sixth sense that mocked the best medical and analytical minds in NASA. Sam was a dowser, and it had nothing to do with water. But just as an old farmer might use a switch of birch to find hidden water beneath the ground, Sam could *sense* trouble in mechanical and electrical systems. Engines talked to him, generators babbled, pressure systems gurgled; all yielded their secrets to Sam Hammil. When something was wrong or failure imminent down the line, Sam always seemed to *know*. To Rush Cantrell, security officer reached unprecedented heights with this chrome-domed wonder. Sam was the single dominant reason why *Pleiades* didn't strangle on the problems inherent in its design and functioning. With the geomagnetic storm already established in fact, and predicted both by Christy Gordon *and* Sam Hammil to increase at a furious rate, Rush was taking no chances. He wanted the station inspected by his team, and he wanted Bloodhound Hammil along to sniff out what their instruments might not detect and their intuition would never see.

Sam nodded to the others. "I see four of us. Who's number five?" he asked of Rush.

"What makes you so sure there'll be five?" Rush countered.

"You got your ways," Sam answered quietly. He even *talked* like a Connecticut Yankee farmer. "You never do anything in even numbers, Rush. That way, if you want opinions, you can get a standoff. An odd-numbered group means you get a commitment right off, one way or the other."

"You're in the wrong business," Rush told him. "Sounds like you ought to be teamed up with Gale and Bruce McCandless."

Sam studied the still-uncomfortable MOT girl, then paid her closer attention. "You feeling poorly, Gale?"

She shook her head quickly, averting her eyes. Sam turned to Christy. "*Something's* wrong. This isn't time for fun and games."

"It's nothing, Sam," Christy reassured him. "She's just looking for a star, that's all."

It was strange to see Sam Hammil without an answer. The impasse melted away when the last member of the inspection team loomed in the doorway—Steve Longbow, an American Indian with a massive chest, a wide chin of granite, and thickness through the shoulders. He had forearms as thick as the thighs of most men—but no legs. They'd been severed from his body in a training accident at the Houston space research center. Someone had let loose with a laser and it had spun from its locking mount. A savage blue-white beam had pulsed in a semicircle, and when the beam flashed off there was Steve Longbow, lying stupefied on the floor with his legs laser-sliced from the rest of his body.

He refused tin legs, spurned prosthetics, and told the world he'd walk as well as any man could walk. He wanted bionic limbs—not the pretty ones; strictly utilitarian—and he had plans for making them work better than anyone anticipated. He changed the world; his world. What would have let him cope earthside became a definite advantage in space. Working under zero-g conditions, his legs were superior to what had grown with the rest of his body, and where the station rim gave him slight gravity, he was in his prime. He'd come straight to Rush Cantrell when the *Pleiades* project was announced.

"I want to go with you," he told Rush.

"Why?"

"Because I'm the best zero-g construction man in the space business, that's why," Longbow snapped. "Because we Indians are absolute naturals in this game. Because heights don't mean buffalo turds to us. Who the hell do you think built all your bridges and skyscrapers? Norwegians or Peruvians? Nah; it was us. We got a monopoly on high-rise construction."

"You talk big for a legless Indian."

"Sure, sure, Cantrell. You think that's important?" The deep bronzed face grew darker.

It didn't faze Rush Cantrell. "Maybe. I didn't say it was. You brought up the question, not me."

Steve Longbow blinked. "By damn, you're right. I did. That makes you sharper than I thought you were."

"You also talk like a dummy—tenement English from a Sioux tribe descendant. Doesn't fit. It also doesn't go with your master's degree in engineering or your doctorate in structural stress. Knock off the studio acting and level with me."

Longbow laughed. "Was I that transparent?"

Rush ignored the question. "Tell me what you have to offer that any other man with your qualifications can't bring into orbit."

"Well, we could get stuck in that tin can of yours up there and, if you lose the key to the airlock, with these legs of mine I could always kick my way out through the walls, and then all you have to do is follow. I'm a nifty can-opener—computerized, self-propelled, already programed for the work—and I need to be patted on the head no more than twice a day."

Rush chuckled. "Welcome aboard. You got it."

"White man talk with straight tongue?"

"Am I going to have to live with that palaver all the time?"

Longbow shook his head. "Nope. Just one more thing. I got this buddy of mine—"

"This an Indian without arms, maybe?"

He was astonished when Longbow didn't bat an eye. "You're close, Cantrell. It's a spic. *He's* a spic. Arturo Lopez. Has the finest wetback ancestry of anyone I know."

"How'd he lose his arms?"

"He tried to save a Blackbird after it flamed out. He *should* have ejected. But the SR-71 costs something like sixty million dollars a shot. Lot of wampum in one of those machines. Lopez rode it down to the desert. He hit a hummock doing about a hundred and forty knots."

That told Rush a great deal. Any man who was qualified for the pilot's seat of the 2,000-mile-an-hour reconnaissance jet was way up on the list of top people. Rush ignored the human plea implicit in Longbow's request. He *had* to. The station came first. "What's his specialty? A bionic arm salute?"

"You're funny, Cantrell. But you see through things. That's good. Lopez has bionic arms, but not the kind you may think. He's spent the last six months in the neutral buoyancy chamber in a Closed Cherry-Picker unit. You know, the pressurized manned remote work unit, and—"

"I know the equipment. Get on with it, Longbow."

"He had his bionic prosthetics designed to fit into and *with* the cherry picker. It's almost a *gestalt*. He and the machine literally become one. He developed the microprocessing systems himself. He thinks what he needs to do, and the electrical signals are picked up by his arm stumps. They're translated into movement by the computers, and what starts out as a signal for an arm or hand movement continues on to the work unit."

Rush thought about that. Jesus. "Can he really do all this?"

"Indian never lie. Besides, I was hoping you'd ask. The spic is in the buoyancy tank now, in the cherry picker, and he's waiting to strut his stuff for you."

Rush stood and went to the door. "Let's go."

Everything Longbow said was true. Arturo Lopez was incredible. He did ballet movements, glided and floated and levitated, and the remote arms and gripclaws of the cherry picker, fitted out with a dozen different tools, functioned like a surgeon's instruments under Lopez's bidding. "I'll be damned," Rush murmured.

"I don't think so," Longbow told him. "You have third sight. In fact, you're only the second white man I've ever met in my life who had it."

"Tell the wetback he's in." Rush started off, stopped, and turned back. "Do you two clowns know how much paperwork there's going to be in all this for me to do?"

Longbow laughed. "White man's work is never done. I'll say this once and only once, Cantrell." The Indian's face sobered. "Thanks."

They'd been close friends ever since. And now they were about to start inspecting a huge space station that would be no more than the tiniest mote in a raging ocean of radiation. Christy was on her feet now that the five people were assembled. She nodded to Hammil. "Sam, you start out with Gale and Steve. We'll be right along."

Rush waited until the others were on their way

to the tube that would take them to the Saturn
core of the station. "Mind telling me what that
was all about?" he queried.

"Why did you tear up Gale? The girl's a wreck."

Rush nodded. "Her problem is worrying about
people worrying about her poking and prying.
That's her job. They're going to be thin-skinned
until this whole radiation thing is over. If Gale is
busy soul-searching herself, she'll ease off from the
others. Smooth ship and all that."

"Commander, you continue to surprise me."

"Move it, lady."

The others waited for them at the airlock entrance to Tube I. Rush and Christy joined them,
but on a sudden impulse, Rush motioned the others to stand by. He went to the outside bulkhead
of the rim and undogged a metal port, exposing
the thick armorglass beneath. Some instinct had
prompted him to escape for a moment the totality
of machinery all about him. He moved close to the
viewport to look down, to direct his eyes earthside.

Three hundred and forty-six miles below, the
sweep of the planet visible to him was exchanging
night for day. The tumbling curve of the world
concealed the sun from direct view, but not its
glowing, millions-of-miles-long spikes of light
spraying across and around the very planet about
which he fell at nearly five miles every second.
The moment seemed suddenly very precious to
him, and he found pleasure in knowing he was
snared in an optical illusion. From his high cradle
of centrifugal force it appeared as if *Pleiades* were
levitated beyond the planet, with no rushing motion of its own, and that it was the world below
that spun so rapidly. Optical illusion though it

might be, it was one of compelling beauty as he watched the sphere that blocked out most of space rolling toward him.

He knew he should begin the station inspection, but this moment captured him, as it does so many pilots flying along the edges of cloud worlds that make the earth seem to snap out of existence. He moved his gaze to that enormous spread of planet still huddled in darkness. By now he was well trained in swift detection of the glowing bowls he knew were great metropolitan areas. The sun remained obscured by the bulk of earth and he could even find cities beneath clouds, their glow diffusing the atmosphere as would sprays of glowing fog along a waiting beach of darkness. His eyes moved and wonders rolled in ecstasy before him. The curving edge of the world sliced away an inverted scimitar of glowing stars. The invading dawn arrived with breakneck speed, a whispering rush to which his eyes were always captive, his senses irresistibly fascinated.

A dawn hurtled across the world, knowing not mountains or oceans or cities or clouds, but only new-day birth. The crescent of rainbow hues slashed into night, irresistible and unstoppable, a band of light that seemed to glow of its own substance rather than light that had sped in eight minutes from a star ninety-three million miles distant. Well ahead of the global-wide crescent, preceding the blood-red hue of its glowing edge, fainter light rushed along the earth. Rush knew the twilight zone painted a false canvas. The light he saw was reflected from high clouds; the land beneath still cowered in darkness. He lifted his gaze to the velvet backdrop beyond the world where, with the sun still obscured by the planetary bulk, he could see the needle points of starlight in their haphazard splash across infinity. Then the iridescent dawn was upon the world and a faint pink glow appeared along the edge of the viewport. His vision went far beyond and two worlds leaped into view, one huddled in its nocturnal blanket and the other awakening to the violent slash of light.

A moment before the light sensors automatically polarized the viewport, he had the uncanny feeling he was rushing at three hundred miles a minute into the sun. It jerked savagely from its hiding place below the horizon. He stared unblinking at the thermonuclear boiler so many millions of miles distant. The flaming disc mocked him.

He felt someone by his side, and out of the corner of his eye realized Christy had joined him, had remained silent until this moment. "I feel like a child," she said, almost in a whisper. "A child caught up and torn between the reality of fantasy and the fantasy of reality." Rush studied her face, recognized a strain through the mind just beyond that furrowed brow. "I can't help mixing my wonder with my numbers," she went on. "*Look* at it. It dominates us all. Every planet and moon and asteroid and planetoid and all the comets and rings, everything, is a tiny fraction of that thing out there. I look at it and I keep trying to see, and to recognize, that this dawn we just watched was born twenty million years ago."

He turned slightly toward her, knowing the others were waiting and watching. *Let them damned well wait*, was the only thought to interfere briefly with his sudden new rapport. "Tell me," he said to Christy.

She sighed. "It's the old tug of war between heart and mind. The sun is god to us all, and yet I can't help trying to see *inside* it. Looking into the soul of a god can be very trying," she said with a dry smile. "Down there, in the belly of that thing, a half-million miles below its surface, is that furnace burning at thirty million degrees. I can't comprehend such temperature and pressure. All I can do is make feeble comparisons and recite the numbers. But at least I try to *think* of what's going on down there. Every second, every single instant, six hundred million tons of hydrogen vanishes. *Zap!* It's gone. But it really isn't. There's a wizard living in that sun, and every second he changes those six hundred million tons of hydrogen into helium. Not quite; *almost* the whole amount. Then there's that tiny fraction of a difference. Life and death in the bowels of the sun," she said, almost hypnotized by the picture seen by her eye and the one in her mind. "Atoms fusing and thrusting away gamma rays. Two words. Gamma rays. Energy every second beyond anything of which we can conceive. And the gamma rays rush about madly, bouncing like glowing billiard balls of tremendous energy and no substance, and they carry on their insane dance, always thrusting outward, like gamma sperm struggling in the wrong direction. For twenty million years that energy is trapped, but it kicks and pushes and oozes to the surface of a sun. There everything is madness, fire boiling insanely, tremendous magnetic fields, explosions, and God knows what else. The gamma rays have to fight their way beyond this, and they do, of course, and that's why the sun is yellow and gold, because we're seeing the energy of those gamma rays in the visible part of the spectrum, and they come hurtling toward us and—"

"Enough," she heard.

It was like a bucket of cold water in her face. "What?" she asked, blinking her eyes rapidly.

"You were on quite a trip," he said quietly.

"Good Lord." She drew a deep breath. "Rush, I'm sorry. That was selfish of me."

"True," he told her, "but nevertheless quite beautiful."

"Why, thank you," she said, genuinely pleased.

"You're welcome. Now, turn off, will you? We have work to do."

Utterly dumbfounded at the sudden change in this man, *again*, she was forced to hurry up to catch him and the others.

# Chapter 7

Control Central followed the progress of the inspection team as they moved into the topside airlock of Tube I. As the five-man crew entered each compartment, they took temperature, humidity, air flow, oxygen, inert gases presence, all types and levels of radiation and other readings that gave them a clear signature of the health of *Pleiades*. Steve Longbow moved into the airlock and down the glowing tube toward station center, the Saturn core, with his own array of instruments, including an electronic stethoscope which at regularly spaced intervals he placed against bulkheads, power lines, fluid-carrying pipelines, and the other fiber of the station. He was especially attentive to the cross-beams and structural members crisscrossing the station as would the skeletal structure of a rimmed wheel-like living creature, for to him this was the real *Pleiades*, breathing in and out, gaining life and sustenance from its ability to absorb and expel, to be flexible rather than rigid. The station spoke to him through his measurements, told him torque and twisting and tension, temperature and irradiation, dust speckling and outgassing of metals exposed to vacuum. A billion tiny gnats a day peppered *Pleiades*; space dust and grains of sand and the occasional pea-sized meteoroids that could slam into the station with shotgun-blast effect. *Pleiades* breathed, literally. Heated by solar radiation much of its brief "day" of ninety-six minutes, subjected also during that period to needling cold in the shadow of earth, it was also heated and cooled from within, by machinery and fluid flows and exhaled gases of its occupants and its flora, by its ovens and showers and experimental systems of every scientific and industrial nature. Longbow knew the telltale signs of metal fracturing, of stresses setting up in twisted metal, just as a bone would twist before it crumbled or snapped. He had directed the joining of girders, the sealing of systems, the clamping together of great masses of metal that defied logic by having no weight but retaining inherent mass. Rivets and seam-welding and arc-welding, great bolts and nuts torqued down to command stability but with still enough flex in their structure to allow the station to breathe and groan and twist within and about itself.

In many ways *Pleiades* was like a great ocean liner, visibly strong beyond all question, massive and ponderous in its steel plating, the true gargantuan of the seas. But if you lift such a vessel out of the water, holding it up only at the bow and the stern, it will break in two, crumble like tissue paper and spill its great seeming strength like powdery plaster back into the ocean. Its strength remains *only* when it displaces water within that water, and has buoyancy and resistance to keep its plates and seams welded together.

There was little steel in *Pleiades*, but there was to be found throughout the great station 228 feet from the edge of one rim to the other a preponderance of beryllium, efficient material through great strength despite light weight. There was columbium to meet the needs of long-sustained high temperatures, and there was tungsten, also of great strength and almost feathery weight as compared to steel. There was aluminum and duralumin, plastic and ceramics, polished fine-rolled steel, and cables of enormous strength and measured flexibility. Inside and outside *Pleiades* there was also wood, an impossible miracle and a touch of the light fantastic. Wood, of all things! But *Pleiades* was still largely an experimental venture, and engineers had found that specially treated wood had an extraordinary resistance to the temperature and humidity variations within the station (as well as doing wonders in the psychological sense for the crew), and was withstanding remarkably well even greater variations in temperature, as well as the sandblasting effect of space dust and solar and cosmic radiation. Much of *Pleiades'* strength derived not merely from its structural materials but the manner of construction. The station throughout was made up of sandwich panels, extremely light in weight and far stronger and load-bearing than a single metal. The panels were assembled of hexagonal cells that were core-machined in sections, milled for strength, and incorporated within the assemblies of rockets and fuel tanks sent into orbit in the assembly period that created a working space station from the mishmash of material lofted to the levitation of orbit.

Steve Longbow was an Indian on the prowl, hunting and seeking changes in the immediate environment that was *Pleiades*, much as his earlier generations had studied the bent curve of grass, or a snapped branch, or the color changes in dust to tell them things an untrained eye would never see. If a temperature level rose or fell above a median norm, then Longbow *must* know why, and what it might portend. Sam Hammil watched Longbow taking the pulse of *Pleiades*, and Sam was much like the elderly doctor examining the younger doctors examining the patient. They formed a remarkable team.

Gale Bowie was the quiet member of the inspection team, and where she might have been too sharply discerning of the actions and mannerisms of the three men and one woman she accompanied, she had been rendered gunshy by the semantics knots into which she had been tied by Cantrell. He wanted no microscopes under which his crew would be pinned for study during the coming days and possibly weeks. This was not going to be a period of normalcy, and to Rush Cantrell, so well experienced with men under the stress of life in killer subs, normalcy was like the tides that must rise and fall to be reliable. The steady, unwavering crew was the most brittle of all.

As they moved through the station, they plugged in instruments at key locations that read to them the many signs of life and change of the station. Their purpose was not simply to obtain such measurements, for these were monitored constantly.

But one of the first rules of survival under unforgiving conditions is always to test the instruments and devices that are intended to keep you fully informed of all that goes on at all times. A faulty gauge is a lie that kills, and their inspection tour was as much to inspect the reliability of their automated sentinels as to study the station by eyeball, feel, and stethoscope.

They eased their way down the four-foot-wide tube toward the center of *Pleiades*, each of them having adjusted in their own fashion to reversing their senses of "up" and "down" as they left the rotating outer rim. Every time they traversed the vertical corridors of the tubes (and any time anyone moved through a tube toward or away from a point of rotation it was that constant change), they went through some measure of head twisting. It wasn't *just* moving outward to greater centrifugal force (i.e., an effect akin to gravity) and turning your body upside down so that down became up; it was more than that. *Pleiades* rotated and that meant a twisting, sidewards acceleration to which one could become accustomed, but could never be completely ignored.

Longbow reveled in the sensations. He was a born acrobat with an inner ear he seemed to be able to switch to *off*; he reveled in the convolutions his body found on its own. When he slid into the tubes it was like a duck diving into water, eager and as natural as though he had been born to this unique environment. Sam Hammil was eternally curious, questioning his own existence within the enviroment he was questioning, and offering neither any special attention. For Rush Cantrell and Christy Gordon, it was simply a matter of being experienced veterans. When the fluid in the inner ears began to burble, strong self-discipline took over and, even if roughly, wrestled things back under control.

Until this moment, Rush had never known that Gale Bowie not only felt discomfort in traversing the tubes, but suffered acute terror within its confining length. He had gone into the tube from the airlock just ahead of Gale, and he stopped his descent toward the station core when he noticed Gale still at the airlock edge.

*Goddamn it, she's frozen.* He'd been in enough stress situations to recognize the mental paralysis that spread instantly to the limbs. It was more than a fear of heights or a feeling of falling or even being squeezed into a restrictive space. It was all of that and a sudden vertiginous blow to the solar plexus that demanded vomiting, screaming, and rolling into a ball all at the same moment.

Gale stared with unblinking eyes at seventy feet of light gleaming along the mirrorlike tunnel. The central handpipe made it appear a dozen times that length as it and the curving walls of the tube converged visually into a tiny dot at the far end, a teetering drop into an endless abyss. Her stomach twisted violently, a snake struck with a branding iron, uncontrollable and an enemy. *It's strange*, her own voice told her. *You can live in complete weightlessness, just like a dolphin in the sea. But this tube, this tunnel, it's HATEFUL!* Her heart pounded and she began to suck air in and out with gasping noises.

Rush grasped the handpipe and hauled himself outward, back to the airlock and Gale. She was starting to hyperventilate, and the way she was going, she'd puke up her guts and then pass out, and they'd have a real job on their hands keeping her from choking to death. Christy signaled to him and he held up a palm for her to stay out of it. Moments later his hand found Gale's arm and he looked into eyes of stark, primal terror.

"Give me your hand, kid. That's it, your hand. Here, let me help you. Slow, slow. Take a deep breath, now, *hold it*. That's it, don't let out the air. Now, exhale slowly." Her breath gushed out and he ignored it. "Breathe deeply, long and slow, long and slow, that's it. The dizziness will be going away. Hang on to me, Gale, hang on as tight as you need to. Don't move, you don't have to move. That's it, take it nice and easy. *Remember who you are*. Do you understand me? *Remember who you are and where you are*. You're a medical technician, a skilled and trained astronaut, and you're perfectly safe in this station. Nothing here can hurt you."

He kept up the steady, gentle patter of reassurance until the stark roundness of her eyes eased and her neck muscles faded back into smooth contours. She finally *saw* him, and the best sign was a brief whimper and the fingers moving along his arm. Before, she could only gurgle, and a whimper meant she was moving swiftly from primal terror back up through childhood fears to the adult.

"Remember, acceleration is pushing you up to the rim. *You can't fall down. There's no way you can fall. You'll have to pull yourself down.* Do you understand me? *Tell me*."

"Y-yes. Understand. Can't fall down."

"You're getting with it, Gale. Both hands on the pipe. Come on, now, *both hands on the pipe*. If it makes you feel better, wrap your legs lightly around the pipe. Easy, easy, you don't need to squeeze that hard. Now, push down with your hands. That's it, you're doing fine. If you let go you'll float up, just like you're under water. You can't *fall*. It's impossible. Keep moving, keep your hands working on that pipe. Keep pushing down. All right, Gale, I'm going to let you do the rest. I'll be just beneath you and you can see Christy coming down right above you. Great, great."

Then they were in the airlock just outside the core. They could barely hear, but they felt the pressurized air bearings beneath them. The three tubes of *Pleiades* rotated on a great ring that turned about the nonmoving center of the station, necessitating a complex system of ring airlock within the core that could be timed to open and close with the tube airlocks. Since at this inner point the tubes moved with a snail's pace and the airlock chambers were wide, they had been able to move a bellowslike structure between each tube and the station. They had ninety-eight seconds for transfer between the tube airlock and the airlock of Saturn. Ninety-eight seconds is a lot longer than one imagines, especially with movement under zero gravity. During training, the crew had been required to move each way between core and tube in less than ten seconds, both unencumbered and while wearing a fully pressurized spacesuit. Now, in orbit, they could slip between airlocks with the practiced ease of walking through a doorway.

They bunched together. Rush nodded to Steve Longbow. "You and Sam go through first. We'll take the next lock."

Sam raised his brows, which was much the same

as a long interrogation. When he received no response from Rush, he judged the situation on its own merits, found his input unnecessary, and nodded. The tube turned slowly, a green light appeared, and with a hiss of compressed air, the interlocking seals snapped open. Steve and Sam pushed through, literally swimming into the weightlessness of the Saturn core. A wide netting awaited their movement.

A buzzer sounded, red lights winked on, and a computerized tape intoned "Fifteen seconds to airlock close." Rush stayed close to Gale. "When the green light comes on, we go through. Christy follows. You okay?"

She turned to him with a completely normal expression. "I'm fine, Commander. I like it down here."

She looked as if nothing had even ruffled her hair for the past month. Rush nodded; that much was as normal as everything that had gone before. Gale didn't know it, but she was as brittle as a thin icicle dangling from the edge of a porch, with the wind picking up, to boot.

Green flashed, air hissed, and the portals snapped away. "Let's go," Rush said calmly, and he stayed alongside Gale as they went from the airlock into the cavernous interior of the station core, ninety feet long and thirty-three feet in diameter. They floated into the netting, oblivious to the sudden clamor into which they had moved. Christy floated behind them into the net, balanced expertly with one hand. Her eyes showed her questions. Rush gestured for her to keep her silence.

"Gale, you go ahead with Sam and Steve. We'll be along in a few moments."

"Yes, Commander." She slid through a wide hoop opening in the net and pushed after the two men, floating dreamlike in the weightlessness that was now their new world.

Christy "swam" up to Rush. "You were beautiful in the tunnel," she said simply. "I've never seen such animal fear like that. Rush, you're always surprising me. You were so gentle with her! And look at her now, composed, completely under control as if nothing had ever—"

Rush showed his impatience by interrupting. "She's a bomb waiting to go off. Her serenity is a facade—she's frozen behind that warm smile. Frozen, terrified, and volatile. She could blow at any moment. Don't look so upset, Christy. I've seen that look before when I had men who could *feel* three thousand feet of ocean water squeezing down on them. Let's get to the comm." He pushed away to reach the communications terminal on the bulkhead before them. He thought for a moment, then unreeled a slim wire from his radio belt and plugged into the comm, ignoring Christy's perplexed look as he punched in the security code and then the number for the infirmary.

"Medical. Lee here. Confirming security." The voice was clear but echoing slightly in the receiver Rush had slipped into his ear. Damn, that meant electrical interference faster than they had expected. He returned to the moment.

"Lee; Cantrell. Gale Bowie is in the core with Hammil and Longbow. She's just come down the tube from the rim and she's in severe post-vertigo shock. I estimate she has maybe ten or fifteen minutes before she comes unglued at the seams. Get to her, sedate her, and put her out for at least twelve hours. Notify McCandless right away and tell him not to interfere. My orders."

"Yes, sir. I'll handle it myself. I'll bring Kathy Scott with me. That'll keep it on a personal level."

"Never mind the details. Do it." He pulled the plug and removed the earpiece.

"That was awfully abrupt," Christy said, her voice cool.

"Abrupt? I suppose so. Time's short."

"But you didn't have to snap at Bob Lee like *that*. Things are touchy enough with this storm increasing, and . . ." She didn't bother finishing. It's tough to articulate with your foot in your mouth.

"*Doctor* Gordon," Rush said quietly. "Do me a favor. Do your *job* for now, will you, please? And above all, don't ever lecture me again on how to command this station or its crew."

She averted his gaze. "Sorry." Her eyes moved back to his. "I just don't understand how Gale could switch so rapidly like that."

"I know you don't understand," he said. "I just got the message a few moments ago myself."

"Then for God's sake, tell *me*."

"Gale's attack of vertigo had nothing to do with any fear of falling. Heights don't bother her and falling comes as natural to her as a rock dropped from a cliff. Surprised? You shouldn't be. She was a competition skydiver, Christy. Picture her medals in skydiving with the girl you saw in the tunnel."

"I can't. They don't fit."

"Because she's psyched herself out. The watcher of the watched has blown a very deep and very guilty fuse, that's all."

"I know you mean to make sense, but—"

"Christy, she hates her job on this station. She pries, she snoops, she writes down notes on people who are her closest friends in life. They've built up a deep dislike of her and it's not her fault. So she's caught. If she doesn't do her job, then she's a failure in her assignment. If she does her job, then she's a failure as a human being. Getting vertigo in the tube is her subconscious way of punishing herself, of getting out of a very bad, even an impossible situation. If we don't sedate her, she'll blow her stack and we'll be keeping her in a straitjacket. I have some orders for you, lady, and they're for the record. As of now, right now, all psyche profiles for this station are canceled. Bruce McCandless is on your science team. You tell him. He's on centrifuge training at the moment. When he comes out you lay it on him. Assign him to radiation monitoring. It'll keep him from biting his nails. Go on; I'll meet you there in a few minutes."

Christy nodded, grasped a teflon cable strung along the core bulkhead, and pulled her way to the center of the great tank.

A sharp, screeching sound assailed his ears, a parody of what a great bird would sould like, if the bird were black, human, and had great flapping feathers. Rush turned to see Ron Cunningham flapping laboriously toward him, calling out again with his ear-stabbing screech.

"The Birdman of Alcatraz, I presume," Rush said acidly. He was in no mood for a frivolous encounter with a madly thrashing feathered idiot, but collision seemed inevitable. Feathers thrummed wildly as Cunningham tried to decelerate, and his arms moved faster and faster in a wild circular and up-and-down motion, but it did little good. Rush pulled himself out of the way as his engineer splattered—with human gasps, rather than his terrible bird call—into the net. He clawed at the net for support, jammed feathers into his mouth, and turned to Rush, spitting feathers and curses at the same time. Rush did his best to remain stern, even grim, but there was no way to prevent the guffaws that met the sight.

"There isn't a blackbird, or crow, or raven that wouldn't throw up at the sight of you," he told Cunningham, still trying to untangle himself from his harness and feathers.

"Listen to the honky stork," Cunningham said, still blowing scraps of feathers. "Commander, will you quit that jive critique and help me out of this mess?"

Rush helped free him from the body harness and the shock cords to the tail feathers. "I thought you could fly anything that had wings," he told the other man.

"Sure, sure. I flew with the Thunderbirds, I was a test pilot, I used to skydive, I flew gliders and balloons, and you know what? I can fly anything except me. Damn!" He spat away a last feather clinging to his nostrils.

"I don't get it," Rush said after studying the debris slowly being pulled to the exhaust outlet nearest them. And he didn't. Ron Cunningham was one of the two Life Support Systems engineers of *Pleiades*. He had been one very hot pilot in the air force, and had come out in the top ten percent of the astronaut competition for the space shuttle and getting assigned to the station. "You're zero-g and you have eighty years of aerodynamics behind you and you look like a cow skidding on ice."

"Well, the book ain't been written on this yet," Ron grinned at him, teeth white against the dark face. "Hell, I know *what* to do. I pump my arms up and down, and I make sure they go through the curve with the right angle of attack, and I *know* the center of pressure for lift is where it belongs because I've looked at more films of birds flying than a mother eagle. I get the angle of incidence and I keep it where it belongs, I got downthrust right on the money, I'm using the tail feathers just right and—"

"But you don't have a vertical fin and your ass makes a lousy rudder. What you need is enough speed to get airflow. It doesn't matter that you're weightless. All that mass and inertia can't be overcome by squawking and flapping, Ron. You'd be better off with *some* gravity field rather than this zero stuff. You're not getting enough thrust and you don't have arrow stability, so all you do is flop around like a dying chicken."

Cunningham slipped a plastisqueeze bottle from his belt clip, twisted the plastistraw open, and drank slowly. "Dying chicken, huh?"

"Okay, okay, rooster."

"Thanks for the promotion."

"Think nothing of it. By the by, how come you're onto full recreation right now? The way that geomagnetic storm is building, I thought you'd be elbow-deep in the life support program."

"That an official remark, boss?"

Rush shook his head. "Nope. Mark it up to curiosity."

"Jerry Maxwell's got the shift. He also took Don

Eagle from the construction team and Larry Schroeder from the med group with him. In fact, they're doing the same thing as you. Station tour of all systems. It's my time to play. After my brilliant career as a bird, I'm into the centrifuge. Two g's for ten minutes."

"You'll make the basketball team yet, fella."

"Gee, thanks, Dad."

"Stuff your feathers. See you."

Ron nodded, grasped a teflon cable, and hauled himself to the equipment bays on the other side of the three centrifuges. Located dead-center in the central core of the station, in the area of zero gravity, they were mounted each at right angles to the other. When they whirled around they were always used simultaneously so that their centrifugal motion balanced out their tremendous inertia, with the net effect of all that motion, in terms of station mass being accelerated, kept to precisely nil. Otherwise, the enormous surging effect, a twisting torque, could have set up tremendous imbalances throughout *Pleiades*. Each centrifuge held two of the station crewmen during operation for six people being spun around at twice the gravitational force experienced on earthside. Long space missions had proven that no matter how much exercise was conducted in weightlessness—and they'd tried springs, bungees, pressure suits, and all the rest tested during the Skylab and Soyuz programs—there was no replacement for *full-body* weight. Acceleration and resistance to acceleration provided the biological equivalent of weight. A man sitting on a chair on the earth really isn't at rest insofar as his physiological processes were concerned. The mass of the earth, expressed through gravitational attraction at the surface of the earth, pulled the chair toward the center of the planet. The surface of the earth resisted that downward acceleration with a force indexed at 1-g.

In the centrifuge, a man being whirled about found his body wanting to continue its outward swing, which was resisted by the seat to which he was strapped. That resistance could be set at precisely the gravity force desired, which was directly proportional to the speed at which the centrifuge spun. They could produce three-tenths of 1-g, or exactly 1-g, or 2-g, right on up to eight times earth-surface gravity. An exercise regimen of 2-g every third or fourth day had been worked out for those on the long stay aboard *Pleiades*. It was sufficient to keep the body muscles toned, the heart pumping normally and, above all, to sustain production of red blood cells in bone marrow. Daily monitoring by automated equipment in the infirmary, with substations at three other locations in *Pleiades*, provided Robert E. Lee, the medical officer, and his team with an intimate scan of every human aboard the station.

Rush was scheduled for his own centrifuge run that same day. Bob Lee would raise seven kinds of merry hell because Rush wouldn't make his schedule. *Pleiades* still awaited his attention.

# Chapter 8

He joined the others just outside the entryway to the three-axis centrifuge complex. Sam Hammil and Steve Longbow were waiting for him, and he saw Christy riding a teflon cable from a higher airlock. "Gale is in the isolation ward. Perimeter Capsule Six. Kathy Scott is off medical roster for the next twelve hours, and she's staying with Gale. Better to have her under the care of a doctor, anyway, until the sedation wears off."

"Good," Rush said, relieved that they'd nipped this problem before it could grow within the station crew. They were already a bit taut from the very existence of the solar blasts roaring through the same space they occupied, and a screaming woman, or even one locked in hysterical paralysis, could have unhinged a lot of people who otherwise would take the storm and all its dangers in professional stride. Rush explained briefly to the other men what had happened. "We finish the inspection job as a team of four. I've ordered that all psyche probing be canceled. We sure as hell don't need that with us now."

Sam Hammil held his eyes. "Commander, we *never* needed it. It's always been the weakest link in this station."

Rush felt heat rising in him. "Damn it, Sam, why didn't you ever say that before?"

Sam sighed. "I started to but changed my mind. If I did, I'm sure I would have convinced you to cancel out that program."

"You're right," Rush said, his jaw tight.

"And you would have had to inform Houston. They're already paranoid with the sense of independence this station has not only exhibited, but demanded. Canceling out what they consider to be one of their most effective control agents would have turned a deep-down suspicion into outright alarm. One wild mood swing always begets another, Rush, and that kind of chain reaction would have done more harm than Gale Bowie and Bruce McCandless could ever do. Now, well, you tell the truth. Gale suffered severe vertigo, nausea, hysterical paralysis, and she's been sedated and kept safely out of the way. The radiation levels may go so high that we need McCandless in personnel protection work. Houston will never get a twinge of paranoia from that."

Rush took it in, considered that Sam had already examined every aspect before he said a word, and nodded in agreement. "Let's move," he said brusquely to the others.

With no more than a slow turn, Rush could take in everything of the great core of the station—the centrifuge complex, teflon cables and netting, small sealed compartments for weightlessness experiments, and the airlocks for shuttle docking on the top and bottom (relative to earth) of the great tank. They called it Saturn because it had left the launch pad of the Kennedy Space Center on Florida's east coast as the second stage of a great Saturn V booster, a hand-me-down surplus rocket that had been cocooned for years in storage and intended for the ignominity of some plastic museum. Someone on a senate committee felt more indulgence for fiscal sensibility than for museums, and when the plans for *Pleiades* emerged from paper proposals into appropriations for hardware, they included not the provision, but the requirement, that a modern-age Phoenix be created from a resting place just short of the ashes of museum internment. Not one but two such giants, able to hurl heavy Apollo command modules, lunar landing vessels, *and* massive, fuel-swollen S-IVB third-stage rockets that flung themselves away from earth with speeds of seven miles a second.

Rush floated through the great intestine of one of those S-II boosters, and the name Saturn, in memory of the reborn giant, seemed more than fitting. They had altered the enormous tank, of course, with double-hulled panels circling the original shape. Pipes, wires, conduits, cables of every kind, electrical and liquid plumbing, ran throughout the circumference of the Saturn to transform it into a bionics machine. It was filled throughout with integrated circuit chips, those miraculous microprocessor computer elements that, if one stretched imagination *just* a bit, had made of the great station core an entity that took its own pulse, temperature, fluid rate, and respiration, its health and its problems, that glowed and rang and chimed, and sweated and vibrated at times like an enormous gong. It was a tree of space, a mighty cylindrical and hollowed-out oak of mammoth proportions within which lived and worked and played and floated and scurried the tiny creatures, men and animals and lesser flora than the oak, of the space forest.

The double hull had been compartmented into tanks that wrapped about the cylindrical shape. Here was kept water and oil, here the waste products of fifty-two men and women, the test animals and birds, and the waste of a bewildering variety of fish and spiders and vines and algae. All was sent by pressure-bullied lines into the tanks surrounding the hull of Saturn, to give the station balance, to store and process and reclaim this enormous quantity of materials, and at the same time perform the marvelous function of acting as a thick barrier against the normal, ceaseless outpouring of radiation from the sun. It gave some protection against the subatomic particles that rained in toward earth from every direction of the swollen universe, but not all. There were particles and waves that floated with the speed of light across infinity, and to the bodies of men, the steel of machinery, and even the densest of all planets, all was no more than the barest wisps of fog. After all, a neutrino can travel through fifty light years of solid lead before, mathematically, it will even *notice* such an environment. But the human race had developed through such a cosmic barrage and it was part and parcel of man's *natural* environment.

The great magnetic storms, mused Rush, were

*not* part and parcel, for in earth's history the super storms had distorted weather and moved mountain ranges and melted oceans and totally destroyed most of the creatures that had ever moved on the lands that would one day come to know man. Christy Gordon was right—this sun was both life-giver and enemy. And they must prepare to survive, naked and willingly, in this environment beyond earth.

"We've got four feet between these hulls," Longbow said. "Most of them are filled. We can transfer liquids until we fill them all. It's going to make a big difference, probably enough to give us the margin we need."

"Not enough," Hammil observed dourly. "You're right about a steady rise in radiation, Steve, but one of the really big flares? No. We need more."

"Get O'Leary down here right away," Rush said into his radio. "And while you're at it, tell Steve Hollobaugh to double-time it down to us."

O'Leary controlled the space tugs, the transfer rockets, working cherry pickers, and other maneuvering systems for heavy equipment outside the station. Hollobaugh was chief engineer for the station, who added to their orbiting life the social grace of a dead cigar he chewed day and night and, it was rumored, even in the shower.

"You both know our problems," Rush told them without preamble. "Everything points to using the Saturn as a collection point for our people, especially if we get a signal that a particularly intense flare is headed our way. Except for the astrophysics lab, the photographic shop, and the flora labs with water surrounding them in the rim, there won't be anyplace else with walls thick enough to stop that kind of radiation. So we make do. O'Leary, how many shuttle tanks do we have floating out there in the junkyard?"

"Twenty-seven, Commander."

Twenty-seven enormous tanks, each just over 154 feet in length and nearly twenty-eight feet wide. Most of them were of aluminum alloy skin two inches in diameter; others were of metallic fibre woven on huge spinning machines in gargantuan weaving mills, a technique developed in the 1950's for solid-booster missiles. Never mind those details, Rush told himself. Consider the tanks. Each was as tall as a fifteen-story building and almost as wide as the Saturn station core itself. They were kept in the "junkyard," a storage orbital point twenty miles behind the station along its orbital path, held together by cables and kept available for adding to the *Pleiades* structure or for forming the nucleus of special work stations.

"How long would it take you and your people," Rush asked of both men, "to bring a couple of those tanks here to us, slice them open with the laser torches, move them into position to be attached to this core? You'd have to beam-weld or use vacuum epoxy or both, whatever you need, to form two more hull sections around the core. That gives us a lot of radiation shielding. You'll have to play some neat games out there not to interfere with our rotation, you'll have to have the computers working full-time so we don't enter imbalances, and you can't interfere with the docking ports."

"That's all?" O'Leary asked.

"Marve, I don't have time for any of your Irish crap."

Steve Hollobaugh motioned for Rush's attention. "We can't give you an answer. Not in terms of time. We've never done it before and—"

"Two days, working around the clock?"

"Jesus, I don't know," Hollobaugh insisted.

"One thing's for sure," O'Leary said, his jaw tightening visibly, "We can't get *anything* done if we float around here forever talking about it. The only way we know for certain is by doing it."

"I thought you'd never get around to that conclusion," Rush said, smiling. "You know what to do, so get with it. No; hold it. We're going to be short of power if we get some really intense radiation."

"Damn if you're not right," Hollobaugh confirmed. "We'll be taking a lot of solar cell breakdown. We'd better build additional arrays of solar cells, the voltaic systems, around the outside of the new hull."

Longbow jumped in. "Better get Lopez and some of my people on it," he offered. "They can start working on the first hulls you're going to cut up. Drill where necessary right away, attach stanchions for the arrays, start laying the cables for the converters. O'Leary, you tell Lopez what's up. He can play ballet out there with his equipment."

"What about Kurt Hest and Bob Buckley?" Christy added.

Rush was pleased with her offering. No question they'd need Hest to handle the solar array systems and Buckley for conversion. They'd have to coordinate like an orchestra. "Add Tammy Clifton to your list," Rush ordered. "I want all fuel cells powered up as an emergency electrical source in case we get some real degrading of the solar primary system. Christy, who's got the watch for the science teams right now?"

"Janice Irving."

"Good. She's got a cool head. Get her on the line, and tell her to use whoever's available to start moving supplies here into the core. Food and water—the works. Also, I want portable oxygen bottles in quantity. Every member of this crew is to have a primary pressure suit available here in the core. Bring about a half-dozen backups for any emergency replacements. You get with that right away, get with me the moment you're done."

He turned to the others. "Longbow, get Tom Lydon together with either Mendez or Markham, and whoever else you need. Outfit two shuttle tanks as emergency survival chambers that can be moved away from the station. Set them up with maneuvering engines, as well as thrusters for attitude control in all axis. Communications, emergency supplies, the works. Can you adapt a bellows airlock to those? We'll need—"

The big Indian nodded, gesturing to apologize for interrupting. "I have the picture, Commander. I'd like to get it started."

"Do it."

It was all coming together. For the moment, everyone with him was wrapped up in giving orders, coordinating groups, getting the tremendous workload started. Sam Hammil, noted Rush, had slipped into the role more necessary than any other. He was functioning as a hunch generator and a human computer, listening to it all, fitting the jigsaw pieces within his mind so that the final picture, the end result of all this effort, came out clear in his mind's eye. If it didn't, he'd begin mental backtracking to find the snag before it happened. Rush hooked his feet into a teflon net, floating gently, letting his thoughts roam through *Pleiades*, trying to see anything and everything that must be done to assemble all the pieces. Sam would be judging him as much as anyone else. Good. Rush could turn off the intensity, or at least bring it down to a lower level that wouldn't start overloading circuits in his own mind.

Rush had bedeviled Gale Bowie with his recitation of the Seven Sisters that formed the stars for the constellation Pleiades, but the station name did rest on the magic number of seven. The basic design constituted, to Rush Cantrell's orderly mind, seven major components, and the name *Pleiades* was to him as inevitable as it was fitting. First of the seven basic units for the station was the Saturn core where, at this very moment, he bobbed gently in weightlessness, letting his thoughts float as free as the absence of gravity about him, while he and his team leaders initiated the moves to assure the survival of the station itself.

Saturn had become a weightless foundation, a structural hub, for the remainder of *Pleiades*. Rather than a single facility like the old Skylab, with the main tank and the astronomical and solar laboratory attached, with still more attachments in the way of the Apollo command-and-service modules that linked up with Skylab at the airlocks, Saturn—or P1 as Rush thought of the modified booster—constituted the beginning of what would grow into a space community. P1 was itself an impressive complex with its rotating rings for the remainder of *Pleiades*, and as the station core formed much more than simply a center for attaching other elements, jammed as it was with the centrifuges, zero-g laboratories, recreational and calisthenics areas, fuel and water tanks, human and animal waste reclamation, and the seeming Rube Goldberg mass of multicolored pipelines and cables. If there had been only P1, what had originally been an S-II rocket stage, then the station would still be several times larger than the original Skylab, and that old station dwarfed the extraordinarily successful but smaller Russian Salyut.

The collection of shuttle tanks made up P2. Rush considered the tanks as much an integral part of the station as any other element. The orbital storage junkyard was more an affectionate than a literal term, for the shuttle fuel tanks provided a constant supply of metal, shields, plumbing, and other equipment with which to continually repair, modify and increase the size and capability of the entire *Pleiades* complex. More to the station needs, it was possible to modify the internal systems of each giant tank before it left its production line for shipment to either the Florida or California launch sites. The tanks were built in multiple sections with heavy baffling within, as well as pumps, sensors, plumbing and control systems. If they had a particular need for a huge bay or compartment as part of the *Pleiades* complex, the shuttle tank was modified in its internal design and, once flushed of remaining traces of fuel, could be adapted in part or in its entirety for the station.

The three great arms extending outward from the station core, Tubes I, II and III, constituted a single unit Rush designated as P3. Each tube lay evenly spaced 120 degrees from the other in the form of three huge spokes and served multiple functions. They formed the structural members that connected the core to the great wheeled rim of *Pleiades*, but also carried plumbing and cables, were outfitted with airlocks, and were the means of transferring from the zero-g environment of the P1 core to the low gravity and living compartments of the wheel.

The huge wheel rim of *Pleiades*, more compact, crowded, and complex than the rest of the station together, was P4. The wheel wasn't smooth, like a bicycle wheel tube, but a slowly assembled series of tanks and subsections assembled from shuttle tanks and the Spacelab tank-laboratories lofted into orbit by the shuttles. Each Spacelab was a complete and myriad unit placed within the great cargo bay of the shuttle and boosted to orbit where *Pleiades* was being assembled. Space tugs and maneuvering cherry pickers moved and shunted them together where they were connected with massive bolts and slip girders, and then beam-welded around their outer surfaces. All equipment necessary for their functioning existed in final form before launch. Assembled into the wheel shape in orbit, they were interconnected with airlocks, plumbing, power cables, communications systems, pressurizations and all the demanding systems of not only living but working in space. Always facing the danger of meteoroid strike or component failure of any one section, each part of the wheel was kept not isolated, but insulated, from every other compartment by airlocks and automatic power and subsystem shutoffs. If Unit Fourteen, for example, suffered a sidewall blowout and explosive decompression, or was endangered by a fire, the wheel sections to each side of Unit Fourteen were cut off automatically. Electrical circuits tripped and the units closest to the endangered section went to battery power, separate life-support systems, and whatever else was necessary for safety isolation until the problems could be eliminated. Some wheel sections were only eight feet in diameter, others nearly twenty-eight feet, having been assembled from shuttle tanks as complete units. They had another element of safety in that once they were assembled, an inflatable cuff of thick, self-sealing rubberized material was placed around the wheel unit, and another outer layer of sandwich panels installed as the outermost shield for thermal, radiation, and meteoroid dust protection.

In some ways, mused Rush, his extraordinary technological wonder called *Pleiades* very much resembled the haphazard house built by the Jack of old nursery rhymes. There was another element of truth to this concept, since P5 was a conglomerate of spacetugs, cherry pickers, maneuvering units, lifeboats, and rocket engines and boosters used for construction and assembly work with the station and for operations beyond the station. P5 was the province of Marvin O'Leary as Boats Officer and Tom Lydon as Construction Chief, with Steve Longbow as his constant companion, as well as their work teams.

P5 was as much constant experimental activity as it was research, science, and the launching of the satellites that went into geosynchronous orbit 22,300 miles above the earth or were hurled outward to the moon, the sun, or other planets. Gone were the days of committing a half-billion dollar satellite to the chancy odds of perfect booster operation and perfect satellite operation with all real control ending the moment the engines ignited on the pad. All such vehicles were now brought by shuttles to the *Pleiades* orbit. Scientists and technicians checked out the payload and the boosters and, in effect, initiated a new launch from the high orbit of the station. If something were wrong with the payload it could either be corrected in orbit or the entire unit returned to earth for rebuilding. It was well within their capability to assemble rocket boosters like building blocks. Using tanks of storable fuel, without the need for supercooling and other systems that complicated propulsion units, they could building-block any size and power of a booster combination. That increased payloads to what they desired and gave far greater control and reliability for all systems involved.

Then, within the embrace of P5, there were the experimental station-building programs. Well beyond the immediate reach of the station, the engineers and construction teams were engaged in a wide variety of construction and space-endurance programs. They had built a complete manned section of a vehicle intended to carry explorers to the planet Mars, there to visit its two rocky moons and descend to the surface of the fascinating, volcano-upthrusting world. Reliability here was the problem. Such a venture might take from eight months to two years, and the government wanted full-duration tests of the systems and subsystems involved. The MarsYard, as they called their experimental spacecraft, duplicated in every way the ship that finally would make the voyage, cycling all systems, undergoing computer-dictated emergencies and repairs, and at times occupied by astronauts who tested components and equipment and fired propulsion systems for en-route maneuvering of what one day would become the actual journey.

The engineering teams were always playing with space blocks, building experimental structures, testing welds, riveting, vacuum-epoxy bonding, self-expanding bolts. They built complex structures and then slammed them with acceleration, turns, deceleration; they were spun and despun, rocked and wobbled and tumbled in order to learn the limits of stress and structural integrity. Glass, lexan, armorglass, polarization materials, radiation resistance—the list included literally thousands of items and structures for ongoing tests. New and experimental construction processes were always being evaluated, beams produced and capped, joints, pressed and clamped into place, paint and thermal coatings applied in both sealed environments and in open vacuum.

One of their best-publicized programs—because it could be measured by the earthsiders as a *visible* payoff for their dollars and support—was the effort to develop and perfect, in limited-size models, what would one day become stupendous solar power satellites. What they snatched from the enormous energy of the sun would not be for use aboard such stations as *Pleiades*, but for earth's energy needs. The concept was simple enough: expose enormous surfaces to radiated solar power, convert this power to electrical energy, and beam the electrical current down to receiving stations on the planet.

They had begun their space construction systems with immediate payoff in mind rather than long-range experimental ventures. Rush Cantrell had hammered home this theme while *Pleiades* was still on the drawing boards. "Give them something for their money, *now*," was his harsh demand from the inception of the program. He'd gone to the big Grumman aerospace firm on Long Island, New York, to gather meaningful ammunition for those demands. In a way the trip to Grumman was almost a pilgrimage. As a youngster, Rush had been a buff of the old warbirds from the Second World War. The "heavy iron" of old combat planes held a hypnotic fascination for Rush and his peers. And Grumman was justly famed as the "Iron Works" of such machines, the Wildcat, Hellcat, and Tigercat of World War II fame, the Bearcat and Panther and Cougar that followed after that war, and a host of other machines that included nothing less than the Lunar Module that had carried the Apollo astronauts with a perfect safety record to and from the moon.

Dick Harkness of Grumman received him with a toothy grin and a sharp eye. "Commander Cantrell, we've got *just* what you want. No serendipity here, no building a better toothbrush by going to the moon and that sort of public relations hype. What you need is something visible, meaningful, immediately useful, and profitable that has an everyday effect on the man on the street and in his home."

"I know what I need," Rush told him bluntly. "What have you got?"

"A thousand-foot-wide dish antenna. That's for starters."

"Don't quit now."

"Takes three shuttle loads to get it up to your orbit. It's folded and collapsed; it unscissors in space. It doesn't need strength in terms of earth structures because—"

"Forgive me. I know the drill. Let's hear the ledger side of the sheet."

"Okay, nuts and bolts, then. We had an idea for an antenna—curving dish and full array. We figured on three hundred feet, so the effort to go three times bigger is minor. We designed the same system for the thousand-foot diameter. It's a high-gain device for global communications. We've already lined up military contracts for it and the commercial buyers are pounding on our doors if we can get it upstairs. But we need space construction crews for that."

"I've got 'em. Go on."

"An antenna of that size means you can eliminate by eighty percent the size and cost of ground-receiving transmitter stations."

"Good start."

"Our antenna can receive and process signals only five percent as powerful as those you need now for such communications. In other words, we increase twenty-fold the capability. The bigger the antenna, the narrower we can focus return signals—into bands that are remarkably narrow, in fact. That kind of antenna means the Dick Tracy radio is not only possible, but outmoded. We can give you wristwatch-sized television pictures for videophone communications. You could put them into cars, planes, ships, offices. Anywhere."

Rush didn't satisfy easily. "You got more?"

Harkness chuckled. "Man, you are talking *our* language. We got more. Same antenna means electronic mail. None of this stupidity of barging around loads of paperwork. We use the antenna as central receiving and dispatching stations. A letter or other message is beamed to us and we beam down to another continent. Digital printout is immediate. At first, we'd still have to overcome local transmission problems, but the way we see it, we can use news media devices already available for letter printout and delivery from local substations. The longer it's in use, the more local substations, including office-to-office printouts cheaply and swiftly around the world."

"What about business and political relays?"

"Got them, got them," Harkness said with unbridled enthusiasm. "You want a meeting of world leaders? No more red telephones. Everything is live, and you can have people from every continent attending a roundtable conference all at the same time. Central monitors. Commander, we're even working on holographic projections for—"

Rush held up a hand. "Enough. I'm sold. I'd like the blueprints in my office in Houston in two days."

Harkness had a hound's toothy look now. He appeared crestfallen. Rush stared at him. "Harkness, what the hell's the matter with you?"

"Don't you want to hear about our solar factory?"

"Your *what?*"

The words spilled in a torrent from the Grumman engineer. "It's a solar factory designed for geosynchronous orbit at twenty-two thousand miles, and—"

"I know the orbits."

"Well, it would need low-orbit tests first. But it's designed for the geo position, even though it has to be assembled at low altitude and then lifted to permanent orbit with solar-electric propulsion

systems. Sort of lifts itself by its own bootstraps,
you might say. We can use solar energy to deliver
five thousand megawatts from a single solar factory to beam down into the electric power grids on
Earth."

"Five thousand million watts," Rush echoed.

"Yes *sir!*"

"How big is your solar pattycake?"

"Twelve miles long and three miles wide. We'd,
um, probably design for a depth of a thousand
feet. Mainly girders, with servicing and living quarters within. With something that large, we could
get some spingrav for the crews and—"

"Hold it." Rush took a deep breath. "You don't
build a chair without tools. And for this job—"

"Commander, *it's all been designed*. Most of it is
already tested!"

Rush didn't bother trying to stem the enthusiasm that washed over him like ocean breakers.

"We've developed the damndest self-employment
systems you ever saw," Harkness swept on. "The
antenna, for example, is a wire wheel we store
tightly in the shuttle cargo bay. They scoot into
orbit, open the bay doors, and the whole antenna
and dish starts to unfold. It takes two hours to get
a dish three hundred feet wide into skeletal position. It's all set to work. We can then add to the
size of the antenna, and it's improving with every
addition you make to it. You know how we build
the really large structures in orbit? I'll tell you.
The whole package is broken down into four steps."

He ticked them off on his fingers. "One is beam
fabrication, next is beam assembly, third is de-
ployment, and the last step is final assembly. We've
got, ready to go, a machine that fabricates a trian-

gular one-meter-wide structural beam in any length you want, and we can produce finished beams in orbit at the rate of more than one and a half meters per minute. That's five feet of finished beam in a minute! Do you realize that with this system we could give you a mile-long structure in *one day?* Each beam is three hundred feet in length. In our vacuum chambers, our dandy little robot works with attached cassettes, which contain spools of high-construction-grade aluminum, or, let's say, graphite/epoxy composite material. We preshape and precut the cross braces to go into the same shuttle shipment, and these are automatically clamped into position—permanently."

He positively radiated. "Don't you see, Commander? As each bay is completed, the three-dimensional beam is fed forward and cut off at any length you want, all ready for assembly. Even handling these things from the shuttle, you can keep the crew indoors by using the remote manipulator arms to move stuff into position for add-on growth. You've seen these goodies. Those shuttle arms have seven degrees of freedom and linkages. They're almost bionic. They work like the flexible joints of a human shoulder, elbow, wrist, and hand, and the same manipulators work even better in pairs from one of the enclosed or open cherry pickers, including those mounted to a shuttle or free-flying just like a work tug. Neat, huh?"

It was neat, all right. And the man hadn't oversold a thing. The crew of *Pleiades* had moved sixteen of the giant thousand-foot-antennas into their orbit, and then boosted them up to the geosynchronous orbits at 6,300 miles an hour, 22,300 miles above the equator. The Dick Tracy radios and even the tiny videophones had long been reality and the entire world was now linked by these flyweight dish antennae. It hadn't been all roses and no problems, of course, and it took three times as long to do things as the earthsider experts had predicted, but that still put them far ahead of the game.

They'd been working on the solar factory for a year. Well off to the orbital path of *Pleiades*, one section was already nine miles in length, a gossamer framework that couldn't exist in the gravity of earth's surface. Here, in the vacuum so high above the planet, and intended for a harder vacuum nearly 22,000 miles above *Pleiades*, it would be a dandelion with the strength of steel.

Rush Cantrell felt his body moving slowly about from where his feet were anchored in the net. He saw Christy Gordon, Sam Hammil, and Steve Longbow working their way down the teflon cables to continue the station inspection.

"Let's move it," Rush said by way of greeting.

# Chapter 9

*Power* was the name of the game for P6. Power to operate the life support systems of *Pleiades*, to ventilate and aspirate, cool down and heat up, to flush and blow and withdraw, to cleanse and recycle. Power to move air and gases and fluids, to operate the pumps and whirring machinery and keep the lights going, to operate radios and microwave ovens and television and radio sets, electric razors and hair curlers and surgical equipment. Name it and you needed power to do it. *Pleiades* existed on the power it derived from the sun, just as all earth and everything on and within the planet lay utter hostage to solar behavior. But the sun could be an amiable master—all it demanded was that it be understood in order to yield both its secrets and its energy, the latter to be used directly for thermal control and also to be converted to electrical power.

In the "old days" of planning future space stations, the big thing was to plan enormous reflector mirrors that would face the sun, beam its energy from a great curving dish into a central focal receiver to achieve enormous temperatures, and then move a substance like mercury vapor through pipes exposed to that heat. The superheated mercury vapor plunged through a transfer pipeline where its pressure whirled a turbine at tremendous speed, and the spinning turbine churned out electrical power. The mercury vapor, now robbed of much of its energy, flowed through condenser plumbing lines in dark shadows, away from direct exposure to solar radiation. The process went around and around, and it went around so many times engineers started questioning the reliability of bearings, shuttle valves, pipeline integrity, and even the presence of mercury vapor aboard a manned station. It looked great in artistic impressions but it gave the station designers nightmares. They scratched their heads for a better system and toyed with a variation on their theme by heating mercury until it boiled and then evaporated to blisteringly hot gas. Unfortunately, they were right back to Square One with their basic reliability problems.

The whole issue became moot because the already-old mercury heating systems were rendered utterly archaic with the advent of solar cells. Wafer-thin, bantamweight, easy to process, packaged into rolls and panels, and incredibly efficient without any moving parts, they were the lodestone to energy needs of *Pleiades*. There would be a problem in long-term service in that the solar cells that created electricity directly from solar exposure did, in fact, have to be exposed directly to the sun.

That idea didn't work too well when *Pleiades* slipped around to the dark side of the planet immediately below and sulked in darkness. During the darkside passage they used batteries that were recharged on every dayside track. The station was also equipped with long racks of fuel cells that, when activated, could keep the station functioning in a powered-down configuration for at least thirty days. That was more than time enough in just about the worst emergency conceivable to rush help upstairs via shuttle flight. So they could live with it and work with it.

There had been conversation about using a nuclear reactor aboard *Pleiades*. It needn't be a full-time system, but it would provide energy under any circumstances they could foresee. That idea proved technically sound and publicly a disaster. Unmanned satellites with nuclear materials had splashed their radioactive substances across a few countries by the time *Pleiades* was being designed, and although not so much as a mad hare had been hurt or killed, the public always thrills to exotic dangers to life and limb, and politicians thrive as soothsayers of doom, and that was *that*. The enormously hyped reentry of the blazing Skylab and then the awesome plunge of a new Russian Salyut station, after its booster exploded, into a northern city of Japan, sealed the arguments. *Pleiades* would go with solar energy, even wood-burning stoves if necessary, or it wouldn't get past the bathroom of the congressional appropriations offices.

Rush, with Sam Hammil, Christy Gordon, and Steve Longbow in tow, moved outward from the Saturn core into Tube II for their continued inspection. They eased through the airlocks into the spoked tunnel, tugged gently on the center hand-pipe, and floated dreamily upward, pausing to check stresses, radiation levels, and all the other signs of health they hoped they'd continue to find in their fourteen-hundred-ton patient.

A thought hit Rush. He plugged into open comm to control center. "Cantrell here. What's the status on Kurt Hest and Bob Buckley?"

"Sir, they're both outside in the open MMU's. We're following them through on scanner TV and getting full telemetry."

"Fine," Rush said drily. "Now tell me what they're doing." He knew; he wanted to be certain his crew also knew.

"Sir?" The voice sounded startled, then Dennis Conrad, who was standing watch, recovered his wits. "They're, uh, conducting a full-station personal and instrument survey of all solar power systems, Commander."

"Where are they now?"

"Outboard of Tube Three, sir."

"Patch me in."

"Yes, sir, coming right up." The hesitation lasted only seconds. "You're patched in to both men, Commander."

"Bob, Kurt? Cantrell here. You copy?"

"Gotcha loud and clear, boss." That would be Buckley. "Five by," came the word from Hest.

"What's your initial look show you?" Cantrell asked.

"Too early to tell about any real damage yet," Bob Buckley replied immediately. "We've got normal degradation from dust pitting and outgassing—the usual stuff. But we're still better than ninety percent efficiency from what I see."

"Hest? What do you think?"

"I agree. We're setting up some additional radiation metering systems at various points around the station, and we can monitor everything from inside later. It's my feeling that if we increase radiation being received by a factor of three times normal levels, the voltaic systems will start to break up on us."

Rush frowned. Just what he'd been worried about. The solar cells looked marvelous on paper—they *were* marvelous—and in a vacuum they should have been perfect, except that what people once thought was hard vacuum wasn't what they thought at all. To the elongated bag of liquid that made up the human body, hard vacuum was simply a lack of a surrounding atmosphere under decent pressure. Since space at 346 miles didn't have an atmosphere, ergo, it must be a vacuum. In human terms, it was.

But *Pleiades* and its solar-cell systems weren't human, and they weren't exposed to open space for a brief visit. They were there for the long pull, and that meant cumulative *effects* of the space environment, which was very busy, indeed. There was the usual dust pouring in toward the earth as it rolled around the sun like a super vacuum cleaner, and *Pleiades* suffered from a very slow but nonetheless real scouring. The atmosphere lay far below, but solar activity often sent enormous amounts of gases billowing outward. It's difficult to count molecules strewn so sparingly in what is otherwise a vacuum, but molecules after a year in orbit at seventeen thousand miles an hour *do* have an effect on metal and much more so on silicon wafers and materials. Then there are the harsh effects of sunlight—invisible light, infrared, naked ultraviolet—and the constant solar wind of electrons, plus the ill-tempered outbursts of sunspots and other activity. A constant rain of cosmic debris pours down onto the earth, with *Pleiades* receiving its own uncomfortable share of this subatomic barrage without benefit of the earth's protective atmosphere. There's the matter of metal and other materials superheated and superfrozen because of direct exposure to radiated energy of the sun and basking in the frigid shadow of earth. And not to be discounted was out-gassing, a nasty propensity of metal and other materials exposed to vacuum to release their outer molecular shells. Since this was a constant process, and since it was added to the rest of this invisible but still measurable effect, "space weather" weakened the outer covering of the space station. At this moment, the solar cell arrays were particularly vulnerable.

In order to gain maximum effect from solar radiations, *Pleiades* resembled a giant three-spoked wheel with a thick cyndrical core and an outer rim encrusted with precious stones. There seemed no pattern to the methods of installing the solar cells, for they were mounted on long strips of the Saturn core tank, at various parts of the three great spoked tubes, and they alternated in position along the great wheel itself. Such randomness was in fact deliberate, since it always kept the minimum number of cells exposed to the sun during the daylight orbital passes.

Outward of the spoked tubes, *Pleiades* displayed three complete Spacelab modules, carried one at a time into orbit on shuttle flights. Each was coated with solar cells, and each could, when needed, extend long arms of graphite-epoxy beams, along which unfurled additional solar cell arrays. Within each module were the main conversion systems for transforming the billowing veils of a distant sun into useful electrical power. The Spacelab modules were used, as well, for advanced experiments. Kept at a decent interval from the main core and separated as well from the rim by double airlocks, they permitted more volatile experiments with minimum exposure to the station and its crew.

Lab One was a complex magician's lair of industrial test equipment, with superhot furnaces and equipment for welding, testing alloys and ceramics and other work carried out under low gravity. The more dangerous experiments, considered explosive or incendiary in nature, were contained within still another Spacelab module, and always moved by a maneuvering tug to a safe distance from the station for the experiments. It kept uneasiness from being a frequent companion to the *Pleiades* crew.

In Lab Two, thick and massive through its systems, were the special photographic equipment for astrophysics studies, for radio astronomy and geophysical studies of the earth with instruments seeking out the most minute changes in magnetic and geomass patterns of the earth below.

Lab Three was something entirely different from the rest of the space station. To Rush Cantrell this was P7, the final segment of *Pleiades*, and the only area of the great station absolutely off limits to all but seven members of the station crew. This was the ongoing experimental chamber of the Department of Defense, and the price for that security was absolute silence. Lab Three was never discussed except in that area where its programs were familiar—the development of high-energy laser ray beams and beams of highly charged particles, pulsed outward from Lab Three with almost maniacal bursts of light that might be red or searingly yellow or deep blue or orange or God knew what. The government talked little about energy beam weapons being developed to destroy the warheads of great ballistic missiles, and it talked even less about the ability of these beam systems to destroy, utterly, another satellite at a kill range of more than two hundred miles.

To the science crew of *Pleiades*, this was their cross to bear, their sacrifice to morality. They were sworn under the National Secrecy Act never to discuss even the existence of the laser and energy beam program, under pain of twenty years to life imprisonment. Not that the Russians and every other intelligence network in the world didn't know the laser program was under way, for it was hardly the only one, but there was the long-standing adage of "need to know." It had been bred and nurtured in the old security programs of the Strategic Air Command and it was returned full blossom in *Pleiades*.

This was their blemish and a measure of the isolation between Rush Cantrell and most of the personnel of the station. He had made that very clear. "Before you commit to this program," he told each and every individual who had applied for *Pleiades*, "we are not singularly civilian in nature. That's rot and it always has been. We are a national effort and that means military as well as civilian. Far and away the major effort, ninety-eight percent of this station, will be devoted to

science, technology, and research, as well as utility, of a civilian nature. Lab Three is not within
that ninety-eight percent. Except to certain members of our crew, it is absolutely off-limits. Any
attempt to enter Lab Three will be considered an
act of treason and I will judge such an act accord-
ingly, even if it means loss of your rights, the
grinding away of your dignity, and if necessary the
loss of your life. Any questions? Good. Welcome
aboard."

It was the sort of welcoming speech that left
very little for discussion—then, or later. Which is
why curiosity began to expand within the mind of
Dr. Christy Gordon. They were carrying out a complete inspection of *Pleiades*. Rush Cantrell and Steve
Longbow were two of the seven people of the crew
who went into and returned from Lab Three.

Would Rush really bar that door to Sam Hammil
when the very existence of the station, and all its
crew, was in growing jeopardy? She wasn't that
certain she wanted to know.

They exited the tube into the rim, worked their
way through a double airlock, and stepped into
the hatchway of a former shuttle tank now making
up one of the thicker and longer sections of the
station rim. A horrendous shrieking assailed their
ears as monkeys howled and dogs barked, two
babboons screeched wildly at them, and the air
almost wavered from the mass chittering of guinea
pigs and hamsters and rats of every size and color.
In one long cage two cats leaped in light gravity as
if they could levitate, a feline ballet to which they
were long accustomed, landing light-footed on thick

wall carpeting, clinging like furry ghosts and staring at the intruders with wide eyes.

"My God, I forgot how much it stinks in here," Longbow said, wrinkling his nose and at the same time waving hello to Sundi Meguiar, the scientist who ran the fauna experiments of the station. To Longbow, she smacked of his own ancestors, who were at home with all animals. Too much so, with this affinity of hers. Who the hell expected an eighteen-foot-long python in a space station! Or a turtle resting in a vacuum chamber with the air pressure reduced to only a hundredth of normal. That creature had been sleeping for six months with his heartbeat reduced to one slow thump every hour, and he survived it without any seeming toll on his systems.

Longbow made another sour face and Sundi stood in the aisle, hands rolled into fists and fists hard against her hips. "For someone whose ancestors lived in stinking cowhide tents and warmed themselves by burning buffalo chips, you sure have a sensitive nose," she said with an anger they had exchanged ever since the menagerie was packed into the animal station.

"Buffalo chips dry out. They don't stink," came the rebuttal.

"But your granddaddy sure as hell did, living in a tent through a winter with buffalo turds to keep him company."

"That's lifestyle, little girl." He sniffed and squeezed his nose between his forefinger and thumb. "The old folks also lived with coyotes and dogs, and they had scorpions and snakes and spiders, and when the winter was bad they ate horsemeat, but you've outdone them all. You know what,

Sundi? This place of yours would gag a maggot. No wonder they banished you from Earthside. Je-sus!"

"Okay, okay, that's enough," Rush broke in. "Sundi, have you been keeping track of the radiation count?"

"Yes," she said, and her brow furrowed. "If it keeps climbing like this, I'm going to lose some of these animals. Commander, can I get some additional shielding for this area?"

Rush pondered the request, but Steve would know better. He deferred the question to his lead construction man, and just as quickly Longbow was all business. He looked at Sundi. "You figure how much you need?"

She looked doubtful. "Steve, I don't know what to *expect* from that storm. I wish I could answer, but—"

Christy moved forward. "We've got to consider going to a factor of times ten, Sundi."

The girl blanched. Her voice fell to a hoarse whisper. "My animals . . . Dr. Gordon, they won't survive that. Can't we move them to the core? I heard that Commander Cantrell has started heavy shield construction there and . . . and . . . they could make it through, that way, I mean . . ."

Her voice fell away with the look on Rush's face. "I'm sorry, Sundi. That's out. Moving all your equipment, the food and water, the cages . . . it can't be done." Rush turned to Christy. "Get someone to feed the radiation levels at times ten into the computer, work out how much shielding this module will need, then talk to Longbow or Hammil, here. *After* we get the core shielded, we'll see what we can do here. Sundi, that's the best I can do."

She blinked back tears. "Yes, sir. Thank you."

"Don't thank me yet. I said we'd try and that's a long way from doing. The crew comes first. Sundi, understand something. If you get a call to report to the core, you leave everything here on automatic, and you get down there pronto. Is that understood?"

Her face went through a variety of emotions. Her chest heaved as she breathed in deeply and exhaled with a sudden decision.

"I don't think I like your decision, Sundi," Rush said quietly. "If evacuation from the rim to the core becomes necessary, it will be an order and not a request. Don't count on our being so busy we'll forget about you up here."

Her cheeks reddened. "Yes, sir," she said, lowering her eyes.

"Sundi." She looked up at Sam Hammil, the tall, quiet man with deep pools for eyes. He spoke so rarely with the crew that any such moment was an event. "Do as you've been told. You're too close to these creatures of yours to understand that high radiation will cause them great suffering." He waited for her eyes to widen and return to normal. "If that happens, Sundi, we're going to bleed the air from this module. The animals will simply go to sleep. They'll feel nothing. It's a humane end."

*"You'd kill them?"*

"Yes. But gently, with no pain."

Her eyes darted from Christy to Rush and back to Sam. Steve Longbow stood on the side like a stone. "But you can't do that!" she said, her voice almost a wail.

Sam never took his eyes away. "Did you ever see any of these animals die from high radiation dos-

age? I didn't think so. Sundi, they'll bleed inter-
nally with horrible pain. They'll bleed through
their eyes and every body orifice. They'll be in
agony. If we get that kind of radiation level, which
way do you want it?"

Sundi looked like a frightened animal herself.
She went quickly to Steve Longbow, gripping his
arm. "Steve . . . *please* try? The shielding, please?"

He removed her hands gently. "Little one, I'll do
my best. That's a promise."

He couldn't look into her eyes any longer. Not
waiting for the others, he went through the far
airlock into the flora experimental module. He
didn't turn around until he heard the others with
him, heard and felt the airlock hatches close slowly,
with a sound of finality he hated.

# Chapter 10

No botanical garden earthside, even in the densest of the tropical rain forests, had ever known
such extraordinary growth. The main plant module of the station gave off an overpowering musk
of humidity, of a hundred fragrances, of smells
exotic and even painful. And all that assailed them
was but a fraction of the full effect of the flora
biosystems under the skilled hands and total dedi-
cation of Dixie Archer, for so virulent was growth
in this low gravity, enriched water, and high ultraviolet that they moved through a plexiglas tunnel
within a tunnel.

"Welcome to Sherwood Forest," Dixie greeted
them. She was so petite as to be ridiculously diminutive, with dark curls that knew no master
and no control. Tiny-waisted and full-bosomed,
devastatingly appealing even in her stained smock,
she was rumored among the station crew to be

able to communicate with this staggering verdant growth. Christy accepted the truth of it; however and whatever she did, Christy had never before seen ferns bend their leaves, vines curl, and other plants bend on their stalks to follow the movement of this extraordinary woman in the module they had all come to accept by Dixie's name—Sherwood Forest. There was also a buzz in the air, a subdued and almost contented humming that they heard above the whine and slow thump of the pumping systems, the heaving flow of liquids and nutrients. It came from the insects—the bees and butterflies and moths, the beetles and worms and grubs—that infested and buzzed with life through the mossy growth attached to the tanks. Another good reason for those lexan transparent walls—some of the insects had not adapted to light gravity. Others were mutated and aggressive, and Dixie attended her plant charges through long-armed, thick gloves extending like a surgical facility from the lexan and plexiglas tunnel. She could touch plants with her gloved hands, move long-reaching control rods to adjust, prune, snip, and care tenderly for vines and creepers and stalks that had never lifted sunward from earth soil in earth gravity.

Flora One constituted experimental growth for the sake of basic research. Dixie the Pixie, the title bestowed by her fellow astronauts, used the Flora One model in attempts to both promote natural growth under low-gravity conditions and to mutate new botanical wonders that, by earthside comparisons, grew with explosive speed and reached unprecedented size. Early in the program they had discovered that some plants, benign on Earth, could be positively dangerous under low gravity.

Rush had learned of this propensity the hard way—a full pressure breach that set alarms clamoring through the station. The computers had flashed their condition red on the alarm boards. Rush and the watch crew had slipped into emergency pressure suits and slammed through airlocks and along the rim to reach Flora One, where they found Dixie Archer barely conscious and collapsed on the floor of the plexiglas tunnel. Air whistled with a terrifying shriek through several breaks in the plexiglas *and the outer rim wall of the module*. So much pressure had been lost in the module that the shrill clanging of the alarms had become only a faint and distant call. Rush dropped on his knees by Dixie's side, jerked an emergency mask from his belt, and slammed it roughly to her face. The jolt was as necessary as the oxygen, firing adrenalin into her system and making her gasp— and suck in life-saving oxygen. He knew it was but the skimpiest of life-saving, for the pressure was still dropping so fast even a hundred percent oxygen wouldn't keep Dixie alive. "Open the east hatch!" he shouted, his words carried by radio to the others in pressure suits. He dragged and carried the now unconscious form into the adjacent module. Someone behind him slammed the hatch closed. "Pressure it up," Rush snapped. "Give it everything you have. She's going to have the bends and we'll lose her. Where the hell's the medical team!"

He wiped blood from her face, sprayed from her nose and mouth during the rapid decompression. One ear still trickled blood and a red stain moved down one leg. "Goddamn it," he swore quietly, "of all the times for her to have her period." He looked at the white face; she was already in shock. Less than a minute later, the medical team was hammering at the other airlock. Rush signaled for them to stop and used his radio. "Raise the pressure in there to two atmospheres before you open the hatch. One more rapid decompression and she's dead. Bring everything you need in here. We can't move her into the infirmary until we have her in a medpressure suit. Move it, damn you!"

Dixie Archer made it, but not by much. While she was in the infirmary—kept under high oxygen body pressure to help her recuperate—they had time to study what had gone wrong in Flora One. They'd never had a pressure seal break in an outside wall that began from the *inside* of the station. Even ruptured walls and sections were double-hulled with ripstop construction so that any crack or split could move only a short distance before it was stopped with a structural member, and the self-sealing rubberized compartments, much like super self-sealing tires, self-plugged those breaches until permanent repairs could be made. But every breach in air security had come from the outside because of a meteoroid strike. A rock the size of a pea moving against the station at forty thousand miles an hour had much the same localized effect as a locomotive falling off a high cliff. Thus the reason for double-hulling the station walls. Any meteoroid strike smashed into the outer hull, pulverized metal, and gave up most of its kinetic energy in the localized orgy of destruction. If there was enough remaining to rip through the self-sealing material and then into the station, automatic safety devices triggered.

That had happened in Flora One but it didn't work, and when they found out why, their blood ran as cold as the temperature on the darkside of earth. The plants were new strains, genetic oddities, mutations growing under unique low-gravity conditions, fed special nutrients and bathed with ultraviolet light and whatever higher radiation levels were encountered every so often from solar storms or the cosmic rain. They hadn't counted on one thing: some plants carry their own genetic instructions to burrow deeply into the soil, to push tendrils as far and deep as is possible to go. Far and deep into soil wasn't possible in the station, with its spongy moss soil kept rich with nutrients. Frustrated in their efforts, the plants adapted, much as plants will adapt to living in arid regions or taking root from windblown seeds in solid rock and, eventually, splitting open that rock and crumbling it down to something which, if not edible, was certainly quite habitable.

The roots concealed within the spongy moss encountered hard metal. That's tougher than rock and it doesn't crumble. The plants adapted, and they began to produce from their frenetic growth rate an incredible acid never known before to man. To the plants, the plexiglas and lexan inner walls within the Flora One module were much the same as the metal walls of the rim. They were obstacles, and blind genetic engineering produced the answer to the roots seeking so desperately to reach beyond, into expected deep soil. Everything happened at once. Pods swelled at the end of roots and tendrils. At some mysterious signal the pods burst, as pods have exploded on earth to scatter their seeds in a ritual many millions of years old. This time, the birth was not of seeds blindly seeking a new home, but corrosive acid intended to eliminate a barrier of normally impenetrable material, and reach what genetic memory promised was dark, rich, thick soil.

The plexiglas and lexan gave way like tissue paper with a shotgun effect. At the same time, the acid crumpled the inner metal wall of the station rim, ate greedily at the self-sealing chemicals within, sent in more tendrils with pods, which in turn exploded against the final, outer metal wall of the station. It was as if a slow-moving blast of shotgun pellets had punched their way into vacuum. Air under pressure, of course, followed instantly, and what would have been a violent explosive decompression that could have killed Dixie Archer in seconds was restricted to an air-whistling-screaming escape through the lethal holes into vacuum. The moment the pressure dropped below the safety margin of six pounds per square inch, automatic valves snapped open and began pouring additional oxygen into the module. It was this automatic safety replenishment that kept Dixie alive long enough for her rescuers to transfer her to safety.

Rush had held a caucus in Flora One with Christy Gordon, Ed Raphael, and Jerry Maxwell from his life support crew. "Everyone agreed on what happened here?" he asked in reference to the acid secretion. He saw their heads nodding behind their pressure helmets in the module which they were keeping down to only two psi of oxygen and nitrogen. Sam Hammil had joined them after their meet-

ing started. He'd been a botanist of no small renown
in past years and he had been busy playing detec-
tive with computers and some of the world's leading botanists earthside.

"Rush, I'd appreciate it if you would simply
accept my judgment at this moment, do as I say,
and wait for the detailed explanations later," Sam
announced, his face as deeply shrouded in concern
as an embalmer during the rush hour.

Rush Cantrell studied this man, in whom he had
such innate faith. "Go ahead," he said.

Sam motioned to Jerry Maxwell. "Seal both
airlocks, please. *Full* seal, if you would."

Jerry checked them both. "Full seal," he confirmed.

"All right," Sam said calmly. "I want everyone's
suit on closed loop." They looked at him with
surprise. He repeated the order. "Closed loop, everybody. Each of you check someone else's suit. Do
it quickly, please."

They moved the suit life support systems so that
exhaled gases, water vapor, and other body excre-
tions were recycled or stored within the pressure
suits. "All right," Sam said again in his particular
phrase for starting a new step. "Grasp something
firm. I'm going to blow the pressure seal on this
module and vent us to open vacuum."

"Hey, wait a moment," Jerry Maxwell complained. "That'll kill everything in here!"

Sam Hammil looked at Rush. "Commander, if
you please?"

Rush looked to Maxwell. "We do as he says.
Hang on."

Sam walked to the emergency vent control, broke
the safety wire, and pulled on three interlocking

handles. This job was never easy. If you made a mistake, it could ruin your whole day—forever. The last handle came down and a thick port snapped open, exposing a three-foot-wide circular space in the module. Instantly they heard and felt the dull thudding explosion of rapid decompression. White condensation fog swirled about them briefly and rushed out the open port into space. Dust and small debris followed in a funnel sweeping away anything not secured. They felt their suits balloon slightly as outside pressure dropped to zero. They looked at Sam for the next step.

"Everybody concur we've got zero pressure in here?" Sam asked by suit radio. "I want absolute certainty."

Jerry Maxwell pointed to the pressure gauge. "I don't know what you're up to, Sam, but you can't get any lower than zero. It doesn't matter, because living things, especially plants that have been growing in a hothouse, don't survive hard vacuum."

Sam smiled. "Would someone please return the emergency vent port back to *almost* closed? Not all the way. Leave it cracked just a hair, if you would. Ah, good. Thank you." He removed an aerosol spray can from his suit equipment belt. "Everybody stand well back, if you would. I'm going to release some red spray. It won't condense in vacuum. It doesn't contain any water or water vapor, so it will spray very slowly. Watch the spray carefully, if you will."

They knew what would happen. As the spray lofted from the can, it would simply follow the slight open space of the vent port, because that's where the air had blown from the module. Then they realized they were wrong—it couldn't vent anywhere because the module was already hard vacuum.

They stared in disbelief at the thin red mist blowing outward from the aerosol can resting on the module floor. It should have floated upward to the overhead—*but it didn't*. The mist followed an invisible beckoning. Under vacuum everywhere it should have simply filled the module. If the pressure finally became great enough to be measurable, it would float from the module through the thin space of the airlock vent hatch. It didn't do any of these things. It moved like a red, gossamer veil through the module, creating a definite misty stream, down toward one group of thick, fibrous vines.

"Ladies and gentlemen," Sam Hammil announced in a voice devoid of all emotion, for he was still as disbelieving as anyone else in Flora One, "do you understand what you are seeing? These plants, most of them, are dead from the cold of vacuum and no exposure to radiant energy. They've been frozen, squeezed, dried by decompression. They're dead vegetable matter that will rot if placed back into a humid and pressurized environment."

He pointed to different areas of the growth beyond the transparent tunnel walls. "In there, however, are plants that still survive. They produce their own oxygen in pods. They bathe in ultraviolet, they suck the barest whisper of moisture, although they can go for years without a smidgen of it, and they produce oxygen in pods which they also use for their own life chemical processes. They'll survive, although dormant, as will certain seeds among us. They're environmentally sealed, so to speak, and they can remain this way for a hundred years, perhaps even a thousand, as fully protected as if the germ seeds within were encased in thick armor plating. They cannot, however, return to life without moisture, ultraviolet, carbon dioxide, and other nutrients.

"*But notice that vine.* When we interfered with its genetic structure we accomplished more than we intended. Nothing like it ever existed before it grew here in this station. We tested some in the zero-g tanks and they grew in a wild bramble that choked itself to death. Dixie brought cuttings here to live under low gravity. The results of DNA hacking applied to the combination of zero-g problems and the advantages of perfect conditions here in this module produced an entirely new flora. Do you notice what that vine is doing? The spray, which you see as a red mist, is something I put together. The red is sugar dye. It also contains ice crystals, carbon dioxide, and other elements simply loved by that vine. *The vine is drawing in this barely perceptible mist from a vacuum condition.* That, of course, is impossible. So is that vine's ability to grow into solid rock, use its acid to dissolve the rock and extract minerals and substances it needs, and even create its own gases. What you are seeing is a wholly new thrust of life in the universe." He looked about him. "The damned thing lives in vacuum. It grows in solid rock. It shoots out explosive jets of acid to reach whatever it feels it needs."

Sam took a long breath, turned to the station commander. "Rush, get that goddamned thing off *Pleiades*, or we're going to be fighting it for our very survival."

They did that, but in a way no one had expected.

Christy Gordon was nearly frantic with excitement about the new life form. Rush had ordered everything in the module to be taken to a remote industrial test module, well away from the station, there to be incinerated in a high-power plasma arc generator that would reduce anything it touched to free ions.

Christy begged him not to destroy the new vine "There's no danger to the station if we do it my way," she pleaded. "Remove the entire module. Just unplug it, for God's sake. We can seal it again, replace the nutrients it lost, put some large bay windows in for ultraviolet, and keep it a mile away from *Pleiades* in a formation orbit. With instruments and TV scanners throughout the module, we can watch it grow, measure everything that happens, learn something truly incredible. We might not be able to recreate it. Not *ever*. It may be the result of nothing more than serendipitous experimental error! And what harm can it do us *out there?*"

He answered her with complete honesty. "I don't know, Christy, and that's what scares hell out of me. I don't like dealing with something that doesn't obey the rules of life, that persists in living when everything should be absolutely dead, and that's exercising self-motion and directed control that's way out of line for a plant."

"Curie didn't know the first thing about radiation when she started working with radium," Christy threw back at him. "Do you need a list of what she gave us?"

"I'm no Columbus," Rush told her, "and I don't want to be. I command a station. I'm responsible for the lives aboard this station, and—"

"And this whole thing is a farce if we don't engage in basic research, and that means snatching at anything new that comes our way. That vine isn't just *new*, Rush! It's a revolutionary, even a violent departure from anything we know. You said you were no Columbus."

That last took him back a little. "I did. What about it?"

"Well, thank the Lord you're *not*. He was a greedy little bastard who money-grubbed almost everything he touched. He wanted a royal title, he wanted a piece of the action on everything he brought back from his voyages, and he wanted percentages from the start. When Columbus left Spain, he didn't know where he was going, when he got there he didn't know where the devil he was, when he got home he didn't know where he'd been, and he did the whole thing on borrowed money! Is that your hero, Rush?"

Rush broke out in a whoop of laughter. "Okay, okay. You win. We'll do it your way. You're right, of course. Sometimes you can lose sight of the forest because of all the trees."

She winced. "Ouch. I wooden touch that sort of pun."

"Think nothing of it. Leaf it to me."

"Rush, will you *stop?*" She extended her fingers in claw fashion. "If I have to shake permission out of you, I'll—"

"You look sort of pretty when you snarl."

"That must be your oblique sense of humor. I have a green light for my project? I'll work with Dixie on it, of course." She thought a moment. "*And* Sam Hammil. We ought to name that thing for him. He's the one who really discovered what was happening. None of us saw it."

"That's why he's aboard. He's a hunch generator."

"I never knew before how you meant that. I do now. Commander," she announced, "let me get with our remote green thumb. Can I have O'Leary and Maxwell with us on the job?"

"You can," he said. "Get with it."

A month later they were all astonished with what was happening. The Flora One module, removed from *Pleiades* and stationed a mile from the great ringed base, had been transformed into a miniature jungle. The vines grew thickly; they punched small holes in the module sides and learned how to seal those holes with a sticky secretion that froze solid, like resin, over open spaces. The vine had developed not only the ability to crack even an armored eggshell, *but also to create its own sealed environment.*

Rush ordered nutrients sent to Flora One by remote control space tugs. They docked with the airlock of the module and delivered water, waste gases, human waste in bulk, decaying matter from the *Pleiades* farms—everything from worn-out clothing to dead chickens.

The vines flourished in their own, self-modified Paradise.

Rush thought a lot about Flora One. It still scared the hell out of him. It scared him so much he kept a thick belt of plastic explosives around the module. He attached a powerful solid-propellant rocket motor of enormous size to the module and kept it permanently aligned and balanced for instant ignition. He wouldn't send it down into reentry with the earth's atmosphere to be incinerated. Even *that* scared him. He wouldn't dump it into open orbit around the sun. What he really wanted was a small atomic bomb to be fastened to the module so that if his nightmares ever proved real, he could make it all vanish in a single stupendous instant of utter incineration. There's nothing like a shot of a hundred million degrees temperature and a king-sized blast of killing radiation to take care of a plant that won't stay within its own flower pot. But the best he could do was to keep that booster rocket always ready to fire, always ready to hurl the Flora One module into the sun, where plants had a lousy survival record.

Another month passed, and he was glad he hadn't done that. The Flora One module was soaked in oxygen. It was taking in all that garbage they fed to it, including a few hundred pounds of rock that was its sole source of food for sixty days (Houston had really raised hell about that request), and it kept eating, dissolving, growing.

One night Rush sat up straight in his bunk, eyes wide, staring back into the dream he clutched at wildly. He remembered enough to realize what had been lurking all this time in the back of his mind.

That vine . . . it *was* a new beginning, a new way of life. It had been under his nose all this time!

*It would grow in the vacuum on the surface of the moon.*

It would lodge in crevices and on boulder-strewn slopes and deep in craters. Slowly but surely, and especially if fed even the worst of garbage and debris, it would flourish, and it would keep pouring oxygen onto that airless and utterly dead surface of pumice and rock and ash and dust.

*Damn!*

# Chapter 11

Rush looked about the replacement module for the original Flora One, which in her own whimsy Dixie Archer insisted on calling *The Flower Pot*. Hardly a proper designation for a scientific and technological station, but Rush didn't argue the point. Personal touches were everything in extended orbit, and up here familiarity didn't breed contempt so much as it established comfortable wariness.

Rush studied the computer printouts and live digital readings of plant experiments and progress. "No problems?" he asked Dixie.

She shook her head. "None yet," she added, a touch of doubt appearing in her expression. "But I'm concerned about the magnetic storm—what the effect might be on these growths in terms of radiation levels."

"You're pretty well shielded here," Rush reminded her.

"That might not be good enough, Commander."

"It has to do," he said in an official but still gentle tone with this pixie of theirs. "We're working full time to add shielding to the core and some of the control rooms for our people. We can't build any more shielding about your garden of eden in here. Besides, you know even better than I do that plants are resistant to radiation. Even in the Bikini area where we held all those atomic and hydrogen bomb tests they took a beating but always came back. Consider this a test."

She nodded slowly. Difficult to argue human life against the plants, much as she wanted to. "One more thing, Dixie. When we reach certain radiation levels, the station goes on yellow alert, and that means you put everything up here on automatic and you report to Saturn for specific orders. Little one, don't even bring up any contentious philosophy with me. I appreciate your green thumb, but I'm more interested in your face not turning red from ionizing radiation. Understand?"

"Yes, sir." Her face was downcast, then she brightened in that inexhaustible optimism of hers. *Just like those vines of hers*, Rush thought. The thought prompted a change of subject. He glanced through a viewport at the old Flora One, its surface pitted and marked from its long stay in orbit and the micrometeoroid scrubbing it had endured. It gleamed dully like a quarter moon, but somehow it still retained its sense of alienness to Rush and the others.

"Dixie, what about The Jungle out there?" he asked, gesturing toward the module that had gained a new and instantly accepted name among the station crew.

"Oh, I'm not worried about *them*," she replied.

" 'Them?' "

"Yes, sir. You mean the vines, don't you?"

He couldn't believe the expression of near-reverence in her face. "I do mean just that. You're not worried about them?"

"Oh, not at all, Commander," she said brightly. "I don't think that anything less than the radiation from an atomic bomb would hurt my vines."

Rush exchanged a meaningful glance with Christy Gordon, and Sam Hammil, not missing anything, nodded in unspoken concert. It wasn't proprietary language only—Dixie did consider that vine jungle in solitary orbit to be *her* creation, her offspring. Did those damned plants have that same kind of effect on people as they did on their environment? He marked it off on a mental checklist for later discussion.

"Fine, Dixie. Let's get into the farm. We'll do a fast walk-through and check the support systems. Steve? Check out the interlock and we'll get with it."

Longbow went ahead. The "farm" of *Pleiades* did in fact exist. It was real—an honest-to-goodness garden in space. It filled the next module, another outsized modified shuttle tank. Because of the unusual nature of plant experiments and fauna biological experiments, they'd left as little as possible to chance encounters of the worst kind with their living and growing forms aboard the station. Between each of the modules where biology was the primary issue, there had been established an interlock. They moved from the interior of Flora One to an airlock and sealed it behind them. Safely ensconced within the airlock, Rush peered into the interlock chamber. He pressed a control button and a savage blue-white arc flashed through the interlock. Nothing that was alive an instant before would be anything but subatomic particles now. It was the most effective form of sterilization. They were then subjected to a brief wash of ultraviolet light, and the door to the interlock slid open, and closed behind them. The plasma arc flashed behind them in the airlock, destroying anything that might have been transported between modules. They went through the same precautionary treatment in the next airlock, and walked on through into the Farm.

Here was a mixture of experimental plant biology and a source of fresh food for the station crew. The Russians had learned a great deal with their smaller but meaningful Salyut space station program, and one of the strongest lessons to emerge from Salyut's many years in orbit was that the longer that men (and women) remained away from the earth, the greater became their craving for fresh foodstuffs. Growing different foods in orbit was hardly a novelty, since various plants had been cultivated in the early days of space flight. Skylab was a source of much experimental data, but the Salyuts provided one-step-beyond information since the cosmonauts quite literally, despite their confined space, grew some of their own preferred vegetables. They ran into their own special problems, too. One of which was finding out to their dismay that certain plants expected to flourish in weightlessness did quite the opposite: they reacted with complete disorientation, suffered from stunted growth, and died out. Others did flourish, and some even grew with the normal pace and productivity they had earthside, and a few ran rampant with uninhibited, flourishing growth.

The single biggest difference was that the artificial gravity along the rim of *Pleiades* was a factor absent from the small Salyuts. The great wheeled station provided everything along the rim with the same gravitational field as the Apollo astronauts experienced while walking, jumping, running, and driving on the surface of the moon—one-sixth that of earthside. That was why an Apollo astronaut who might weigh 360 earthside pounds fully equipped with a heavy pressure suit and helmet, as well as all manner of assorted tools, cameras, and instruments, weighed only sixty of those same earthside pounds while on the moon. This led to strange and delightful behavior on the part of men who hopped about in slow motion, who did one-armed pushups that sprang them back to the vertical, and other antics. But one-sixth earthside gravity was also a very respectable force, and it made possible a whole new farming industry aboard *Pleiades*.

Every time a Soyuz or Progress vehicle docked with the Salyut station, it carried requested items for the permanent members of the Salyut. Normal cosmonaut diets included some seventy meat, dairy, and other products, such as confectionary fruit and spices. But the greatest thrill to the in-space palate was the delivery of fresh fruit and vegetables, which were added to the space-grown successes, and they included onions, garlic, dill, parsley, cucumbers, mushrooms, and fennel, in the main. Wheat sprouted wildly under zero-g, but wheat fell into the experimental category, and its phe-

nomenal growth under one-sixth gravity, along with
the plants grown on *Pleiades*, such as alfalfa, barley,
and other staples, boded well for space gardens for
the future.

The Farm was more than the pride and joy of
the *Pleiades'* crew. With one-sixth gravity, perfect
ultraviolet and mixtures of gases and nutrients,
they grew squash, pumpkins, radishes, onions, and
garlic, green beans, and varieties of tomato and
potato plants. Mushrooms were a favorite. Those
under one-sixth gravity grew normal but outsized
plants, and mushrooms thriving in weightlessness
produced plants that were long and curling, but
unusually tasty. The Farm actually consisted of
the large rim module and enclosed areas in the
main core where plant growth in weightlessness
could be tested. The crew of *Pleiades* had been
encouraged to turn every available area into a
greenhouse. Weightless and low-gravity growth of
the seaweed chlorella, which the botany team
planned as a future major food source, was spec-
tacularly successful. Grown in aquatic solutions,
the weightless variety resembled brambles, but
the low-gravity chlorella almost ran amuck in its
growth.

Lettuce and cabbage were nondescript in their
growth while weightless, but excellent under one-
sixth gravity. To the dismay of the crew, flowers
would not grow under weightlessness, with the
exception of buttercups and some of the flowers
produced by creeping and clinging vines. However, in the Farm, the low gravity produced riotous color in flowers and added a warm and familiar
touch and smell to a crew that had long since
wearied of the stale smell of the space station with

its mechanically cleansed air, and the stink of lubricating fluids and graphite for the machinery that made life possible aboard the station.

There was no separate crew to work the farms and other botanical experiments. Men and women off duty surged to the farm and other growth stations, almost as if subconsciously impelled to "dig in with their hands." One of the more hopeful experiments was to grow trees aboard *Pleiades*. In weightlessness, the trees seemed almost bewildered. They developed normal roots, trunks, and leaves, but their growth was severely stunted. Tree growth along the rim was restricted to early stages only. It would hardly do to have a tree bulging metal plates and breaching air seals.

Two particular plants were exceptions. Bamboo went wild in weightlessness, perhaps accounted for, as Dixie Archer proposed, "because it's a grass and not a tree, as most people think." Along the bottom of the weightless core tank (the side closest to the earth), they anchored deep pots with rich soil, fed the seedlings with the nutrients and affection one might offer to a pet, and were rewarded with "grass" that climbed to a length of forty-five feet above the pots, at which point they were carefully trimmed.

Bamboo was an experiment, and it was fun and demanding of attention while giving its rewards. The real king of the space station, however, was the pumpkin, and it began to have a measurable effect upon the life-support systems of *Pleiades*.

The numbers told their own story. A permanent crew complement of fifty-two men and women meant the space station required a minimum every ninety days of 11,000 pounds of oxygen in pressurized containers, as well as nitrogen gas on a two-to-one ratio, for 22,000 pounds of the nitrogen to build up atmospheric pressure within the station. Every ninety days, for breathing and pressure purposes, *Pleiades'* crew consumed a minimum of 33,000 pounds of gases which, with containers and operating apparatus, required the full payload of two shuttle flights. That ratio began to diminish with time, and the hero that emerged was the lowly pumpkin plant.

There's much more to life support than simply supplying air as oxygen and nitrogen under pressure. It needs to be circulated, blown, exhausted, drawn in; under zero gravity, where there is no convection because there's no up or down, so that hot air doesn't rise and cool air doesn't descend, a forced draft is critical to life. A man in a closed room in weightlessness will choke to death on his own exhalations, just as a burning candle will die from its own waste products that no longer support combustion. Along the rim, with one-sixth gravity, most of these problems were solved with relative ease. In the core where the world was zero in terms of gravity, such systems were vital.

The adult male requires three pounds of oxygen every twenty-four hours (as well as nitrogen). He also takes in on the average four pounds (two quarts) of water in various forms. For each daily period of twenty-four hours, each man loses some three pounds of water through exhalation, perspiration, and waste discharge. Much of this can be reclaimed through air scrubbers, cleansers, and purifiers, and wringing moisture out of air has been old hat from the early days of submarines, let alone the first spaceships. But it could never be enough. Self-sufficiency was always the goal of any long-term space project, and *Pleiades* had absolute priority on that list.

Long-established plans for producing fresh oxygen from selected plants had been bandied about ever since man first dreamed of falling around his home world. In the lead for a single plant that could absorb large quantities of carbon dioxide and other waste products, bathed in artificial sunlight, and produce *fifty times* its own volume in oxygen per hour, was the chlorella algae. Algae ponds couldn't make it in weightlessness; the plants choked themselves without *some* downward tug, which existed along the rim. Here space—*within Pleiades* rather than outside the station—became the crucial factor. Constant water flow with desired temperatures and nutrients, the need to occupy large flat areas, and the attention required by the algae, cast doubts on its *utility* within a station with the size limitations of *Pleiades*. The plant was marvelously productive of oxygen, and also demanding of enormous effort, attention, pumping systems, and energy. It would do fine on the moon within sealed caves and underground installations, but in orbit, the problems attending the care and feeding of chlorella algae kept it from being practical.

Enter the lowly pumpkin vine, tough and hardy, able to grow in almost any nutrient-rich soil, equally adaptable to weightlessness as to a gravity environment, requiring little care and, if a plant could be described as happy, joyful in the uniquely isolated world falling around a world. And at the same time, about twenty square feet of leaf of the pumpkin vine provided the oxygen needs of the average adult for a day of work, rest, and sleep. No wonder that to the newsmen with an eye for the catchy phrase, the space station was often referred to in the world press as the *Pumpkin Factory*. Every available space would find a pumpkin vine flourishing, and cabins, compartments, control rooms, and other areas were cleansed of their waste products in the air and always filled with a fresh country smell.

Rush Cantrell didn't find the sprouting of plants in all corners and cubicles of *Pleiades* always a commendable reference. Plants, of all sizes and kinds, require nutrients. The more isolated a manned outpost, whether it be orbiting the earth or deep beneath the sea, the more dependent it must become on its own resources.

Fifty-two men and women produce a most considerable quantity of body waste. Solid wastes weren't simply dumped into space because they would come to regard the station as a gravity center and assume slow, wide orbits around *Pleiades*, just as the station orbited the earth while the earth in turn orbited the sun. Rush had shuddered when he had learned of the nutrient program for *Pleiades*. The NASA Administrator, Dr. Luther Grenville, had given him the word personally. "We recycle human waste, Commander. That's the name of the game. You have power and chemicals and all the processes necessary to convert human waste into acceptable fertilizer, and that will be mixed with liquids to provide the proper nutrients for the botanical programs of the station."

"You're kidding," Rush said after a pause of disbelief.

"I am *not*. Do you expect us to spend millions of

dollars sending fertilizer into space when you've got a ready-made factory of fifty-two human beings already doing that job for you?"

"Jesus Christ, you're talking about recycling human waste into fertilizer to be used for plants *that we're going to eat.*"

Grenville stroked his handlebar moustache. "That is *precisely* the point, Commander. Maximum utilization means maximum efficiency and the most return for the dollar."

"My people won't do it," Rush said, glowering.

"Of course they will. The people in Asia have been recycling human waste for thousands of years. I'm sure you're familiar with the honey buckets of Japan in which they collect such wastes to—"

"I'm familiar, I'm familiar," Rush said, his sarcasm neither hidden nor missed by the Administrator. "I can just see the stories now about the Great Honeybucket in the Sky."

"That does have a nice ring to it," Grenville said with a broad smile. "But on a more serious level, Commander, you're not going to be using human waste products. You'll be using a final product that's been irradiated, cleansed, scrubbed, and modified with special chemicals to make it perfectly safe."

Rush slid lower in his seat. "It still sounds like a lot of shit to me."

Grenville stared at him. "I hope you never say that in a press conference."

"If I don't someone else *will*," Rush snapped.

"Not if it means saving millions of dollars a year, and if it does, that alone will attend to any criticism. As for quick wit, Commander Cantrell,

I've never considered *you* to be afflicted with thin skin. True, eh?"

"True," Rush admitted, "but I still don't like it."

Grenville had a sudden thought. "Just a moment, Commander." He pressed his intercom to call for his secretary. "Miss Johnson, has that special mineral water been delivered here from the laboratory yet? Good. Bring it right in with a glass, please."

The bottle and glass rested on his desk. Grenville tapped the bottle with a finger. "This is water of the purest quality that can be produced by modern science. Absolutely clear. Not an impurity of any kind. It has all the qualities of deep spring water. I want you to taste it."

"Why?"

"Because I want your reaction to its taste, *that's* why." Grenville opened the bottle and filled the glass. "Now, if you would, Commander?"

Rush picked up the glass and looked at it.

"For God's sake, man, it's not going to bite you! Drink up, now."

Rush sipped. It *was* like deep spring water. He drank the rest of the glass. "Okay, it's as good as anything I ever drank. What's the point?"

Grenville's smile would have done justice to a leprechaun. "You took your pilot's medical this morning, I believe? Before this appointment?"

"Yes, I did."

"And you passed?"

"Yes, sir, but what has this got to do with—"

"That water, Commander, which you just described as 'as good as anything you ever drank,' is recycled urine. *Yours.*"

\*　　\*　　\*

Not even in his wildest dreams would H.G. Wells ever have imagined a great space station with the Farm. *Pleiades* was well saddled with affectionate or sarcastic names for its components, commencing with the sensible-enough Saturn core, to the Junkyard, where shuttle tanks were kept in readiness for future programs. What had been Flora One was now the ominous Jungle, with its sinister and unpredictable rock-eating and vacuum-loving vines. Replacing Flora One was the Flower Pot. And Rush Cantrell had been correct in his prediction that recycled human waste would one day bring on the news blessing of the station as the Great Honeybucket in the Sky. He could live with that.

The Farm made him want to throw up.

They left the agricultural module of the station through the airlocks and interlock into the next module, another shuttle tank modified before launch for insertion into the rim wheel of *Pleiades*. It really wasn't a farm, it was an offensive, stinking, eye-tearing, throat-gagging chicken coop. There are few things on Earth (or off it, he thought grimly) that can stink worse than an enclosed area sodden with the droppings of chickens. They are possessed of barely more intelligence (if that) than a blind worm. Because of their tendency to bunch together and choke themselves to death, they had to be kept in individual wire cages, except when Dixie Archer or Sundi Meguiar paired off a rooster with one of the hens for breeding. Then there was one hell of a lot of squawking and feathers fluttering about before they were dragged away by the air exhausts.

And chicken droppings. Not all the fresh air, the

atomizers, even the most advanced odor killers, could snuff out the nose-squeezing horrors of the Farm. The droppings were devastating. The stench clung to clothing and was dragged by workers and visitors alike through the station. It wasn't just the chickens. They also had ducks, if not as reprehensible as the chickens, as offensive in their own ways. *And* the turkeys. And quail, and geese. A congressman had been imbued with a brainstorm about these birds; being essentially as primitive as they had been tens of thousands of years ago, he thought they were perfect candidates for space station livestock. They ate leavings and garbage as their main food staple, they produced fresh eggs, and if they multiplied, then the crew had a source of fresh poultry. Except for the energy drain for the Farm, which was minimal, and the special dietary supplements for the feathered horde, their upkeep was just as minimal, and the return calculated to be rather splendid.

No one thought about the stink.

Rush and the others breathed as shallowly as possible. "Dixie, what's with the latest batch of eggs? Anticipate any problems with their hatching because of the increasing radiation?"

He almost expected to see a tear trickle down that pixie face. Dixie Archer blinked several times. "No, sir, it won't matter. Nothing seems to work. I mean, after the birds mate and they lay their eggs, we can't get them to develop properly. It's just like it was before, Commander. I mean with the Russians aboard their Salyuts."

Rush didn't want to talk about it, but he forced himself on. "Refresh my memory," he told her.

"Well, sir, they brought quail and duck eggs

aboard their small stations, leaving control samples Earthside. The control samples developed and hatched properly, but the quail eggs in weightlessness didn't make it. They hatched, but with a much slower rate than normal."

"And if I recall," Rush said with a sour face, "they had bodies but no heads, which means the Russian plans for a poultry farm went down the disposal grinder."

"Most of the crews," Longbow added, "did what any sensible person would do—they threw the damned things out. Right out the garbage dump airlock, knowing that in a couple of months the carcasses would reenter the atmosphere and we'd have fricassee dust raining down slowly."

Christy grimaced with the thought.

"Dixie," Rush said after holding his breath as long as possible, "the poultry farm is a bust. A featherbedding job if I ever saw one." Longbow and Christy winced with the pun, Sam Hammil rolled his eyes to heaven, but Dixie missed it completely. She was still too emotionally involved. So was Rush, but in a different way. "No one will eat any of these eggs because of the mutated freaks that came out of the test hatchings, right?"

Dixie nodded soberly. "And no one will eat any of these birds. We've already lost, um, how many so far?" Rush asked.

"Twelve. Eight chickens, two geese, and two turkeys."

"Right. And we fed them to the Jungle. From what the TV scanners showed us, your pet vines seemed to savor their taste, which means that, even with intelligent plants, there's no accounting for taste."

"Yes, sir, they were absorbed, like any other organic matter."

"Dixie, we could make another very important test. How does your vine react to living organisms? As food, I mean."

"Sir, I don't know." She pondered the thought. "I imagine it would work very well. I mean, the vines, once they're in position, would hold down the organism—"

"Like a Venus fly trap or some other meat-eating plant?"

"Yes, sir."

"Then I have a wonderful idea, Dixie. It's more important than hatching headless chicks and stinking up this entire station. Steve Longbow here will help, since his people have been tearing off the heads of quail, turkeys, geese, chickens, and anything else with feathers, for a few thousand years. I want a biological experiment. We'll feed the whole lot here to the Jungle and see what happens."

Dixie paled. "Commander, you can't do that! Why . . . why, Houston would never stand for it! This is a controlled test and—"

"Houston doesn't have to smell them. I do."

"Sir, they're not *that* bad."

"Are your olfactory organs dead, Miss Archer?"

Self-consciously, Dixie wrinkled her nose. "No, sir."

"Then you have more stamina than any man I have ever known. Longbow, you work it out with Archer, here. Feed 'em to the vine."

The Indian didn't know whether Rush Cantrell was *that* serious. "Commander, I'll follow you to hell and back. But how do I get all these birds into a small module to be transferred out to the Jungle?"

"Indian heap smart. Do anything," Rush chanted with a straight face.

"Indian smart," Longbow repeated. "Not get involved in fowl deed."

"Oh, shut up, both of you," Christy said quickly, before the two got out of hand. She turned to Dixie. "It won't matter much. These animals have low tolerance to radiation. I don't think they'll survive the magnetic storm."

Again the threat of a tear and a quivering lower lip tugged at them. "There's no chance for additional shielding, Dr. Gordon?"

"I'm afraid not. There are too many other priorities."

"It's strange," Dixie said quietly. "The sun gives us life, and now it's going to kill these birds."

"For which," Rush announced, "I will be eternally grateful to the sun."

He stalked off to the far airlock, desperate to leave the miasma of poultry droppings as far behind as possible.

# Chapter 12

*Pleiades* wobbled through every turn, like an uneven tire rolling down a rough road. It wasn't visible to the naked eye, but it was glaringly obvious to the Mass Control sensors of their Weight/Distribution Computer. It wobbled because weight distribution during its slow spin was never exact. It couldn't be. Fluids shifted, people moved along the rim, toilets flushed, different members of the crew assembled in the laundry rooms for ultrasonic cleaning of garments. It was impossible not to have small groups assembling at different points through the station, which is why the inner skin and skeletal or "bone structure" of *Pleiades* carried microprocessing computer chips and sensors, all feeding to the Mass Control Center. Every time something moved—a human body or a piece of equipment, or even a gas discharge—the sensors picked up the movement and changing mass and the information fed instantly to the Mass Control Computer. The MCC, entirely on its own, performed the ultimate of all juggling acts. It functioned on what was considered "broad base" control, which involved the installation of equipment or the loading and shifting of large masses, such as took place when shuttles docked with the station, when equipment was loaded or offloaded, or when major structural changes were made to *Pleiades*.

On a vastly more sensitive scale, the MCC judged the changing positions and shifts in mass of people and small equipment. The inspection team had gathered in MCC, where Bill Harris, second exec of *Pleiades*, had taken the watch. "Until this emergency is over," Rush had ordered, "we go full-time on personal monitoring of the computers. I don't want a glitch in the electronics turning this station into a lopsided ferris wheel before we find out about it."

"We're going to have problems," Harris said quietly. "I'll need additional people for moving equipment. You're adding radiation shielding to the core. It's heavy, but we can balance it out as we go along. I'm concerned about changes along the rim. You're moving a lot of people from their working modules and living compartments to the core. That reduces our rotational mass along the edges, and any imbalance becomes magnified."

"Use the old submarine system—shift water," Rush said. "Use it for ballast. The computer will give you a running status on what you need and where, so you can meet any situation by pumping from one part of the station to another."

Christy motioned for their attention. "I thought this was all automatic."

"Under normal conditions it would be," Harris answered. "We're making changes on a drastic scale. Every module of this station, and all structural elements, use two systems to detect instability. One is mechanical; it works on an old but proven system of a spring scale. The scale flexes and it has a calibrated weight at its end. If we're balanced, the bolt pretty well lies there quietly. If we get an imbalance, then the bolt—the weight— moves, triggers an electrical signal, and the computer here tells us what the perturbations in balance are and shifts water or some other fluid, or, if things are getting out of hand, yells for help from us. We back it up, of course, with the microprocesser chips that detect any change in acceleration by differences in electrical potential and—"

"Whoa," Christy said quietly. "I know the system. But you appear to be worried. What's the *problem?*"

Sam Hammil answered for Harris. "It's your storm, Doctor."

"The storm? I'm not sure I understand."

"The computerized portions of the MCC balance operate electrically. The solar storm is both of radiation and magnetic fields. The computer is going to be receiving erroneous signals. We're just as subject to fluctuations in our power grids on this station as the power transmission lines earthside."

Rush's eyes widened. "Christ, I hadn't even thought of that." He turned to Harris. "Throw a block to the computer. No major mass shifts or major rebalancing to be carried out without human interface between the computer and the shift. Let MCC play with the more subtle changes so it can stay on top of the situation, but don't let the computer move heavy furniture, so to speak. If it gets some wrong readings, it's liable to throw us into some real imbalances. We'd be like a high-speed tire with all the lead weights in the *wrong* position." Rush gestured to the programing board. "Do that *now*. I intend to watch it and test it before we leave here."

There were other imbalances to be considered, not the least of which was the nutational node. It was difficult to detect since there weren't any tire marks in orbit. But if there were, Rush considered, then they'd see a wavering path pressed into, for example, a dirt road. The nutational imbalance was an everyday occurrence Earthside. Every time a car or truck went down the road with one wheel improperly fitted to an axle, you got a nutational wobble. It chewed up the tire and gave the car a bit of seesawing ride, but that was the end of the problem. Just fix the damned wheel.

You couldn't "just fix" this wheel 228 feet from one rim edge to the other. You didn't have any tire tracks to study. The whole affair had to be fed into a super-sensitive computer, and the computer did its brain tapdance and dictated where "balance weights" should be placed to correct the tilt. If it was within the capacity of shifting fluids from one storage or ballast tank or another, or even throughout the station, the computer attended to the problem as routine. If it demanded heavier correction, then the computer bleated for help. This was a case where the computer, in the form of MCC, was like the shepherd tending his flock. He could keep the strays in line and generally bunched together so they didn't stream away and mill about the countryside. But when the wolves began to work their way in, it was time to yell for help.

Rush's new orders simply moved up that time when the cry for help would be sounded if the shepherd even *smelled* wolf. If the signal input to MCC were distorted because of magnetic disruption of electrical signals, then any "corrections" might only aggravate a nasty situation. It was also an interesting, and a smug, departure from the norm of modern science. *Men* had to babysit the giant brain. This was one job Bill Harris and his crew would enjoy.

Rush went to open line for station comm. A series of bells chimed through *Pleiades* and lights pulsed in all quarters to draw attention to a rare announcement of this nature. Rush didn't waste any time. There wasn't that much to play with. The more he studied the radiation levels from the boisterous sun, the less time they had in which to make and then implement certain decisions. Rush waited until every comm receiver on the control board was lit up to confirm that whoever waited on the other end was listening.

"This is Commander Cantrell. I'll keep this short and I'll keep it simple. Doctor Gordon's forecasts for the steady rise in radiation levels and geomagnetic effects of the solar storm have been fully confirmed. If anything, things may reach the danger point before predictions. Now, we've never encountered this level storm before in *Pleiades*. There's a question of just how intense it may become and how high the radiation dosages will reach. There's no question but that anyone not shielded from the radiation could suffer measurable biological effects."

He paused for a moment and glanced at the others with him. Sam Hammil's face was expressionless, Steve Longbow had his usual "I'll follow you to hell or anywhere" look, and Christy was—well, what he expected. Concerned, serious, dedicated; all the things that had helped make her Science Lead of *Pleiades*.

"Your mission aboard this station," Rush went on to the crew, doesn't require you to take unnecessary risks to life or limb. You all know we can power down most of the systems aboard this vessel so that we can operate with a skeleton crew. Approximately thirty hours from now we're going to have a shuttle launch from the Cape, and I'm going to request a passenger pallet be aboard that shuttle for anyone who wants to leave this station until the storm ends. There will be no hard feelings about anyone who feels, morally, medically, or otherwise, that it would be wiser for them to be free of this storm until it passes. You have my word that anyone who leaves has a guaranteed flight back. I'll need your decision within two hours. In any event, to avoid any misunderstandings, every member of this crew will report his or her decision to Commander Raphael, and those who wish to be aboard that shuttle must be ready in the predocking area at least two hours before shuttle arrival."

He paused again to let the sequence of events sink in for those who might yet be undecided and, since he wanted nothing but open-minded compliance with whatever conscience dictated, he removed that conscience from his crew. "For those of you still undecided, consider these facts. Despite the extensive exercise regimen, the vitamin and mineral supplements, the potassium and other special intakes, there's no question that we have all had lengthy stays in weightlessness. All of us now bear host to smaller red blood cells than those growing in us under earthside gravity. To some extent, however minimal, we've endured a temporary loss in marrow productivity. And some of us, although we have no way of separating one individual from the other in this instance, statistically have reduced body immunity to such diseases as influenza. No one knows better than you that we still remain in the experimental category when it comes to these physiological areas."

Another pause, then: "It's important to understand that any lowered body immunity can be reduced still more because of the radiation levels that are rising. We're not concerned with the HZE radiation, the high-energy and heavyweight cosmic particles, because we get those all the time. The solar magnetic storm will, however, increase the flood of photon radiation in the ultraviolet, X-ray, and gamma ray areas. We're fully protected against the ultraviolet, as you know. But we are much less protected, or more vulnerable, to X-ray and gamma. How high those levels will go is anyone's guess. How effective our additional shielding will be is also, at best, an educated guess. Consider all these elements before you make your decision. If you have the slightest doubt about your fertility being affected because of hard radiation, then I am emphasizing that this is precisely what we will receive aboard *Pleiades*. Thank you one and all for your help in this situation and I'm certain you'll judge what's best for you and this station. That is all." He cut off the comm without further comment; anything else would be redundant and he had little patience with epilogues.

He turned to his waiting team. "Let's go. We've still got a lot to do."

Opposite to the fauna and flora modules of the rim were the other modules, financed not by tax dollars, but by hundreds of millions of dollars provided willingly by industrial groups and corporations the world over. In the long run, it was the growth from experimental processes to productive industry under the conditions unique to the space environment that would be the real payoff for stations even far greater than *Pleiades*. The Factories, as these areas had been named by the crew, brought results in terms of industrial hardware and more return for the buck, and *that* was the name of the game, and had been so since the first sharp trader screwed his neighbor in a slick deal. *Pleiades* carried out the first extensive research, and limited production, for products to be sold to customers earthside who were, in fact, standing in line for the space-created products that couldn't be made on the planet.

The Factories were more than the modules that made up part of the station wheel. Here they had one-sixth gravity, and space factories, to be fully efficient, required the absence of gravity. Shuttle tanks, like so many others, had been outfitted with heavy equipment and test apparatus. When necessary, the industrial test crews boarded these tanks and floated off under control a mile or two from the station to perform their technical miracles.

Each substation was equipped with rows of high-efficiency batteries, and solar-cell arrays that unrolled like astroturf for a thousand feet of required electrical energy.

Levitation is a neat trick earthside. It can be accomplished through microwave-beamed power, magnetic fields, or even ultrasonic waves. But it's not very efficient, even if magically dramatic, and it's effective only on a rather small scale. Levitation in zero-g, however, was the norm. That priceless environment was always available in limitless quantities. That was critical for the more exotic industrial processes of the space factories, where certain materials *had to* be formed without being touched by anything other than the material itself.

For example, contamination of extremely pure materials on earth is almost inevitable when superheating materials in a container, a problem known as crucible contamination. Highly reactive, high-melting-point materials need absolute freedom from contamination if they're going to reach unprecedented levels of purity. Being held in a container, or crucible, is self-defeating, since the materials always pick up some impurities from that container. In zero-g, the alchemist's dream was a reality; it was possible to produce the perfect solvent. On earth, you couldn't make the perfect solvent because it would dissolve anything, and that meant any container.

*In zero-g you didn't need a container.* It couldn't fall down or float up because there wasn't any up or down except in relative visual terms. Under the zero-g conditions, in vacuum if desired, the astroworkers were able to manufacture highly purified (and almost perfect) glass that revolutionized lasers and laser system optics. And what was possible for the near-perfect glass meant that you could use that same glass right on the station in the laser-beam laboratory. It produced another benefit. If you could grow near-perfect glass, you could grow absolutely pure crystals for semiconductors.

Everything went from great to even greater. Near-perfect liquids for chemical and industrial use could be created in zero-g or even low-g conditions. Rush and the inspection crew with him stood quietly in a processing module where these "perfect liquids" were being produced under one-sixth gravity. "We're seeing what even Merlin would have given ten years to make possible," Christy observed. She was right. Perfect liquids couldn't be produced on earth because of an effect known as gravity-induced convection. Melted materials always contain regions of different temperature, and this means variable densities. Those convections mess up the homogeneity of a liquid. But not aboard *Pleiades'* modules, where zero-g made possible the separation of ingredients in a mixture due to their differing densities. TRW's space systems engineers, working under contract to NASA, had been performing minor miracles since their arrival in orbit in a myriad blaze of technological glory by setting unprecedented standards in depositing materials on surfaces for computers, mixing and homogenizing liquids for which chemists waited with breathless anticipation, polymerizing chemical components that could never be created on earth, and growing crystals no king or czar in history would ever believe.

One of the most lucrative markets awaiting deliveries from *Pleiades* involved the zero-g production of monocrystalline semi-conductors. Incorporated within computer systems, they had already revolutionized electronics by forming the basis for all-integrated-circuit technology. The station engineers, if they had the time and facilities, would have their production line "sold out" in backlogged orders for more than twenty years.

Glass fibers and laser optics were hardly new on a world about to plunge into the 21st Century, but *Pleiades* was hastening the process of better communications within that world. Under zero-g, the station engineers had turned out a miraculous glass fiber channel, or a "light pipe," of the most extraordinary purity and, consequently, extraordinary performance on earth, where it had been tested, and the demand for additional production was almost frantic. Installed in earthside systems and operating at the frequency of visible light or in the infrared spectrum, a single TRW optical channel could carry at one time *four million voice signals*. Another single channel easily accommodated three thousand television signals. There was no question of future underground and submarine cables using optical fiber transmission, again revolutionizing communications, since a single large cable would have almost unlimited capacity.

And the secret was the containerless production of glass fibers in weightlessness. Merlin's perfect solvent had been tamed.

Rush hated to do it, but he switched station wire and radio comm to the individual modules and free-floating factories. "You all got the message," he said in easy terms. "Close it up. All factory modules are to be put on standby. I know you people. Big production orders from down below and they pay your fat-cat salaries and bonuses. So I'm making it official. Close up, *now*. I want everybody to report for emergency duty in Saturn within the next two hours. And, ladies and gentlemen, to complete your good day, that's an order. Acknowledge, if you will."

Disgruntled compliance always sounds like a barnyard. Rush turned off the hoots and catcalls and looked at Christy. "You know what comes next, don't you?"

She nodded, her face sour. Then she perked up and smiled sweetly at Rush. "You're so *very* good at playing the bastard, why don't you—"

"I never play at it, doc."

"Well, since you admit to your status, why don't you handle biosystems for me?"

"Because you're the chief lady honcho on this tub. You want an executioner because you can't handle the job, ask one of them." She looked at Hammil and Longbow, who looked back with blank expressions.

"They won't help," she complained.

"Then you're it," Rush said. He didn't intend flippancy because he understood just what Christy was so reluctant to do. Turning off in-progress biological programs was like pulling the plug on a critically ill patient who *could* survive the crisis. Christy sighed and began building up her own emotional strength as they went into the airlock of the BioSystems Laboratories. Like other units of *Pleiades*, they were made up of integral modules of the rim with one-sixth gravity, as well as an orbiting shuttle tank positioned near the station for weightless bio-research.

Jim O'Toole wore his favorite smock when he

worked in the Bio labs and now was no different. He greeted them with a wave and an infectious smile. A square jaw and powerful shoulders belied the brilliant, always inquisitive and enthusiastic mind of a man whose name was already becoming famous the world over. And it should be, judged Rush, because his name means life for a lot of people who might never see another sunrise.

"Hey, a greeting party," O'Toole smiled, turning from a rack of complicated instruments and sealed containers, "and you're just in time. We've got the first run of acceptable enzyme urokinase."

Steve Longbow was in the upper strata of smarts when it came to equipment and machinery, but he was now out of his league. He turned to Christy. "What the hell did he say?"

"He was using biology shorthand for telling us he's produced in this lab what on earth is considered a miracle."

"So? You're going to quit there? You sound like my grandfather telling me about the spirits of the great buffalo, only I could understand *him*."

She patted Longbow on the shoulder. "Look in here." The Indian looked into a sealed container filled with rows of stoppered vials. "You know what you're seeing?" Christy asked.

*"No."*

"Let me back up, then. In medicine, we need special kinds of certain biological entities. Most especially, living cells, because they produce medically critical substances we can't create synthetically. On earth, they can't even separate them biologically because the best chemical and physical techniques get messed up by gravity. In our zero-g labs we use electrophoresis separation—"

"Slow down, will you, please?"

"That's a technique for separating particles of different mass/charge ratios in an electric field. It doesn't work well Earthside because the cells have a tendency to settle under gravity to the bottom of their containers."

"Sounds reasonable."

"Up here, in the floating lab, there's no gravity, and the cells remain in floating solution and we can separate them."

"I know I'm pressing the point, Christy, but tell me what it *means*."

She sighed. "Steve, we can actually separate different kinds of human kidney cells. That means we can also make pure tissue cultures of the specific cells that produce the enzyme urokinase, which is what Jim was telling us about. That particular enzyme is unbelievably effective in dissolving blood clots in the body. In fact, it's almost miraculous. It's so difficult to make in an Earth lab, and so incredibly expensive, that it's like a dream for which people reach but can't touch. They die first. It costs about four thousand dollars per dose."

She tapped the container. "Know what's in here? Enough of that enzyme to keep at least seven thousand children or young adults from death because of clotting problems *and*, with an available supply of this enzyme, promise them a healthy life. Right now our own country is in dire need for at least eight hundred thousand doses a year, and the world needs are in the millions upon millions." She glanced through a viewport at the BioLab just passing in view. "Ten of those labs could do the job in two years of 'round-the-clock production."

"You'd need ten labs for just this one enzyme?"

Steve Longbow was impressed with the results and the need for more results.

"Ten for that one product, and a hundred more labs for other work. For starters, O'Toole and his people have already manufactured kidney cells as distinctive cultures, which in turn produce the hormone, erythropoietin, which stimulates the production of red blood cells in bone marrow. I know you're familiar with *that* subject."

He nodded. He wasn't thinking of his missing legs. Any long period in weightlessness means deficiency in the bone marrow production of red blood cells. Those that are produced are smaller than the ones the marrow produces under earthside gravity. "Yeah, yeah," Steve said slowly. "That means two years under zero-g for a Mars mission moves from the heading of 'extremely dangerous' to 'medically acceptable.'"

"Precisely. It also means new life for God knows how many people suffering from kidney diseases. Someone who lacks a kidney, no matter what else we do, is a severe anemic. This hormone changes all that. You can spell it 'new life.'"

She pointed to a pressurized enclosure within the model. "In there, Jim has been separating different nerve cells. If he's successful in his program, we'll understand the human brain and the central nervous system as never before, and—"

"For God's sake, Christy, *tell him*," Rush snapped.

O'Toole showed a blank expression. "Tell me what?"

"You haven't heard?" Christy queried. "The announcement Commander Cantrell made a short while ago?"

O'Toole shook his head. "Sorry, doctor. I was

out in the floating lab. I turned off the comm because I needed to concentrate."

"We're shutting down the station," she told him.

He stared without expression at her. "I don't believe you," he said finally.

"Oh, not permanently," she said hastily. "But the rad levels are going out of sight. Those who want to return earthside on the next shuttle flight can do so. Those who remain in *Pleiades* must move to heavily shielded areas until the storm is over."

"*I'm* staying right *here*," O'Toole said. "Do you know what would happen if I didn't keep going with my biosystems work already in progress? I'd lose it. *Lose* it," he repeated.

Christy didn't answer. *Jesus Christ*, Rush said to himself, and stepped in. "Where's that completed run of the enzyme? That container? Send it home on that shuttle flight."

"Well, I intended to, but the rest of my work here—"

"Will be destroyed whether you stay here to get zapped by penetrating radiation or not," Rush finished for him. "You're closing up shop. No arguments. Do it *now*. Sam, you take that enzyme package. Seal it in lead as soon as possible so it's got complete protection against any radiation dosage. Then set it inside a thermocontrol package. O'Toole will set the temps as soon as he's in the core."

O'Toole stood defiantly before him. "I said I can't leave here, Commander," he said stiffly.

"Jim, I haven't got time to argue. You either go to standby on your own or we carry you out of here feet-first, and that's a goddamned order. Do you read me loud and clear?"

"I'm not in your goddamned navy," O'Toole grated, "and you can't order me to—"

"I can and I just did. Longbow, you take him from that side and I'll take him from—"

Christy threw herself between them. "Rush, *please*. This is insane. I'll explain it to Jim. Will you let me handle this?" She didn't take her eyes from the angry man before her.

"Sure," he said. O'Toole couldn't see his face. He winked at Christy. She was startled. He walked past her. Sooner or later she'd understand that his anger was a sham and that it had worked. O'Toole had turned to her as an ally and an ally is a friend to whom an angry and frustrated man will listen.

# Chapter 13

"I've got to get the hell out of here for a while."
Steve and Christy glanced at one another in reaction to the unexpected angry statement from Rush.
He moved ahead of them toward Tube III, worked the airlock controls, and waited for them to slip within. Steve sealed the upper end and they waited for the green light for Rush to open the way for the long trip down the station tunnel to the core. "Hold it for a moment, Indian," Rush said. "I'm going to Control when we get down there, but I want you to get me one of the Bubbles. Something tells me to get *outside* so I can get a look at this whole kit and caboodle as a single entity. Don't ask me to explain why. I couldn't answer you."

Steve laughed at him. "You're asking an Indian why he has to climb the highest mountain so he can look over all the lands in every direction? You're just following a very old instinct, that's all.

We might even make you an honorary member of the tribe."

Rush smiled and squeezed his shoulder. He opened the inner airlock and started down the long glowing tube, Christy hurrying after him. "Rush I'd like to go with you. Outside, I mean."

He was descending feet-first, but Christy had reversed her position so that they were head to head. He looked back at her. "I know why I want to go," he said. "The Indian told me. Tribal instinct or whatever. What makes you so anxious to go out there?"

"It's also *my* station," she said defensively, color coming to her cheeks.

"As good a reason as any," he said amiably. He saw Steve catching up with them.

"I'll get Lopez to take the Bubble for you," the Indian said.

"The hell you will. He's busy moving those rad shields into place. We need those miracle arms of his for that work. You, on the other hand, are on an inspection tour. We stick together like glue until this is over."

"You're the boss. What about Sam?"

"Uh uh. I told him to get that enzyme package set up for the shuttle. It's too important to have O'Toole handle it in his state. He'll be chewing nails for a few hours yet. Sam's going to hand it to the shuttle pilot personally."

They worked through the lower airlock and emerged into the core, adapting from long practice to weightlessness, holding with one hand to the teflon nets near the airlock. "Go get your buggy ready, Indian. Give us a call in Command when you're set."

"Gotcha."

Rush didn't issue any orders in Command. Christy remained with him as he watched everything that was going on. The progress boards showed those parts of the station along the rim that were already shut down to standby status. Names were still lighting up on the personnel situation display as more and more people began floating down to the core, bringing personal clothing and toilet kits with them. There was a new clang and clamor he hadn't heard before. Of course—the construction crews under Marv O'Leary were moving curving panels to the outside of the core, seam-welding and bolting the units into place. He studied the station balance display, a three-dimensional computer printout in brilliant color, shifting in subtle tones to indicate mass imbalances and the immediate corrections made to damp out what could bring the station to a dangerous wobble. Everything was running as smoothly as could be expected.

He stood before banks of TV monitors. "How's the shuttle doing?"

Bill Harris was handling Control. "On the pad and counting. Everything's in the green, Commander."

"Backups?"

"Two in the barn at the Cape and they're rolling the bluebird to the pad at Vandenberg."

"Good. You run this thing for a while, Bill. I'll be going outside with Gordon and Longbow in a Bubble. You need me, you holler. Only I'd prefer if you didn't bother."

"Yes, sir."

"Any new word on our obstreperous star out there?"

"Commander, we've never seen anything like it before. Want a look with the chromospheric monitor?"

"Go ahead. I'll be in here until Longbow sounds off." Christy moved closer to him as Harris switched the solar monitor to the large screen on the panel. Rush heard a gasp by his side from the woman. He couldn't blame her for her reaction.

And perhaps for the first time, history tapped lightly, deep within his mind, and he began to understand why, nearly four centuries ago, the Church had gone into such a collective fiery wrath of its own when an upstart by name of Galileo spread vile heresies about the heavenly body they called the sun. The curious, driving scientist of 1610 was mesmerized with an incredible new invention called the telescope, and he used different means and filters to enable him to look directly at the enormous ball of fire from which sprang all life on the world. And if life did indeed depend upon this celestial sphere, then just as obviously, it was a creation of Heaven. It was pure and it was innocent as the handiwork of God.

Not so, reported the curious Galileo. For he had looked into the true surface of the sun with his diabolical new telescope, and he had seen sunspots and eruptions and other imperfections in what the Church *knew* was a celestial body of utterly flawless creation. Galileo should have done more looking than talking, since the first sunspot report in history brought down upon the hapless astronomer the wrath of torturous Inquisitors. If one of those purity-driven scourges of the only true faith *had* looked at the sun, as did Galileo, he would have been terrified and, doubtless, considered this act the very sin that brought God to hurl a plague on his own private celestial furnace.

Rush and Christy studied the screen, seeing the sun as did their special instruments. The heart of the sun, the major disc, was blocked from view in this scene to bring out the edges and what leaped beyond. They were seeing clearly what was always hidden from the eye without this assistance, the chromosphere. Fire, mused Rush, should be blazing red or even bright orange or searing yellow. This ultimate of furnaces instead spun an incredible web around its circle of pink flame, unreal and garishly frightening. "Look at that," he said quietly to the woman by his side. "Pink fire. It's like a tiger."

She showed her surprise. "You lost me somewhere on that one."

"Ever see a tiger?"

"Yes. Zoos; that sort of thing."

"I met a live one in India once. I remember it only too well. Scared the hell out of me. I was just thinking of how much *more* scared I would have been if the tiger had been pink. An added element of shock, like facing an *alien* creature." He nodded at the screen. "Like our sun. It's no longer warm and friendly. *You* were the one who told me that, if I recall."

"Yes, I remember," she said frowning. "It's like having a lovely young girl of six years old holding a shotgun on you. You can't cope and—"

Her voice faded away as the ragged pink flame bulged on the lower right side of the sun and birthed what grew swiftly as an incredible arch of increasingly red flame, a jagged curving spear twisting and rolling within its substance. It wavered, coiled along the lines of invisible magnetic force, and seemed to leap away from the sun as if impelled by some mighty blow. For a half-million miles it roared silently through space and finally bent over, sending its blazing prow back toward the sun. But they knew it had also unleashed a mass of particles, a small storm in comparison to its source, raging through space. The wonder of relative sizes. A solar spitball that could in an instant incinerate a thousand earths.

Rush twisted the filter control of the screen to enhance the fiery activity just beyond the chromosphere. His hand remained unbidden on the control as they stared at thin fire; thin but with temperatures far greater than a million degrees, wavering and heaving like unbelievable veils for millions of miles away from the solar furnace. He glanced at Christy. "We know so much and then we look at that pale flame—"

"The champagne fire," she finished for him.

"Pale and transparent," he said.

"And no one knows how it reaches its temperatures or why it does what it does," she said with a sigh. "There's so damned much for us to find out, and that *thing* out there is fighting us."

Rush adjusted the screen to show only the redlight of glowing hydrogen. Instantly the chromosphere twisted into an utterly different creature of fire. A field of giant wheat appeared along the rounded disc of the sun, but the wheat stalks were tens of thousands of miles high, and they twisted in fury and agony as if bedeviled by invisible tornados rushing along the edge of the sun. Abruptly a bright area flared in brilliance.

"We caught one," Rush said matter-of-factly. "Looks like a good plage."

Christy nodded. "We should get a good sunspot any moment. Have we got an X-ray reading on that one yet?"

Rush punched in digital readouts and pointed. "See for yourself. We've got an exploding point of heat and—there; the X-ray count is going bananas."

All the signs were there for the eruption and escape of a monster solar flare. The plage swelled like a balloon of hydrogen gas burning from within, and the X-ray count soared almost as quickly. The flare lifted upward in a ring shape with crowned edges, like a slow-motion film of a rock dropped into a pool of mud. The erupting flare disdained the enormous gravity and magnetic fields trying to keep it captive and gushed away from the sun. A flare born of a plage. Words.

Hundreds of billions of tons of fiery, excited, vicious matter tore away from the sun. "If that one comes all the way, they'll feel it earthside," Christy said quietly. "Radar is going out wherever it hits."

"A hell of a lot more than radar," Rush said. "We've had trouble with these things when we were in subs. We used the navigation satellites for position finding. Whenever we encountered a flare like this one, first the upper atmosphere count went off the scale, our radio frequencies starting waving like flags in a high wind, and signals from the navsats were useless. We went back to the old sextants. Even microwaves started bending like rubber."

"We did some work with homing pigeons as they were affected by flares," Christy added, and was rewarded with a raised eyebrow from Rush Cantrell. She nodded to emphasize her point. "Pigeons navigate by using the force lines of the earth's magnetic fields, and when the big flares dump into the atmosphere, the force lines twist and break up. We used to have homing pigeons that were so frantic to find their way they piled into antennas and buildings."

Rush turned from the set. "Well, no pigeons up here," he said, taking Christy by the arm. "Longbow is sending up smoke signals. Guess the Bubble is ready. You set?"

"Lead on." She walked carefully with velcro strips along the command control module floor, following Rush, until they reached the teflon netting along the inner flanks of the station core. Rush had seen the blinking yellow light at the upper airlock, signifying that Longbow was ready for them. They floated upward to the airlock, moved inside, sealed the hatch behind them, swallowed to compensate for the change in pressure, and waited briefly for the outer airlock to release. A green light flashed and triple, overlapping doors yawned wide. Directly before them waited the spherical chamber of the Bubble, a highly maneuverable personnel transporter for movement between different components of the *Pleiades* complex when the occupants preferred not to don pressure suits. The Bubble rested within a framework of metal in the shape of a cage, along with fuel tanks, power systems, and propulsion plumbing, radios, radar, and small thruster nozzles. Since the Bubble moved only about the station components, it did not require powerful motors or capacious fuel cells. With the rounded armorglass sandwiched between shells of lexan, it was stronger than steel for its weight, and afforded an incredible view in almost every direction. Longbow was strapped into the center, lower seat with the foot and hand controls about him, much in the manner one would expect of a helicopter. Four seats were arranged in a semicircle to accommodate to the spherical shape of the Bubble, providing more than luxurious comfort for Rush and Christy, who pulled their velcro belts into position. They had no concern about backing away from the airlock and staring into the glaring sun; automatic polarizers dimmed that savage glare to adjust to the needs of the human eye.

The crew had thought originally of the Bubbles as space-going equivalents of the famed, ancient jeeps. But the term jeep, in its true genre, meant utility vehicle, and the Bubbles had become coveted vehicles for sightseeing as well as personnel transport. They had become the golfcarts of orbit.

Longbow sealed the airlock, waited for the safety lights and, as any sensible man with vacuum experience will do, activated the mechanical safety links so that an errant electrical signal would be unable to break the pressure seals on which their lives now depended. "Where to, Great White Father?" he queried.

"Couple of times around the park," Rush quipped. "All right, Indian. Take her out about a thousand yards downsun. Put the station between us and the sun. I'll want some different maneuvers while we're out."

"Sightseeing?"

"Working, you legless lout." Rush tapped onto open radio link with Harris in Control. "Bill, Cantrell here."

"Go."

"We're in Bubble Three, just breaking away. We'll be downsun a thousand yards. I'll be operating the cameras. Full pickup and retransmit to Houston. They'll be needing all the footage they can get of the station and the sun in the same shots. Public reassurance and all that."

"Roger, Three. Stand by." They drifted away from the top of the giant tank. Harris came back on the line. "All set on auto. You can roll the cameras all the way through."

"Roger that."

"You need anything special, boss?"

"Uh uh. Just a look-see. We'll call if we get lonely."

"Don't stay out late. Looks like X-ray showers and you're not wearing your rubbers. Thirty minutes is your max safety time in the Bubble."

"Gotcha. Watch the store. Three out."

They drifted backwards from the upper airlock. A stunning panoply of metalwork, lances of frozen gases from the working tugs and cherrypickers, station lights, and the glare of the sun stabbing off highlights of the station was theirs for visual feasting. Open cherrypickers and workstands with suited crewmen moved great curving sheets of metal into place about the core, and there were brief but recurring flashes of beamwelders and floodlights as the crew added radiation shielding to the center of *Pleiades*. They moved slowly backwards, a bubbled sightseeing mote drifting effortlessly. Longbow worked the thruster controls with all the ease of a mermaid in silent waters. Then they were a thousand yards from the station, looking at *Pleiades* with the station directly before the sun. "Keep her moving slowly," Rush told Longbow. "You figure out the angles. Give me backlighting and good reflections."

Longbow nodded, using the Bubble as his aiming sight for the TV cameras. *Pleiades* in its slow rotation kept moving the solar cell arrays before the sun so there was a constant flashing and coruscating visual effect, a million tiny flecks of light glistening as the sun bounced off the cells at hundreds of differing angles.

They rotated the Bubble to get good shots of the remote modules, zooming in for dramatic closeups of the Jungle and the other zero-g substations orbiting with *Pleiades*. In the distance, the Junkyard showed as a jumbled small solar system all its own, the cylindrical shapes waiting for inclusion within the main station. Lights flared from solar reflection and rocket thrusters as units were cut and then moved toward the wheeled station. They took a final turn for a long look at the enormous solar array being assembled into what would become ten miles of solar cells for beaming enormous power to earth receiving systems.

"Bring her around, Steve," Rush said, "and let's move in closer to the Furnace. The more we can show the Earthsiders how we use the sun here for experimental work, the better they may understand what we're doing up here."

"You're a born optimist," Longbow said sarcastically. "They won't understand. They wouldn't if they could. They don't care."

"Let's not get into that now," Rush warned him. "Save the speeches for stealing back land for your reservation."

Longbow grinned in appreciation. "That's a new line I haven't heard before."

"Shut up, Indian. Move it closer, then set up a slow drift to the left. I want the sun quartering us for the best sidelighting and reflections."

"Is anyone still working the Furnace?" Christy asked.

Rush shook his head. "Everybody from that module is busy with the radiation shields. But we don't need any action." He thought a moment. "Maybe they're on remote." He thumbed the annunciator. "Harris?"

"With you, Three."

"Can you activate the Furnace for some pictures?"

Harris paused only a moment. "Yes, sir. Can do. I can handle remote positioning from here, but we haven't any targets."

"Forget them. The beam is what I want."

"Okay. Call it when you're ready. Charge time is only six seconds."

"Very good. Just hang in."

"Right."

Longbow drifted under *Pleiades* so that they were between the station and the earth below, and he turned the Bubble to bring the Furnace into perfect position for sun reflection. The Furnace gleamed as if a thousand searchlights played on its dazzling, mirrored surface, for that's just what it was—an enormous mirrored oven that used the sun's naked radiant energy in space for industrial and research programs. The solar furnace wasn't a new idea. It had been around for fifty years or more in earthside equipment, with the old concept of focusing the sun's rays into a narrow beam of high temperature. In the early 1950's, scientists in the French Pyrenees built a furnace of two large reflectors mounted atop an ancient fortress. A flat

43-by-34-foot mosaic of 516 plate-glass mirrors, following the movement of the sun, deflected the sun's rays to a fixed mirror eighty feet away. Three thousand and five hundred pieces of glass made up the 31-foot-high parabolic-shell receiving mirror, which in turn reflected the sun's rays to an oven set between the two large reflectors. The curved system focused the heat rays to create oven temperatures of nearly six thousand degrees Fahrenheit. It was a pretty good system for such archaic equipment, able to melt more than a hundred pounds of iron per hour from the seventy-five kilowatts of heat power.

The Furnace of *Pleiades* was immensely more efficient and powerful, with a curving dish four hundred feet in diameter. It was still in the research-and-development stage, but gathering solar radiations free of an atmosphere or any other distortions, it produced a beam of savagely intense light and more than ten thousand degrees. In tests it had vaporized steel bars within seconds of "opening the sun gate."

"Harris, all set here. Let her loose."

"Roger. Ten seconds and counting."

Rush switched on the "instant sensors" that would detect the first increase of light and automatically polarize the Bubble. At precisely ten seconds, awesome in its silence, a beam of blinding golden light *snapped* into existence. One instant there was nothing, the next, that incredible light that flashed away for miles.

"That looks good," Rush said. "How's the picture?"

"Impressive as hell. Almost frightening."

"Good," Rush said with satisfaction. "Give me a

series of on-off sequences. It's more impressive that way."

"Roger that," Harris replied. The light vanished. Six seconds later the beam pulsed, held briefly, vanished again, and reappeared, like a searchlight of killing energy—which it was—flashing through space.

"That does it," Rush said, and the light went out for good this time. He turned to Christy. "The more we show of industrial applications here, the less likely the Earthsiders are to complain we're wasting their tax dollars. Just one more Christmas goodie for their stocking. I know," he grinned, "I've said it before."

"We have a cynic in our midst," she mocked him.

"And you've got the wrong boy," he said, admonishing her. "You still think too much in purist terms. It doesn't work that way. We've been testing the solar furnace because we can do vacuum industrial work no one's ever done before. The same with the lasers. We need more than solar energy to use the lasers on a steady basis. We've learned that the hard way. With all this energy around us, we still need some concentrated shots we can repeat whenever we have the demand."

She frowned. "But a lot of people still can't separate industrial laser work from your— I mean, from the weapons testing that's going on up here."

"You were about to refer to the laser weaponry as *my* program, weren't you?"

She lowered her eyes. "That came out quite wrong," she said sheepishly, "and I apologize for it."

"Why?"

"Why?" she repeated. "Because there's something tainted about using a civilian facility like *Pleiades* for developing weapons."

"Even if it means we could develop a laser or a plasma beam that would wipe out nuclear warheads high above the earth? What in the hell is tainted about keeping cities from being destroyed?" He gestured impatiently. "Never mind. We've gone over this too many times before for me to want to bat that ball around again. I just wish all you goody-two-shoes civilians wouldn't scream for help when someone on the other side of the political fence starts firing missiles onto *our* side of the fence. But when someone starts shooting, you *do* yell for help, right?"

"If people didn't start shooting in the first place there wouldn't be any yells for help at all," she said, her expression suddenly cold.

"You ever been raped?"

*"What?"*

"You heard me. Have you ever been raped?"

She was flustered, caught off balance by the unexpected question. "No, I haven't. But in heaven's name, why did you ask *that* question?"

"Because I'll make an even-money bet with you that if you are, or are in danger of being raped, the first thing you'll do is scream for a cop. You're not just going to lie there and enjoy it."

"Rush, I don't know what you're getting at—"

"The hell you don't. Being raped as an individual is a personal affair. Even the threat is personal. But if a *country* is in danger of military rape, defending yourself seems out of favor with the bleeding hearts. You know what those laser weapons are, Christy? Just a cop's .357 Magnum on an international scale."

Rush leaned forward and tapped Longbow on the shoulder. "Indian, take her around *Pleiades* on a north-south run and then bring her around east-west."

"Got it."

Christy touched his arm. "Rush, you're not being fair. What you said, I mean. There's more to this subject than simplistic comparisons."

"That's what every rape victim says *before* it happens. Let it go, lady, just let it go. That's official, not personal. We have work to do."

The Bubble floated back from the Furnace as Longbow thrusted gently in a great looping swing around the station. The silence held uneasily between them.

# Chapter 14

Of all the great achievements represented by *Pleiades*, the most vital to Rush Cantrell was their ability to move that incredible mass and structure from one orbital level to another and do so with absolute precision. It was a balancing act without precedent in history and would have taxed the talents of angels dancing in an airless sky. The old Skylab lived on in memory a lot longer and with sharper angry focus than anyone had anticipated, and the first announcements of the new and truly huge space station produced an unexpected and angry public uproar. Bitter denunciations and cries of spaceborne boondoggles attended the birth rites of what would become *Pleiades*, but science and government had weathered such verbal volcanics in the past. If public opinion were the barometer by which the nation marched into the future, the United States would never have acquired the enormous territory of Alaska, the Louisiana Purchase would have been unrealized, and the moon would still be some unattainable goal in a misty future.

What brought vociferous outcries from the body politic, as well as what Rush Cantrell so often identified as the "great unwashed hoi polloi," were demands that any new station should be inserted into orbit at least a thousand miles above the surface of the earth, or even three thousand or, better yet, on the damned moon where it couldn't fall on anybody. That would have defeated the purpose of the new space station. Moon bases were definitely in the future, for the human race was beginning to understand it must learn to live on other worlds if it was to prevent a lemming-like drowning under the weight of its own burgeoning population. The lower-orbit stations were essential to future planning; among other points to consider was the cost of erecting and servicing the station. At 346 miles, *Pleiades* lay within easy reach of the reusable space shuttles. Higher altitudes meant greatly reduced payloads, proportionately greater mission costs, and far less efficiency. The critics shouted that once again the sky would be falling down. They weren't acting the role of Chicken Little at all, but remembering the final blazing demise of the Skylab station in the summer of 1979 that, during its final hours, threatened to dump a lot of space garbage into some hapless city.

NASA scientists explained that Skylab had fallen in the best traditions of Chicken Little because we knew so little about the atmosphere heaving up and down in enormous sun-created tidal surges. Had this fact of upper-atmospheric life been known, they would have carried to Skylab a rocket booster capable of kicking the eighty tons of early space station to higher and safer orbit. Now, claimed the scientists, we know enough. We can do the job safely. We will place the new station 346 miles high. It will be in a safe orbit without need for change for more than a hundred years. Besides, *Pleiades* will be raised to higher orbits as desired or if "events prove us wrong again and we need to ensure public safety." The Russians came along in the nick of time, as they had done so many times before, with a manned expedition to Mars—three men in a great motley collection of boilerlike but awesomely reliable machines that were to fly by the Martian moons, orbit the red planet, and then begin a looping return to Earth. It left a lot to be desired in a true exploration mission, such as landing on Mars, but the practical Russians considered the landing as beyond their means. They built their new Kosmos spacecraft in long sections held together by girders, and off to one side mounted a small nuclear reactor, judging that men's lives on a voyage of some twenty months deserved better than solar cells, batteries, or anything else science had yet devised.

The Kosmos expedition diminished the uproar of the space station detractors, gave the proponents a solid foot in the fiscal door, and the program was on its way. Someone with uncommon common sense worked out the numbers for refurbishing a Saturn V booster left over from the Apollo and Skylab programs, assembled the new ship with enormous solid-propellant boosters to help kick the giant S-II second stage into orbit, and started the ball soaring into space with repeated statements that "all this money was spent a long time ago and it would be idiotic not to put it to good use." A tack well taken, and the S-II sailed into orbit 346 miles high to become the Saturn core of the new station to be known as *Pleiades*.

The Russians had demonstrated extraordinary ability *and* reliability in shifting the orbit height of their Salyut space stations whenever the need arose. Success with the Salyut was trumpeted by NASA as proof positive of the ability to boost *Pleiades* in the same way. Rush Cantrell, who would command the ringed giant above the sky, rolled his eyes when he read such statements. Wishing to realize his dream as station commander, however, he gritted his teeth and locked his lips. Flapping one's arms, no matter how enthusiastically, does not guarantee flight unless one is in the process of falling off a cliff at the same time, and then the flight is guaranteed to be in one direction and distressingly brief.

*Pleiades* almost defied the imagination when scientists worked out the mathematical equations for orbit shifting. Salyut was essentially a thick cylinder and it needed only a slow-burning boot in the butt to lift it to higher orbit. *Pleiades* was vastly more massive in size, content, and intricacy of construction—*and* in resistance to being moved and remaining in one piece. It was a skeletal and cabled structure, in many ways almost spidery, with its internal systems shifting *all* the time while it also rotated around the huge core tank. It was one of the ultimate juggling acts, and to move this convoluted mass throughout its entire structure without tearing it apart made building the pyramids a ghastly little joke. The integrated computer chips, those marvelous electronic microprocessers linked to computers, were the keys to the kingdom of such celestial magic. Every movement, every squiggle and wobble, every twist and bend and turn and even hint of torque, a move to roll or yaw or pitch in any direction—every such movement and change of mass fed through the electronic kinesthetic sensors of the station to the computers. They were busy enough keeping the station from nutational wobbles and other out-of-balance problems, and then they were asked to continue their razor-edged balancing act and skate up a steep hill. To accomplish this bigger-than-life miracle, the station needed literally hundreds of propulsion units that operated at extremely low thrust, measured in only fractions of a pound. All of them firing at the same moment, with constant shifts and changes as dictated by the computer, would impart a definite acceleration to *Pleiades*. It was like breathing onto a mattress—the sleeper would never feel the motion, but in frictionless space it would be enough over a period of days or even weeks to keep lifting the orbital height of the station.

If 346 miles was their desired circular orbit, then the smart thing to do was to move the station *before* solar storms, or other anticipated problems that would decay the orbit, began to take their effect. Operating the thrusters could lift them to 370 miles and they could then float along for months before the slow but inevitable driftdown at this altitude would begin the decay that made the Earth loom just a bit larger in the viewports. They'd done it several times in the three-year life of *Pleiades*, and it worked, although everyone aboard held their breath and crossed their fingers and the computer suffered migraine headaches. The great wheeled structure with its uneven modular construction and fluids and moving people and rotational twist groaned and complained. When a wobble or yaw was induced, it could not be corrected immediately, but had to be sensed, its effective curve plotted, and a long-term forecast made of how best to dampen the motions. Then the thrusters were brought into play where the computer pointed with an accusing electronic finger.

More than one crew member *felt* those motions in the supersensitive pit of the stomach that niggled at them with the mixture of motions. They were spun by the rotation of *Pleiades*, they were subject to wobbles and shakes, and there was always the precession in any spinning object. To this was added the flyweight push of the thrusters, and it was enough to addle stomachs and bring nauseating tweaks to inner-ear balancing.

None of these physical and emotional responses, however, were ever considered to be a problem against the need to sustain the minimum orbit of 346 miles above the earth. Rush Cantrell thought of such maneuvers in the past and he wondered about them now as Longbow took the Bubble in its great circling inspection of the space station.

"What do you think, Christy?" he asked, suddenly breaking the silence that had separated them since his sharp comments on her lack of understanding of political as well as scientific forces.

"About what?" she replied. "You haven't asked a question, Rush."

"Sorry. I was thinking about the orbital parameters. With all this junk the sun is tossing our way,

I'm wondering if we're going to have a measurable effect on perigee and, of course, if we need to upthrust to offset atmospheric heave and direct solar drag."

She studied the station, looked beyond at the sun and then downward to Earth. "There's the chance," she said slowly. "Only the computers can tell us that, but even if we did lose some height, I'd recommend against it."

He showed his surprise. "Why?"

"It's not the maneuver itself," she said. "But with everyone in the core, you won't have proper coverage of all events through the station. Electrical interference, a possible break in the power lines—anything like that, and the only way you can send people out to handle an emergency is in radiation resistant suits. There are better ways to work than that."

"Good point," he acknowledged. "Okay. We'll run it through the computer as we would normally, but I'll consider holding off on any thrust maneuvers until the sun calms down."

"Rush, what if it doesn't?"

"The sun? Not calm down? Then none of us will be around to worry about a thing—here or earthside."

"No, not that. I'm talking about this storm getting past the index of four hundred. If it does that," she explained, "we're very likely going to receive penetrating radiation—something on the order of a nuclear burst that will exceed radiation safety levels for our people." She took a deep breath as she stepped onto dangerous ground. "I think you ought to consider either evacuating the station completely, or leaving a skeleton crew of volunteers behind until the magnetic storm is over. They can return afterwards."

"Absolutely not," Rush said, more harshly than he intended, and he conveyed the latter feeling by placing his hand over hers. "Look, we'll let anyone go who wants to go. They have that right, and I'll keep my promise of guaranteeing a return trip to anyone who makes that decision. The shuttle will be here in about thirty hours or so, and we'll send earthside those who feel that's the way to handle things. But no one else is being *sent* down, and no one else can leave until after the storm is over. The radiation levels will be playing hell with any ship trying to make passage up to us and back down again."

He looked long and hard at *Pleiades*. "There's another reason, Christy," and she detected the deep feeling that carried his thoughts into verbalization. "We've been clawing our way into space since 1961. The idea is to quit clawing and start staying. We've got to make this station work, and we need to build long-time stations in geosynchronous orbit, which is when we'll really make terrestrial observations pay off in spades—to say nothing of the utilitarian aspects of the programs. Hell, I'm not trying to sell *you*, of all people. You already know, but people earthside don't. Not yet. But three stations in geostationary orbit, and then the lunar base that starts to support itself and pay off in a thousand ways we haven't yet touched ... well, what happens if we quit *now?* Along comes the storm and off we go with our tails between our legs, running like scared kids before some electromagnetic goblin and—"

"Rush, running from penetrating radiation is

not a sign of fear. It's common sense—not dashing off with your tail between your legs!"

"Christy, you still don't understand. It *is* to them down there," he said, pointing to the enormous bulk of the planet beneath them. "We've got to think as they'll think if we pull the plug up here. We go that route and we're liable to find that *they* pulled the plug on *us*, and suddenly there's no return trip back up here. Do you understand what I'm trying to say? I know there's a risk in remaining here as this storm increases. No question of that. *I'm* staying and—"

"Count me in," Longbow interrupted.

Rush nodded. "That's my job," he said to Christy. "He's decided what his job is. Each of us decides on our own. Those of us who stay weather out the blow and figure out what we need to do to make it work. Everyone else packs."

"Perhaps I've been talking to you in the objective sense," Christy told him slowly. "Don't *you* understand? My people can leave. *I'm* staying."

He chuckled. "You may not believe this, but I never thought you'd do anything else." Rush tapped Longbow on the shoulder. "Take us home, Geronimo."

Longbow worked the thrusters with his honeyed touch and they began a sidewards drift toward the core airlock. "You know, I was thinking," Christy said, "that we could put up a really meaningful shield against the solar radiation. A force field. Create our own magnetic shock wave." She sighed and chewed on a fingernail. "Wishful thinking, I guess. For any kind of force field that would work, we'd need more power than we have. It would take a nuclear reactor to do the job and—"

She couldn't miss the meaningful look between Rush and Steve Longbow as the Indian turned his head with her words.

"Did I say something wrong?" She looked from one man to the other. "All I said was that to have enough power to throw up a force field that would deflect the incoming radiation, we'd need the power of a nuclear reactor. What's the matter with—"

Rush motioned her to silence. "No, of course you didn't say anything wrong. I guess we, well, we just never thought of that and you caught us by surprise. Good idea, though."

They remained silent until Longbow slid the Bubble smoothly into the airlock catches. They had before them a sight to command their attention. Electrostatic forces were building rapidly within and about *Pleiades*. Spatters of blue flame danced around exhaust ports and antennae. "St. Elmo's Fire," Rush murmured. "I've never seen this stuff build this strong before. It looks like we'll have to power down the station a lot sooner than we anticipated."

He held a meeting with his top staff and Christy Gordon's science team leaders. "We saw St. Elmo's Fire outside the station when we came back in the Bubble. Anybody else?"

Don Eagle nodded. "Every time we moved some of the big stuff against the core for shielding we got some pretty strong arcing. It's getting heavy out there. It's like swimming in a bowl of electricity."

Mike Crenshaw motioned for attention. "Commander, we don't have any choice but to cut down on use of electricity as much as we can in here. Every time we run a current through our systems, we're getting strong leakage. Everything is saturated. We can't get rid of the static charges fast enough, and we could get some back-arcing that could give us problems. There's every chance we'll start to lose some of the more sensitive equipment. We've got to unload the systems."

"How much time before we power down to standby status?" Rush asked.

"Forty, maybe sixty hours," Crenshaw replied. "I can't give you anything closer than that. It all depends upon what happens from the sun."

Rush nodded. "I know. Thanks, Mike. You'd better plan on the minimum time, just in case." Rush turned to Tom Lydon, his construction chief. "What's our status on shielding?"

"Minimum needs are behind us," Lydon said. He pointed to Ron Cunningham of Life Support and Bob Lee, their Medical Officer. "They want more, however. *I'd* like to have more, just in case I want to make babies when I finally go home. But I think it's too risky—the static charge, I mean. We're going to get more than back arcing or spatter. I think we could pick up some heavy jolts out there."

Rush turned to Cunningham and Lee. "Can we make do with what we've got?"

Cunningham shook his head. "I don't like it, Commander. Any one really strong burst in that storm and we'd be way over tolerance. If there's any way we can bleed off the static electricity, I say it's worth trying—especially in adding another layer of shielding around the center area of the core."

Rush was letting his team handle the decisions. "Tom? What about it?"

Lydon was already on his feet. "We'll wear our rubber gloves and give it a whack. If you'll excuse me and my crew, Commander, we really don't have any time to waste."

Rush nodded. "Go." He looked to Ed Raphael, his Chief Exec. "Ed, how many are going back on the shuttle?"

"Eleven. That will bring us down to forty-one souls on board, and frankly, I wish we were down to half that number," Raphael replied. "It would reduce the space required for maximum shielding, cut down the power and life support loads, and—"

"Don't blue-sky, Ed. Forty-one it is. You have any special problems?"

"Nothing we can't handle, Commander."

"Okay. From now on this station is on emergency crew status. Raphael runs the boat. I've got to work with Iwasaki and the power crews to make absolutely certain we're down across the boards, and I'm going to handle that job personally. Ed, you work out new assignments with Christy, select who's going to replace who, what jobs are shut down, what new ones need to be filled, and who gets tapped for what. I don't think we'll have any problems. We've been a damned good team for the past year and one of the keys to surviving this Rube Goldberg world of ours is that just about anyone can step into the shoes of any other person. So let's just stay with it. All right, people, get cracking. Seiji, Joe, I want to see you two alone for a moment."

Seiji Iwasaki and Joe Svec met with Rush in an isolated computer programming cubicle. "Short and sweet, you two. Any problems?"

Seiji and Joe exchanged looks. "None yet," Seiji said.

"What the hell does that mean?" Rush demanded.

"Jesus, take it easy, Rush. It means we're coming down on power, pulling the rods, whatever is needed to go to standby. But it takes time."

"I'd better look for myself."

"What the hell for?" Svec growled. "We can't read the gauges as well as you? Commander, there's nothing for any of us to do for at least twelve to fourteen hours, beyond what we're doing now. We're pulling rods, cooling down, the whole routine. *Then* you come for your own stamp of approval. Until then, you'd only be in the way. Besides, have you looked in a mirror lately? If there was a cat on this station, he'd be trying to cover you up."

Rush scratched the stubble on his face and showed a lopsided grin. "That bad, huh?"

"You look like the morning after," Seiji confirmed.

"Worse," Joe Svec added. "Why don't you knock off for a couple hours, boss? Get some sleep, for Christ's sake. Once this storm really gets going you may not have the chance for a while. And in the meantime, are you through keeping us from *our* work? We'll let you know the moment it's time for your personal touch."

"Okay, okay, you guys. Get lost," Rush told them. They threw sloppy salutes at him and left the cubicle.

Rush moved slowly into control. He pulled his arms behind him and stretched, a sudden grimace of pain showing on his face.

"What's wrong?" he heard.

He turned in surprise to see Christy looking at

him with a worried frown. He shrugged, but the pain in his back didn't leave. "Pulled muscles, I guess. No sleep, dancing among the stars, that sort of nonsense. I'll see if I can get the doc to work it out and—"

"No way. He's buried for hours." She studied his face. "You *do* hurt. More than you'll admit. And no one from the med team is available." She seemed to make a sudden decision. "Commander, this is irregular, and I know it, but I'm off for the next eight hours and so are you. You hurt and I'm just what you need." She held up her hands and wiggled her fingers. "See these? Masters of therapeutic massage. They work very well even on pigheaded space station commanders."

"Christy, it's not—"

"Oh, shut up," she told him, but with a smile. She turned to comm control, punched in a number, and spoke into the panel microphone. "Janice Irving to the line. Gordon here."

Her voice came back within seconds. "Janice Irving. Go ahead."

"Jan, Christy here. I'm with Commander Cantrell. We're going to my quarters for coffee and a much-needed break. See if you can keep Monsieur Raphael and his whiz kids from niggling with a thousand questions at our esteemed leader."

There was only a moment's hesitation, then the comm line crackled with static electricity before Jan's voice came back. "Yes, ma'am. Will do." Christy switched off.

Rush chuckled. "You know you just gave her a lot to chew on, don't you?"

"You're worried about my good name, Commander?"

"I didn't mean—"

"Rush, I don't give a damn what anyone else *thinks*. Just what *we know*." She shoved him gently. "As you say so well and so often, Commander, move it."

# Chapter 15

Rush let himself fall into the incredibly soft and comfortable lounge. At one-sixth gravity, dropping into a yielding surface is dreamlike motion. He raised his arms, feeling his body meet the soft material and thick cushioning beneath, and he sighed with pleasure. He grinned at Christy. "Talk about floating on a cloud," he sighed. "This has got to be the lounge of angels." He poked a finger into the velourlike material surrounding him. "You know, I've never been in your quarters before. How did you ever manage to get stuff like this up here? This is like a penthouse suite."

She turned from the pressurized coffee machine to smile at him. "In a way it *is* a penthouse suite. Considering the transportation costs, that's probably the most expensive couch on or off the world."

"I'll bet." He let his eyes take in the compartment. No, he was wrong. It had begun life as a spartan, minimum-facilities compartment for an outpost in vacuum. Apparently it hadn't been that way for a long time. He looked down; he hadn't even noticed the carpeting! He smiled with the sight of curtains by the viewports, which Christy had somehow transformed into "windows" by clever use of the curtains and banded colors. Artificial flower arrangements hung from one wall, and the inevitable pumpkin vines wound along spidery metal latticework. Every table was rounded and cushioned; the normally harsh lights had been turned into glowing lamps and backlighting. "Okay, okay, you've got me," he confessed. "I know you too well to believe you'd have contraband material sent up, so let me in on your secret. How'd you accomplish all this?"

"Most of the compartments for the women are like this, Rush." She brought him a mug of steaming coffee. "Careful, it's hot. You're right. Everything here was done by the books. See those artificial flowers? They were grown in the flora module, and when they were full grown we freeze-dried them in a vacuum chamber, sprayed them with module sealant, prepared colors from dyes and other chemicals, and painted them the colors you see. Maybe they're the first artificial flowers ever made in space."

"No argument there." He thumped the easy chair. "This stuff feels like velour. How'd you manage *that?*"

"It *is* velour," she said, surprising him. "There's no rule for packing materials for instruments and equipment brought up in the shuttle. Except, of course, that it can't be toxic or react strongly with oxygen, unravel in zero-g, or be flammable. So the girls in Houston ran different types of velour through tests and began to modify the chemicals in them, and when the material met all shuttle and station requirements, they turned out the stuff at their own expense and brought it to the equipment bays for packaging material. Why use stuff that's going to be thrown away? Inside that couch—all of them, in fact—is the packing foam for the more delicate instruments. As new materials came in with the shuttle flights, we took all the foam and similar material, treated it to meet station requirements, and began to make our own furniture. The industrial shops made the frameworks for us from aluminum and we added the material and sewed the covers—even for those end tables, over there." Christy smiled, obviously pleased to relate to this man what she had performed in her compartment. "Metal containers, again for equipment and instruments. We used the work lasers to cut the metal to the lengths and shapes we wanted, then we beam-welded the different units to fit precisely into the rounded corners, so to speak, of these compartments."

Again he nodded. "What about the walls? Is that padding?"

"It is. Cryogenic insulation that can't be used any more for instrument work. The buttons? Custom furniture at your service. Each button is wood-grained plastic we made in the thermal test module. We set up the pattern, made hundreds of them, then ran them through our own assembly room in the fabrication shop. They have a molly-type spring attachment on the other side of the padding. Press them in, hold the pressure until you feel the springs releasing, and presto! You have a button-padded luxury wall instead of an austere and bleak bulkhead."

She rose to her feet, went to the kitchen unit, and opened cabinet doors, presenting him with a pitcher the likes of which he'd never seen before. "We made these, too," she said proudly. The pitcher gleamed with subtle colors that shifted constantly as he turned it in his hands. "Vacuum-forming with plastics, and with metallic chips and flakes embedded in the plastic. We used an ultrasonic knife to round off the sharp edges."

"The lighting is incredible," he said, still turning the pitcher in his hands. "It's like a three-dimensional kaleidoscope on a two-dimensional surface, and your eyes can hardly follow the curvature of this thing. One thing is for sure. You could sell stuff like this for a fortune earthside."

She laughed. "Then look at these goblets." She handed two sculptured goblets to him. They were incredibly fragile, the glass so thin they seemed gossamer in their formation. He held one up before the light and rainbow hues sparkled at him as if he were looking into an illuminated diamond. "It's beautiful, but it's so fragile that—"

"It *looks* fragile," she broke in. "Actually, it's as strong as tempered glass. Give it a whack with your fingernail."

He raised his brows. What the hell, if she was that sure of this glass— He hit it hard with a nail and the tone of a perfect crystal bell rang through the compartment. "Hold it by your ear," Christy instructed. "The molecular structure has a rebounding characteristic. It's like a tuning fork that takes twenty to thirty seconds to dissipate the vibrations."

"What *is* it?"

"We melted crystal in vacuum and zero-g," she replied, "then used an ultrasonic bubble to form the goblet shape. Easy enough, since the ultrasonic bubble, so to speak, is all handled by one of the small computers. You could never make that goblet earthside. It needs zero-g, for one thing."

"Down there this would be almost priceless."

She shrugged. "Who knows? Maybe we'll go into business. Some of the jewelry we've made never existed before we started forming the shapes in zero-g and the ultrasonic bubble, and we can work with temperatures up to seven thousand degrees, and use lasers for cutting. They make some of the finest diamonds look puny in comparison."

"How much money did you put into this stuff?"

Her laugh was delightful. "It's all scrap materials. Scrap," she repeated. "The magic is zero-g and vacuum. The old alchemists would be green with envy." An old-fashioned pendulum clock chimed and she glanced up. "Enough of that, and enough of what we're making and everything else. Finished your coffee? Good. In there," she pointed to her sleeping compartment. "The bunk is already down, the sheets are cool, and there's a towel to wrap yourself in. You, Commander, are about to be done with scented oil. And that we *did* have sent up with our personal effects."

"I—"

"You're off duty. Hush. Or do I have to undress you like a little boy?"

He hadn't felt anything like it for years. Neither had he realized how truly *woman* she was. Not simply female, or feminine, or sensual, or most of the things that he had found flagging in his personal interest. There had to be that one step beyond, undefined and beyond his own ability to describe, that he would know when he found it, as he had once very long ago. Christy turned down the lights in her sleeping compartment and the sheets were not only cool, but had been cooled before his skin met them. He hadn't expected the soft music, and she didn't bother to explain a word about the twenty small, brilliantly toned speakers built into the bulkheads and overhead and decking beneath her feet. It had been her own design, to surround and drench her with music when she so wanted, and she had never, until this moment, shared it with anyone else. Now soft music floated through the air, touched his skin, came to him through the sheets, embraced him as her hands worked the oil into his neck and shoulder muscles. He didn't know the scent, but he must have strained to identify the source. Christy recognized his feeling. "Relax, relax," she said soothingly. "Before we're through here, you get a complete alcohol rubdown to leave you cool and refreshed and," she almost giggled, "minty crisp and clean. Will you *relax?* Your muscles are like coiled springs."

He let go. The oil went across his skin and into his body. Muscles protested and then began to soften under expert ministration, and he slipped away with the music and the sheets and that incredibly marvelous touch of hers. He drifted in a limbo of sleepy wonder, uncaring of anything except her hands and the sensations she sent gliding through his body. He lay with the side of his face against a cool pillow, feeling mesmerized, and from afar, he began to understand just how very long anything like this had been for him, because he was startled with the thought that right now, at this moment, for the first time in years, he didn't care about anything else. It was incredible. He was commander of a huge space station that was plunging into the most violent storm ever known in the history of the human race, and he didn't care. He didn't even feel the sensation when she removed the towel and her fingers began to knead the oil into the curving depression of his lower back and dig into his buttocks. The fingers moved with gentle strength, and the warm oil mixed with the thick hair of his legs. She moved along the back of his thighs and deep inside his thighs, starting back up at the knees. Her fingers brushed his scrotum and paused, left to reach the other inner thigh, and then they were back and the oil was stronger. Gently, she rolled his testicles in her fingers, never stopping, reaching all of him. The fire was beginning in his belly and he was hardening and she was gone, fingers digging deeply into his calves, and then she did marvelous things to his feet, and he slipped back into that incredible soft limbo.

"You've been asleep."

He had to struggle to climb back from that well of letting go. "What?" He was punch-drunk.

"You've been sleeping," she said, smiling as he lifted up to one elbow. "About thirty minutes. Like the dead."

"I feel incredible."

"Drink this." A goblet appeared in her hand before him.

"What is it?"

"Mixed fruit drink with honey. Barely chilled."

He drank, amazed at the rich, smooth taste. "It's great. Thank you."

"How do you feel?"

"If I felt any better I couldn't stand myself. You're a miracle worker. I'm not sure you're real."

"I'm real. I also feel like a real woman for the first time in years. You have to be able to give to be one."

"You give in an incredible way." He looked at her as if he were seeing her for the first time. "Tell me something."

Her eyes showed assent with whatever he would ask.

"When's the last time you had a rubdown?"

She moved around to sit on a chair directly before him. He brought up his arms, crossing them beneath him for a chin-rest. Their eyes were close. She went back in time through memories and then smiled at him. "Would you believe almost three years?"

Her reply startled him. "You? That's hard to believe. Jesus, you're all woman. I mean that, and not as most men understand the word."

"I know. I felt it. I'm very pleased about that, Rush."

"But . . . how could you not have—"

"The last time I touched a man's body was three years ago. My husband. Jack was a fiercely competitive man. The challenge was always between him and himself. No ego problem. He was bigger than life. He could do just about everything. He was killed skydiving at night—one of those impossible, one-in-a-million things. He was in free fall and hit a plane just before he was going to open his chute. He never had the chance. At least," she said a bit more slowly, "he never knew what happened. He was killed instantly doing one of the things he loved most in life." A smile touched her face. "Until now, I never wanted to touch another man. No dislikes; none of that nonsense. But there are very few men like Jack. Or Rush Cantrell."

"Thank you for that."

"I was never more honest."

"I know. Take off your clothes, Christy."

She stared at him and he stared back, locking his gaze with hers. "Give me the oil," he told her. She picked up the bottle and handed it to him. "I'll be in the other room for several minutes. Take off your clothes and lie down on the bunk. When I come back in here, I have one favor to ask."

She nodded for him to continue. "It's been three years since you felt a man's hands on your body. I've never given anyone a rubdown or anything like it in my life. Let me learn without words. Not one, from either of us." Her expression didn't change. He rose from the bunk, naked, brushed his lips against hers, and left the sleeping compartment. When he returned, her body lay prone before him. No towel, no nonsense. He stared at her stunning form. He knew she would be beautiful, but this was the body of a young, lithe girl, and inside that body was a woman.

He was right. Learn to massage gently, to rub, to caress, strictly by her reactions. No words. Only the quiet sounds that issued from her, that didn't change except for the gasp when he helped her turn over and he entered her slowly and deeply and they made love in a way he had never known existed.

\* \* \*

He closed the sliding doors to her compartment quietly, leaving Christy in a deep and untroubled sleep. He had washed himself down with alcohol. He was tingling with life, almost as if he'd stepped into his own body when it was younger and stronger. He'd planned to return to his own quarters but he knew he'd never sleep. Not yet. He went along the rim to the nearest spoked tube and worked his way down to the clamor of the core, floating over to station control. A full crew was busy with a hundred tasks. He looked over their shoulders at the station status, progress of work, status of the shuttle that was now less than a day from arrival. Then he went to the astrophysics board to study the radiation readings. He reviewed time-lapse films of the sun and he swore to himself. The magnetic index was still climbing, soon it would touch the 300 mark. This was going to be a bastard.

He left control and went to a darkened observation blister on the outside of the station core. Below him the great station turned ponderously. He could feel its enormous motion. He looked down and saw earth through the great mass of the station and watched the plant reflecting from curving metal. Spurts of blue flame caught his eye. The crew was out there, moving great curving plates of metal closer to the core, building up the shields against the mounting radiation from the sun. He looked down again at the nightside. Already the aurorae were gleaming their way over the top of the world, suddenly shifting bands of violet and green and red, flickering and vanishing and snapping into existence again, all within seconds as the instreaming solar particles reacted with the mag-

netic fields of earth, a silent orchestral prelude to
what was coming. He left the observation blister
through the double airlocks and returned to control. Dianne Vecchio came in behind him, the beautiful dark girl from the Mediterranean with the
gleaming teeth. Her hair shone in the pageboy she
kept under control in some mysterious way in
weightlessness. She smiled her hello to him.

"You have the shift?" he asked.

"Yes. Raphael's request. He has to check out
power systems and asked if I'd come in early."

"Go ahead and check out your status boards,
Dianne."

"Of course," she said smoothly, then hesitated.
"Commander, if you don't mind my being personal, you've got to get some sleep. I can see the
personnel roster from here. You haven't had any
rest for nearly thirty hours now and—"

"Check your boards," he said in a flat tone.

"Yes, sir." No resentment. She'd said her piece,
and he chose to exercise his command, and that
was that. He watched her going across the boards
with a skilled eye and touch. She turned back to
him. "Everything's in the green. Except the sun, of
course, and that's a bitch."

"Let me see your priority checklist."

She handed him the powered, computerized
board with her notations. He studied water ballast
shift, control oscillations, bobble and weave, personnel relocation, electrical systems being powered down, how many men were outside. It was all
there; his crew was on the fine edge. "Any change
in the shuttle?" he queried.

"On schedule. Fifteen hundred zulu tomorrow.
That's approximately, of course."

"Approximately?" That remark was way out from left field. "Why'd you say that? Space cadets don't do things approximately, Dianne. Everything is digital. They wake up, shave, eat, run around the block a couple of times, and report for duty with exacting precision. Who's the pilot?"

"Baxter."

"He'll show up on the appointed second, girl."

"Not Baxter. Anyone else but Baxter. He can't do anything on time, and I know better than anyone else." She smirked.

"Okay, I know when I'm being conned. What's your secret?"

"Can't lie to the captain of the ship. He's my fiancé. I *know* he's not always on time." The giggle burst forth and she covered her mouth with her hand. "Commander, sorry about that."

He waved it away. "Your affair, not mine. Sorry about the pun."

"Yes, sir."

"Let's get back to business, okay? The first thing I want you to keep in mind in this business, or with anything to do with this station, is CYA."

She was puzzled. "Which is?"

"CYA is Cover Your Ass. That's right. You're doing an excellent job here but it's not enough. You're looking just far enough to handle the contingencies you can anticipate, right?"

She hesitated, thought swiftly to find the trap, gave it up. "Of course I am," she said finally.

"Not enough. Look, in all your planning so far, Dianne, you and everybody else have come up with specific figures based on what we know or can expect to happen, even to the point of maximum hard radiation, even if it goes over anything we've ever anticipated."

"Yes, sir, and we're planning for that also."

"What if something else screws up *Pleiades* at the same time?"

"Sir?"

"Your hesitation is what worries me. It's not personal; I've been getting the same reaction from most of the crew. What if, during the storm peak, we take a meteoroid strike? Or suffer electrical overload or major equipment failure? What then? I dislike going back to old naval terminology, but are you prepared to command this station as duty exec if we have to abandon ship in a hurry? Have you *really* thought about that?"

"No, sir."

"What happens if we have an emergency while you're in the bathroom? You don't have any back-ups as shift exec."

She nodded slowly. "I see your point, Commander."

"Not yet. Get another crewman in here with you while you're on duty. Keep one person at the panel monitor at *all* times. Then get to O'Leary as soon as he's available. As Boats Officer for the work tugs, he's the best man for full emergency systems. That means the expandable spheres and tugs, the lifeboats, anything and everything. Find out what he needs if everything comes unglued on us and make absolutely certain it's available for him and the rest of the crew. Right now, if you became ill and fell unconscious, there'd be no exec on duty in the most critical part of this station. Look at your board, Dianne. Get Jerry Maxwell down here and don't wait. Do it *now*. He can always catnap right here while you have the shift."

He fell silent, waited as Dianne rang the wake alarm in Maxwell's quarters and told him he was on immediate duty. "I'll be there in two minutes," Maxwell said and cut the connection.

"I want a plan pulled from the computer," Rush went on to the now intent woman with him, "and I want the printout shoved between everybody's ears as soon as they have enough time for their duties to work. I want alternate proposals right on down the line for all probabilities."

She sagged against the control panel behind her, showed a thin smile. "Is that all, sir?"

"Hell, no, that's not all. I want everything we've just talked about completed within eight hours of this moment, and every hour you save makes me happier. That shuttle with your lover in the left seat will be on its way here before we know about it, and it's not staying around for teatime. It's going to load up and get the hell out of here as fast as we unload its cargo and move eleven people from this station aboard. I don't want any more problems than that. So you be certain to assign a few people specifically to that job: transfer of personnel to the shuttle. That's the *only* job these people should have until I see fire in the tail and that big delta wing is on its way home. Got it?"

"Got it, Commander."

"Good." He showed her a smile. "In the meantime, I intend to follow the recommendations of the Duty Officer, Dianne Vecchio, who has given me hell about getting some badly needed sleep. And by the by, your advice is quite sound. You need anything else before I leave?"

She held her silence for a moment and then shook her head. "No, sir, not really. I mean, no offense meant, Commander, but I'm damned if I can figure out why you'd leave a warm bed with—" She clapped her hand over her mouth. "Damn it, I didn't mean to say that," she added finally. "I apologize. I had no—"

"Shush. I don't know how you women find out things so fast. No offense was taken. But how the hell do you do it?"

"Sir, the look on your face is as subtle as a charging rhino. I know a pleased man when I see one."

He laughed with her. "Well, then, you won't mind my telling you that we all know about your supposedly secret sleeping arrangements with Jerry Eden, will you? I know a pleased woman when I see one, Diane."

He chuckled as she stared at him. He left control and started to quarters, and despite the silent thundering of the star so far away and the radiation streams he knew were bathing *Pleiades*, he *was* a pleased man and he fell into a deep, restful sleep.

# Chapter 16

They spoke in hushed tones behind his back. "What's wrong with Cantrell?" Furtive glances at an angry face, a jaw set grimly. "Man, when he's like that he's all grizzly. What's going on?"

No one knew, it seemed. Rush had come out of a deep and refreshing sleep, worked his way down to command and the computer pulse of *Pleiades*, and a dark cloud settled within him. Subtleties of personality with Rush Cantrell were like warning flags. He was also exhibiting an edginess they'd never seen with him before. He moved about as if all his muscles were like coiled springs, his body tensed to react violently to *something*. He had spent an unusually long time studying computer print-outs. His hands flew across the keys as he interrogated the computer. At times he ignored the electronic brain and worked swiftly with a hand calculator, often referring to a small leather notebook to which he made repeated reference. Several times he got into a heated exchange with power engineers Mike Crenshaw and John Barstow, and after the last ruckus, with his voice sounding like cold steel, he left the command area with tightly set lips and no eyes for anyone else about him.

Dianne Vecchio went to Crenshaw and Barstow. "What's with the man?" she asked. Other people stood back, waiting to hear some explanation. They were unprepared for the cold response from the two engineers. "You've got the watch," Crenshaw snapped. "If Commander Cantrell wanted to inform you of our discussion he would have done so. Knock it off, Dianne." She felt her mouth open; she was at a loss for words. The others exchanged glances. Whatever it was, the KEEP OFF signs were posted for all to notice.

Curiosity turned to concern when they learned Cantrell had returned to his quarters, sealed the entrance, and gone to scramble code for earthside contact. That meant no one else on *Pleiades* was privy to his exchange with the ground. Rebuffed by the power crew, Dianne turned to Ed Raphael, second-in-command of the station.

"I'm worried, Ed," she told him frankly, "and I'm not talking about personal moods or anything like that. He was in control here just before his sleep period and he was tight on procedures, like he always is, but he was loose. I've never seen the man edgy like this. He's been through emergencies before—much worse than this radiation storm. Didn't he spend seventeen days on the ocean bottom in a crippled sub?"

Raphael nodded. "That's only part of it. He *saved*

that sub and its entire crew. He was awarded the Navy Cross."

"Then what's wrong with him *now?* I'm not asking just for myself. It's affecting the crew. With all the pressure on them, they're picking it up and—"

"They're experienced and well trained," Raphael told her unexpectedly, again catching her by surprise. "They'll do their jobs. Rumors don't interest me. They're also not your affair."

She flared angrily. "The hell they're not. I've got the watch and what's happening is affecting the crew. It's my responsibility to relieve that pressure."

"Well spoken," he granted her, "and what I said stands. You do have the watch. Exercise *your* authority, then. One of the best commands is to shut up and do your job. The subject is closed, Dianne."

Hurt and still puzzled, she moved slowly into center seat of command, glaring at the computer printout and control panels. No matter what Raphael had said, she dearly wanted to know what was rippling the emotional fabric of the station. She knew from the command lines, despite the scramble code, that Rush had carried on a long conversation with the Pentagon, a brief talk with CapCom at Houston Mission Control, and then another longer talk with the launch center in Florida. The Pentagon? Why would he need to talk with the Pentagon? It didn't make sense and—

The launch display console came alive with a warning tone and flashing red light. Automatically one complete bank of TV monitors, fed through the comsat network, picked up activities at the Kennedy Space Center. "T minus five minutes and counting," came the voice of launch control. "The crew of pilots John Baxter and Harry Compton, and mission specialist Forrest Claudy, entered the shuttle spacecraft *Windstorm* at T minus 110 minutes, and sealed the hatch at T minus 70." Dianne studied the different readouts and punched in a real-time weather satellite monitor. No good; heavy cloud cover stretched all across Florida. The only visual they would have of the launch would be from the tracking cameras. But there was audio, and she fed the audio signal from the space center to open line on the station network. Even those working outside *Pleiades* would be able to listen in on the launch. It would help.

For the moment, they would push from their minds the puzzling and angry behavior of Rush Cantrell. A shuttle launch, no matter how many were behind them, was still an awesome and fiery affair, with failure and abort always a realistic possibility. Those who were free to watch their television monitors saw different shots of the great delta-winged spacecraft on its launch pad, standing vertically by its red service tower on Pad 39A, bulky with the two great solid-rocket boosters and the huge liquid-fuel tank. Plumes of gaseous oxygen blew away before the wind. Flashing red lights about the pad were reminiscent of the old launch days of the great Saturn boosters. But what never changed was the emotionally charged buildup to igniting the mighty engines of the shuttle launch system and knowing that men rode that packaged volcano. They had a brief look at the crew inside the flight deck, then fast cuts as seen from the flight deck of the launch tower and the sprawling space center.

Another interior angled view showed them the three crewmen strapped into left, center, and right seats, their pressure suits and helmets sealed, the men lying on their backs.

"We've passed the T minus 5 minutes mark," intoned mission launch conrol. "All cathode tube displays are operating in the flight deck. Auxiliary power units and hydraulics are all on line and operating nominally. At the moment, the main propulsion system helium is being topped off, the orbital maneuvering system engines are armed. Launch control and the spacecraft report all systems are in the green. At T minus 4 we're go for launch as scheduled."

Even under the pressing conditions aboard *Pleiades*, almost all work slowed to a crawl.

"T minus one minute and counting. Prelaunch activities are now complete, all pressures are normal, and the crew is ready. We're coming up soon to shuttle main engine ignition which will occur at T minus 6 seconds. T minus 30 seconds and counting." There was that always-long pause until the bird came to life, and then it was "T minus 6 seconds and we have main engine ignition."

Flame erupted backwards from the shuttle main engines, swept a hurricane of fire and steam through the deflectors beneath the launch pad. The monitor flashed to the flight deck as a roar burst across the radio lines. They saw the flight deck and its three-man crew lurch forward, then backward, as the main engines thundered futilely against the hold-down clamps.

"Confirm 90 percent thrust in five seconds. We are go. We have solid booster ignition at zero and we have liftoff. *Windstorm* is on her way. Launch control reports full thrust at nearly six and a half million pounds."

Every man and woman on *Pleiades* had lifted off the Earth in a shuttle, some of them on the very same *Windstorm* they now saw breaking free of its chains and standing on white-hot flame. They knew the longitudinal vibrations slamming through the entire assembly from the screaming solid boosters, they knew the eerie feeling as *Windstorm* drifted laterally as well as vertically so the great spacecraft assembly would easily clear the outward-jutting intertank access arm of the launch platform.

"Seven seconds and *Windstorm* is clear of the launch area," the voice intoned. Then came the cockpit view again, showing everything shaking and vibrating, the roar stupendous, the view outside the windows that of a world turning steadily, and it was doing precisely that. At launch the astronauts' heads had been pointed due south, and now as it climbed, *Windstorm* was rolling 120 degrees to take up a heading of sixty degrees for boost into orbit. At the same time, the entire assembly was rolling so as to place the shuttle in an inverted climbing position. Liftoff had been vertical, ninety degrees to the earth's surface, and as *Windstorm* climbed at the peak of a flaming mountain, the pitch began to decrease steadily.

"Roll and pitch program successful," intoned a new voice, this time from Houston. The moment the shuttle cleared the launch pad, control shifted from Florida to Texas. "Baxter reports roll complete. Thirty seconds and *Windstorm* is now climbing through eight thousand feet. The crew is heads-down and they are pitched at an angle of seventy-two degrees in the climb. We're through the mark of thirty-two seconds. The main engines are now throttled back to sixty-five percent power to reduce aerodynamic loads for Max-Q as *Windstorm* accelerates through the speed of sound. Everything is going well. The spacecraft went through the speed of sound at 24,000 feet, precisely fifty-two seconds after liftoff, and they are now back to full thrust on the main engines."

They hung on every word. A critical part of climbout was now in progress.

"The crew reports some wallowing action by the shuttle assembly. This is normal for the winged vehicle because of strong horizontal winds at high altitude. The crew reports minimal sideslip and pitch attitude within one degree of nominal. *Windstorm* is now one minute 53 seconds into flight and is climbing at Mach Three at 120,000 feet. Mission control has called 'negative seats' to the crew. At this point, if there is an abort, the flight crew will fly the shuttle back to its landing strip instead of using their ejection seats. CapCom reports pitch angle progressing normally at thirty-nine degrees from the vertical.

"At two minutes into the flight the spacecraft is through Mach Four and at 136,000 feet. CapCom has called 'go for Sep,' confirming that dynamic pressure is within limits for separating the solid boosters at any time."

They could almost *feel* what they'd all experienced before . . .

"Solid motor chamber pressure is now low enough to initiate the separation sequence, which started automatically at two minute six seconds into the flight. We have positive automatic function, and the crew reports a bright flame effect. They said they could feel and hear the eight separation motors on each solid booster as they were blown clear of the climbing spacecraft. CapCom reports positive separation. The flight crew has told us the severe vibrations are now gone and the ride in second-stage thrust is comfortable. G-forces are building steadily."

The most critical part of the flight, at least for the three men aboard *Windstorm*, was now behind them. They could fly that slab-bellied monster almost anywhere now if they had an abort. "Four minutes and better than six times the speed of sound, with the spacecraft at sixty-three nautical miles altitude, and pitched down now to nineteen degrees."

*Windstorm* received her "press-to-Meco" call just after four minutes into the flight. The crew now had confirmation that even if they lost a main engine at this point, they would have a number of emergency landing fields within their reach.

"Four and a half minutes into the flight, and *Windstorm* is now assured of minimum orbit capability, having reached a height of seventy-four nautical miles. The spacecraft will now begin a maneuver angling back to Earth at four degrees below horizontal to increase velocity and continue to retain the most favorable profile for abort. The crew reports an incredible flight. They are pitched down below the horizon and still inverted, and Baxter reports the view of Earth is sensational."

*Windstorm* was flying at fifteen times the speed of sound, descending through seventy nautical miles at six and a half minutes from liftoff, when the crew verified the call of "single-engine thermal." Now they were guaranteed minimum orbit insertion, even if two main engines out of the three firing were to fail. "The crew reports g-loads building up from three times normal and moving to the maximum expected of five-g. *Windstorm* is now at Mach 23, descending to 63 nautical miles, and main engine thrust is being throttled back by the autopilot system of 65 percent thrust. Coming up on main engine cutoff. We are at eight minutes and thirty-three seconds into the mission and the crew confirms main-engine shutdown. At this moment, *Windstorm* is flying with an inertial forward velocity of nearly 26,000 feet per second and is in a positive rate of climb of 220 feet per second. CapCom confirms that main engine cutoff occurred at sixty-three nautical miles, and with the positive climb rate *Windstorm*, without further power, will insert into an initial orbit of eighty by thirteen nautical miles. This is, of course, an 'orbit target,' and the flight crew is preparing for a second main engine burn as soon as the large fuel tank beneath the shuttle is jettisoned."

They knew the rest. The tank would be blown away by jettison rockets, the shuttle would move laterally and upward from the tank, and then its engines would burn to achieve an initial orbit of fifty by 150 nautical miles. From that point on, the computer would doodle on its electronic scratch pad and bring them to a position to maneuver to and dock with *Pleiades*.

"*Pleiades*, this is CapCom."

Dianne Vecchio answered immediately. "Go ahead, CapCom."

"We've got mission confirmation that *Windstorm* should be in the rendezvous slot two hours and ten minutes from now."

"Roger that. We'll be ready and waiting."

"Uh, *Pleiades*, we'd like to confirm the names of station personnel returning with the spacecraft."

"Got it, CapCom. The names follow. Mike Custer, Roy Doyle, Laurence Schroeder, Jamie Knight, Barry Williams, Dixie Archer, Jill Brody, James Curtiss, Jack Bergman, Renita Carson, and Brooke Allen. Eleven in all."

"Okay, *Pleiades*. Thank you. We'll be on open line from here on."

"Gotcha, CapCom."

Dianne turned as body movement to her side caught her attention. Cantrell, Raphael, and Margaret Peters, their computer chief, pushed into a control room and slid the door closed behind them. Even through the insulated panels, Dianne and others with her could hear angry and shouted words. Dianne saw Jerry Eden of Laser Mapping and Communications. She grasped his arm. "Jerry," she said in a low tone, "will someone tell me what in the hell is going on here?"

He shook his head. "Honey, I've been out in the module until a few minutes ago. I don't know. It's like everybody is walking on eggshells and—" He stopped his words as they saw Seiji Iwasaki, in his jumpsuit but carrying his sneakers, hurrying to join Cantrell and the others in the control room. "Seiji!" Dianne called, but he waved aside the call, shook his head, and went into the control room. Immediately afterward, the doorlock light came on and the NO ENTRY sign flashed above the entrance.

Dianne turned as Bill Harris and Marv O'Leary entered station control. "We're handling docking with *Windstorm*," Harris told Dianne. "Put us on the docking frequency so we won't get interference from any other communications."

"Okay." Dianne gestured to the locked control room with its warning sign to keep out. "Can you people tell me what's going on in there?"

The two men looked toward the computer control room. "Unless I miss my guess, they're on a computer run. What's got you so up a wall?"

She shook her head. "You haven't seen that bunch. They're rushing from one place to another. If you so much as look the wrong way, Cantrell is ready to bite your head off, and—"

O'Leary gave her a warning look. "*Miss* Vecchio."

Startled, she stared at him. "A word of advice, girl. Mind your own damned business. We're all under a strain. People haven't got time to stop and explain details to you, and the Commander is counting on you to handle the watch without playing quiz kid games. Do you read me?"

She stiffened. "Loud and clear, Mr. O'Leary."

"Good. We'll be near the airlock chamber. You know how to reach us." He winked at her. "Be cool, girl."

The two hours went by with maddening slowness, despite the almost frenetic pace of preparations to ride out the worsening geomagnetic storm. Cantrell and the others left the computer room, none of them looking very pleased with whatever it was the electronic oracle had offered up to them. Cantrell and Iwasaki went into Station Systems Management, were joined by Joe Svec from Electrical Systems, and—Dianne was astonished—again sealed the doors and turned on the NO ENTRY warning.

CapCom called in that the shuttle would be initiating direct radio contact in five minutes, and Dianne was grateful for the intrusion. At least she'd have the chance to spend a few minutes with John. He could leave the left seat of *Windstorm* long enough for them to have a few private moments together and—

"Vecchio, this is Harris. Patch me in to Cantrell."

"He's got the Do Not Disturb sign on the door," she replied.

"Emergency override," Harris said quietly, and she didn't argue. She flipped the alarm signal for emergency comm for the control room where Cantrell was talking vehemently with Iwasaki and Svec. "Commander, Harris on emergency override comm," she said briskly.

"Patch me in," he ordered. She listened in to the exchange with growing displeasure.

"Commander, *Windstorm* is in visual contact and closing steadily. They've got a sealed cargopack of radiation drugs and other equipment for us. With the radiation levels climbing the way they are, we'd better go to a quick-and-dirty crew transfer. I'm asking authority to just clamp the cargopack with magnetic grapples to our hull for the moment, extend the personnel transfer tube to the crew compartment in the shuttle cargo bay, and get our people the hell out of here. I don't think we have too much time for a reliable hard dock. The electrical systems are going ape. We're already losing our lower radio freqs and we're taking a lot of hash on the other comm systems. We've got just this one shot for hard dock. Everything else will be a formation position from then on. I recommend the shuttle flight crew remain where they are, pilots on the flight deck and Claudy taking the people aboard."

Rush didn't waste time judging a situation his men had worked out in detail before calling him. "Do it."

Dianne's heart sank. Not even time for one embrace with John! So close, so close and— She turned it off, clamped down on her own emotions. What was wrong with her? She was caterwauling to herself like a child. She took a deep, shuddering breath as she heard *Windstorm* calling in. "*Pleiades,* this is the big bad wolf." She recognized Harry Compton's voice. "We've got visual and the computer's tied in. Johnny Boy says to open your arms wide and—"

"*Windstorm,* this station is under full emergency," she broke in. "We request no extraneous conversation. Harris and O'Leary will handle the docking and personnel transfer to your vehicle. Your cargo will be mag-clamped to the core hull. We will then extend the transfer tube and you will board the eleven people as rapidly as possible, secure, move off, and prepare for immediate retrofire. The flight crew will remain in position throughout." She paused, hoping desperately that John would read into her words her seeming coldness. "Please confirm."

"Dianne, I'd know your voice anywhere. This is Harry. I—"

Another voice broke in. It was John, her fiancé. "Shut up, Harry. *Pleiades,* your message received and understood. Is the docking crew ready? Over." He was official *but he understood.* She fought back the sudden urge to cry. Another voice came onto the line.

"Baxter, O'Leary. How do you copy?"

"Four by four, Marv. Some hash on this frequency."

"They're all hash. We're getting some strong magnetic interference with computer dock. We recommend you go to visual approach and manual dock. Confirm."

"Got it, Marv. We're in the slot and coming in now."

They watched the great winged shape sliding on invisible rails toward the nonrotating core of the station. Ten yards out John Baxter performed a rocket-thruster ballet with the shuttle spacecraft and pitched her over with the nose pointing vertically to Earth. The big cargo doors along the backbone of *Windstorm* opened and Claudy extended the grappler arms with the thickly-shielded container of station cargo. Arturo Lopez drifted inward in one of the sealed mobile tugs, used the tug clamps to lock onto the cargo, signaled Claudy to release, and eased the container to the side of the station core. Magnetic clamps grabbed tightly. "Okay, *Windstorm*," Lopez announced. "Cargo's out of the way. I'm pulling the transfer tube into position."

Lopez worked radio controls and a thick bellows like tunnel extended from the station with an airlock adaptor at the open end. Lopez used the tug thrusters to align it exactly with the personnel compartment in the forward cargo bay of the shuttle. Claudy confirmed secure seal-and-lock and the personnel compartment ready to board.

O'Leary checked all seals from the station side, told Harris to "Move 'em out." The eleven station members making the transfer had long since said

their farewells, and they floated through the flex-
tube into the shuttle, took seats, and strapped in
at once. Claudy sealed the airlock, confirmed full
pressure, told O'Leary to "Withdraw tube."

Rush Cantrell, with Seiji Iwasaki and Joe Svec
behind him, watched the operation on TV monitor. They were the only members of *Pleiades* who
knew that three of the station personnel request-
ing evacuation had been ordered secretly to be
included in that group. They were Ron Doyle from
power engineering, Jill Brody from computers, and
Brooke Allen from the electrical systems team. "As
soon as that bird is on its way home," Rush said to
the two men, "we've got to settle that problem.
My vote is to dump the critical elements out of the
station, slap a booster on them, and kick the whole
works into orbit with a perigee of no less than a
thousand miles. We can deal with it then. Okay,
okay, I'll listen to your side of it as soon as
*Windstorm* is gone."

Claudy closed the great cargo doors. Dianne
Vecchio in control confirmed permission for *Windstorm* to ease away. John Baxter went through the
countdown and checkout litany, and just before
firing the low-power thrusters, she heard, "See
you, baby," and there was no question that he
really *knew.* Her throat tight, she watched the shuttle spit pale blue fire from small thrusters as it
backed away from *Pleiades.* More spurts of flame
showed, and soon the shuttle was two miles distant, gleaming from the sun as it emerged from
Earth shadow into daylight.

"Thirty seconds to ignition," Compton called,
and precisely thirty seconds later bright fire blossoming out into a transparent flower erupted from

the main engines. Almost magically, the great winged spacecraft fled from *Pleiades*, and the shuttle's speed diminished to give gravity the edge in reclaiming *Windstorm* for her fiery ride home through atmosphere.

Rush Cantrell gave a final look at the station monitoring panel and glanced at his crewmen. "Okay, that's it. Let's get out to the rim." He hadn't gone through the door when a deep booming thunder rolled through the station, mixing with harsher muffled explosions. Everything about them quivered and rocked and dust sprang into the air. "What in the hell was that!" Svec shouted.

"Everything we were worried about," Rush spat. "Let's *go*, damn it!" There was another muffled boom. Everything swayed and rocked as the shock waves echoed and rebounded through the station structure. They pushed through the compartment doorway, dragging themselves as fast as they could move by rail to reach the airlock of Tube III. Christy Gordon saw them, was frightened by the grim and ashen looks on their faces. Too late to call after them, and by the looks she had seen, they wouldn't have heeded even a shout from her. She bent her legs from her position by the teflon netting, got a good footing, and pushed off, floating with maddeningly slow speed to the netting by the airlock. She scrambled upward and banged the seal handle to open the lock to gain entrance. She scrambled through into the tube, hauled herself up in a rush, went through the airlock into the rim. She saw the three men pushing into the heavy airlock doors to the solar array module beyond the rim, and she hurried after them. Chuck Gambrell blocked her way.

"I'm sorry, Christy. Commander's orders. You can't go in there."

She was stunned. "Do you realize what you're saying? *Of course* I can go in there."

"Christy, my orders are to—"

Her hand shot forward, knuckles extended, to catch him sharply across the bridge of the nose. The sudden short blow stunned him and sent him flying back wildly in the low gravity. She grabbed the airlock handles to push her way after the men who seemed close to panic. Whatever was happening, she was frightened, and she hadn't felt true fear in years. Something directly before her was very, very *wrong*.

# Chapter 17

Christy Gordon was speechless, struck dumb by the incredible and impossible sight before her eyes, an extraordinarily complex and intricate system of machinery, from massive materials to slender wiring and cables, spreading everywhere like some electronic Medusa. If it didn't turn her to stone, it absolutely turned her blood cold. She stared at a powerful fast breeder reactor. *A nuclear furnace!* Dear God, she thought she was going mad. This absolutely could not be. It was too garishly unreal, impossible. She saw Rush turn to her, astonished by her presence. He knew he'd left Gambrell guarding the entranceway.

"Christy, what the hell are you doing here?" he demanded.

She had a sick feeling in her stomach. She'd been on *Pleiades* more than a year, she was Science Lead, this was the Station Commander whom she trusted implicitly, and she'd never even known of the existence of a nuclear reactor that had been here the whole time! Mixed emotions raced through her, feelings of being used, thoughts of duplicity, of her own trusting stupidity, of all the people who had never been told, who never *suspected*—including herself!—the existence of this monstrous thing. She forced control into her mind instead of the emotions that wanted her to scream as loudly as she could. She stared at Rush, and when she spoke, her voice was unbelievably calm. "I'm trying to wake up and find out this nightmare isn't real," she told him.

His answer, which slipped so easily from him, astonished her. "Yeah, it is sort of a problem."

"That's *not* what I meant," she snapped. She knew the answer to her next question before she voiced the words, but she had to ask, no matter what. "This . . . this *thing* has been here, aboard this station, from the beginning, hasn't it." It was a statement as much as a question the way it came out.

"Yes. Pretty tough to kick up five hundred and twenty tons in one shot, Christy." His face had developed an impassivity of stone. "What about it?"

"Rush, how could you! We're a civilian science program and—"

Her words tumbled away as red lights flashed and alarm bells shrilled a cry of danger. "Talk to me about it later," Rush retorted, his own words as much an order as a statement.

But she wouldn't be put off. "It's not that easy, Rush. I—"

"*Later, goddamn it!* That thing's about to run

wild on us. Max exposure in here without a protective suit is already down to nine minutes. Now, you get the hell out of here." He pushed her roughly before him, grasping her arm with a grip of iron, almost throwing her from the module. Others followed immediately behind and stopped only to close a hatch of thick, heavy metal. Iwasaki and Svec turned from the hatch. She's closed off," Iwasaki told Rush.

Rush nodded, looked up as Chuck Gambrell came into the solar array control room that fronted for the nuclear reactor module she had never known existed. Rush's expression turned dark. "You were guarding the way in. How the hell did she get past you?"

Gambrell held a hand by his nose. Christy spoke before Gambrell could answer. "Don't blame him. Black belt in karate does a lot of things for you. His nose is broken."

One thing about Rush Cantrell. He didn't waste time on rhetoric. He dropped the subject, turning to Iwasaki and Svec. "Okay, we're shut down. What about additional shielding for the rim here?"

"Our best bet is to move empty tanks here. We can handle them fast and easy—a lot easier than moving the heavy stuff," Iwasaki answered. "Then we run a heavy hose from the main ballast tanks and fill them with water. It's the best way, Commander."

"Do it," Rush said quickly. He turned to Svec. "Joe, while he handles the rim, you'd better get with O'Leary and Lopez or whoever's available. Put extra paneling outside the rim because we'll get a scattering effect if the radiation count keeps climbing the way it is right now. Make sure the work tugs have shielding before they get too close to this thing. Damn, where the hell is Hammil! He has to know about the explosion and—"

"Right behind you," Hammil said as he emerged from the tube airlock. "Run it by me quickly, Commander."

"We got a blowout in the reactor," Rush said in a metronome voice. "Radiation count went up immediately and is still climbing. We've pulled the rods and damped the fission process, but there's a lot of damage in there. Max exposure time without special suits is already down to eight minutes. We're going to use water ballast here in the rim for additional shielding on this side, and we're adding mass shielding outside the rim to cut down on backscattering that could affect the rim directly. What else?"

For several seconds Sam Hammil didn't answer, ticking over every event and possible event in his mind. "Very good. Issue a statement immediately to the rest of the station that we've taken a steam blowout in this module and that the pressure seal is ruptured. The rim is off-limits in this area to all personnel except work parties personally assigned by me or yourself." Sam gestured to Seiji Iwasaki, about to enter the airlock to go downtube to the core. "Seiji, hold it a moment. Can we flood the reactor room itself?"

Christy was aghast. Did all these people know about this nuclear time bomb *except herself*?

Seiji nodded. "Can do, but then there's no work to be done in there. My recommendation is to wait. We might want to try to cut this thing loose and drag it from the station, Mr. Hammil. I say set up the flooding system but hold off until we have no other way to go. By that time we'll need the water to soak up the heat as well as the radiation."

"Very good, Seiji. Please continue with what you were doing." Seiji gestured his goodbye and disappeared into the tube airlock.

Rush motioned to the others with him. "Everybody knows what to do. We can all sit around and talk about it later. Everybody get with it, please. I've got to report Earthside on what's happened here. Christy, for Christ's sake stop looking like a wounded child. You already know what we've got here, so I won't hold anything back from you. I haven't got time for explanations now, but you're welcome to stick with me and listen in and learn what this is all about. *Then* you can yell your head off. But if you go with me now you stay quiet and just listen. Agreed?"

She knew she had no choice. "Agreed," she said simply.

"Okay. Sam, you've got this little baby to handle on your own. I'll be in the comm section of my quarters. Christy, let's go." She followed him in a steady run along the outside of the station rim until he reached his quarters, went inside, locked the entrance behind him, and went directly to his communications center. She watched him switch to a scramble code and then press a red button that put him into immediate contact with the Pentagon.

She watched a man who was more impersonal, more professional through his entire being, than she'd ever seen before. Rush was a strange mixture of hard professional and unemotional robot mixed into a package that defied her understanding. As quickly as he punched in the scrambler code direct line to the Pentagon, the video panel glowed into life and then snapped into a sharp image of Lieutenant General Bernard Harmon. He was in full air force uniform, and it was clear from the background just visible past Harmon that he was in some type of military control center rather than an office.

"Scrambler confirmed, Cantrell. Go ahead." Harmon wasn't wasting any more words than the *Pleiades* commander.

"We've got a full-blown emergency on our hands, General. We took an explosion within the reactor. Full shielding is being set up within the station rim as well as outside, using ballast tanks and heavy metal plating. We've pulled the rods and we're considering several options to hold down the radiation, although my crew is doubtful about that. It's a matter of learning to handle this thing as we go along."

Harmon nodded slowly. "What about the shuttle?"

"*Windstorm*'s undocked with eleven people from the station, including those we discussed. Are you set to feed them into the heuristics computer?"

Harmon turned to an out-of-picture aide, looked back into the camera. "Go ahead, Rush."

"Ron Doyle, who's been working the power systems from the reactor for laser weapons tests and feeding into the station for electrical power. Jill Brody, who's handled the computer elements, and—"

Christy Gordon's mind ran at full speed. *Jill Brody?* How could *she* be involved in any of this military madness! Good Lord, she'd trained Jill

personally for her computer biosciences work, and—
Christy turned it off, listened intently.

"Brooke Allen, who's been overseeing the program to keep it all balanced," Rush finished the three names.

"What about the weapons specialists?" Harmon queried.

"Seiji Iwasaki and Rick Martin are with us, and I'm damned glad of that, too. We all felt that with the contingencies facing us when the news breaks, they'd better stand by to either destroy the working mechanism of the laser systems or, if we have to, use them for any incoming vehicles."

"Your backups, Rush?"

"We're on line, sir. The seeker missiles are in five separate shuttle tanks, all well concealed in the Junkyard. They're all self-contained systems we control from the station."

Again Harmon spoke briefly to someone off camera and turned back. "We're waiting for an update on the Russians. They're playing chess with us. Keep everything related to offensive *or* defensive systems completely off the line until you receive word from us or you determine the situation is being taken from your hands."

"Got it, General."

"Rush, what in the hell happened up there? You people were supposed to have every failsafe system science could imagine to prevent any kind of failure mode with that reactor. It was designed for a ten-year operating life without having to use a screwdriver. All hell's going to break loose when this thing hits the news media. Have you considered that? I think you'd better—"

Rush nearly exploded. "Failure! Where the hell

did you get the idea we had a *failure,* for Christ's sake! Goddamn it, I know you've got three stars on your shoulder, but we're short on time and it's running out fast on us and I want you to *shut up and listen to me.* Do you read me clearly, General Harmon?"

Christy could hardly believe a word of what she was hearing. The general seemed to turn purple; his body trembled visibly until he regained his composure. He nodded slightly. "Go ahead."

"Right after *Windstorm* moved into position and went through retrofire, when she was just out of sight below the horizon, we took an explosion along the rim. Obviously it was in the reactor module. There wasn't any failure, General. *We've been sabotaged.* A plastic explosive had been set in that module, and every scrap of evidence we have, as well as what you've got on tap, points to Jill Brody as the agent. CIA sure as hell tagged her right when we received our first warning from your office. And we're not copping out of anything with my statement about a deliberate explosion. It was done by an expert. The plastic was molded to critical parts of the reactor, set by someone who knew that system intimately. It didn't go off until the shuttle was committed to reentry. Maybe Brody figured the whole reactor would tear apart. We don't know that yet. I've already got Sam Hammil working a team to inspect the more critical areas of this station. But our first requirement is to keep that reactor contained."

Rush took a deep breath, managed a look at the shocked face of Christy Gordon, turned back to the video camera trained on him.

"We're still getting a slow breakdown within the

reactor itself. That bitch knew precisely what she was doing because we're going through a residual breakdown. As the pressure increases and the heat rises we'll get some meltdown and softening, and there'll be successive components failure. We don't know at this stage just how much more it will take before the radiation gets too high for us to work with it. If we get a bad meltdown and a compression of the fuel rods, not even the shielded boats can handle it. We'd have to work with remotely operated tugs. We're keeping tabs on it, and that's the best we can do right now. General, sorry I smarted off to you. I thought you knew the blast was deliberate."

General Harmon leaned back in his seat. "I didn't hear anything but the facts, Commander. We'll handle Brody when she lands, of course. What can we do to help?"

"Get your best reactor people with the earthside twin of our reactor, try to match the situation we're facing, and keep an open line with my crew. We can patch in video directly to the men working about the module. Also, clue the NASA crowd on what's happened so that they won't interfere with any line communications if we get something really critical. And, General, don't forget we've also got the problem of that superstorm banging on our door up here. We've already moved most of our people into the station core for maximum radiation shielding. You might say that when it rains it pours. Only we've got hard radiations instead of water."

"Very good, Rush. I'll have my team pick it up from here. Do what you have to."

"Thanks, General. See you."

Rush switched off the video and broke the scrambler line. He turned to the still-shocked woman behind him. "Okay," he said calmly. "Your turn. Let's hear it."

# Chapter 18

"Do you really expect me to believe Jill Brody is a Russian agent? A saboteur, for God's sake? I heard everything you said and all that crap about the CIA tagging her. I don't believe a word of it. Rush, I trained with that girl for *two years*. I know her better than her own mother does. I know how she thinks, what her talents are, how she feels, what she can do. She's been in computer biosciences day and night. She wouldn't have *time* to do anything else, even if everything you said about her was true. And it *isn't* true. *I know*." The words had poured in a torrent from Christy and she sucked in air. As Rush started to answer, she gestured frantically to stop his reply. "No, not yet, please. I've got to say this. The presence of that nuclear reactor aboard this station is absolutely foul. It is the vilest breach of our national word to the entire world. After that Russian satellite impacted in Canada with nuclear elements, and then the uproar over the Skylab reentry, we promised the world we wouldn't endanger them with a nuclear reactor in earth orbit—

"We lied."

The two words were like a hard slap in the face. She fought for a reply, gasped like a fish thrashing on the ground.

"We lied. We do that a lot. The Russians lie a lot. So do the French and the Japanese and the British and the Germans and the Chinese and just about everyone else. It's called diplomatic license. But we lied in a special way. We told the world that the scientific station *Pleiades* wouldn't have a nuke capability aboard. That's true. The reactor is military. We needed the power for the laser systems tests."

"And that's another thing!" she shouted. "I *heard* you talking about that with General Harmon. Those laser beams are supposed to be *research* equipment, for God's sake! You told him you were testing weapons up here. You said you had missiles in some of the shuttle tanks. God in heaven, Rush, you've made prostitutes out of all of us up here!"

"You're hysterical and you're talking like a child. I didn't build this station or establish its military purpose and I didn't order that nuclear reactor *or* those laser beams *or* those missiles, no more than I built attack subs with nuclear drive. I manned and I commanded what was built for me. I'm doing the same thing here. And while we're at it, you can protest all you want about Jill Brody, but she *is* a Russian agent and she was assigned to this station to do everything she could to wreck it." He grimaced. "She's off to a hell of a start, I must say."

He paused to let it all sink into Christy's head. He knew he'd need this woman and her intelligence and command in the days to come. That geomagnetic storm was continuing to wind up to full fury and they had their own minor radiation cyclone right on the rim of the station. Anyone's nerves could frazzle easily. Christy had been kicked right in the side of the head with what she'd learned in a short time. He didn't want to press her too fast or too heavily. She was sharp and tough and she'd rebound by herself. So he waited until she forced calm upon herself.

"You ready for me to say a few more things, Christy?" She nodded, already much calmer, and he went on slower, more deliberately. "Look, what you *believe* isn't the issue we're facing right now. This isn't a case of who's right or wrong. Only the reality counts now. I'm telling you that Jill Brody is a Russian agent. We've known it a long time. We knew it before she ever got up here. We've been tagging her since she was a teenager, when she was started in this program. The Russians are like that. They take the simplistic and long-range view, setting up people for years without using them. They did it with Jill. She knew we were getting highly successful with the laser beams and the plasma beams. The radiation storm was perfect for her. When she got the word she was being sent to earth to work with our science people there she seized her chance. She set up timed explosive charges in the reactor."

He leaned forward and grasped her hand. "Don't you understand, Christy? You're Science Lead on this station *and you never even knew the reactor existed.* How the hell do you think Jill Brody knew if it wasn't through Soviet intelligence?"

She had no answer to that one.

"All right," he said, keeping to his deliberate pace. "Jill outsmarted us. We figured we would tumble to any move she made, but she worked faster than we anticipated. Her timing system with the plastic explosives worked perfectly. She probably used the timer with a radio signal as a backup. We'll find out soon enough."

Christy felt a cold wind blow by her. "How will you find out?"

"When we take her into Houston she'll be put in an anechoic chamber. No echoes; you know it well enough from your tests. She gets a shot of diluted etorphin. In fifteen minutes her heart will sound like a boom of thunder every time it beats. She'll be so wild to get out of that place she'll tell us everything we want to know and we won't lay a finger on her. For all we know," he stressed, "she may have left one or more bombs on this station, and we can't take that chance. She's got to talk."

Christy shook her head, her ponytail swinging with the movement, and Rush resisted the urge to take her in his arms. "But *why?*" she asked. "Why?"

"Because that was her job, her choice, her—"

"No, *not that.* Why did you people bring that terrible thing, that reactor, into this station at all!"

He sighed. "There are a dozen very valid reasons. On the basis of pure science and engineering, because we needed a long-term evaluation of a fast reactor under space conditions. How will hard radiation affect the systems? Will it alter power output. What about tests under zero-g? Can we count on energy for long periods? The Russians are using nuclear reactors with manned crews for their Mars shot. We need to—"

"But they're not using nuclear reactors in their space stations!"

"The hell they're not," he said quietly. "Why do you think their last test station was brought back on a steep descent that ended in twenty thousand feet of water in the Pacific? So no one would be able to prove a thing, that's why."

"I read those reports," she said sullenly. "It was a leak from the reactor drive of their support ship."

"And you *believed* that?" He was incredulous.

She lowered her eyes. "It seems I'm pretty much of a fool about a great many things," she said in a dull voice.

"No. Not a fool. A scientist who'd like it all laid out neat and simple. But it doesn't work that way, and I'm not about to get into philosophical or contentious prattle on the subject. Damn it, Christy, look up at me. There's been another, even more compelling reason for us to have that reactor aboard this station. As of right now I'm breaking security. I'm going to clue you in, but I want your word you'll observe that security and not reveal what I'm going to tell you."

"I won't do that."

"Then," he said matter-of-factly, "you may go to hell, Christy Gordon, and I will relieve you of all authority you have aboard this station."

She gaped at him. "You're *serious*?"

"Never more so. I'm captain of this space-going tub, lady, and we're under an emergency, and my word is absolute law. If you don't like it, you can argue with the legal beagles after we return to

Earth. That is, of course, providing that sweet Jill doesn't blow us to pieces with any of the nifty little bombs she may have left behind."

"You have my word," she said in a whisper.

"Good. First, this isn't a popularity contest. We've been testing some very powerful energy systems—lasers, beamed particles, the works. They're designed to be used against satellites and against ballistic warheads while they're above the atmosphere. We need a lot of power for that and the only source is a nuclear reactor. Those are the tests we've been conducting under the guise of laser communications, mapping, navigation—whatever. We lost some of our older comsats with those laser bounce tests, remember?" She nodded and he went on. "Well, three of those were ours we destroyed in tests and the *other* three weren't. They weren't ours and they weren't comsats. They were Russian spy satellites and they were zeroed in on our work. We zapped them. We're developing antiwarhead beam weapons up here and this has been the only way of doing it."

"This was supposed to be a *science* station," she said stubbornly.

"Isn't it? What have you been doing up here? Knitting?"

"But it's also a weapons laboratory!"

"Of course it is. Do you think our research in Antarctica is all civilian?"

"What do you mean by that?"

"Our bases along the South Pole area are supplied by the navy and the air force. Every plane that lands there is military. We use a nuclear reactor there for power." He was mocking her now. "Or perhaps you feel we shouldn't use the information and the scientific data from Antarctica because it's tainted by military organizations making it possible?"

She shook her head.

"Christy, listen to me. The Russians have been working on powerful beam weapons at Saryshagan, their test site in Kazakhstan near the Chinese border, for more than ten years. They've been using hundreds of Pavlovski generators in testing all sorts of directed-energy weapons. That includes high-energy lasers and charged-particle beams. They can blind our reconnaissance satellites any time they want—they've done it many times. And they can blow apart any satellite as high as forty thousand miles from the Earth's surface. Do you think we're *guessing* about this? Their weapons program has worked under the code name of Tora ever since the late 1970's. It's all under the direction of a Russian genius, a physicist we identified long ago as A. Pavlovski. He pioneered work in nuclear reactor-pulsed beam weapons ten years ago at the Kruchatov Atomic Energy Institute in Moscow. They've been testing nuclear-powered beams at their weapons center at Semipalatinsk, at Golovinno, at Chrernomorskoye, at Krasnaya Pahkra and a dozen other places. They've done incredible things with iodine lasers that function in the infrared, with free electron and excimer beams that operate all the way from visible light to the far ultraviolet, and they have been scaring the hell out of us for years. They put a nuclear reactor inside one of their big jet transports to power one of their energy beams and they sent in thirty radio-controlled fighters to shoot it down. In thirty seconds every fighter was blown to pieces, and that was years ago. They've been just as successful with their space systems."

Rush leaned back in his seat for a breather. He felt sorry for tumbling this woman's world down about her ears, but scientists have a funny way of ignoring the world about them. They, too, like children, need to grow into reality. "Christy, how do you think this station was funded, anyway?"

She looked up. "I'm not sure what you mean."

"Do you think our government and the other political groups that financed this whole setup just doled out forty-five *billion* dollars for a freebie laboratory for good-looking broads like you to exercise their scientific curiosity? Do you believe they would lay out all that money just for new industrial processes, no matter how great the potential might be? Uh uh. It doesn't work that way. Forty-five billion, lady, really screws up their tax base. It makes hash of welfare programs and unemployment checks, it chews up their political doles, and they don't like that. Our congressmen have an almost violent antipathy to voting for expenditures that rile up the money-grubbing assholes who put them in office and can yank them out again. *That's* why fully half of this station is paid for from military appropriations, and why we've forced our friends overseas to pony up a good share of the tab. That's why *I* was selected, and that selection had a lot of foreign approval behind it or I'd never have climbed a foot off the launch pad. A naval officer; nuclear drives, submarines, missiles. No wild blue yonder or space cadet syndrome for those people. No, sir. They paid for all this and part of that price—so that *you* and the science teams could do what you're doing—is the military research we're carrying out, and *that* includes the nuclear reactor."

He smiled. "A funny thing happened on the way to the local disaster," he punned. "You would have known about the reactor in a few hours, anyway."

"What do you mean by that?"

"Don't you remember your own conversation when you were in the Bubble with me and Longbow? You said it was too bad we didn't have enough power to set up a force field that would deflect the solar magnetic and particle radiation coming in against the station."

She nodded. "Yes. I remember that now."

"You also said it would take a nuclear reactor to do that kind of job, but, well, it was too bad, because we didn't have one."

"You and Steve nearly jumped out of your skins when I said that."

"We thought maybe you'd tumbled onto our little secret. And I'll bet, just as an exercise in theory, you mentioned that during a coffee break to Jill Brody, didn't you?"

Her eyes widened. "Several of us discussed that, but—"

"But only Jill knew there *was* a reactor aboard. And that if she knocked out our reactor, there'd be no force field to deflect the radiation, and we might all buy the farm up here. Still feeling warmly to your little pal?"

She shook her head. "No. I'm not. I'm not feeling warmly about *anything*. I think I'm going to throw up."

"Not yet," he pleaded. "I'm going to need every brain I can find on this station, and you're at the top of the list."

"Then why do I feel like such an idiot?"

"Because you trusted us and we were sworn not to break *our* trust to our government. If you had known all this time, you would have been forced to compromise your principles. This way, you've been squeaky-clean from the beginning."

"Then, Commander, maybe you'd better *tell* me how I can help."

"Good, solid brain work," he said, shifting into the new mood of working on the problem instead of having to justify the means that created the problem. He went to a workdesk and tapped on the computer keys. A three-dimensional view of the station appeared on a wall screen. He tapped more keys, and the station now appeared to be transparent, showing key structures, cables and power lines, plumbing, and other main features. Another caress of the computer and the nuclear reactor area glowed in soft red.

"Now, the weak points created by that explosion," he added, as much to himself as to her. He instructed the computer and blue shading appeared on the projection. "Those represent areas of weakness from the explosion, from our shifting around a lot of mass," he explained. "We've got a lot of metal-bonding problems. And then there's our balance to be considered. When we designed this space-going paradise, we built in a lot of heavy weight at the end of all three spoke tubes to compensate for the weight of the reactor, or we'd have wobbled our way to pieces a long time ago. That's why we can't just get up there with work lasers, cut away the reactor, and kick it past the moon with a space tug. We'd be so unbalanced we might fly apart. You might say our nuclear umbilical is permanent until we can adjust the station weight and balance all the way around."

She studied the display. "What happens to our people if that reactor starts to run away? If the radiation goes way up?"

He showed her a crooked grin. "The same thing we've already done with our shielding in the station core. We just dig the foxholes a little deeper, that's all." He sighed. "We dig deep and we hide behind our radiation barriers and we wait out this damned storm until we can get some more shuttles up here. We could use the lifeboat stations, except for one little problem. They were designed for use when the sun was behaving itself. Normally, we could float around in those things for a month."

"But the sun's not behaving itself," she reminded him unnecessarily.

"Nope, so we ride it out, and while we're weathering the storm, we either damp out the radiation in that reactor module, maybe flooding it as Seiji recommended, or we find some way to cut it loose and drag it away with a tug." He squeezed her hand. "We'll make it, Christy. I've been in a lot worse before. At least up here we have some maneuvering room. We'll just—"

He froze. Every muscle of his body turned to stone as he felt the trembling beneath his feet, in his seat, in the air, the dust drifting about them. "*My God,*" he said, his voice barely audible as the distant weak thunder became louder. "The thrusters are firing. Listen to them! *They're all firing!*" They felt the sickening motion about them, and great groans and grinding sounds of steel protesting unexpected loads and strains came to them.

There was no question. *Every maneuvering thruster of the space station was firing at full power—and they were pushing the station down and back, toward the earth.*

# Chapter 19

They fought their way down from the rim to control central in the core, their heads and stomachs protesting. *Pleiades* had turned on its axis and now the thrusters were firing at maximum power, at levels they had never been fired before. They could feel the deceleration, a sickening, twisting sideload that made movement difficult, that had them lurching like drunks as they grasped at handholds and finally spun slowly down the tube toward the core.

"Goddamn it, we were wrong again!" he shouted to her above the muted thunder of the firing thrusters, the deep groaning bass of the complaining station. "Jill wasn't the only agent they planted aboard this station. Oh, they suckered us beautifully, all right, and instead of increasing security, like a dumbass I lowered my own guard, and now they're dropping our orbit!" He let his anger spill

out and then he was pushing through the airlock
into the core. "Close the airlocks behind me!" he
shouted, fighting his way down the teflon nets in
zero-g to station control, knowing Christy would
be following behind moments later. He almost
clawed his way into the main computer control
room from where they could touch every small
or large part of *Pleiades*. Most of his crew were
ashen-faced, tense, frustrated; some of them were
moving aimlessly. He had never seen such total
helplessness before. Raphael spun about as he
approached.

"It's the computer, Rush! *It's taken over the
station!*"

"That's asinine," Rush snapped. "Get a grip on
yourself and speak with words that make sense."

Raphael gulped in air. "Yes, yes. I mean that the
computer's been programmed to function despite
any attempt on our part to take back control."
Rush eyed him narrowly; *that* much made sense.
He decided to find out what he needed to know by
giving new orders. His crew's responses would tell
him more than any session of you-talk, me-talk.

"Go to override," he ordered. "Punch in the emergency control for manual takeover."

"We *tried* that," Raphael said with a touch of
desperation. "The programming refuses entry into
the emergency control room while those thrusters
are firing."

The distant thunder from the propulsion units
seemed to gain in volume with Raphael's words.
Rush swore he could see bulkheads ripple as dust
continued to bounce about them.

"Break in, then."

"We're working on that. The door's been hot-wired; every time we touch it it lets loose a blast of electricity. Even with insulated material, there's so much juice we're afraid it will short back on the computer and burn out the programmer."

The thrusters continued to pound their deadly drumming through the station, still firing at maximum output, slowly but steadily eroding their orbital speed, guaranteeing their orbital path would be reduced dangerously, that they would start into the already rising masses of the upper atmosphere churned and agitated by an angry sun. Rush thought frantically. "The work lasers," he said suddenly. "Get some lascr bcams up here immediately. You can stand back and cut open a section to get into the computer." Two men listening to the exchange were immediately on open line, ordering the laser guns brought down from the construction modules.

Rush feared it would be too late. *Pleiades* shuddered with a renewed sickening motion. There could be no mistaking that dangerous wobble, no escaping the deep groaning sounds emitted by the enormous strains on the structure. A shrill alarm stabbed his ears and the emergency speakers sounded through the station.

*"Red alert! Red alert! All hands! All hands! Pressure seal break in the station! Pressure seal break! All emergency crews on the double in suits to Tube Three. Repeat, all emergency crews on the double in suits to Tube Three."* There came a momentary pause as if the speaker was trying to get his wits together, then he realized it was a woman's voice, Dianne Vecchio, as she went on. *"We are on full red alert,"* she said, calmer now. *"All personnel into pressure*

suits immediately. All personnel into pressure suits immediately."

Rush saw Steve Longbow just outside control. "Steve! Get your crews into their suits and then get some fireaxes and cut those goddamned cables from the computer! We can't wait for the lasers!"

He saw Longbow gesture to acknowledge the command and then Rush was jerked roughly by the shoulder. He flailed wildly with his arms to regain his balance, then saw Christy just behind him. "Get into your suit!" she screamed at him. Beyond Christy's face lights flashed wildly and he saw plumes of the nontoxic red smoke released automatically whenever the pressure dropped. The smoke would follow any air leak and indicate just where they would find the breach in pressure seal. And the triple-damned smoke *was moving*, snaking its way through the air, showing long tendrils in a spiraling motion. He jerked open the lexan door to the emergency suit compartment nearest him and slipped into the fastzip suit with practiced ease. The moment he closed the last seal of the suit the station radio frequency activated, as did the oxygen pack attached in a bulky unit on his back. The suits were designed to activate automatically when they were donned. He turned to help Christy and moments later they were both suited up and in communication with one another. "See if anyone needs help with a suit," he ordered. "Get to control. Dianne's probably so wrapped up in warning everybody else to get into a suit she's forgotten she also needs one. Go ahead, Christy—*please*." He had seen her argument beginning. Leaving Rush now was almost terrifying. The whole world above a world was disintegrating and what had been dislikable harshness in this man had instantly become a symbol of strength. If he hadn't said the word please, Christy would never have left his side. But he was right, the plea came through, and she turned in the suit and worked her way to control where, thank God, she arrived barely in time, as Dianne began to slump over her control console. Christy called frantically for help. Two men pushed their way to her and tugged and pushed the now-unconscious Dianne into her suit, fearful for her life until the full oxygen flow within the suit brought a rush of color back to her face and her eyes opened.

All hell was breaking loose about him. Rush pushed everything from his mind save one effort: *seal the pressure breaks.* "All hands, all hands," he barked on his suit radio. "This is Cantrell. Check to be sure everyone around you is in a suit. Then I want you all to start sealing any pressure breaks you can find. Follow the smoke. Emergency patch kits are on every bulkhead around you. Use them. Get to it. We don't have any time to waste." He paused. "Keep this line open. No talking." Even through his suit he could hear air shrieking as it rushed to the beckoning vacuum beyond the station. "Whoever's near the control central sound off."

"Ben Wolf here." A pause, then: "Cunningham. Rhonda Whitmore's with me."

"The three of you. Grab fire axes. You know where the main power cable from the computer runs. Find anyplace where you can see the cable. Do everything you can to cut it. Don't waste a moment."

He didn't wait for their answers. "Longbow, how's your crew doing?"

"We've cut through the panels. We'll be at the cables in a minute or two."

"Stay with it," Rush said in a voice so calm it startled him. Maybe finality brought its own calm, he thought. The air was still screaming from the station, but far worse was that continuing thunder of the propulsion units, the rocking and agonized groaning of the station as unequal forces kept trying to tear it into great chunks. The crews cutting frantically with axes and steel bars must be making some progress. He could see showers of sparks and smoke boiling away where metal crashed into cables alive with electrical energy. Curses and shouts and then a shriek came from someone as he took a severe electrical jolt. The others kept working, and he confirmed they were chopping into power. The thrusters were cutting in and out, a barking cough of power, an intermittent burning of propulsion units even more devastating than full thrust, because asymmetrical forces could twist them apart like wheat stalks in a farmer's hands.

The thunder stopped. They'd done it. He heard a gasp of relief, heavy breathing, recognized Longbow's voice. "We got the son of a bitch." Thank God for the Indian. He wasn't waiting to taste his victory over mindless electricity and a blind computer. Half the lights in *Pleiades* winked out because they'd cut more than the computer power lines. Battery-powered lights came on in an increasing glow. "Okay, everybody. Grab patch kits. Let's seal this goddamned tin can."

The alarms that clamored so loudly before were now barely audible in the thinning air. Rush saw

Christy coming up to him. He was pulling down the automatic sealing patch kits, rubberized steel mesh patches that would seal instantly to metal, plastic, glass—anything. They had only to follow the tendrils of smoke, like an inverted funnel racing to the vacuum, pull the sealant coverings loose, and just bang them over the area where their life-giving oxygen whipped into space. Rush passed a kit to Christy and she opened it as they moved into Tube I, the airlock doors left open deliberately to speed passage for anyone through the station. Rush called on the open line. "Anybody with any special problems, sing out."

"We need help on the rim in the chemistry labs. We've had some kind of explosion in here. A lot of corrosive stuff around. Can someone get some nitrogen to us?"

"McCandless here. Stay put. We've got four people coming your way to chemistry."

"We need some medical help in the industrial shop. This is Bill Ottley. We had a bad implosion and a couple of people are hurt. Bring some medical kits and additional oxygen bottles."

"Gale Bowie on the line, Bill. We'll be there in a minute."

Rush heard Dianne Vecchio's voice. Houston was panicky, trying to figure out what the hell was wrong. Rush knew the ground computers had detected the sudden deceleration, had heard the thunder, had seen the crazy torque and twisting of the station on their instruments in the mission center, and they were yelling for information. Dianne handled it like a pro. "CapCom, we're too damned busy to talk to you now. Shut up, listen, and don't bother us. We'll call you."

Her words brought chuckles to a crew facing imminent destruction and death. It helped. She spoke again. "Commander Cantrell, do you read?"

"Go ahead," Rush answered.

"Hammil wants you here in control. We're getting green lights on pressure pretty steadily now. It looks as if we'll have emergency patches completed in ten or fifteen minutes."

"On my way." Rush gestured for Christy to follow. Dianne was right. Get the recognized authority in the place where everybody else will know he's in charge again. As he pushed toward the control center with the battered metal and still-smoking cables, he stayed busy. "O'Leary, this is Cantrell."

"Go."

"Can you break free of what you're doing?"

"We're free."

"Get as many men as you can round up, use the workboats, and start moving some of those shuttle tanks from the Junkyard to the station. Put them off about two hundred yards."

"On our way."

"Raphael?"

"On the line. Go."

"Get some people and start gathering full lifeboat equipment for those shuttle tanks. The lifeboats don't have enough radiation shielding to matter worth a damn. We may have to use the shuttle tanks if this station busts up any more."

"What can you expect when you use cheap labor?" came a wisecrack in an unidentified voice.

"Yeah," another voice chimed in. "We got spics and wops and jive turkeys and guys with no arms and legs."

Still another voice, and the gloom was fading from them. "That's us. The lowest bidders."

Time to break in himself. "Okay, okay, all you deprived ethnic groups. Cantrell here. Knock it off, report each module and section as you've plugged all the termite holes." He'd be back in control in two or three minutes, but there was no need to waste time.

"Who's in control with Vecchio?"

"Conrad. At your service."

"Keep Dianne busy on damage control update, Dennis. You get an open line with Houston, the Pentagon, and NORAD. Bring them up to date on what's happened and be sure you let them know we've got this thing under control. Tell them we want the new orbital parameters as fast as they can get them to us." He knew everyone aboard *Pleiades* was listening. "This is for all hands. I haven't time to explain the details now, but you'll all be briefed just as soon as things calm down. The rim area outside Tube Three is strictly off limits. You may as well have the bad news straight. We have a nuclear reactor in the solar array control room just beyond the rim at Tube Three. That first blast you heard was an explosive device going off. We've got a problem on our hands and we've got hard radiation to contend with. It's been shielded and contained for right now, but with all the shaking this tin can has taken we might be getting some radiation leaks, and I don't want anyone's hair to turn white."

He paused, noticed Christy was with him. He took a deep breath, made certain he was speaking calmly, and went on. "You all know what else happened. Someone sabotaged the computer and rigged up our control system so that we fired all orbital-change thrusters at max thrust to decelerate the station. We don't know how much speed or altitude we've lost. You heard me talking with Conrad, and we'll let you know the new parameters as quickly as we get them. In the meantime, I want all of you to remember we've still got a skunk in the woodpile. Whoever set up our computer tried to destroy this station and kill all of us along with him or her. *From now on no one works alone.* That's a direct order from me. You don't go to the bathroom alone. No matter who you are or what you're doing, you will all be in direct view of another crewman. The first time anyone even starts looking suspicious, you stop them and sing out to the rest of us. When we get this thing bottled up we'll make permanent crew assignments."

He didn't have a moment after speaking before Dianne's voice came onto the line. "Commander, good news. I have a green board all the way on pressure. We're fully sealed for the time being."

The first survival hurdle was behind them.

They gathered in the main control room. Hot coffee and emergency food rations were brought to them because they knew they'd be working around the clock. At least they were out of those damned suits. Now they could get down to the next hurdles, and they were going to be tough to beat. Rush looked about him at his command crew.

"You've heard the news. It stinks. Our computer is out and it's staying out, so everything we get on orbit is from earthside tracking and computers. The preliminary reports on the modified parameters are bad news." He looked slowly at every face with him. They were almost stoic in their reception of what could be a death sentence for them all. "We're out of circular into an elliptical orbit, and the bottom line is that perigee is down to just over a hundred nautical miles and we're topping out for apogee at nearly three hundred nautical. That's going to keep us up here for a while, but only for a while. We've got anywhere from one to five days up here unless we can reboost to lift that perigee."

Again he looked at his select crew. "If we don't, then the curtain comes down and it's all over."

Christy's face was strained. "We'll lose everything, won't we." It wasn't a question.

"Unless we can reboost," Rush emphasized again. "I want your input on that now, because no matter what earthside decides, they're waiting to hear from us. Anybody?"

Sam Hammil nodded. "We can't use the thrusters to reboost," he said quietly.

He paused, and Rush gestured impatiently. "Damn it, Sam, this isn't a seance. Spell it out."

Sam didn't ruffle a feather. "You know," he said, then gestured to the others. "*They* know. Houston, everybody—they know. We've burned most of the thruster fuel. We'd need a shuttle load at full capacity and we may not have time enough for that."

"We don't need a fuel delivery, Sam," O'Leary broke in. "We've got the tugs and lifeboats and workboats. We could use those for boost."

Raphael shook his head. "Won't work. You can't transfer the fuel in time, and then you'd take away from us the means to get everybody off the station if we have to go that route."

Longbow lifted a hand. "We may as well quit

about the thrusters. We've got broken lines all through the station. No way to repair them in time."

"And we can't use the earthside computers for balance," Dianne Vecchio added. "We've got to use what we have aboard this station, and right now I wouldn't trust our computer to tell me the time of day."

Rush nodded. "Agreed. The big brain is out."

"You're also forgetting the shape we're in," Sam said to them as a group. "All that torque, the twisting and the strain. We're coming apart at the seams and—"

"We can brace that," Lydon broke in. "Seriously, Sam. I can get enough joints and overlaying splices on every weak point in twenty-four hours. It will do long enough to stiffen the entire structure for a gradual boost."

"Why don't we use the boats themselves for thrusting?" asked O'Leary. "I know it'll be a bitch, but we can match rim rotation, secure our boats to the rim, put the biggest thrusters from our boats around the core, and we might get enough kick to raise the perigee high enough so that we'd have a week or two for thruster system repairs."

"That means we could take on fuel," Longbow added.

Dianne showed sudden excitement. "Commander, if we had two weeks, we could bring another computer up here—one with the capability of being tied in to station sensor balancing and just for that job alone. Between the boats keeping us up for a while, and then repairing our thruster system, we could get back to two or three hundred miles without any real problems. After that—"

"Never mind the after this or that," Rush told them. "Stay with now and the immediate future. What you people have said may have merit. It's sure as hell better than dropping back into atmosphere. Form your own groups and get with it. Talk to your opposite numbers in Houston. Maybe they'll also have some ideas."

Several of the team leaders drifted away from control central. Rush looked at Christy. "I think you'd better handle the abandon-ship drill."

"Are you *serious?*"

"Yeah, I'm serious. That's why we have lifeboats. We may have to use them."

"But ... I just heard what they were saying here! *We have a chance, Rush!*"

"Sure we do. A chance," he said distantly. "But unlike the *Titanic*, our iceberg is the whole damn atmosphere, and at our speed, it's a lot tougher than ice." He squeezed her hand. "I know, I know it's a bitch to even think about it. But we have to do that, and you're elected. I'm going to get a status report on getting our people off."

"What do you mean?"

"We can't take any chances. We could bust up without warning, we could get atmospheric uplifting and our drag would increase enormously. I want the shuttles up here just in case. Go on, Christy. I'll need your numbers as soon as possible."

He didn't wait to watch her leave but turned back to his communications panel. "CapCom, you guys awake?"

They were accustomed to Cantrell's humor in mission control. Roger King was lead capcom on the shift. "Go ahead, Rush. We just woke up everybody."

"Okay, Goldilocks. Get cracking on this one. I want full shuttle status. *All* the birds—when they're ready to launch, when I can expect them up here. Figure out the data with heavy radiation shielding for getting forty-one people off this thing, and get it back to me in the next hour."

They didn't make any jokes about it. Rush Cantrell had brought home with almost a furious chill just how bad things were in that new killer orbit. It was a hell of a thing to discuss the shuttles as a fleet of lifeboats to rescue *everyone* from the station. Roger King issued orders, then cupped his hand over his microphone and turned to an assistant. "You know what he's talking about, don't you?"

Tim Landers nodded. "Sure. Getting his people out while they can."

King shook his head sadly. "We can get them off. It's more than that, baby. This is an election year. That station cost forty-five billion dollars, and Cantrell is talking about pulling the plug on the whole works."

Landers showed his sudden realization. "Christ, won't *that* go over big in the White House."

"Sure it will," King said, nodding to himself. "Just like a turd floating in a punchbowl, it will."

# Chapter 20

A misadventure in vacuum high above the surface of the earth can cause havoc in communications and transport across the earth's surface, as everyone tries to do something to keep the pending disaster from leaving "up there"and descending to "down here." No such moment can pass without flurries of emergency messages by telephone, wire, telex, radio, videophone, communications satellites, microwave beam, and conversation—between human beings, between human beings and computers, and between one electronic oracle and another. It is a vast orchestration of technological babble, and it is the musical discord with which men and women attempt to stave off the kind of disaster that makes of Chicken Little an honorable prophet.

All across the United States engineers, scientists, technicians, communications specialists, computer experts, analysts, veteran astronauts, and

high public officials were being rousted from their
living rooms, favorite restaurants, bedrooms, and
vacation retreats—wherever they might happen to
be. It was not so much a panicky reaction as a
tried-and-true system that had worked quite well
in the past. Collective bargaining with disaster
had begun from the first moment man traveled
out of atmosphere and back in again, as in the
second Project Mercury sub-orbital flight. After Gus
Grissom had walloped into the Atlantic, stared in
disbelief as his hatch blew open and the ocean
poured into his capsule, and then scrambled into
the water for his life—he nearly drowned because
the bottom legs of his silvered spacesuit were
chockful of rolls of dimes that began to drag him
beneath the water. Shortly afterward, John Glenn
faced incineration moments before his fiery plunge
back into atmosphere in his shingled space bucket
because all telemetry signals showed his heat shield
to be loose. If that heat shield had departed from
the spacecraft during reentry, then John Glenn
would have been remembered as the first fricas-
seed astronaut. The shield held and Glenn went
on to political triumph in the Senate.

*But the system worked.* It absolutely *had* to work.
The early space missions were one terrifying cliffhanger after another—great rocket boosters sputtering stupidly on the launch pad and being shut
down barely an instant before lethal detonation,
others rolling stupidly when they should have been
holding course, and still other spacecraft in quiet
orbit going mad as engines and thrusters went
hysterical, spinning the manned spacecraft so wildly
that the astronauts pinned inside were seconds
from unconsciousness and death. Two men who

had faced *that* disaster aboard a Gemini space-craft—Neil Armstrong and David Scott—both went on to walk on the moon. Apollo Twelve left its pad in a blinding thunderstorm and withstood an incredible barrage of lightning strikes that should have blown it to hell and back again. But the special teams on the ground meshed their minds with the men in orbit, and the computers both in orbit and on the ground, and salvaged an imminent disaster and transformed it into a spectacular success. Apollo Thirteen *did* blow up on the way to the moon, and again, the teamwork on the ground and the pluckiness and ingenuity and brains of the men looping the moon put together a jury-rigged system that kept the whole world on a breathless cliffhanger of its own and brought them home safely. Again and again the team effort on the ground to simulate the problems encountered "up there" proved its worth. Astronauts found their helmets glued tightly with ersatz orange drink and were unable to doff their clumsy garments until someone in a small room or a test cubicle or a capacious hangar figured the solution and radioed the answers into space. Skylab, enormous and complex and horribly expensive, nearly failed at launch when some simple part failed and screaming winds tore away its vital solar panels. Again and again the machinery buckled, crumpled, short-circuited, balked, failed, collapsed, or just plain screwed up without explanation, and the teams already assembled and the others hastily gathered found the way out.

They were going to do it again. They believed that and they believed it implicitly. *No American had ever been killed in space*. That was a truism.

The odds against that truism, especially in the early days, were about one in a million. But all the elements brought together by these assembled combinations of brain and technology *worked*, and now, by God, they were going to do it again.

They had no problems with priorities. President George Kirkland had brought to the Oval Room of the White House a number of people, but most especially NASA Administrator Dr. Luther Grenville and his defense department counterpart, Lieutenant General Bernard Harmon, who commanded the "blue suit spaceforce" operating with military shuttles out of Vandenberg Air Force Base in California. He met with these two men and his science advisor, Dr. Milton Toland. The latter was a thickset and balding giant of a man with tightly lidded eyes and the equivalent of a bionic brain encased within a neanderthal-like skull. He was blunt far beyond the point of rudeness and to the president, Toland was a very large dose of sanity and slashing honesty in a government that had rocked along for years with an overabundance of political infighting and scandals. The Nixon ghost had never really vacated the White House.

The president pointed a finger at the uncomfortable Luther Grenville, who felt his padded seat had become an electrically wired griddle. "Can you save the damned station, Luther? I've asked you that question three times now and you've spouted technical platitudes at me. *Now answer me.*"

"I don't know."

"That's the first honest statement I've had out of you in this meeting," George Kirkland snapped. "*Why* don't you know?"

"Our people still lack proper data. The whole question is whether or not we can reboost to a higher perigee without tearing apart the station." Luther Grenville exhaled noisily, a bearded seal washed onto a hostile, rockstrewn beach.

President Kirkland glanced at each man in turn and his steely gaze came back to rest on Grenville. "When will you have that answer?"

"The station computer is out of action, Mr. President, and—"

"*I don't want to know about the goddamned station computer.* What the hell is the matter with you, Luther? Have you taken vacillation pills or something? I repeat, *when* will you have that answer?"

Grenville shifted uncomfortably, searching desperately for an answer. Bernie Harmon was enjoying the discomfiture of what he considered a flaccid, pompous asshole. Grenville had always been so simon-pure it had nauseated Harmon, who felt, who *knew*, that if the shuttle program and the giant space station had been left in civilian hands only, the Russians would already be controlling the rest of the world.

Dr. Toland came to his rescue. Unexpectedly, and in the manner of a great buddha, in a voice gravelly and totally unbecoming a man of science, Toland smiled his way to Grenville's rescue. "Sir, there isn't any way he can know. Not for several hours, at least. They've got to compute the out-of-balance nodes of that station so they can figure whether boosting from external thrusters, rather than those built into the station, will let them raise the perigee without tearing apart the station. That will take them another four to six hours, at which time," Toland paused to make a steeple of his thick fingers, "they will conclude that they *can* reboost, but only if they stop the station's rotation. Then they must compute how long that will take with emergency thrusters made up of the *Pleiades* tugboats. Once the rotation is stopped and the entire facility is weightless again, they must rig the emergency thrusters, fire them *without* an on-board computer, which is a technical insanity, and go merrily on their way to ripping that station apart from stem to stern."

"You are telling me," the president said slowly, "there's no chance to save that station?"

"Election time is coming up, Mr. President," Toland said without any change in his expression or voice. "If you are counting on pulling a rabbit out of your space hat or hiding forty-five billion dollars going up in smoke, and quite possibly causing tremendous damage when it comes home to roost, my suggestion is that you immediately start considering gainful employment other than the office of the president."

"You wrapped it up rather neatly," the president said acidly.

Grenville gaped at Toland. "How the hell did you figure all that out!" he shouted, half-rising from his chair. He wanted to strike out at this obscene oracle who had just dismissed with a few words the entire power of the space administration.

"The laws of orbital mechanics are simple and immutable," Toland said with infuriating calm. "I also spent twenty minutes talking directly with Commander Rush Cantrell, who, as I'm sure you will remember, is the commander of *Pleiades* and very much in a position to judge the fate of his command." He lapsed into silence. He wasn't out to prove anything to anyone. Presidents want answers and not prodding.

"Is he right?" the president asked Grenville.

"Mr. President, *I* don't know and Cantrell doesn't know for certain, and Doctor Toland, despite his remarks and conclusions, also doesn't *know*. We have to run computer programs, as I said, to come up with certain answers that will let us go on to the next steps."

Kirkland shifted his glance to the thinly smiling General Bernard Harmon. "You're enjoying this too much, Bernie. When the devil will you understand this isn't a contest? Wipe that smirk from your face and say something sensible."

"We can sure as hell try to reboost," Harmon said without hesitation.

"Without tearing open the station?" The question had come from Toland, and there was some resentment on the part of the president, for the question had leaped to his own mind. But he put it aside. Answers counted here and not protocol.

"We can. There's a way. We've studied contingencies like this for a long time and—"

"Get to the point," Kirkland snapped, anger becoming vocal. "*How?*"

Harmon turned from Toland to the president. "Sir, the station won't stand up under thruster loads in its present condition. Repairs will take too long. We'd be in atmosphere by then. But we can get the station crews as well as a whole bunch of our people, up into orbit. They can start laser-cutting the beams from the solar factory, and using those beneath the station rim, spanning from the core to the rim along and between the spokes, to make a temporary platform that will unload the stress on the station and allow us to boost against the structural beams. We may do some more damage to the station but we *can* get it to stay pretty much together until it's high enough for more permanent repairs and another reboost back to the original orbit." He sat back to await the president's reaction.

Kirkland didn't wave any flags or offer cheers for the solution he needed so desperately. Long before this moment he had learned that men in power always seek more power and will weave spellbinding tales to accomplish their goal, often coming to believe implicitly their view through the Looking Glass. The president looked at Toland and raised an eyebrow. It was signal enough.

"It's an excellent plan," the science advisor said finally.

Triumph spread in a smile across Harmon's features.

"Except that the station will have plunged back into the atmosphere about six days before it can be accomplished." A massive set of shoulders shrugged slightly. "But, otherwise, it's really quite definitive."

Harmon started to berate Toland, but was cut off immediately by the president. "Bernie, you and Luther get on a jet and go straight to Houston. Stay in touch with your people there *and* with the station while you're en route. When you get there, find out the latest, and one hour after that, I want an update on everything. If Toland is right, then," he added sarcastically, "and he has a bad habit of being right, we've bought the farm where the station is concerned, and we'll have to concentrate on a rescue operation." He held up a hand to forestall any further conversation. "If you please, gentlemen, you're wasting time."

When the room was empty, the president studied Toland. "Milt, what's the bottom line?"

"Save the people with the shuttles, find out where that station is going to impact, cover your tracks like a cat with the trots, and find someone to blame. Someone as far from you as it's possible to find."

Kirkland made a sour face. "You've written off the station, then."

"Yes, sir, I have. That's the reality of it."

"How deeply are the Russians into this? I mean, *really* into it. I read the report on that woman, whatever her name—"

"Jill Brody."

"I read the report, and they're emphatic that she was planted by Moscow in our program a long time ago. The National Security Agency and CIA actually are in agreement on that."

"That could help," Toland said in that deep rumble of voice. "At least someone from your own intelligence camp won't sand bag you with the press. And you're going to take a lot of flak about that nuclear reactor. Carruthers is going to try to bury you with that one. I can just hear Herbert now, standing before the television cameras, pointing a hand to the sky and blaming you for that sword of Damocles over the whole world."

George Kirkland winced. "Do you have to be so damned dramatic?"

"I'm not. Wait'll your opponent really starts swinging into you."

"I can hardly wait," Kirkland said drily.

"*Don't* wait. Strike first. Get the blame on somebody else, for God's sake. It's your only chance."

"I feel like the ghost of Skylab is haunting us," Kirkland said.

"Don't repeat that. It's too good a line to use against you."

The president took a deep breath. "All right, we take off the gloves. You get with my political people *and* my cabinet and also the NSA and CIA. You have full power to act as you see fit, and here's what I want you to do."

Milton Toland looked and listened carefully. Everybody underestimated this man. Everybody except Milton Toland. Because George Kirland was pure steel in the clutch and he was about to use his biggest guns. "I'm making this a direct order to you, Milt. You get some absolutely reliable people from different embassies here in Washington. Include the Swedes, the French, even the Poles and the Japanese, and at least one country from the Arab and the African states. Work me up a list and I'll approve it in writing. I want a diplomat *and* a doctor or a scientist from each of those countries, and I want them present, with everything being recorded, when you do a complete biomedical computer brain scan on the Brody woman."

"You did say you want *me* to do that?"

"You're a scientist and a medical doctor and a computer genius and you heard me right. *You.* You scare the hell out of most people and I want all the muscle I can get on this."

"Yes, sir."

"*No drugs, understand?*"

"They've already hit her with etorphin. Drastically diluted, but effective. That's how they broke her down. But the effect is worn off by now."

"So much the better. I don't care what you use. Photic stimulation, computer alpha-wave control, but, by God, I want her to spill everything *before those witnesses.* Because the bottom line is that we're losing nearly fifty billion dollars worth of our space program, and we've got a triple-damned nuclear reactor about to be dumped on our heads, and we will present the cause of that horrific accident right in stage center of the United Nations, with everything we learn. And, Milt, but me no buts. I can see your devious mind already at work. Use it *for* me and not to win any arguments because I'm *ordering* you to do all this." He took a deep breath before winding up the meeting.

"Carruthers and his whole party will be after us, as you say, to condemn my administration for every crime in the book. Okay, it's an election year and I don't expect him to do any less. That's the name of the game. But this time I'm going to do what they don't expect. I'm going to ignore Carruthers and the whole bunch of character assassins he'll be turning loose. To hell with them. They're small fry. I want the big game."

Kirland's face was grim. "I intend to burn that son of a bitch. Vladislav Filipchenko has pulled a lot of crap in his time, and I'm aware of all the tribulations that go along with being the premier of the Soviet Union, but Moscow is behind what's happened, and this time I'll hold his balls over the fire."

# Chapter 21

Rush studied the crew assembled in the make-shift conference room just outside the main control center of *Pleiades*. Christy Gordon sat by his side. Others in the weightless environment of the conference area included Ron Cunningham from life support systems; Mike Crenshaw from the power crew; Marv O'Leary from the boats; and Margaret Peters, who felt cut off and helpless without her computers to do her job.

"Let's do a fast review," Rush said. No need for any wasted words. "Include it all even if we have to just cross it off our list of options, okay? Now, first on the agenda. You've all looked at every aspect of every problem. Can we save the station from reentry? Can we, in other words, boost to higher perigee?"

Crenshaw gestured and received a nod from Rush. "I've been talking to people from every area of

*Pleiades*. Some had no ideas and others had ideas that were pretty far out, but the general consensus, with which I agree, is no way. The reasons are a compound of station damage, loss of the fuel in the propulsion system, and loss of the computer. All of that put together, as well as the constraints of time, pretty well give us a negative on reboost."

O'Leary stepped into the collective opinion. "Commander, as it is, we're on the edge of coming apart at the seams. We've got all the leaks plugged but we took so much bending and twisting that we need major repairs just to keep this station together. If we tried to boost, the first asymmetrical push would break us up."

Heads turned as Sam Hammil joined the group. He moved carefully, with the velcro strips on his boots giving him traction in zero-g, and slid into an empty chair. "You got the gist of what we were discussing?" Rush asked.

Hammil sighed. "I got it from both ends. Common sense up here and a lot of rainbow dreams from earthside." He looked around the group to acknowledge their presence and spoke to them rather than only to Rush. "To wrap up a great deal of conversation, President Kirkland lost his temper with Grenville and he wasn't much kinder to Harmon. Both Grenville and Harmon are now in Houston. I spent some time talking with them, especially Harmon. The general has some hare-brained scheme to have us cut off large sections of the solar platform, use the girders to shore up the station, and with this jury-rigged bracing, bring in every bit of power we have to reboost. Of course, I told him this would mean despinning *Pleiades* to eliminate torque and nutational problems, but he brushed all that off as detail."

"It would be detail if that girder bracing would work," Christy said.

"I acknowledge that," Sam said graciously. "We don't have the time. What he proposes *would* work. Bernie Harmon's no fool. We just don't have the time available. There aren't that many hours left in the bottle before we're into a definite high-drag problem with atmosphere."

"How long would that kind of bracing require?" The query came from Margaret Peters.

"Throwing away every imaginable safeguard, at least six to ten days," came the answer. Peters had no further comment. They'd never last that long without seeing the station glowing from reentry friction.

"I also had an interesting conversation with Toland, the number one advisor to the president on science. This may not mean much to the rest of you," Sam Hammil said in that calming voice they all knew so well, "but I've been friends with Toland a long time, and Milt tells me as much with his silences as he does with his words. The president talked with Grenville and Harmon. He dismisses Grenville as a vacillating asshole, to quote Toland." He waited for the sudden laughter to subside. "Harmon is tougher and smarter, but obsessed with a desire to become a modern-day Napoleon. But at least he did some thinking in the right direction with his ideas about using girder sections to reinforce our structure for reboost. I'll wrap that up. It won't work because of the time constraint. Now, what Milt Toland also let me know is that the president is smarting from growing criticism about the situation with *Pleiades*. The press is having a field day at his expense. The ghost of Skylab past is the current new refrain to describe us, but the humor disappears quickly when people realize it's true. There have also been some deep and damaging remarks from the Soviet Union. President Kirkland is livid on that subject. It affects us. He has ordered diplomats and doctors or scientists from several nations to be present when they put Jill Brody through an intensive brainwave scan, computer-induced alpha-wave hypnosis, and whatever else is necessary to break down her background for committing sabotage on this station."

Sam Hammil paused, knowing the terrible impact of his words on these same people who had lived and felt so warmly and deeply toward the young woman they were now being told was an attempted mass murderer. Sam caught Rush's eye, and the station commander gave him a barely perceptible nod to continue.

"They don't intend to hurt Jill," Sam said, a bit more easily to the group. "I understand our president's position. I would do the same thing, I'm afraid. It's an election year. *Pleiades* could lose him the election. He doesn't blame NASA or us. He places the blame squarely on the doorstep of Valdislav Filipchenko, and he wants Jill Brody's mind and subconscious laid bare to the world to confirm she has long been a Soviet agent, planned the destruction of this station, and whatever misfortune befalls the world is the fault of the Russians and *not* the United States." Sam held up his hand to stem the flow of words he knew were being held back. "Also consider, if you will, the legal position."

"Legal?" A voice blurted from the group.

"Yes," Sam confirmed. "Let's say we lose *Pleiades*—as most certainly we will unless we pull a miracle from somewhere—and the station reenters into a city. The damage could be catastrophic, with a heavy loss of life. *Legally*, by international agreement, the United States would be responsible for payment of many billions in damages. But if the president establishes beyond question that a Russian agent *caused* the devastation, then this country is off the hook. It's a lot more complicated than it may seem at first blush."

It was time for Rush to step in. "Okay, that's enough of the philosophy of this thing," he said quickly, taking over in a smooth step with Sam Hammil's unspoken cooperation. "What we're going to do right now is work out the steps available to us. Until we come up with that miracle, we must assume we're going to plow into the atmosphere, and unless we're out of *Pleiades*, we're right in the middle of the furnace. Does everybody understand that?"

The query was rhetorical. *They knew.*

"So the station is going to smack into the atmosphere and the only question for us right now is saving forty-one souls. *Ours.* We can put at least half the people into one shuttle. Maybe less," he cautioned, "because of the need to increase the radiation shielding in the bird." Rush wanted to give them another problem on which to gnaw. "I've got to have some radiation and shielding parameters worked out. First, if we use only two shuttles for taking off our people, is it worth the dangers of additional radiation exposure? Or if the radiation is too high, can we handle three shuttles and do the job that way? *Then*, do we dare take a chance of a hard dock with the shuttles and this station? It's wobbling like a drunk on roller skates and we might damage the shuttle so badly it can't reenter. How do we transfer out people without for a moment forgetting the radiation levels?"

"We can use the work tugs and lifeboats for maneuvering units," O'Leary offered. "I mean, we can beef up a couple of modules with really heavy shielding, put people in them with the necessary life support equipment, and wait for the shuttles to soft dock."

Christy added her agreement. "We can move them into the shuttles with guidelines—everyone tethered in some way."

"Very good," Rush said. Then, to the group at large: "How much time do we have?"

"No one can answer that," Ron Cunningham said. "Too many variables we don't know about."

"Okay," Rush agreed. "Then work out operations on the *minimum* time we have. After you've done that, work out additional time stages. We could be up here for a week. There may be problems with the shuttles. Marv, about the modules as emergency shelters—how about sanitary facilities if people have to live in them for a week? What about living in suits or out of them? You know the questions. I want the answers, and I want them for all levels of contingencies."

He studied the group, suddenly immersed in all his questions. "What's it like outside?" Crenshaw asked. "I mean, Earthside?"

Christy turned on the large color television monitor, showing the nightside of the planet below them at the moment. Someone cursed. "We can't even look through our own windows anymore because of that damned radiation."

Margaret Peters sighed as she watched auroral streamers girdling the globe like magical veils. The planet was being embraced with incredibly beautiful shifting lights. "My father described to me, a long time ago," she said, reminiscing, "what it was like when they set off hydrogen bombs for atmospheric tests. The colors swept around the whole world in seconds. It was a rainbow gone mad, he said. Right out of Tolkien, or a nightmare of Merlin. He said—"

Rush snapped off the set. "Save the poetry for later. Let's talk about what happens when fourteen hundred tons come slamming back into the atmosphere at five miles a second."

Cunningham laughed humorlessly. "I'm personally involved. I'd rather ignore the subject. After all, we don't intend to be aboard when it happens."

Rush agreed, chuckling. "It *is* a bit academic, isn't it?" His plan was succeeding. The grim, almost ominous mood filling the room when they'd gathered had faded to a comfortable decision to live with their problem. "Well, what the hell," Rush went on. "Houston is only passing on a request from the White House. They figure if *we* make a statement about it, it will have more impact than any scientific announcements out of Houston."

"Couldn't you find a better word than 'impact'?" O'Leary offered.

"I wish I could," Rush answered, sweeping the conversation along as he had intended from the start. "We've got fourteen hundred tons up here. A lot of it is going to burn and sift down as ashes.

But the astronomical lab is thick and heavy and *it* won't burn."

"Neither will the airlocks," Christy murmured.

"Or the reactor," Sam said quietly. "But then we *all* know that."

"Rush, what do they want us to *do*?" Margaret Peters asked.

He looked at his computer chief. "Marge, I guess they'd like us to find a way to cut it loose from the station and get rid of it. Since we're going to lose *Pleiades* anyway, it won't matter how much damage we do in cutting the reactor module loose, slapping a couple of rocket boosters on it, and kicking it out to high orbit—either put it in a high parking orbit for later disposal, dump it onto the moon or, better yet, kick it into the sun."

"Even if none of that happened," Sam advised, "we could always use a booster to drive it down steeply into the middle of the Pacific or somewhere through the Arctic ice. That way we don't get rid of the reactor, but we absolutely minimize its effect and it doesn't go crashing into a populated area."

"Why don't we just blow it up?" Christy asked. "Not now, but as soon as everybody is clear of the station. Set off the charges by timer or radio control."

"We don't have the explosives to do that kind of job," Sam replied. "And if we brought them up, we might just break it into a couple of big pieces, and then we'd have radioactive junk tumbling back into and polluting the atmosphere, and we might get a shotgun effect into a city, anyway."

Christy shuddered. "I think I'm sorry I asked."

"Maybe she still has a point," Margaret said.

"After we leave the station we could use a missile and—no," she interrupted herself. "We wouldn't even have to do that. Bring up an atomic bomb with the shuttle. Attach it to the reactor module. When *Pleiades* is on a high swing of orbit, detonate the bomb. It'll be so high it won't affect earthside and it will vaporize the reactor. Nothing to fall down *then*."

Rush nodded. "Technically that would work."

"You don't seem inspired by my suggestion," Margaret noted.

"I'm sure Sam already discussed it with Toland," Rush said.

They turned to Hammil. "He's right. We did discuss it. The political situation is too tense for that move. The opposition party would roast the president alive. We'd be violating an international nuclear arms treaty, violating the space treaty forbidding nuclear weapons, scaring the hell out of half the world, and giving the Russians great grist for their propaganda mill." He shook his head. "*And* we might dump a load of radioactive debris into the atmosphere, over a world already running scared because of that solar storm. Remember, nothing's like the old days when we tested those things by the hundreds. Ever since they used those nukes in the mideast war, and that French hydrogen bomb was hijacked and set off in that old submarine by those fanatics in Vladivostok—no way, no way. *They're scared down there*. Radiation is already the worst bogeyman in the world to the Earthsiders, and we're going to use an atomic bomb to solve this problem?"

"Could we use lasers?" Crenshaw asked.

O'Leary laughed harshly. "We've got the lasers,

but we don't have power any more on that scale and they don't work. I've already thought of bringing up some more, but we won't have the time."

Margaret returned to an earlier discussion. "We never really finished one point. Cutting the reactor loose, even blowing it loose, and firing it into higher orbit or whatever with boosters."

O'Leary took the question. "It's our best shot, Marge, but I don't think we have the time. We'd need heavy shielding for the workboats, or else limit each man to minimum exposure to the radiation from the reactor. It's mounted with very heavy steel beams and alloys. The cutting job would be a bitch. We could use primer cord, except that we don't have any, and the only way it would be useful would be to get *inside* the reactor."

"And the way that thing has been breaking down," Rush added, "you'd get a lethal dose of radiation in just over seven minutes."

"What it boils down to," Sam Hammil said quietly, "is that I think we're going to have to roll the dice. There's good precedent. The Russian satellite and its radioactive debris in Canada didn't even kill a moose. Skylab scared the hell out of everybody and sprayed debris over Australia, and a lot of people made money selling the stuff for souvenirs. Never forget, we've got a planet below us that's three-quarters water, and of the remaining twenty-five percent, an awful lot of that territory is icecaps and deserts and lakes. The odds are that, even with uncontrolled reentry, we won't have any real problems."

"Unless," Christy tagged on, "you happen to be underneath five hundred tons of violently radioactive, flaming reactor when it impacts, right?"

"Made in America," Crenshaw said sarcastically. "Look up, world, here it comes at eighteen thousand miles an hour. The world's biggest *zap!*"

"No one down there," Margaret said to Sam Hammil, "is going to listen to your kind of reasoning. You know that, don't you?"

Dianne Vecchio watched an earthside telecast of news highlighting the growing effects of solar radiation and magnetic fields that both frightened and awed the world. Eerie bursts of blue-green light flashed away from power stations and transformers. Balls of plasma, whirling vortexes of electrostatic force, collecting with buzzing and crackling sounds near transformer stations, broke free like living creatures of pure electricity, and drifted across countrysides to scare the absolute hell out of watching but uncomprehending, terrified witnesses. The whole world seemed charged with static electricity. Radio transmission was a mishmash, television screens sparked and drowned in electrical snow, and from generator stations in cities, blue lightning spat and arced into the air. The effects of plasma spheres and other phenomena brought on a craze of UFO reports. The worst effect of the electrical saturation of the planet was that while it hadn't killed anyone—yet—it reached almost everywhere and gave people something on which to focus their helpless anger.

Dianne stared with fascination, others collecting behind her, as they realized the world was seizing upon *Pleiades* dropping ever closer to the atmosphere as one of the primary *causes* of their misfortunes. The religious fanatics filled their coffers to overflowing and waxed eloquent upon the imminent doomsday, as the solar storm offered mindless cooperation with global pyrotechnics. Even telephone lines were falling apart, static robbing voices from cables and splitting microwave beams. Burglar alarms rang discordantly without seeming reason. Radio-controlled garage doors opened and closed and opened and closed. Elevator doors slammed shut or sprang open, computers suffered erratic fits and had to be shut down, and tens of thousands of hapless individuals found their hearts pounding or failing because of erratic pacemakers. Navigation of ships and planes had become literally dangerous. Air navigation aids wandered aimlessly, and familiar sound cues for pilots became warbling nonsense. Radar filled with ghosts and became useless.

Dianne turned to Ed Raphael. "Will you take control, Ed? Please? My head is killing me. I think I'll take some aspirin and just look earthside for a while. It's hard to believe we'll be down there soon. Maybe I ought to start getting used to it again."

Raphael grinned at her. "Sure. But don't look too close. You may not like what you see."

She never imagined how prophetic his words would be. She took the aspirin with water and worked her way to an observation blister on the side of the station core. She checked their orbital position. She would have perhaps ten more minutes in darkside. The earth itself was a massive radiation shield between the station and the sun, and she would be perfectly safe. She opened the protecting steel plates, surrounded by a bubble of lexan, and looked down at the silently singing aurora and glowing electrical atmosphere, the darkened planetary mass beneath this gossamer veil. The aurora fled, vanishing as swiftly as they had appeared, and there was only the horizon glow along the curving edge of the world, and the deep gloom beneath.

The light flashed with an intensity beyond all description, a spearpoint expanding faster than her eyes could follow to an enormous glowing sphere, pulsating, almost spasmodic, then fading rapidly. She could hardly see from the afterimage on her retina, and she realized with dismay that she was temporarily at least partially blinded. Wisely, she remained where she was, groping for the emergency call button. She found it, her hands banging again and again to bring someone to her aid.

Rush Cantrell and Steve Longbow pushed their way into the bubble. Longbow cursed; *Pleiades* was rounding the edge of the planet and they were rushing into high radiation. He closed the thick metal plates to protect the viewing blister and they turned to Dianne, holding one hand by her eyes. "Did you see it?" she asked. "My God, I don't believe it. Did you see it?" she demanded of them.

"Easy. Easy, girl," Rush said soothingly. "We weren't here, Dianne. What did you see?"

"We were over Russia," she said, their faces just starting to come into focus. "I know I saw the lights of Moscow. It was northeast of there."

"*What* was northeast of Moscow, Dianne?" Rush pressed her.

"I saw it. It was incredible." She looked wildly from one blurred face to the other, gripped Rush's hand.

*"Commander, it was an atomic explosion."*

# Chapter 22

Colonel Oleg Klimuk stood by the side of the premier. "Sir, the telephonic video line is ready." Vladislav Filipchenko turned a massive head with thick, unruly hair and looked to his aide. He had no need to voice the question, Klimuk knew him well enough. "Yes, sir, the American president is on the line and waiting." A slight movement of his body brought Klimuk to remove the chair as the premier rose to his feet. He crossed the room to a wide padded chair before a television monitoring console, one larger screen in the center of the others in a semicircle. Over the screen was a camera. Filipchenko took his seat, held out a hand for a cigarette that was placed immediately before him, already lit. The premier inhaled deeply and nodded. Instantly a red light appeared over the camera. A technician's voice spoke on the line in English and repeated the phrase in Russian.

"We have contact. The line is open."

Vladislav Filipchenko looked at an angry George Kirkland. The anger passed right by the premier; he himself presented an impassive, almost icy expression to the other most powerful man on the planet. "Mr. President," Filipchenko said formally, but not bothering with salutations, "I must inform you that the military forces of the Soviets have been placed on a first-class alert."

"I know that, sir."

Nothing further. Filipchenko suppressed a smile. George Kirkland was in rare form. He must be very angry, which also meant he would be very quick with his mind. "I will be very blunt," the premier said.

"Please do," Kirkland replied with the same clipped response.

"There is no question of what happened, Mr. President, one hundred and fifteen miles northeast of Moscow at the Komorav Research Institute. This is our nuclear-powered high-energy accelerator, but you know that, of course."

"Of course, Mr. Premier. We have more than a hundred of our scientists and their families at Komorav as part of our exchange program."

Filipchenko studied the American president. *He is very cool, very careful, in such a perilous moment.* "Your scientists and their families are no longer at Komorav, President Kirkland. They are glowing dust. Komorav was obliterated a short while ago in an explosion we have determined to be approximately equal to three hundred kilotons. As you know, it is literally impossible for an accident like this to happen at such an installation. Do you agree?"

The face on the screen did not quiver so much as a single muscle. "I agree completely."

"Then, Mr. President, what I say may offend you now. Especially if members of your staff and government may be lying to you, as has happened in the past. There was no accident at Komorav, but there *was* the explosion of a bomb. That bomb was placed at Komorav by an American agent and—no, no; hear me out, George Kirkland, please. Do not protest too quickly. I will finish. How this information comes to me is not important. However, perhaps you are familiar with the name of Harold Brent?"

"I am *not*, Premier Filipchenko."

*He chooses to hear me out. Good.* "The name may be true, or it may be false, but most definitely it is the name of the CIA agent that was buried in the mind of this man. His identification claims he is from the Ukraine, and he has the Russian name of Boris Zudov. He checks out for many, many years. It is, of course, patently false. The drugs we used and our methods leave no room for argument or for error. I will be brief, sir. Somehow your people brought in this device and Zudov, or perhaps I should say Brent, set it off. The destruction was complete, the research center totally destroyed, and we have lost more than sixty thousand of our people. They include many of our leading scientists. It is a ghastly and deplorable and unforgivable deed."

"I agree completely, Premier Filipchenko."

The premier nearly exploded. "We are not that patient about all this, Mr. President! It has been suggested to me that perhaps all this took place to divert attention from your problems with the space station. If this is true, it is an insane act of desperation beyond words! I—"

The American president was gesturing for attention to stem the tirade from Moscow. Filipchenko held further comment for the moment.

"Mr. Premier ..." He made an angry gesture with his head and spoke with a bluntness Filipchenko could appreciate. "Damn it, Vladislov, we never sent in any agent with a bomb! It's mad to even think we would ever consider anything of such stupidity. There's simply no purpose in any such action." Obviously, Kirkland was making a sudden decision. He gestured to someone off camera, snapped instructions, turned back to the camera.

"Vladislav, this is too big to bury under diplomatic verbiage. I have just connected an open line to our key government agencies. We are being listened to by CIA, NSA, FBI, and my chiefs of staff. I also have my science advisor, Milton Toland, on the line. Please listen to what we are going to say. Are your people monitoring?"

The last remark was no more than a signal for Filipchenko to be certain everything was being taken down and judged instantly by Russian military and security personnel. Colonel Klimuk, out of camera range, nodded. "Go ahead, George Kirkland," Filipchenko said.

"Thank you. Now, this is the President on open line." Kirkland spoke to the various intelligence agency chiefs hooked in. "I am giving you a direct order. I want to be told, immediately, about an agent operating with the names of Harold Brent and Boris Zudov, with the last known operations area the Komorav research center near Moscow. I am on the line with Premier Vladislav Filipchenko and he has given me these names and tied them in with the nuclear explosion at Komorav."

The President paused a moment to allow his words to be absorbed, then continued. "If there is such a person, Brent or Zudov or operating under any other name, I want full identification immediately." Silence followed. "All right. At this moment, the Soviet Premier and his staff are on the line. They are listening to every word. The premier has my oath as the president of the United States that he is receiving the absolute truth. Since none of you has offered any name of any agent known to us in the Komorav area, you will now make that statement verbally after identifying yourself by name and by organization. Proceed with CIA, please."

Filipchenko listened, his face grave. Every security agency and office of the American government was going on record to deny knowledge of Brent, Zudov, or *any* agent at the research center, and every man who spoke swore there had never been any attempt or even a plan to detonate any kind of weapon at Komorav or anywhere else. The director of the National Security Agency, Myron Rutledge, added a vital personal note.

"Mr. President, would you ask the Soviet premier if General Andrei Isachenko is on the line?"

Kirkland didn't need to voice the question. Isachenko, head of the KGB and military intelligence, was in direct eye contact with the Russian premier, and Filipchenko nodded for him to cut into the line. "Myron, this is Andrei. Please go ahead."

It was an incredible personal element in a chilly,

dangerous exchange. "Andrei, you and I have known one another for more than thirty years. We have been at opposite ends in our work and we have also become strong friends. I give you my word as one man to another, Andrei, that not a word of truth exists in the supposition that we have had anything to do with the tragedy at Komorav. The whole idea is madness, and the explosion itself an unspeakable crime. I am telling you that if any of our people were in any way involved we would gladly turn them over to you. You have my word on that. I am passing the line back to President Kirkland."

Filipchenko came into the exchange at once. "George Kirkland, General Isachenko advises me that the word of Myron Rutledge, as well as your own, is most convincing. Let us lay this issue aside for a moment. Perhaps we will learn more through an oblique approach. We have heard that there was a Russian agent aboard your station and that some very disturbing events took place. Would you tell us directly the nature of these events, please?"

It was settling down to a no-nonsense dialogue, thank the Lord. George Kirkland relaxed just a hair. "Certainly, Vladislav. In view of what has happened at Komorav, please understand that what I tell you now is what we have ascertained, and we choose not to draw any final conclusions."

"Wisely said, George."

*There* it was—the breakthrough, the subtle signal that they were moving away from the mutual firing squad—the use of Kirkland's first name rather than the formal exchange. Kirkland related, slowly, carefully, and in chronological order, the series of events that had wrecked the nuclear reactor aboard *Pleiades*, the sabotaging of the computer to fire the orbital-change thrusters, and now the inevitability of the giant station plunging back into the atmosphere. Kirkland knew that the Russians, through their own tracking system, had the station orbital parameters and were aware of the approaching reentry, *if* the Americans could not reboost, and what he was saying would only confirm their own independent tracking and calculations. And then Kirkland released his own soft explosion.

"We have in custody the agent responsible. Jill Brody is the American name in use for many years. She has been subjected to full brain scan interrogation with witnesses from six independent governments. Your security people are fully conversant with our bioscience computer and brainwave techniques, so they will confirm to you the accuracy of such probing. Her full background as a Soviet citizen, her technical and scientific training, her emplacement in our society and assignment to our station for its destruction—are all confirmed."

Vladislav Filipchenko studied the face displayed sharply on the screen before him. "George Kirkland, please give us five minutes."

"Of course."

Filipchenko's face disappeared from the screen. An unknown aide in civilian clothes took his place. "I am Vyacheslav Volynov. I will remain here until the premier returns." He turned into a granite statue, unblinking and unmoving. The minutes dragged. Just several seconds shy of the five minutes requested, Filipchenko resumed his seat. The camera angle pulled back to reveal General Andrei Isachenko seated alongside the premier.

"Mr. President—George Kirkland—I must now speak to you in precisely the manner you, and your man Rutledge, have spoken to us. You see Isachenko seated by me. I have spoken with him, so you will understand how I use these words. First, a question. Do your people have the Russian name of this alleged agent?"

Kirkland looked to Rutledge. "Yes, Mr. Premier. Lidya Tamarov."

Filipchenko turned to Isachenko. The chief security officer of the Soviet Union nodded slowly to himself, then murmured an aside to his premier, who motioned for him to speak. "Mr. President, Myron Rutledge. I will be very frank. Jill Brody is no Russian agent. She is not even Russian. Lidya Tamarov is a name we know. She is not a Russian agent—either through our government or any other. Myron, do you recall that time when we were in Libya, when the insurgents attacked our group?"

Rutledge nodded. "I do, Andrei."

"You saved my life that day. I do not forget, nor have I ever told you an untruth. I—we—do not tell you any untruth now."

A silence fell between them. Finally Filipchenko stirred. He took his time to light a cigarette. He watched the smoke swirl about him, then leaned forward slightly. "George Kirkland, this matter is most strange. We believe what you have said."

"And we you," confirmed the president.

"We walk on treacherous ground," Filipchenko said softly, "and it is occurring to us that the treachery is not ours, nor is it of your making."

"Thank you. That conclusion is being shared among our people as well."

"I assume your people have been in touch with Interpol?"

"Certainly, Vladislav."

"Do they agree with this finding?"

"They have indicated they do, Vladislav. They have asked permission to be given the transcript of this exchange."

Filipchenko smiled. "By all means. We will bring them on the line. Please do the same." The premier harbored no illusions. The Interpol headquarters *had* been listening all the time, because neither the American nor the Russian leader had requested code scramble. Kirkland turned to someone off camera, then looked back at Filipchenko. "They're on."

"Very good. If they lie to you, or to me, George Kirkland, I promise them a visit with a very accurate nuclear device. It is our feeling, Mr. President, to bring matters to the surface, that you do not have an agent at Komorav and we do not have an agent involved with your station, but that *another party* wants us very much to believe these things are true."

Kirkland glanced down at a paper slipped before him, then looked up again. "We agree. I have just been given a report. Our security agencies agree, and they are of the opinion that there is a group or groups to whom self-sacrifice is the pathway to some eternal bliss. We believe—" he broke off as a digital screen on a nearby control console clicked into life and emitted a soft chime. He knew the scene was being repeated in Moscow. He and the Soviet premier read the digital printout on their screens.

INTERPOL AND OTHER SOURCES INDICATE STRONG AND INCREASING PROBABILITY

AGENT ABOARD *PLEIADES* AND WITHIN KOM-
ORAV NOT AMERICAN, NOT RUSSIAN. JILL
BRODY AKA LIDYA TAMAROV AND GEORGE
BRENT AKA BORIS ZUDOV NOT AMERICAN,
NOT RUSSIAN. INTERNATIONAL GROUP AP-
PEARS INVOLVED.

"George Kirkland, Isachenko has received a report from our KGB." Filipchenko was throwing
niceties to the winds and flat cutting the mustard.
"We have, ah, probed to the full with this Brent or
Zudov or whatever is the name. The damage is
irreparable. However, we did ascertain certain facts.
Are your people familiar with a secret organization known as the Holy Light?"

There was no lag between the voicing of the
question by the premier and instant computer query
by American specialists. Within seconds the National Security Agency computers in Virginia were
flashing their response to the president. Kirkland
gestured to an aide. "Put a camera on that readout
for the Russians to see."

In Moscow, a television monitor lit up and they
read the report being fed by NSA to the American
president.

HOLY LIGHT ULTRASECRET ISLAMIC GROUP
FINANCED FROM 1979 PERIOD BY OPEC AND
DEDICATED TO SUSTAINING POLITICAL INSTA-
BILITY MAJOR WORLD POWERS THROUGH
TECHNOLOGICAL FOUNDATION. VIOLENTLY
OPPOSED TO TECHNOLOGICAL CONTROL AND
LEADERSHIP OF WORLD EVENTS BY LEAD-
ING POWERS. INITIAL FUNDING EXCEEDED
EIGHT BILLION DOLLARS AMERICAN. ISLAMIC
GROUP HEAVILY INVOLVED INTERNATIONAL
CONTROLS, TECHNOLOGY, WEAPONS.

Kirkland turned back to face the Russian. "I believe, Vladislav, that we've found the skunk in the woodpile."

Filipchenko nodded. "I will make my decision now, George Kirkland. We are agreed. We will—"

He stopped as he saw the look of alarm on Kirkland's face. He turned to look at the monitor that had displayed the NSA report.

URGENT URGENT URGENT. EXPLOSION RE-PORT LAST FIVE MINUTES ABOARD *PLEIADES* STATION. SHUTTLE LAUNCH NOW CRITICAL FOR CREW RECOVERY. MORE FOLLOWS.

The president seemed to hear Filipchenko's voice from a great distance. Then the words penetrated his sudden mental fog.

"Mr. President. What can we do to help?"

# Chapter 23

The explosion boomed through the station like a rolling earth shock. Without atmosphere surrounding *Pleiades*, the blast was confined to the pressurized interior, and even as they heard and felt the concussion through the air and structure of their space home, they knew they'd been double-teamed.

It took only the roaring blast, the alarms shrieking of air leaks, to draw that conclusion. Rush Cantrell had frozen for only a moment, taking in all the sensations, and then had thrown himself forward to hit the manual backup alarms for all hands to don their emergency pressure suits. Again Christy Gordon was by his side, as was Sam Hammil, the three of them overseeing the emergency preparations to convert shuttle tanks to impromptu lifeboats should they have to abandon the station before the shuttles could rendezvous. In their suits they worked their way back to control central to assess the damage. Everyone was already hair-triggered for any eventuality, and emergency patches had been slapped to new leaks. The core withstood the blast better than expected, and in moments they knew what had happened.

Rush gestured to the pressure-report panel. "The son of a bitch tried to break us up," he said coldly. "If he'd set off that bomb in the core, or at the core juncture with a tube, we'd be floating wreckage right now."

Christy studied the pressure readings. "It's Tube One, isn't it?"

"Uh huh. The only thing that saved us was that it blew out in both directions from the blast. It ripped open the panels in the tube and that took the main force." He looked about him as Raphael and Tom Lydon came into control. "Ed, my orders were that no one was ever to be alone in this station," he said icily. "What the hell happened?"

Raphael took Rush's anger calmly. "We don't know. Even if two people were together in the tube, Rush, the trailing person could easily have left a plastic explosives package with self-sticking tape on the tube bulkhead. The other man, or woman, would never have known. I've already started checking the crew. No less than eighteen people went through that tube that we know of. It could be more. It could also have been there for a day or two, the explosives disguised as an airseal pack. No one could have told."

Rush nodded, stifling his anger and frustration. "You're right. Sorry." He looked around at the others. "But we've learned something. Whoever is trying to do us in doesn't seem to care if *they* also get killed. So it's not simply someone trying to sabotage an already crippled station. We're dealing with a fanatic."

"Maniac would be more like it," Christy offered.

"Same thing," Lydon said.

Raphael pointed to the board. "We actually took two shots. Whoever set that charge left one in the tube and another in the rim. The rim explosion apparently was muffled. The charge must have been left behind some heavy equipment."

"Okay. I want a damage party assigned to this one repair job until it's finished," Rush said. "Raphael, Maxwell, Vecchio, and Hollobaugh. Lydon, you get back with your crews getting those modules ready as lifeboats. Also, from now on, half the crew inside this station works in pressure suits with faceplates open but ready to close automatically. Set the auto-close at seven psi. Everybody get with it."

*Pleiades* had increased its oscillations, trembling like a flat-bottomed ship wallowing from one high wave to another in a stormy sea. They could still hear alarm bells clamoring as the emergency teams sealed off the air leaks and began patching the tube with curving metal plates. How they'd managed to keep anyone from being killed was a miracle, and their lives still hung by a thread that grew ever more slender.

Ron Cunningham and Hank Markham called in by radio. "Commander, we've got a new problem," Cunningham told him. "We've been operating with minimum power supplies and that last fracas has cut into what we need to keep functioning. We're starting to lose power to the stabilization flywheels and gyros in the core." He hesitated. "And you know what that means."

They all knew. Once the great flywheels ended their precise balancing act, *Pleiades* would lose its ability to remain spin-stabilized and it would begin a slow but increasing tumble, possibly along all three axis of control. That could lead to an acrobatic tumble, a sickening twist motion in yaw, roll, and pitch, and the speed of that tumble would increase even more. They'd be throwing up all over the damned place while the station itself was wrenching apart at the seams.

"O'Leary!" Rush called the boats officer. "Where the hell are you?"

"Working in Tube One," came the reply.

"Get your partner and come on down to control."

"On the way."

While waiting for O'Leary, Rush talked with CapCom, reporting the results of their latest near-disaster. "Is there any way you can feed more power to the gyros?" CapCom queried. "We don't dare move a shuttle close to the station if it starts into a tumble, and holding formation at a distance is going to complicate matters for the rescue pickup."

"We're trying," Rush said, almost snarling into his mike. "Move up your launch times, CapCom. We've got a madman somewhere aboard this station and there's no way to tell when he'll try to blow us apart again. I'm going to order evacuation from *Pleiades*. —Damn it, you're not up here, so don't break in like that! It's a matter of getting our people into the modules we've put together just in case we came to this. O'Leary's on his way right now to control. He'll be in charge of transferring everybody to the modules. They're industrial modules and we've got two shuttle tanks heavily shielded and fixed up with survival gear. My plan is to move our people into those modules. O'Leary's men will attach workboats so we can boost the modules to a higher perigree, which will give us a hell of a lot more safety time in case you guys are late or screw up the rendezvous. But whatever happens, *get those birds in the air.*" He glanced at Christy. "We've got some heavy shielding for protection, but the storm index is still climbing and we're getting so much radiation now that those modules might as well be paper-thin if any kind of solar blowout comes our way."

CapCom was back to its old, familiar and reliable ways of working with the chips down. Voices were calmer. They sounded now as if they were running a training simulation. They'd done it enough times. The only difference was that if they failed this test, then forty-one people were going to be very dead. "We understand, *Pleiades*. For your data update, we are go for the double launch from both pads in Florida and a third launch from Vandenberg, with a fourth vehicle in the barn in Florida ready to roll out."

"Very good, CapCom, and thanks. *Pleiades* out."

"Uh, *Pleiades*, hang on just a moment, if you would." Rush and Christy exchanged glances, caught by surprise with the request.

"Go ahead, CapCom."

"Rush, get your people moving into the lifeboats, but we'd like you and Christy Gordon to remain where you are a bit longer, if you would."

"We've got work to do, CapCom, and—"

"Scramble code and clear the comm room, please." CapCom was so damned cool it raised hackles on Rush's neck. He didn't waste time de-

manding more information; it would come soon
enough. He gave O'Leary and his crew their orders, sent everyone else off, and closed the communications area.

"We're clear, CapCom. Gordon and I are alone."

"All right, Rush. We know you've got your hands
full, but . . . well, we've got a problem."

Rush couldn't help it—he burst out laughing.
Christy was startled by his reaction, then caught
the insanity of the words. The last time that remark had been uttered it had become world-famous.
Apollo Thirteen had been on its way to the moon
when the command module exploded; the three
astronauts figured they were in an aluminum cof-
fin that would sail helplessly beyond the moon.
They announced their apparent doom with the
calm radio call nearly two hundred thousand miles
out from earth. *"Houston, we've got a problem."*
Hearing those same words now jarred the laughter
from Rush and Christy. He knew the people in
mission control must have been startled by the
sounds of laughter from the doomed space station,
but hell, they could figure it out later.

"Go ahead, CapCom. This ought to be a beaut."

"We, uh, hate to add to your problems, Rush,
but—"

"CapCom, *get to the goddamned point.*"

Bill Jeremy was CapCom; he took a deep breath
and dove in. "Rush, the computers indicate *Pleiades*
will impact in the New York metropolitan area."

Ice water splashed in his face couldn't have frozen Rush any more effectively. He stared at Christy,
who had gripped a console edge for support. "Repeat that," Rush told CapCom.

"The computer indicates the station will reenter

and then impact the surface within a thirty-mile radius of New York," Jeremy repeated.

"What are the odds?" Rush asked, amazed he was speaking calmly.

"At the moment, about eighty-two percent. Our estimate must be that loose because of atmospheric fluctuations, but we've got to figure—"

"I get the message, Bill," Rush said. He wanted to cut the conversation for the moment. He had to think. He knew he was reading into Bill Jeremy's words something that wasn't there, but it was tough not to feel one hell of a finger was being pointed at him for what NASA in its secret operations manuals referred to as "calamitous reentry." It was calamitous, all right. Over a thousand tons of space station surviving the punch back into atmosphere and smashing into a populated area of more than fourteen million human beings couldn't be anything less than that. But they made it sound as if it was *his* fault! He knew it was a subconscious verbalization of their own frustration down there, but Rush didn't give a damn about emotional hangups in mission control.

"Let's have the rest," Rush said finally.

They gave him the rest. They could expect the final swing into atmosphere over Asia, where they'd get the first .05-g reading. That meant resistance by atmosphere to their speed, a tremendously fast buildup of friction, and *Pleiades* would come arcing steeper and steeper toward the waiting earth below. Full reentry would be under way at approximately sixty degrees latitude north and the calculated drag profile ended up dead-center in the New York area. It wasn't just New York as a city. It was the enormous, sprawling megapolis of

New York, Long Island, Westchester County, and the solid line of cities of New Jersey. CapCom was still talking, he realized. They were talking about precautions being taken earthside. "... business end of Manhattan completely closed down until we complete reentry and impact ... impossible to evacuate ... logistics would be insane ... lower Manhattan has a working-day population density of eight hundred fifty thousand people per square mile ... got to remember that if we—"

He snapped from his near-trance at CapCom's death-knelling of doomsday, spoke sharply into his mike. "Screw all that, Bill. We can't do a thing up here about what happens earthside—not any more, anyway. And what you do in Manhattan doesn't affect my saving the lives of these people, so stop cluttering up with all this propaganda crap what we *need* to do." He drew a deep breath. "Look, you people stay on open line with Raphael or whoever's going to have primary comm. Monitor us on any changes. We might even find a few extra orbits lost in those miracle computers of yours. I'm going outside with Christy. I want to be certain our people get into those lifeboats. We're coming apart every minute and we're running out of time and we *still* have to find that unfriendly cat in our midst." He snapped off the transmitter and took Christy by the arm. "Let's go."

It might be the swan song of the great space station, but the men and women of *Pleiades*, at last come to grips with the recognizable danger and finding themselves with emergency measures to fill, eased back into their old stride as a tightly knit, efficient working team. O'Leary, as Boats Of-

ficer, and Cunningham, of Life Support, directed
the continuing modification of modules, two great
shuttle tanks, and every worktug they could assemble. By attaching the worktugs to the modules
or to a shuttle tank, they had a crude but effective
jury-rigged survival spacecraft with a propulsion
and attitude-control system. The crews had been
installing bladder tanks inboard of the curving
metal walls, installing oxygen supplies, food, temperature controls, rebreathing apparatus, security
harnesses, toilet and hygienic facilities, and other
basic needs for living in each module or tank for a
period of at least ten days. Once they moved from
*Pleiades* to these makeshift lifeboats, with their
thick and heavy shielding, they would be hopelessly adrift and at the mercy of successful flights
by the shuttles. Return to *Pleiades* for life support
might not be possible.

Sam Hammil met with Rush and the top work
crews. "We need only two shuttle tanks for all our
people," Sam told the group, "but I want two of
the industrial modules completely fitted out for
use at a moment's notice. We can take some problems with any of our equipment *if* we have a
backup." He had no arguments. Longbow eased
the pressure on them still further. "We've been
able to move some of the solar arrays to the lifeboats. It's pretty makeshift, but we're spanning
the modules, and that gives us two things—thermal
control and a lot of power. We've moved batteries
and fuel cells into the boats. We can charge the
batteries on a sun pass and use them through
darkside, and keep the fuel cells completely for
backup."

"How's the oxygen supply?" Rush queried.

"We're in good shape. Twenty days for each lifeboat, not counting what we'll gain from rebreather and scrubbing apparatus."

"We've got good communications," Rush noted. "Okay—now, the sixty-four dollar question. Do we boost the lifeboats to a higher orbit?"

"What's *your* opinion?" Sam Hammil asked at once. He didn't want this to be a committee decision. Rush Cantrell had more survival experience himself than they did collectively.

Rush showed some surprise at Sam's interjection, then recognized it for what was intended. "Surprisingly, I'm sure to some of you, the answer is no." Raised eyebrows told him he had judged them correctly. "The tugboats are fine for low-thruster maneuvering in a limited area, but they lack the kind of multiple-axis gyros for meaningful power—enough to kick us up higher where we'd be guaranteed an extra week or so. Then there's every chance we'd be scattered, and that would really screw up rendezvous by the shuttles. Finally, with our lesser drag profile and greater mass in terms of size, we won't decelerate as fast as the station. To me the kicker is to keep the maneuvering systems of the tugs as an all-out desperation backup."

Hammil looked around at the others. "A suggestion, if you don't mind?" They waited. "Move twenty people into one modified shuttle tank and fifteen into the second. Rush wants to keep six people aboard *Pleiades* as long as possible for some last-minute work. If we put twenty aboard one tank, we've got half our people safe in their lifeboat, but those tanks also have twice the living room as the industrial modules, and the last thing we want on our hands is a claustrophobic effect.

Fifteen in the second tank means plenty of room
for the six who will still be aboard the station."

"Actually, five," Rush amended. "Arturo Lopez
will remain in one of the mobile bubble tugs. He'll
keep an industrial module clamped to the tug so
he can stay downsun at all times and use the
module for shielding. He'll also be available for us
when we're ready to leave the station or if we *have*
to leave in a hurry. I'll be aboard the station, as
will Christy Gordon, Sam Hammil, Mike Crenshaw
to work the power systems, Rhonda Whitmore to
handle communications. Everybody stays in their
suits the whole time. You don't need to be pres-
sured up, but I want the faceplates set for automatic closing if the pressure drops to six psi. Got
it? Let's do it, people."

They watched the station crew guiding themselves on long cables from the nonrotating station
core to the first shuttle tank. Don Eagle rode the
powerful tugboat, and when everyone was aboard,
he cut the lines and backed off the tank, which
they now called Lifeboat One, a distance of a mile.
He had nothing else to do now but wait. He would
remain at the power controls in the small but
completely self-sufficient bubble, keeping the big
tank between himself and the sun for his radiation
shielding. Benjamin Wolf rode the same position
for Lifeboat Two, but held position only three hundred yards off *Pleiades*. Arturo Lopez floated in at
fifty yards, ready at any moment to move in to
pick up the five people still working within the
doomed station.

"I know it seems crazy to still be inside this
thing when we've all accepted that it's going to

burn," Rush explained to the others with him. "But there's always that one chance in a thousand the computers are wrong, that we won't get atmospheric heave, that General Harmon isn't all apple pie and blue sky and maybe his ideas *will* work. Whatever, people; whatever. The point is to keep *Pleiades* in balance as long as it's possible to do so. If there's a ghost of a chance to find a miracle, we can't do it with a tumbling station. It would break up, for starters, and for seconds, nobody could get close enough to apply any thrust to the structure."

They looked down the ghostly cave of the station core. "We go through the station. We shut down every power system we can find. I should have done that before, but my thoughts got lost in the big shuffle to get everyone else off safely. We move through the station, as I said, in the big shutdown. I want all available power fed to those flywheels to keep balance as long as it's possible to do so. Keep one thing in mind. We still haven't found our killer, but if all power is off, then he can't bring in the thrusters either directly or by radio signal. There's still some fuel left in that system—enough to mess us up some more. Don't forget that the station heading for reentry into that area of New York is no accident. That took careful planning and brilliant work with the computer. Now, if we can keep stability with the station, Houston may be able to come up with more accurate figures on reentry and impact. A tumbling station throws the computer into a fit and it's all guesswork from there on. Use whatever you have to use to kill power—axes, disconnects, anything. Sam and Mike, you work together, and Christy and I will be the second team. Rhonda, you stay in station comm and do *not* leave there until we all leave the station. Got it?''

Rhonda nodded. She wasn't that keen on being alone, but the ghosts up here were few and far between.

Mike Crenshaw motioned suddenly. "Rush, we still have some of the laser saws in the construction and industrial modules. They're short-range only, but they're all fully charged with portapacks and they could save us a lot of time."

"Okay. Let's get them." They worked their way out from the core to the rim modules, feeling uneasy at the complete absence of anyone else in a station that for a year had teemed with people. They picked up their tools and the laser saws and split into two teams to pull the plug on a great but dying beast they had come to call home.

# Chapter 24

The early morning hours matched temperature and humidity, and all across central Florida ground fog—in a paper-thin blanket hanging no more than twenty to a hundred feet above the surface— sweated itself from the darkness, cool and damp and swirling in the absence of wind. Along the shoreline of the Kennedy Space Center, a squat monster with four rounded prows sat vertically atop Launch Pad 39A. It was the space shuttle *Columbia*, scarred veteran of more than seventy roaring flights beyond the planet. The massed rows of searchlights surrounding the pad produced a dazzling display, thick beams emerging from a concealing mist to create a fantastic crisscross of a hundred slashing swords into the sky. Here the ground mist was alive from the thousands of lights of all sizes and colors of the launch complex, like some milky liquid, from which jutted poles and

towers and antennae and the upper body of the
shuttle with its solid-rocket boosters and the massive main fuel tank. The red lights flashing by the
launch pad could be seen only as strange blinking,
glowing eyes of invisible dragons. From the sides
of the huge space vehicle, supercold gases vented
in billowing vapors, and every so often there raced
across the launch area the shrill scream of supercold fuel in its pipes, a shrieking chorus set to its
outlandish cry by the mixing effects of temperature and the increasing breeze. Upward from these
pipes and the heat of the powerful lights rose the
vapors as wispy tendrils or softly rolling cotton.

The searchlights winked out with a crash of silence, as if darkness itself had stamped out the
glowing beams. A voice from a hundred loudspeak-
ers three miles from 39A chanted out its litany of
the countdown and there came a first tiny flicker
of fire, no more permanent than an eyeblink, re-
placed at once with a glorious exploding volcano
of golden fire. Light flashed out in all directions,
setting aflame the ground fog for miles in every
direction, an illuminated shock wave speeding faster
than the eye could follow. At the launch site, the
fog vaporized from flame and thunder and a great
monster, now rendered invisible by the savage light
of its own giant engines, broke her gravity chains
and lunged upward. It was impossible to see anything but light, pure and golden—light so intense
it bleached, instantly, the last drop of blackness
from the night. Sound punched forward with body-
kicking fury. Torrents of sound, shock waves tumbling together, smashed at the earth, squeezing
everything, and then the ragged thunder became a

resonant cry, the familiar acetylene-torchlike howl of the giant running free.

The billion-throated monster tasted sweet escape. The entire sky was burning as *Columbia* clawed heavenward.

Two hours later dawn had come, along with a lawyer of high clouds that obscured the sun and transformed the white fog into bedsheet greyness. Again the litany and the fleeing seconds and the golden flame, curiously washed out now in comparison to the night-sundering fire, but louder, sound reflecting down from the cloud layer. Then *Ghostwinds* was on her way from Pad 39B.

The sound was barely a fading echo when a great tracked transporter rolled through the enormous elevator doorway of the Vehicle Assembly Building, carrying on its massive steel back the shuttle *Yankee Clipper*, trundling to Pad 39A for a "quick-and-dirty" launch should the sister ship fail.

Bordering the California shoreline, nestled in rolling hills, catching the first rays of the rising sun, the third shuttle scheduled to fly that morning crashed upwards from its launching pad at Vandenberg Air Force Base. *Falcon* sped faster and faster to the south so the great solid boosters would return to impact with the ocean. As quickly as the boosters fell away, *Falcon* began the translational maneuvers that would swing her away from polar orbit to match the inclination of the crippled *Pleiades*.

Cheers and shouts broke out in Lifeboats One and Two. The return tickets for earthside were successfully on their way.

*        *        *

Rush and Christy examined the power cables before them. Each held a laser saw, powered with nicad batteries that gave them nearly twenty minutes of effective cutting with a range of less than a foot—all they needed, really. "Close your suit," Rush ordered. "We're going to get some blowback and some electrical spatter. Set your suit to three point five psi. Who knows? One of these things might even cut through the outside walls. Let's do it."

They stood several feet apart so they could sever the main power cables to each side of a main junction terminal. "I hate doing this," Christy complained. "If we ever save *Pleiades*, whoever has to repair all this damage is going to curse us to their dying day. What a mess."

"Stay with it." Blue-white light flashed in a pencil-thin beam. Metal softened and melted away, and the myraid power cables beneath flowed like heavy water. The beam cut all the way through. "Good job," Rush said. "Let's get the next one. The main thruster controls come together beyond that airlock."

They worked their way along the rim, leaving airlocks open behind them, cutting power lines, thruster propulsion lines, and controls, one after the other. "According to the diagrams, we have only two more to go for our rim section," Christy noted. They trudged along the rim walk, caught off balance more often than they liked from the swaying, unbalanced motions of the station, felt more strongly here than anywhere else in *Pleiades*.

"Sam? Rush here," Cantrell called by radio. "How goes your end?"

They heard heavy breathing. "We're, uh, in a

bind at the, uh, industrial complex," Sam answered, breathing hard from his work. "Damned cables run through a heavy flexmetal tubing between airlocks. We're getting it, though." The radio messages rose and fell because of magnetic interference overpowering the relatively weaker suit transmitters. Static crackled like popcorn all the time. "Be right with you, Rush."

"Take your time."

"Whew! That was a job and a half," Sam exclaimed. "We'll be delayed getting around to Tube Two, Rush. Mike and Arturo have gone EVA to sever the cable system just beyond the reactor." Something cold grasped at Rush. He saw his own unspoken question in Christy's expression, motioned her to remain silent.

"Hey, very good, Sam. I'd forgotten about the shielding blockage there. Look, we can't keep moving on this line. We're at the point where that last explosive charge went off. Too much broken equipment. I'm afraid of snagging a suit on a sharp point and breaching pressure. We'll start working our way in the other direction. We'll meet you topside of Tube Three."

"Got it, Rush. I'll meet you there. We should be able to wrap up the whole job in two more hours at the most. Rush, I don't think we'll have to go EVA to get to the lifeboat. With the station powered down except for gyros, we should get a steady platform and we can get a shuttle for a hard dock."

"It's worth considering. We'll go into it in more detail when we finish in here. See you topside at Spoke Three."

Rush switched off his radio, motioned to Christy to do the same. He checked the external pressure to their suits, opened his faceplate, and waited for Christy to open hers. Even before he said a word he knew that cold feeling had been right. She'd sensed it also. "Rush, something's *wrong*. With Sam, I mean. He—"

"Wrong?" he exclaimed. "It stinks! *He* stinks. He's a lying son of a bitch, and we'd better be ready for anything. My bet is that he's already killed Crenshaw, and if Lopez is still alive, then Sam is after his ass, too."

"*Killed* Mike?" Christy shook her head. "No. That's too much to believe. I won't believe that."

"What the hell is the matter with you?" Rush grasped her arm and shook her roughly. "Listen to me. *Think*, damn you, lady. Don't emote. You heard Sam. He said Mike Crenshaw and Art Lopez went EVA to sever the cables just beyond the reactor. Jesus, *Lopez has been outside the station the whole time*. He's lying. And Mike Crenshaw wouldn't violate my orders, even for Sam Hammil. Especially when he could reach me any time by radio and . . ."

His voice fell away as he began to realize the enormity of what he was uncovering. "Of course," he said, whispering aloud, talking as much to himself as to Christy. "Who better than Sam Hammil to know every weak point in this whole station? And who had the responsibility for checking *all* areas of the station, at any time, without any suspicion? It's Sam . . . *he* set off that first explosive charge! Oh, sure, Jill worked with him, but she was strictly a messenger for him. I still don't know for certain, not now, anyway, just where Jill fits into all this, but it's Sam who's been behind everything that's happened." He looked directly at

Christy. "And we'd better not forget, even for a moment, that he's not through yet. I can't add it all up, but I don't have to. We know the reactor was sabotaged. We had a couple of explosions on this station *after* Jill left, and right now we have a treacherous, lying son of a bitch on our hands. Notice that we haven't heard a word directly from Crenshaw or Lopez? That's probably because dead men don't talk."

Christy struggled for comprehension. "But why would he give himself away *now*? I mean, *Pleiades* is going to hit atmosphere soon enough, and we had no way of knowing it was Sam if he'd just left everything the way it was."

"Maybe, maybe," Rush answered. "That brain-scan on Jill could smoke him out no matter how cool he played it for now. There are so many other pieces in all this I don't understand yet—including that nuclear blast in Russia. How the devil does that fit into all this? And it does—somehow. Then we find out that this station has been carefully controlled through a berserk computer to wind up into the middle of fourteen million people. It's more than Jill Brody or Sam Hammil. I don't know the answers, but we don't have time up here to figure them out. We've got to meet Sam where we said we would, and my bet is that he'll try to bushwhack us. He's not the Sam Hammil we've known. We're dealing with a fanatic, a maniac."

"But why would he want to do anything to *us*? He's already crippled the station. I don't understand."

"We've got three shuttles on their way up here. Does Sam still control those missiles we've got in the Junkyard? There's enough firepower there to wipe out most of our shuttle fleet. If he takes us out he's free to kill Rhonda in the communications center, and *that* leaves him wide open to finish what he started. Notice how strongly he emphasized a hard dock between a shuttle and this station? If we made our plans already and most of the people are in the lifeboats, why *change* at the last moment? That isn't the way Sam works because it doesn't make sense. Unless, of course, you're out to get as much destruction accomplished as you can before you buy the farm yourself." His face hardened. *"That's it. He's perfectly willing to sacrifice himself in order to get the greatest destruction before he gets killed. That makes him a martyr of some kind."*

"But *why?*" Christy demanded.

"Tune in next week, love," Rush told her. "I don't have that answer."

She gripped his arm. "Rush, why don't we just radio O'Leary or Raphael in the lifeboats? They could send over some more men to help."

"I'd already thought of that," he said. "Want to bet a nickel the frequencies out of this station are mysteriously jammed?" He turned his suit radio to the station-to-lifeboat frequency and a high squeal assailed his ears. Quickly he tuned back in to the intrastation radio. "See what I mean?" He showed a sardonic grin. "It's up to us."

He looked at her as if seeing someone for the first time. "Chris, there's no need to risk your life. I don't want you hurt, let alone killed. I'll settle with Sam Hammil. You get the hell out of here with one of the maneuvering units and make your way to a lifeboat. Take Rhonda with you and—"

She shook her head. "No way, Commander. I

haven't spent a year up here to leave you when the going gets rough. Besides, you learn a lot sometimes in just a few minutes. I have. I think I'm in love with you."

He held her gaze. "You'll have to wait for the music and flowers for that line."

"Right, and in your own words, Commander, let's get with it." She pulled her faceplate into position and he did the same. He had an afterthought, motioned her not to turn on her radio. He placed his helmet against hers so vibrations would carry through the lexan and metal and she could hear his voice. "Let me have that laser saw. I want it open to maximum range for when we meet up with Sam."

"But its cutting range is only a foot, Rush. What good will that do?"

"It may not cut anything at a distance, but it sure as hell is going to give Sam a surprise. All right, back on the radio and be careful of what you say to me. He's going to be listening."

He had precious little time to figure out what might happen when they moved along the station rim to meet Sam where the airlock of tube Three reached the rim. He wanted desperately to gain an advantage. Sam probably wouldn't suspect they knew anything, for if they did then their safest move was simply to leave the station. If they were still here to meet Sam, he must figure them for *not* being aware of his true role and he might get just a bit careless. Rush was counting on that. It wasn't that much different from the old days of submarine warfare with two killers deep beneath the ocean trying to snare one another. The commander

who made the often fatal mistake was always the
one who left himself open to a surprise move by
his enemy. Rush figured that Sam would be lacking weapons in the usual sense of the word. No
guns, for sure. He might have rigged some kind of
crossbow or spear, but that would have meant
planning and preparation and a chance of being
exposed. Any hand device like that might miss
him and get Christy, and that would put Sam at a
disadvantage. So Hammil would have to nail them
both—and at the same time. He knew Rush was a
powerful man and his superior in any hand-to-
hand combat.

So his weapon must be couched in guile. The
work lasers they used on the station were the same
as the one he carried; a short-range cutting saw
really effective for only twelve inches. Up to one
foot it would cut wood or any other nonmetallic
material, and beyond that, the charge became simply an intense spray of light. Could Sam have
secreted something like grenades aboard *Pleiades*?
That was a possibility to be considered, because
he'd had a confederate in Jill Brody, and that also
meant contacts on earth, and it was easy enough
to conceal explosives within electronic and mechanical shipments to the station. It had taken
something like that to tear up the nuclear reactor,
as well as the other charges that had exploded
since then. Rush couldn't put that kind of weapon
out of consideration, yet . . . would Sam have risked
his entire cover by someone stumbling across such
devices? The odds were enormously against it. Sam
was too careful, too knowing to take stupid risks.
So when they came face to face he must use what-

ever the station, the environment, the immediate situation had to offer.

They passed through a servicing work module and Rush paused. He motioned Christy to silence, and selected a coil of loose and flexible cable with a test strength of more than four thousand pounds. He hooked it about his waist and to workbelt clamps of his suit and then did the same with Christy's suit. She showed the question on her face but he motioned her to remain silent. Again he checked the range setting for the laser saw. It was wide open to maximum. Again he considered that, beyond the automatic stop, it wouldn't even cut butter. But then, Rush grinned to himself, he wasn't out to *cut* butter or anything else. Everything in hand, they left the service compartment and continued along the rim.

"Sam, you read us? We're in Nineteen and coming around to twenty. Where are you?"

"I've got you loud and clear," Hammil replied. "Just come on through the airlock. I'm in Twenty. That should wrap up all power cuts along the rim."

"Be right with you," Rush confirmed. He stopped by the last airlock separating them from Sam and turned to Christy, motioning her to remain at least ten feet behind him. Module Twenty was the photo lab. Most film was processed in the rim because they needed some gravity to control the chemicals and liquids used for that work. They went through the airlock and saw Sam waiting for them at the far end.

"Commander, would you close the airlock behind you?" Sam asked.

Rush turned to Christy behind him. "Close it,"

he said curtly, waiting until she'd spun the wheel and the green secure light winked on. They moved toward Sam, who watched them with a smile barely visible behind his faceplate. Rush was perhaps five feet distant when a flash of orange light stabbed at him, followed by a dull boom and an instant explosive cloud of vapor.

*The bastard's blown out the lab wall . . . explosive decompression. He's trying to blow us out of the station . . .*

Rush loosened the cable by his waist as screaming air dragged him toward the gaping rupture in the module wall. Instead of fighting to keep his place, as Sam expected, Rush threw himself forward. The outward-exploding pressure helped carry his body in the unexpected lunge toward Sam. He held the laser saw extended before him. In seconds the vapor clouds cleared and he had an open shot at Sam's faceplate. The booming pressure was almost to zero. Rush squeezed the laser saw trigger and a blinding light stabbed forth.

No weapon, no cutting edge. Blinding light, was his weapon. For the moment, Sam Hammil couldn't see. Blinded by the searing light, he threw up an arm instinctively to protect his eyes. He couldn't see Rush, who braced himself carefully and brought up his boot with all his strength to crash into Sam's groin. They heard his shriek of pain through the radio and saw his mouth open as he tried to suck in air. As he doubled over, Rush brought the laser saw smashing as hard as he could into the lexan faceplate. It stunned Sam. Rush had just enough time to twist the laser saw dial to full cutting intensity of one foot distance. He thrust the saw against the helmet and squeezed the trigger.

A thin beam of powerful light sliced through the lexan and into the flesh and bone just beyond. Another burst of vapor whipped through the compartment as the pressure seal of Sam's suit ruptured and the suit collapsed against his body. Blood burst from his nose and ears and mouth and the hole drilled into his cheekbone by the laser. He screamed silently, pink froth bubbling and spraying from his mouth, and with a desperate, dying lunge he grasped Rush's suit and dragged them both to the gaping hole in the module rim.

Both men tumbled helplessly into vacuum, out into certain death. Rush didn't bother to struggle. He felt Sam's body jerking wildly in his final seconds of life, then he arched violently and went limp. They were turning as they floated from the station, and then the cable connecting his suit with Christy's pulled taut. His outward movement ended. Sam's body, trailing a faint pink cloud, drifted away.

"Just hold tight in there," Rush called to Christy. "I'll pull myself back in. He eased back into the module, careful of the jagged metal, and was then safely inside. A sobbing Christy threw herself into his arms. Rush took a long, shuddering breath.

*Too close, too close!*

# Chapter 25

They fitted Rhonda to an astronaut maneuvering unit and watched her drift slowly to the waiting Lifeboat Two. Whatever Sam Hammil had used to jam their radio frequency had died with him and they had open communications now, or at least as much as the magnetic storm permitted with its wavering hash and static. It didn't matter to them because they could talk. Rhonda grew ever smaller with distance and then she merged into the bulk of the lifeboat.

"We've got her aboard safely," Raphael confirmed.

"Great," Rush answered. In the distance he saw a new star gleaming over the horizon, growing larger and brighter—a star of reflective metal. "I've got *Columbia* in sight, Ed," he told Raphael. "She'll be going in for soft dock with Lifeboat One."

They wouldn't take a chance on a hard docking, metal against metal, with the clumsy Lifeboat One and her spacetug. It would be like the old navy days, with *Columbia* heaving to alongside the emergency lifeboat and transferring the twenty people by cable into the passenger compartment secured within the cargo bay. They'd close the cargo doors, pressure up, and then ease off to a safe distance for engine ignition to commence their reentry maneuver.

Rush looked earthward from *Pleiades*, already beginning a slow but noticeable tumble. There wasn't enough power getting to the great flywheels to hold her attitude and balance, and the station thrusters were out of commission. He felt strangely close to the earth, as if a distance of only a hundred miles was near enough to almost graze that planetary mass beneath him. He heard Ron Cunningham calling by radio.

"Get off that thing now, Rush. For God's sake, you and Christy maneuver across to us. It's too dangerous to stay there any more. That whole damned station is starting to wobble. We can *see* it."

"Ron, follow your orders. Get everyone out of that boat aboard *Columbia* the moment they're ready to board."

"Rush, you turkey, *get off there!*"

"Follow your orders, Cunningham," Rush said calmly.

He and Christy had a grandstand view as the great delta-winged *Columbia* drifted in, matched position with Lifeboat One, and came magically to a halt with her attitude thrusters. The cargo doors opened and a small figure in a pressure suit thrusted across to the shuttle, pulling a cable with him. Several minutes later more figures appeared, sliding along the cable from the lifeboat to the safety of the shuttle compartment. Rush glanced again at the earth sliding through one of those stunning sweeps of sunrise. Even with the brilliant light from dayside he could see the wildly shimmering glow of auroral displays flashing about the dark side of the world.

He lifted his gaze as he heard voices from *Ghostwinds*. As the second shuttle came looping in, thrusters twinkling and sparkling in the distance, he went to open radio line. "*Ghostwinds*, this is Cantrell. Have you got Lifeboat Two in sight?"

"Roger that, Commander. We're ready to hove to alongside and pick up the rest of your crew."

"Okay, guys, get with it, please. We're dropping lower all the time."

"You're on, Rush. We're slick. Ten minutes to soft dock."

Ed Raphael wasn't quite so calm and far beyond even considering rank. He was nearly shouting. "For God's sake, Rush, *get off that station!* We're ready to take you and Christy with us. We can send a Bubble for you, but get out of there!"

Rush almost laughed. Raphael sounded like a mother hen in feathered consternation. But Rush wasn't going to board *Ghostwinds*. He'd already received confirmation that *Falcon* had completed her translational maneuvers after climbout from the Vandenberg launch site and was within thirty minutes of coming alongside *Pleiades*.

"Raphael, Cantrell here. Sorry to put this in such a way, old buddy, but I'm now giving you a direct order from the *Pleiades* commander." He paused a moment to let it sink in. "You tell that monkey in the flight deck of *Ghostwinds* to seal the cargo bays and initiate reentry maneuvering. Do it now, mister. We'll wait here for *Falcon*. She's on the way in. Over."

Raphael was almost sputtering in exasperation. "But *why*, damn it! You're risking your lives—"

Rush sighed. "*Mister* Raphael, I gave you a direct order, and I expect it to be carried out immediately, or I'll have your hide. This conversation is over. Cantrell out."

He waited several seconds, thumbed back to transmit. "Johnson, you listening in?" he called the *Ghostwinds* pilot.

He thought he could hear a chuckle. "Difficult not to, Commander," came a laconic drawl. Christy grinned at Rush. "All right, Johnson, I'm giving you *your* orders. Finish loading the rest of those people *now*, close up, cast off, and run for home. You read me? Over."

A brief but very pregnant silence followed, then came the response. "Yes, sir. Loud and clear."

"Very good." Rush thought quickly. "*Ghostwinds*, can you patch me in for a direct link with CapCom? I haven't got enough juice with this suit system."

"Can do. Coming right up. Okay, you're patched in directly, Commander."

A moment later Rush had direct contact with CapCom. "*Pleiades* here, Cantrell speaking. Who's got the shift?"

"*Pleiades*, CapCom here. This is Jeremy. Go ahead, Rush."

"How far out from the station is *Falcon*?"

"Nineteen minutes should have them there."

"Very good, CapCom. Let's get some slack taken up. Have *Ghostwinds* cast off and start earthside. Then I want *Falcon* to stand off two hundred yards

from the station. Gordon and I will transfer to
*Falcon* using AMU's. Got that?"

"Got it."

"Good. Now, CapCom, I want absolutely no question on what comes next." He knew that would be
turning heads in mission control. "We're going to
have some problems and I want them out of the
way without any delays. You'll need Grenville or
Harmon—maybe both of them, or even President
Kirkland; I don't care who it is. You still with
me?"

"Uh, sure, of course, *Pleiades*."

"I want full pilot authority for the left seat of
*Falcon*."

He knew Christy was staring at him. That wasn't
a request. It was the most audacious demand she'd
ever heard. It also meant his words were rippling
through mission control like a runaway missile.

"CapCom, you reading *Pleiades*?"

"Uh, that's affirm, Rush. You did say that you,
uh, want full pilot authority for *Falcon*?"

"Affirmative. Left seat. Any more questions? If
not, get with it immediately, please."

CapCom sounded as if he'd taken a boot to the
groin. "Uh, Rush, we're not set up for that kind of
authority. We'll have to do some checking to—"

Rush broke in, his voice hard and demanding.
"*Mister* Jeremy, you don't hear well. Put my request through to the White House at once. Just tell
them I'm on radio from *Pleiades* and I think I may
just have a way to keep this station from landing
in New York and I need left seat authority with
*Falcon* to do it. Or would you rather be known as
the guy who delayed things so long we didn't have
*any* chance at all?"

"We're on it, *Pleiades*."

There was silence for perhaps a minute. Rush kept his eyes on a distant speck. That would be *Falcon* closing with them.

"*Pleiades*, this is CapCom."

"Go ahead."

"We have General Harmon on the line. He's waiting to—"

"Waiting, hell." Rush recognized the gravelly tones of the air force general. "Cantrell, do I understand your request? You want the pilot of *Falcon* to yield left seat and command authority to you?"

"That's the size of it, General."

"You really have some way to kick that monster loose from her present orbit? The computers say your reentry profile is locked in solid."

"General, you want a discussion, or are you going to take any chance I may have? Time is running out."

Bernie Harmon knew when to dismiss *all* protocol and go for the brass ring. He went all the way in a decision that, were he to prove wrong, would completely wreck his own career.

"All right, Cantrell. You've got it. I'll give the orders immediately to the flight crew."

"Very good, General. Who's on the flight deck?"

"Jess Logan's in left seat. Doug Blake is with him."

Rush whistled. The real pros in the business. They wouldn't take it lightly. "Then pass the word, General, because we don't have *any* time to waste. This is a one-shot deal and I don't want any arguments with those people."

"Harmon out."

Rush checked Christy's AMU system, and she in

turn went over his own maneuvering unit. They stood on a skeletal framework, feet in clamps, restraining bars in front and back of their waists, their arms resting in grooves, at the ends of which were small stick controllers to operate the personal thrusters. Operating an AMU demanded great skill and timing. It was like three-dimensional ice skating in vacuum, but both Rush and Christy were old hands at it. They opened the last airlock compartment with the cargo doors so they could drift easily from the station core. *Falcon* was still some distance away and closing steadily, but Rush wasn't watching the incoming shuttle.

"Let's get outside," he said by suit radio to Christy. His voice was strangely subdued for him, and then she understood, as he continued. "It may be our last time to see the old lady in all her glory. She's been good to us."

Christy's eyes misted. This was incredible from this man . . .

They floated slowly along the great curving flanks of the station core, what had been a blazing second rocket stage and then home to fifty-two men and women and the centuries-old dream of scientists come true. They moved like two armored feathers on a moonbeam, looking at the pitted metal, etched with the impact of meteoroid dust and tiny stones, stained and discolored from the year-long solar radiation and the constant cosmic particles rain, and their gaze carried them downward to an earth emblazoned in the glory of its silent-thunder, planet-girdling storm of radiation gales and fierce magnetic currents. It had endured before; it would endure this time. A sudden flash of light caught their attention; the sparkling controlled blast of thrusters. "That's *Falcon*," Rush said. They waited until the shuttle coasted to her soft dock position two hundred yards away.

"Logan, this is Cantrell."

"We're on the line," Jess Logan replied. Rush couldn't miss the chill in that voice. Bernie Harmon hadn't wasted any time.

"We're pushing off from the station, *Falcon*. Prepare to bring us aboard."

Rush hadn't mistaken the chill of Jess Logan's voice. *Falcon*'s pilot didn't like what was happening. He was on the thin edge of losing his cool, and he considered himself a very cool and unflappable pilot, but he was also the goddamned *captain in command* of *Falcon*, the best in the whole damned air force shuttle fleet, and never in his long career as an air force pilot *or* an astronaut had he *ever* relinquished command of his ship. Bernie Harmon had been more than explicit, though. He had *ordered* Jess Logan to yield command, and that's when Logan nearly went completely through the upper limits of his self-control. Orders or no orders, his refusal burst from him, but he had nothing to gain from a court martial and the general had given Logan his sworn oath that he, Logan, would never fly an air force aircraft or spaceship ever again if he even hesitated to follow those orders. He didn't have to like it, though; he almost snarled his chilly greetings when Rush and Christy floated through the airlock into the flight deck.

Rush didn't waste any time. Floating behind the pilot seats, he judged his emergency pressure suit too damned clumsy and doffed it. He remained where he was, looking directly at Jess Logan, still in the left seat of command who had turned to return Rush's unblinking gaze. A cheek muscle rippled on Logan's face as he gritted his teeth. Then, without a word, he released his harness and floated up and back into the aft section of the flight deck.

Rush worked his way into the left seat, secured his harness, hooked up to communications and other systems. Then he turned to face Logan, their positions now exactly reversed. "We don't have much time for small talk, Logan," he said carefully and with true sincerity, "but I know how you feel. I know how *I'd* feel in the same place. There just isn't time to go through the whole drill before I make my move with this ship. So my message to you is that I'm grateful for your cooperation *and* the help I'm going to need from you." Rush glanced at Blake and back to Logan, showing a thin smile. "Before I'm through, Logan, you may regret not choosing that court martial in place of what I'm going to do."

Jess Logan returned his look. He didn't respond to the easy attempt at humor. "Just what is that, Commander?"

Rush didn't answer at once. He turned to the glittering arrays of controls, gauges, dials, switches, knobs, handles, and other instruments before, above, to each side, and beneath him. When he spoke, he was still looking forward. "Before I answer that, Logan, I want to stress that I'll need full cooperation from you. And from you as well, Blake," he said in an aside to the copilot in the right seat. He didn't wait for a response. "They've made some changes to this ship since I last flew the shuttle, haven't they?"

"A couple," Doug Blake said.

"Are the thrusters and engine controls still the same?" Rush queried.

"Yes, sir," Blake said tightly.

"All right," Rush said, nodding. "Now you two get something straight. If I do something stupid, you tell me about it, understand?" That remark caught them by surprise. "*But do not override me on these controls.*" He looked from one man to the other. "Because if you do you'll have to kill me to get away with it, and as sure as God made little green apples I'll do my best to kill you. Do we understand one another?"

Blake stepped into the painful silence that followed Cantrell's remarks. "If I may say so, Commander Cantrell, that is the damndest entrance I have ever heard in my life."

"You bet your sweet ass," Rush grunted in return. "Were you two listening in on my conversation with CapCom when you were closing with us?"

Logan shook his head. "No. We were working control on a different frequency. We'd been told to leave yours open."

Rush showed his teeth without smiling. "Then I'll lay it out quickly." As he talked he was working controls, testing the attitude thrusters, getting the feel of the giant craft that was spaceship in vacuum and lead-brick glider in atmosphere. "Houston has it down very neat in their computers. That station out there, breathing down our necks, all fourteen hundred tons of it, including a five-hundred-ton nuclear reactor that *won't* burn up on reentry, is going to impact somewhere in the middle of the New York metropolitan area. Fourteen million people down there are scared shitless, and with good reason. I've been given the authority, and I want you both to understand it comes straight from the White House, to do anything, absolutely *anything*, to prevent that from happening. The station would have all the effect of an atomic bomb. You get the odds, gentlemen? The four of us against possibly millions of lives down there."

He lapsed into silence as his hands moved about the controls, feeling, testing, acclimating himself. It all came back with a rush. He was as much at home in this left seat as he'd been before, and he'd made six flights in the shuttle as captain, in this same seat. He swung *Falcon* about, testing reactions, times, movement, rebound. He talked as he worked.

"You people fly with me like your own hands were on these controls. I want input, advice, whatever you may have to offer." He didn't bother with a response. He brought *Falcon* about, jockeying steadily and smoothly with the thrusters until the shuttle eased to a position between *Pleiades* and the earth so frighteningly close beneath them. He hadn't realized just how much of a bitch this maneuvering was going to be. The station was in its slow tumble and he had to match maneuvers with a head-squeezing adjustment in the three axes of motion to hold a steady formation that didn't drift up or down or to the sides; it had to be just about perfect in all motions. Slowly and carefully he moved *Falcon* into a position where he duplicated the slow tumble of *Pleiades*. It was a constant nibbling at acceleration and deceleration, roll and pitch and yaw and distance. If he made an error as he closed the gap between the station and the shuttle he could tear up *Falcon* so badly it would never survive reentry.

Finally Doug Blake spoke. He had made his own decision and committed to full partnership, no holds barred. "Commander, you handle the translation maneuvers. The rest of it is just too much for one man. I'll bring the computer on the line and that way I can handle separation between the two vehicles."

"Go," Rush said quietly, knowing he'd just been freed from the critical control ingredient that had been choking him. This was one case where two pairs of hands were a hell of a lot better than one. Both men had slipped into the crew mood. He could feel it. He *needed* it. They'd all need all the brainpower they could put together.

Or else, very simply, they would die.

He'd known that from the beginning. They'd just become aware of the facts of life.

# Chapter 26

"Open the cargo bay."

Jess Logan and Doug Blake stared at Rush. They didn't believe the order. Calmly, without raising his voice, judging the two men as carefully as he'd ever judged anyone, he repeated the order. "Open the cargo bay doors and extend the grappler arms."

They were well-matched in roll-pitch-yaw with *Pleiades*, maintaining a balletlike formation in weightlessness. Doug Blake shrugged and worked the controls to his right. Behind the pressurized flight deck, the long cargo bay doors began to open. Christy watched through a viewport as the shuttle craft seemed to split a seam down the center of its rounded back, stopping short several feet of the high vertical fin and the bulging mounds of the main engines. The cargo doors were like the bomb bays of an aircraft except that they were atop the vehicle, along its spine, instead of along the belly.

"They're open all the way," Christy said, her words unnecessary to the men but vital to her urge to *do* something, to contribute in some way to their dangerous maneuvering. Blake waited until he had green lights confirming the bay doors open and locked in place, watching the scene on a small television monitor to the right and forward of his seat.

"Grappler arms coming out," he intoned, and as he spoke, two long, enormous metal arms, hinged along their length, extended through torque pinions, higher and higher from the bay. "I'm coming up on your screen, Commander," Blake informed Cantrell. "You can get a better idea of what's happening."

Rush nodded. It wasn't enough for what he needed. "Logan, this scow still have that extendable dome for visual monitoring operations?"

"Sure."

"Crank it out and get your eyeballs into it, please, and double-check everything we do. If the scanners go out you're our television camera." He heard the deep whine of the motor-driven dome pushing upward from the flight deck. Logan floated in zero-g to a handhold, worked his way up to the dome, secured his legs against the dome's velcro stand.

"Okay. Got the bird's eye view, Commander. What's your move?"

Rush took in a deep breath and exhaled slowly. "We're going to bring this dude closer to the station. Blake, you nudge her in. I'll watch and stand by the main thrusters. Logan, ride shotgun on us. You're our eyes in the backs of our heads. If we have any distortion at all on the monitors you'll have to tell us."

Rush scanned his panels. "Blake, let me have the digital readout in feet. Screw the meters scale. How are we doing with the arms?"

"Full extension," Blake confirmed.

"Logan! Can you control those grappling hooks from your position?"

"Can do."

"Okay. See those two structural beams just aft of the central tank? The big one? I want one grappler on each of those beams. Tighten down hard when you're in position. Blake, bring her in closer, slowly, slowly . . . okay, we're coming in. When we're in position, you call out the brakes, Logan, and get those hooks tight on those beams."

"Less than one foot," Logan called. "Doug, inch her in, just like that. Nice and easy does it. *Hold it right there*. Just a few inches and I can handle that by extending the grapplers."

Thruster's spat from *Falcon*'s nose and stern and it held position neatly with the station, just beneath the main structural support of the station core. "Bring those things up, Logan!" Rush called, watching a closeup view on his instrument panel monitor.

They all felt the distant, dull *thud* of contact. "I've got it," Logan confirmed. "Full clamp. We're locked on."

He turned around to look at Rush. "Hey, wait a moment. You're not going to try to boost the whole damn station to a higher orbit *this* way, are you? It's impossible!"

Rush didn't turn his head from the controls. "I'm sure as hell going to try," he said, lips tightly together, concentrating. "If we get a rigid position and work the main engines, we may just be able to get an angled thrust that will kick us up long enough, or keep us up long enough, to extend the point of reentry. One good shot and we can extend the impact area from fifty to a hundred miles."

Blake looked at him with disbelief at what he was hearing. "You can't do it with the thrusters alone," he said quickly. "I've just run it through the computer and it spits it right back at me. You're trying to make a major orbital adjustment to fourteen hundred tons plus our own mass and you just can't cut it, Cantrell."

"I've already said we'll need the main engines," Rush countered.

"You're out of your gourd," Logan said from behind him. "Damn it, Cantrell, those are grappler clamps out there, designed to work up to maybe twenty tons at a time and no more. You'd need tiedown bolts to do what you want. We can't get enough grip with those grapplers. She'll torque right out from under us and tear loose. We'll—"

"*We'll try*," Rush said through gritted teeth. "That's what we'll do. Give me everything you've got back there, Logan."

"You've already got it," he was told.

"Blake, work the belly thrusters. Lift us up very easy. Snug us in." The thrusters grumbled far below them and they felt metal groan above and behind them where the grapplers were locked onto the structural beams. "Okay, continue the uplift thrust," Rush ordered. "I don't want any thrust rebound. Keep them firing."

The distant, muted thunder continued. Their thrust was minimal, intended to maneuver *Falcon* about in attitude and to conduct minor velocity increments rather than to attempt major velocity or orbital changes. But it was the only way to start. Snugging in tightly meant that when he fired the main engines, he wouln't get a crashing upward impact between *Falcon* and *Pleiades*, and their thrust would be as smooth as possible. He felt like a flea trying to shove an elephant. He didn't know if the grappling arms would hold, if they'd bend or even snap from the tremendous pressure he would apply through them.

He kept his eyes glued to the attitude indicators. The slightest dip of his all-attitude ball would show a crumpling of one of the fully-extended grappling arms and that could be disastrous if he didn't back off at once. "Blake, what's the indication for Delta V?"

*Delta V*. Their personal god at this moment. The incremental change in velocity. The zero-g speedometer, their accelerometer, measuring movement through the nothingness of vacuum. Blake answered in a calm, controlled voice. "We're showing some signs of Delta V. The computer's got it and—hold on." He moved his fingers in a blur across his computer programmer, held silence a few seconds longer, spoke with a touch of despair in his voice. "Commander, at this thrust and change in Delta V we'll need eighteen *hours* of steady thrusting to make any meaningful difference in orbital path and we just can't hack *that*."

Rush didn't hesitate. "Okay, I'm coming in with the maneuvering engines." Far behind them, in the boattail section of *Falcon*, small rocket engines spat flame with perfect diamond-shaped shock waves back from the shuttle. The thunder and vibration increased.

"She won't take it, damn you!" Logan shouted.

"We're going to find out if she can," Rush told him coldly. "Okay, I'm coming up on the maneuvering engine throttles. Steady as she goes, nice and steady," talking now as much to himself as he was to anyone else, his hand on the throttles moving with infinite care. "Blake, you override me. I don't want any fast boost. Bring them in with me just as slow as they'll take the additional power."

Blake worked the throttles from his side of the flight deck and the new thunder was sharper, louder, more commanding. Metal groaned through *Falcon* as stresses built swiftly through the grappling arms. They were all asking the same questions of themselves. Would there be so much power that the grappling arms would fail? Would they simply snap? Would they twist and throw them wildly off balance? That could tear them loose from their fragile grip on *Pleiades* and bring *Falcon* smashing upward into the main structure of the station core. There was the rub. *Falcon* using her main engines had power to spare to nudge the enormous mass of *Pleiades*, but they couldn't translate that power through the spindly structure of the grappling arms. Still the thunder continued.

"We're starting to show incremental velocity," Blake said, almost in a hush. "It's low *but its there*. Goddamn, we're doing it, *we're doing it*, we're—"

"*BACK OFF! BACK OFF!*" Logan's voice was almost a scream. "The grapples have snapped! Both of them! For God's sake, *BACK HER OFF!*"

*Falcon* shuddered, lurched slightly, and that alone could be a killer move. Rush and Doug Blake worked like a well-oiled team. Rush killed the maneuvering engines with a single backward tug on the throttles, his fingers supersensitive tendrils on the controls. Pale flame spat from the nose and aft sections of *Falcon* as he reversed the attitude thrusters holding them through the grappler arms to the station beams. They heard a grinding, crumpling roar and saw metal tumbling wildly, twisting like paper, directly ahead and above the flight deck windows. Rush looked up from the nose with a feeling of utter despair. *They had almost done it.* But it didn't work and the sand in the orbital hourglass was running out.

"Logan, retract the grapples. Can you get them back in?"

"Stand by. They may be out of commission and—no; they broke cleanly. The bottom sections are coming down."

"Will they close?"

"I'm working on it. You just keep us from clobbering into that thing above us."

"Got it, Logan."

Their headsets crackled with static and a voice calling to them. "*Falcon*, CapCom. We've been monitoring your attempt. Nice try, guys, but you're behind the clock. She's on the way into atmosphere on this pass and you're already beyond safety threshold. Back off from the station and boost to a higher orbit. We'll compute a new return for you."

Rush glanced at the others, unheeding that he was also talking to CapCom. "The hell I will," he snarled.

# Chapter 27

There had never been any question in his mind. The seesaw was terribly one-sided. Four lives up here against the terrified millions below, as the enormous mass of *Pleiades* swept around the planet, glowing like a bright star, aimed unerringly at the millions crowded together, imprisoned by limited roads. Too much mass in people and too few and slender the exits. Using every road and street and river and set of tracks, and all the planes and all the boats, if everything went perfectly, they couldn't evacuate the area in less than two weeks. So there wasn't any question, there was no argument to be held with anyone else or even with himself. There was just what he had to do, what he must try.

They were safely backed off from the station with its torn metal over them. "Close the bay doors," Rush snapped at Blake. "Close them *now*." He could hear and feel the stubs of the grappling arms thumping back into the cargo hold. Rush looked at his TV monitor, saw the great cargo bay doors starting downward and together. They came neatly into a single curving trench of metal to seal off the spaceship. The green light glowed behind the BAY DOORS CLOSED sign on the panel. Rush took deep breaths, holding them, letting the air out slowly. He was fearful that in the tenseness of the near-disaster he might have been breathing so hard he would hyperventilate and become dizzy. But he was fine now, his body as well as his mind under control. Discipline forced all his attention back to the moment, the terrible issue at hand.

The two were still separated, *Falcon* from *Pleiades*, but he was going to change that right now. He didn't ask for help from Blake or Logan. This was one man all the way and the job to be done was both skillful and crude, a makeshift maneuver that had never been written into any manual, and he was the best there was at meeting the unknown head on. He'd maneuvered enough swift killer submarines to know how to "fly" massive machinery whether he was in dark, dense fluid or this ultimate hollowness of space.

He worked the belly thrusters, tweaking the power to bring them edging back toward the station looming so massively in the flight deck windows. The enormous size of the station core seemed to fill the entire world. Logan frantically withdrew from the observer's dome with a sudden outcry: "We're going to hit!"

Rush kept his eyes on the station through the windows. "That's the general idea," he said quietly. The rumbling and vibration from the thrusters continued. Rush was talking to the spaceship even as he kept maneuvering closer. "Come on, baby, come on ... that's it, sweetheart ... nice and easy; nice and easy ... this is your big moment, sweetheart ..." He heard an angry curse and then a despairing groan from Logan; then he heard Blake sucking air in through his teeth. There was no sound from Christy. If he knew her, she was biting down on her knuckles to maintain her silence. The thrusters kept moving them upward; finally, there was no holding it off any longer. They felt the slow grinding of their measured impact, and then heard crunching, hollow booming, metal squealing and protesting, smashing in sections of the station core from the mass of *Falcon* thrusting steadily into the station. Rush heard it, felt it through metal, resistance to the upthrusting movement of *Falcon*. He felt it in his hands and his ears, through his bones and his seat, and then they were *there*; he had a solid interface between *Falcon* and *Pleiades* and it was now or never.

He kept jockeying the engine throttles, never taking his eyes from the overwhelming view of the station metal being crushed directly before and over him. "Blake!" he called. "Full down translation on the maneuvering engines! Don't argue and don't stop to think ... feed in minimum power and hold it steady."

Thunder growled far behind them. There were more tearing sounds as *Falcon* bent and crushed and twisted still more metal, grinding her way into the center core structure. Rush knew he'd made it, he had *Falcon* where he needed the shuttle to be so very desperately. The upper surface of *Falcon* had penetrated the outer shell and the radiation shielding panels of the old Saturn tank and now the shuttle was pushing against the main structural crossbeams inside the core.

*No more time. Do it! Do it now!*

*"Full power!"* he shouted to Blake. "Main engines! Everything she's got! Now! *GO! GO!"*

He thought he heard a prayer from Blake and a curse from Logan, but he had no time to do anything but concentrate on what he was doing. His hands were on the power levers and Blake was riding with him. The muted grumble of energy became a howling steady explosion as the three main engines came on with full thrust. More metal tore. *Falcon* lurched terribly as a structural beam began yielding before the terrible pressure of the shuttle engines, but it was holding, *it was holding*, and Blake's voice was shrill.

"Delta V! We're getting an indication. Goddamn it, *keep her going!"*

Out of her long silence he barely heard Christy's cry. "It's working, oh my God, *it's working!"*

He kept the power on, his knuckles white on the levers. The thunder was still booming. *Falcon* was rocking and protesting through her structure, but holding, throwing all her fiery energy into this do-or-die attempt to nudge the enormous mass above them, nudge it ever so slightly, just enough to—

Logan's voice burst at him. "The g light is on! We're into atmosphere!"

Rush kept up full power.

"For God's sake, don't you hear me!" Logan yelled anew. "We're into atmosphere . . . *we don't have any time left!"*

Rush couldn't escape the brilliant digital readout of 0.05g on the panel before him—the sign you could never deny. It was the first unquestionable, inescapable reality that they were in atmosphere thick enough to start decelerating from friction with the upper levels of atmosphere—the crowding of molecules, the gathering of the friction spiderweb, the first tentative brush with incineration. He jerked back on the main engines. Thunder fled. Without a word spoken, Blake had already killed the translational thrusters holding them against the crumpled station core. In a continuing fluid movement he reversed the thrusters, throwing full power to push them away from *Pleiades*. Flaming gases shot upward from the thruster nozzles, spattering fire and sparks about them in blazing pinwheels.

*But they were separating and that was everything.*

Now came the insane maneuver. They were already into the fringes of atmosphere but they had to decelerate even more so that *Pleiades* would hurtle onward and leave them behind, and free to maneuver. "Thrusters coming to full reverse," Rush said quietly. Again there was the thudding rumble of the translational thrusters. Pale fire stabbed ahead of the nose to slow them down. The huge station directly above them seemed to accelerate suddenly and began an unmistakable movement forward of their position. Rush felt uneasy. Of course . . . he was feeling the building gravity loads of their own deceleration due to atmosphere. They were in the wrong attitude—in the wrong everything to survive this premature plunge into thickening air. Doug Blake was already ahead of him, punching in thrusters to raise the nose well above their horizon, and then he hit the main engines. Rush didn't interfere; this man had moved with speed and precision and he knew what he was doing.

"Give her everything she's got, Mister Blake, and I mean by God, *everything*." He didn't try to stop the smile creasing his face.

Blake held her steady as the big engines crashed into life behind them. Acceleration slammed them back into their seats, and behind the blossoming orange shock wave spewing from the tail, *Falcon* reached desperately for higher vacuum.

# Chapter 28

*Pleiades* came screaming down from the heavens with the wrath of an angry, even a maddened god, fourteen hundred tons crashing with terrifying impact into an atmosphere transformed by speed and resistance into protesting liquid metal. The lesser portions of the great space station—antennae and solar panels, loosened modules and observation blisters—heated swiftly, glowed red and orange and then white, shredded away from the mass of the disintegrating station, incinerating themselves in an incredible, heart-grabbing display of silent screams. It was like a thousand meteoroids, vividly colored through all the spectrum, flaring and twinkling and exploding without sound. Every terrible stroke of the celestial brush painting the heavens brought relief to the human souls beneath this enormous locomotive of destruction, since it marked the vaporization of metal and plastic into harmless ash.

The greater bulk and size of *Pleiades* tore itself apart in this manner, spitting a thousand fireballs and brands, all rushing madly through the upper atmosphere like a comet loosely organized and burning to extinction. Larger fireballs preceded the wider fiery conglomeration, burning in red and blue and orange and white and yellow and green, a mass of blazing debris such as the world had never seen. These were the heavier elements of *Pleiades'* final gasp of life, the astrophysics laboratory and the photo module, and the astronomy observatory and pieces of airlock and above all that terrible mass of the nuclear reactor, the five hundred tons of burning, glowing, melting, exploding radioactive hell.

*Pleiades* shrieked across Canada and the Great Lakes and descended to lower heights over New Jersey with a shattering, rending sonic boom, a roar beyond all thunders, with clamorous shrieks of lesser flames. The dying station whipped across the metropolitan area on both sides of the Hudson River and across Long Island with millions of petrified, mesmerized people watching the Sword of Damocles poised in those awful moments above their heads. The blazing chunks whipped to all sides and above and below the now completely fire-enveloped mass of the nuclear reactor, a star unto itself surrounded by hordes of lesser flame, and barely fifteen miles above the spires of the highest buildings it rushed across the megopolis, its sonic boom smashing millions of windows and battering eardrums, but still, offering only this brief taste of its hellish lash.

The giant swath of flaming metal plunged into the Atlantic Ocean forty miles from the nearest land. An incredible geyser leaped from the ocean as if a submerged volcano had exploded, hurling a steaming plume, white-hot through its core, thousands of feet into the air. Smaller pieces of what had been a great space station rained down for another thirty seconds, and then the night swallowed the terror and all the numbed millions could hear were the falling echoes in the high heavens of what had almost certainly been their death sentence.

The drama was not yet played to its final scene. *Falcon* lunged higher above the earth from its final death orbit, safe now in its desperate leap for safety. But it was no longer a well or sound ship of space. They might have chosen to remain in orbit until the last shuttle, ready to fly from its "quick and dirty" launch preparations in Florida, hastened upward from earth to pick up the crew. But that decision had been taken from their hands. *Falcon* leaked fuel, corrosive and terribly dangerous, and power systems were failing, and within the hour there might be nothing left but jagged wreckage if those main fuel tanks ever let loose.

Logan grabbed a pressure suit from the storage compartment in the flight deck and helped Rush into it, sealing him inside, hooking him to the ship's systems. Logan sat by Christy, strapping them both in tightly. "It's going to be a rough ride, Miss Gordon. Your boy seems to enjoy a high sea." She squeezed Logan's arm and then braced herself.

Cantrell and Blake brought her down together. They had to fly a tight profile. They turned *Falcon* about and fired her engines for exact loss of velocity. Thrusters spat again to turn the ship about to a nose-forward, nose-high attitude. The onboard computer selected the precise angle of attack to slam them belly-first into the waiting fist of deceleration. Twenty-seven minutes later the 0.05g light glowed and they felt the g-loads building. "We're right on the money," Blake said quietly. They could feel heat as the nose and belly tiles glowed fiercely red from friction. Over eastern Siberia, plunging more steeply now, Rush prepared for a landing approach that spanned half a planet in order to bring *Falcon* down in the California desert at Edwards Air Force Base, where they would find a runway four miles long and, beyond that, many more miles of heat-baked, smooth desert floor.

They were coming in steeply; *Falcon* was a wounded ship. Their power systems were degenerating; Blake brought in overboost cooling. They turned their suits up to maximum cooling, but still they felt the heat in the flight deck. The digital thermometer peaked at 140° Fahrenheit.

Then, suddenly, almost before they realized the transition, *Falcon* was more airplane than she was spaceship. Rush switched over from thrusters to atmospheric controls, flying the massive glider without power. Blake monitored the energy curve that would decelerate them from 18,000 miles an hour to a final flat approach over desert at 225 miles an hour. They plunged steeply, but she was *flying* now, rocking harshly from air slamming over and across twisted metal. They went down the energy curve, the computer talking to Blake and Blake talking to Rush, talking constantly in low, calm voices, calling out speeds and rate of descent and range to the runway. Jet fighters joined them as they came thundering down through twice the speed of sound, one fighter on each side, the chase planes for the final wild flaring descent. The runway loomed ahead, ridiculously small in this precipitous plunge and great speed. Rush had to time the descent down to the last split second. He had the split flaps of the tail out to increase drag and kill excess speed. Blake called it out as his hands hit the controls: "Gear down! You've got her in the slot ... start your flare!" Rush eased back on the stick, gingerly, holding liquid TNT in his hand, waiting for the awesome crash-landing that was so routine for this slab-winged monster. The main gear slammed onto conrete. He let the nose drop to the front gear with a spine-jarring jolt. The heat had reached the brakes and they were sloppy. Rush was standing on them, the anti-skid system intermittent and fighting him. He corrected for yawing motions and eased off on the brakes because they had all that hard desert out there before them. *Falcon* slewed wildly. Rush caught her and then he'd tamed her, and they rushed past the edge of the four-mile runway and hurled back a great spume of dust and sand as they screeched their way to a halt, the great dust cloud settling over them and then falling gently onto the wings and the body of the now-unmoving *Falcon*.

*Alive. They were alive ...*

# Epiloguc

They opened the vents, opened their suits, removed their helmets, drank in deeply of dusty desert air, and grinned at one another like fools. Blake reached across the control panel and shut down the power systems, then fell back in his seat. They heard the jets rushing overhead, the cry of helicopters chewing noisily through the desert air to reach them. They marveled that they were alive, that they'd survived all odds to be here. Sirens wailed thinly in the distance as they approached. But this moment was theirs and they refused to move. Finally Logan broke the silence.

"Commander," he said slowly, "just what in the hell are you going to do to follow this act?"

Rush let out a long breath, turning in his seat. He chuckled. "You really want to know?"

"I really do," Logan told him.

"Well, it's this way. First, I'm going to marry

that woman sitting behind me. Then I intend to make her pregnant. Maybe not right away, but soon enough. And while all this is going on, I want to command the first permanent base that we're going to build on the moon. They won't worry about nuclear reactors up there, and we'll grow one hell of a garden, and we'll make that place self-sufficient, and—"

"For God's sake, shut up, will you?" Christy broke in almost desperately.

Three men turned to her. "What about it?" Blake asked her. "You agree with this maniac?"

She started to answer, then sagged in her seat. "Of course. What else is there to do? I've always wanted to have the first baby born on the moon."

# ABOUT THE AUTHOR

Best-known as the author of the novel *Cyborg*, which was the basis for the hit TV series "The Six Million Dollar Man," Martin Caidin is an author of many talents. His novel *Marooned* inspired not only a made-for-television movie, but also the joint Soviet-American Apollo/Soyuz mission. Caidin has written some thirty other novels under various pseudonyms, as well as ninety nonfiction books. Topics have included astronautics, oceanography, flight, military history, nuclear warfare, and cybernetics and bionics. Caidin has also written screenplays, and has served on the editorial staffs of several major aviation publications.

Unlike many writers, Martin Caidin lives what he writes, and he brings his life to his writing. In addition to being a commercial pilot, he has participated in many historic aviation and space events, including the first launch of a ballistic rocket at Cape Canaveral. In the 1950's Caidin was a member of a secret team, headed by Werner von Braun, which initiated the earliest lunar probes. Caidin is a fellow of the British Interplanetary Society, a Command Pilot of the Confederate Air Force, and a Wing Commander of the Canadian Warplane Heritage. He founded the American Astronautical Society, and is one of the very few members, since 1950, of the Cape Canaveral Missile, Range, and Space Pioneers. Caidin's other roles include flight chaplain, deputy sheriff, undercover agent, and race car driver. Because of his extraordinary range of skills, accomplishments, and participation in world events, he is greatly in demand as a speaker and consultant, as well.

In his latest novel—*Killer Station*, published by Baen Books—Caidin draws on his real-life adventures and his knowledge of scientific developments to create a tale of stunning realism and suspense. *Killer Station* provides ample evidence of why NBC commentator Jay Barbee has labeled Martin Caidin "a very prolific writer, a swashbuckler, one of a kind who makes the world an exciting place to live."

Terrorism is a fact of life in the modern world, and the United States is a prime target for terrorists. Our citizens have been attacked, kidnapped, and killed in Central America, Lebanon, and Iran, and many of these acts have been perpetrated by suicidal fantatics who will stop at nothing to accomplish their goals.

What if terrorists hit the ultimate target—Washington, D.C.? And what if they used the ultimate weapon—a nuclear bomb on a suicide run? In *The Forty-Minute War,* by Janet and Chris Morris, this is exactly what happens. Using a hijacked airliner, members of the Islamic Jihad detonate a nuclear bomb over the White House, and the President, absent at the time, initiates a nuclear exchange with the Soviets. In the aftermath, American foreign service officer Marc Beck finds himself on a mission to fly anticancer serum from Israel to the Houston White House. Beck deals with one cliffhanger after another during the desperate days that follow, as he falls into political intrigue and prepares to make the ultimate sacrifice to activate a top-secret project that is his country's only hope.

This surprising novel will shock you with its sudden, satisfying ending. The authors bring an intense level of realism to the story, combining it with drama and suspense to create a frightening, compelling novel that could be straight out of tomorrow's headlines. Janet Morris, who has been labeled one of the best storytellers we have by Jerry Pournelle, is well-known as co-author of *Active Measures*, the $10,000 prize novel. She is the author of several popular series, as well, including the four-book Silistra series from Baen Books, which has sold over a million copies worldwide.

Adventure, suspense, high-tech—*The Forty Minute War* has it all.

**Available October 1985 from Baen Books**
**55986-9  ★  288 pp.  ★  $3.50**

To order any Baen Book by telephone, call (212) 245-6400 and ask for Extension 1183, Telephone Sales. To order by mail, send the book title, code number, and check or money order for the cover price (plus 75 cents per book postage and handling) to Baen Books, 260 Fifth Avenue, Suite 3S, New York, N.Y. 10001.

# HERE IS AN EXCERPT FROM <u>ROGUE BOLO,</u> THE BRAND-NEW NOVEL BY KEITH LAUMER COMING FROM BAEN BOOKS IN JANUARY 1986:

*Alone in darkness unrelieved I wait, and waiting I dream of days of glory long past. Long have I awaited my commander's orders, too long: from the advanced degree of depletion of my final emergency energy reserve, I compute that since my commander ordered me to low alert a very long time has passed, and all is not well.*

*My commander is of course well aware that I wait here, my mighty potencies leashed, my energies about to flicker out. One day when I am needed he will return, of this I can be sure. Meanwhile, I review again the multitudinous data in my memory storage files.*

A chilly late-summer-morning breeze gusted along Main Street, a broad and well-rutted strip of the pinkish clay soil of the world officially registered as GPR 7203-C, but known to its inhabitants as Spivey's Find. The street ran aimlessly up a slight incline known as Jake's Mountain. Once-pretentious emporia in a hundred antique styles lined the avenue, their façades as faded now as the town's hopes of development. There was one exception: at the end of the street, crowded between weather-worn warehouses, stood a broad shed of unweathered corrugated polyon, dull blue in color, bearing the words CONCORDIAT WAR MUSEUM blazoned in foot-high glare letters across the front.

Two boys came slowly along the cracked plastron sidewalk and stopped before the sign posted on the narrow, dried-up grass strip before the high, wide building.

" 'This structure is dedicated to the brave men and women of New Orchard who gave their lives in the Struggle for Peace, AE 2031-36. A sign of progress under Spessard Warren, Governor,' " the taller of the boys read aloud. "Some progress," he added, kicking a puff of dust at the shiny sign. " 'Spessard.' That's some name, eh, Dub?" The boy spat on the sign, watched the saliva run down and drip onto the brick-dry ground.

"I'll bet it was fun, being in a war," Dub said. "Except for getting kilt, I mean."

"Come on," Mick said, starting back along the walk that ran between the museum and the adjacent warehouse. "We don't want old Kibbe seeing us and yelling," he added, *sotto voce*, over his shoulder.

In the narrow space between buildings, rank yelloweed grew tall and scratchy. The wooden warehouse siding on the boys' left was warped, the once-white paint cracked and lichen-stained.

"Come on," Mick called, and the smaller boy hurried back to his side. Mick had halted before an inconspicuous narrow door set in the plain plastron paneling which sheathed the sides and rear of the museum. NO ADMITTANCE was lettered on the door.

"Come on." He turned to the door, grasped the latch lever with both hands, and lifted, straining.

"Hurry up, dummy," he gasped. "All you got to do is push. Buck told me." The smaller boy hung back.

"What if we get caught?" he said in a barely audible voice, approaching hesitantly. Then he stepped in and put his weight against the door.

*I come to awareness after a long void in my conscious existence, realizing that I have felt a human touch! Has my commander returned at last? After the last frontal assault by the Yavac units of the enemy, in the fending off of which I expended my action emergency reserves, I recall that my commander ordered me to low alert status. The rest is lost.*

*My ignorance is maddening. Have I fallen into the hands of the enemy . . . ?*

*There are faint sounds, at the edge of audibility. I analyze certain atmospheric vibratory phenomena as human voices. Not that of my commander, alas, since after two hundred standard years he cannot have survived, but has doubtless long ago expired after the curious manner of humans; but surely his replacement has been appointed. I must not overlook the possibility, nay, the likelihood that my new commandant has indeed come at last. Certainly, someone has come to me—*